"Hollows fans rejoice! . . . . k
into her world of coexi. . . . . n
many of the beloved characters and all of the fast quips and
high-stakes magical action of her previous books."
—*Library Journal* (starred review)

"A fun outing, a welcome and unexpected return to a world
I'd thought we'd left behind."   —*Locus*

"Will keep series fans up all night."   —*Booklist*

"Harrison's world is incredibly rich. She's mastered the col-
lision of the real world and every fantasy story and fairy
tale. . . . A wonderful addition to the universe of Rachel
Morgan and Kim Harrison."   —Paperback Paris

"Kim Harrison's masterful character development and
world-building shine."   —Fresh Fiction

"Classic Kim Harrison. . . . *American Demon* was like
coming home again to find your favorite people sitting
around the living room with smiles of welcome on their
faces."   —Wicked Reads

"It was emotional, tense, and powerful in all the right ways.
Best of all, we were given a chance to see all of the characters we've come to love once again. . . . It felt so good to be
back."   —Word of the Nerd

BY KIM HARRISON

BOOKS OF THE HOLLOWS

AMERICAN DEMON

KIM HARRISON

ACE
New York

ACE
Published by Berkley
An imprint of Penguin Random House LLC
penguinrandomhouse.com

Copyright © 2020 by Kim Harrison

ISBN: 9780593101421

Ace hardcover edition / June 2020
Ace mass-market edition / April 2021

Printed in the United States of America
3   5   7   9   10   8   6   4

Book design by Kristin del Rosario

For Tim

PREFACE

INDERLAND SECURITY
Internal Document DOX W 143.1739
Fact Sheet: Rachel Morgan 2000 to present
Document Shepherd: Jeffory Gradenko

INTRODUCTION: Rachel Morgan successfully terminated her I.S. contract in 2006, buying her way out by implicating Trent Kalamack Jr. in the illegal bio-drug trade. Several years of antagonism between them were rubbed out after she helped him regain sole custody of his out-of-wedlock child, Lucy, from his ex-fiancée, Ellasbeth Withon, in 2008. Morgan currently freelances security for Trent on an as-needed basis.

SPECIES: Witch-born demon who survived infancy when Trent "Kal" Kalamack Sr. applied illegal genetic tinkering to bypass the lethality of the Rosewood syndrome, a suite of lethal genes that ancient elves cursed the demons with to stunt the magic capabilities of their children, with the intent to commit slow genocide. It's unknown if this was Kalamack Sr.'s intention, or if it was accidental, but with the ongoing feud between the demons and elves, it seems accidental.

> **NOTE:** *Kalamack Jr. seems to be continuing his father's work, as there are currently more than a dozen children surviving the Rosewood syndrome. They are collectively called the Rosewood babies and are to remain under close I.S. observation, as they have the potential to bring about a rebirth of the demons.*

RESIDENCE: Currently lives aboard a gas yacht (*The Solar*) docked on the Ohio River at Pizza Piscary's in the Hollows, KY. Previous residence condemned after a vampire mob consisting of several camarillas destroyed the back of the church because of the mistaken belief that Morgan was responsible for bringing the souls of the undead back from the ever-after. Further damage was sustained in a separate attack from the elven Goddess.

POLITICAL RAMIFICATIONS: Morgan has a surprising number of political contacts, both in and out of her favor.

The Federal Inderland Bureau: Morgan has a solid in with the human-run FIB through her association with CAPTAIN EDDEN and his son, MATHEW GLENN. It was Edden who arranged for the payoff on Rachel's I.S. contract.

Demons: Though currently the only mature female demon, Morgan maintains an uneasy relationship to her "kin." This is in part because of her past association to the elven GODDESS and her continued dabbling in elven magic, and in part due to her ongoing relationship with elf TRENT KALAMACK. The demon collective overlooks her nonconformity, as she and her gargoyle (BIS) created a new ever-after (and hence a continuation of magic) when the original was destroyed by the elves in yet another attempt to eradicate the demons. Demons range from neutral to antagonistic toward her, apart from her instructor, AL, and possibly the demons' self-proclaimed leader, DALI.

NOTE: *It was the elves' miscalculation, not Morgan's, that freed the demons to walk freely in reality, but the I.S. sees no reason to correct this misunderstanding.*

Elves: Trent's ongoing relationship with Rachel has caused a deep rift between Trent and both the elven's political group, the ENCLAVE, and their religious order, the DEWAR. His refusal to reunite with ELLASBETH

WITHON and his relationship with Morgan have resulted in the loss of considerable political power, turning him from a prince-in-waiting to an outcast. The income from his illegal bio-drugs is gone, and Trent spends much of his time and many of his remaining assets staving off blackmail from previous buyers. In the absence of his usual political tasks, Trent has been developing his magical skills. His mother (FELICIA "TRISK" CAMBRI-KALAMACK) was a spell caster of considerable note, and though he's improving quickly, the I.S. sees no threat apart from his association with Morgan.

The Goddess: Though not being actively hunted for anymore, Rachel remains vulnerable to an attack from the elves' goddess, a deified energy being. She's the source of all magic, as her mystics (tiny, independent motes that function as her eyes) power the ley lines as they bring images and elven prayers from reality back to the Goddess, who exists in the space between particles of mass.

Both demons and elves can bypass the ley lines to utilize the Goddess's power directly through prayer, though it's only the elves who do this ever since the Goddess's betrayal of the demons thousands of years ago and the demons' subsequent enslavement. That Rachel performs elven magic is grounds for severe punishment, but again, demons are ignoring this, as she not only saved them from extinction but forced modern society to grant them citizenship.

Before becoming the Goddess in a fight for supremacy, demon NEWT changed how Rachel's soul resonates, to hide her aura from the mystics who would otherwise swarm Rachel and force her to join the Goddess, which would destroy Rachel in the process. It's believed that elven magic is currently not working well because Newt is now the governing force in the Goddess.

Vampires: Rachel is currently enjoying a balanced to good situation after thwarting the latest elven attempt at world domination—when the elven dewar and enclave under the leadership of LANDON worked to pull the souls of the long undead from "storage" in the ever-after, allowing them to roam in reality until finding their original bodies and committing suncide.

Morgan remains a person of interest to the I.S., as she was successful in capturing the departing soul of a living vampire (NINA LEDESMA) at her first death and installing it within the body of living vampire IVY TAMWOOD. It has resulted in a surprisingly stable undead vampire who, unlike her undead brethren, remembers how to love and therefore has a reduced need to feed. Ivy and Nina remain under observation as this new kind of "undead master vampire and scion" pair holds the potential to end the vampire curse—but it is fraught with its own complications and there's much resistance from the old undead.

Under the original curse, living vampires are molded by the vampire virus before birth, giving them increased strength and sharp, normal-length canines useful in dealing with the undead on a daily basis and serving as their main means of acquiring blood. Being alive, living vampires have no light or religious limitations, and are accustomed to doing the daylight work of the undead, as is expected. An undead's favorite, or scion, maintains special privileges as well as enjoying heightened strength and senses, as well as an increased blood drive due to sharing blood with their master on a regular basis.

After their first death, living vampires become true undead. Even reflected light will cause their second death, and they must feed on the living to take in not only blood but, to remain emotionally stable, the auras of those they feed upon. Though having no morals, they police themselves and hide much of the ugliness from humans lest society become afraid and take action against them.

With Ivy holding Nina's soul in addition to her own, Nina is in the unique position of taking in her own aura while feeding on Ivy, resulting in an almost normal emotional baseline. It has been noted that though Nina displays many of the sultry, powerful characteristics of the undead, she looks to Ivy for direction, not the other way around. Simply put, because Nina is dependent on Ivy for her aura, Nina is recessive and Ivy is dominant. This needs to be examined in detail before allowing any more such master/scion pairs to develop, as, in time, the living may control the dead, not the dead control the living.

NOTE: *Emotionally damaged by the thought of regaining his soul, RYNN CORMEL is no longer effective as Cincinnati's master vampire. Replacements are being considered, and the master/scion pair of Nina Ledesma and Ivy Tamwood is fulfilling his function in the interim with surprising efficiency.*

Weres: Rachel no longer has a contractual link to the Weres after abdicating her alpha position in DAVID HUE's pack. Though it's not widely known, Hue still retains the focus artifact that Morgan gave him, enabling him to gather multiple Were packs under his will at his discretion. Hue is savvy enough to know to lie low, but he should remain under observation for future problems.

The Order: Morgan is currently a potential target of this humans-only, highly funded vigilante task force that has been illegally catching, judging, and incarcerating Inderlanders.

The Dewar: The elven religious order, currently under the leadership of Landon after BANCROFT's mystic-induced suicide. The dewar is actively trying to discredit Morgan to gain political security. Having once enjoyed moderate sway with the dewar, Kalamack is on the outs with them due to his association with Morgan.

The Enclave: The elven political faction is also currently siding against Morgan, though that stance is beginning to shift to neutral as Kalamack works to rebuild his once-considerable pull with them and regain his Sa'han status. It's unlikely that Kalamack will ever regain his past strength if he continues to shun his responsibilities with Ellasbeth Withon in order to create good relations with the demons, something neither the elven nor the demon societies are interested in.

HAPA (Humans Against Paranormals Association): Due to Morgan's actions, HAPA is currently in disarray after she identified their leader/mole deep within the FIB and helped the Order capture and incarcerate her. It's believed there are several HAPA sleeper agents remaining in the FIB.

Additional: Though Morgan does not hold sway with any subspecies of Inderlanders, it should be noted that her association with a particular pixy, JENKS, is causing small waves that might evolve into long-term societal impacts. Having been cursed to extend his life, Jenks is the first pixy to own property (1597 Oak Staff, Hollows, KY) and the first to remain alive after his spouse's death. He's currently the oldest living pixy at twenty, and he's creating innovative ways to function in a world that still affords him few rights or responsibilities.

Also of note, Morgan is responsible for the release of the demon hostages taken as familiars over the last several thousand years. Though they are lying low and many are suffering from culture shock, they are a potential threat, as they see Rachel as their savior and might react if she finds herself attacked. This has led to upper management's continued hands-off policy concerning Morgan.

KNOWN ASSOCIATES:

IVY TAMWOOD—Living vampire. Rachel's former roommate, now Nina's scion.

JENKS PIXY—Urbanized pixy who acts as Rachel's backup when needed. Loyal to a fault.

TRENT KALAMACK—Elf. Recently lost most of his wealth and political clout because of his continued close association with Rachel Morgan and his refusal to condemn demons.

AL (GALLY)—Demon. Morgan's onetime adversary, now teacher and pain in the ass.

DALI—Demon. Al's "parole officer" and leader of the few remaining demons.

NEWT—Formerly the demons' only female demon, crazy from knowing too much. Now incorporated into the elves' Goddess and causing mischief at will.

SAMUEL EDDEN—Human. Captain in the Federal Inderland Bureau (FIB). A friend and backer of Rachel from the beginning, he fights for more understanding between the species.

MATHEW GLENN—Human. Edden's adopted son. Used to work for the FIB, but is believed to have been lured away to the Order.

QUEN HANSEN—Elf. Kalamack's head of security and confidant.

JONATHAN DAVAROS (JON)—Elf. Kalamack's publicity adviser and personal assistant.

LUCY KALAMACK—Elf. Child of Trent Kalamack and Ellasbeth Withon. Born out of wedlock.

RAY HANSEN—Elf. Child of Quen Hansen and Ceri Dulcet. Born out of wedlock.

BIS—Gargoyle. Adolescent gargoyle (fifty years old) who bound himself to Morgan.

MARK (JUNIOR)—Witch. Once an employee of the coffeehouse Morgan frequents, now the owner.

ELLASBETH WITHON—Elf. Kalamack's ex-fiancée, currently trying to win her way back into Trent Kalamack's and Lucy Kalamack's lives.

LANDON—Elf. The current head of the elven religious order, the dewar.

ZACHARIAH OBORNA (ZACK)—Adolescent elf. Leader-in-waiting of the elven religious order, the dewar.

BENNY—Elf. Until recently, the only dewar representative in Cincinnati.

WEAST—Human. The leader of the human-run Order.

MATTIE—Pixy. Jenks's deceased wife.

BELLE—Fairy. A wingless assassin fairy who has taken on a few of the traditional duties of a pixy wife in Mattie's absence.

KU'SOX SHA-KU'RU—Demon. A psychotic, failed attempt to bioengineer a fix to the demons' fertility problem. Originally freed from his prison by Kalamack Jr. and later killed in a joint effort between Kalamack and the remaining demons to cement future good relations.

MIA—Banshee. Incarcerated after allowing her infant child to recklessly feed on the auras of multiple humans and Inderlanders to the point of death.

CERIDWEN DULCET (CERI)—Ancient elf. Al's longtime familiar rescued by Morgan. Ray's birth mother. Died while attempting to kill Ku'Sox to save Lucy.

NICK SPARAGMOS—Human. Morgan's ex-boyfriend who died in Newt's oubliette after aligning himself with Ku'Sox.

PISCARY—Undead vampire. Former city master vampire and owner of Pizza Piscary's. Ran the city through his contacts with the I.S. Died his second death when DOROTHY CLAYMORE killed him in a jealous rage over Ivy Tamwood.

KISTEN FELPS—Living vampire. Piscary's former scion and restaurant manager. Both Ivy Tamwood's and Rachel Morgan's boyfriend, though not at the same time. Died his first death when Piscary gave him as a blood gift to an undead vampire after he refused to kill Morgan, then died his final death to protect Tamwood and Morgan.

RYNN CORMEL—Undead vampire. Served as president of the U.S. during the Turn; since retired to serve as master vampire in Cincinnati. Author of underground bestseller *The Vampire Dating Guide*. Emotionally damaged from the thought of getting his soul back.

STANLEY SALADAN (LEE)—Witch. The only other known witch whom Kalamack Sr. saved from the Rosewood syndrome as a goodwill gesture. Runs the drug cartel west of the Mississippi and is in friendly / not-so-friendly competition with Kalamack Jr.

CHAPTER

1

"THAT'S AN UNFORTUNATE MISCONCEPTION THAT I'VE been working hard to correct," Landon said, and I stared at the radio, not liking that the priest's professional, tutored voice had lost none of its elven persuasion through my car's speaker. I was parked at the curb outside the church, waiting for Ivy and Jenks—who were late. Late enough that my to-go coffee was gone and I was down to listening to the news to try to stay awake. Landon spouting his lies on Cincy's radio circuit was better than a double espresso.

"So you claim it wasn't poor spell casting that sent the rescued souls of the undead back to the ever-after, but Mr. Kalamack?" the interviewer said, and I drummed my fingers on the steering wheel, imagining Landon's fair features and thin lips curving up in a reassuring and fake smile.

"I do." Landon's confidence was absolute as he lied. "The spell to return the undead their souls was cast by the entire elven religious dewar and our political enclave. It fell due to Kalamack's tampering. Which is why the witches joined us on our second attempt."

"Ha!" I exclaimed, my voice coming back hard in my tiny car. "Trent didn't mess with your lousy charm. It was bad spell casting. Hack," I added, then angrily changed the channel.

"—possible food contamination being tied to the recent spate of domestic assaults in the greater Cincinnati and Hollows area, having just this morning taken its first human victim."

I turned the radio off. Food contamination did not lead to violence, unless it was the now-extinct T-4 Angel tomato.

Leaning back, I stared at the car's ceiling and tried to "let go," as Jenks would say. Landon had been spouting his alternate version of reality for months. It was frustrating that no one—not Al, or Dali, or Trent—had come forward to say anything contrary. Every time I brought it up, Trent would pull me into a hug and tell me that things were being said behind closed doors and that to make the argument public would make me a scapegoat.

Nervous, I tucked a tickling strand of my curly red hair behind an ear and fiddled with my empty coffee cup. A gentleman's agreement between Trent and Landon to keep my name out of the news was more than likely. And my name *had* been suspiciously absent. Not that I was complaining. I didn't know how much more collateral damage my life could take.

Dropping the empty cup into the holder, I settled back to wait. The ticking of my shiny red MINI's engine cooling in the sunny morning was a gently slowing rhythm, and I felt myself relax despite Landon's lies. Walking into the silence that gripped the church without Ivy and Jenks had all the appeal of eating toasted butterfly wings. Besides, it was warm in my car, and I didn't think the heat was on in the church yet.

Late November was cold in Cincinnati, and I squinted up through the tinted band of windshield until I found Bis's lumpy shape sleeping beside the steeple. New gray shingles covered the hole the elven Goddess had blown through the roof in frustration, but the kitchen and living room were still missing, and boards still covered the busted windows. The colored glass that Jenks had been so proud of glittered like jewels among the lengthening grass and fallen leaves. "Please bring coffee," I whispered as my head thumped back against the headrest and I closed my eyes.

I'd gotten up way too early for this, but Ivy was coming off of third shift at the I.S. and David had been available. Jenks, of course, was up. But my sleep had been restless, my dreams running the gamut from Ray grown-up and marrying a Rosewood baby to me in an insane asylum, being visited by Trent. I was tired, and almost immediately I felt myself begin to fall asleep, the familiar sounds of my street soothing after two months of living on Kisten's boat, *The Solar*, now docked at the quay next to Piscary's old restaurant.

My eyes began to twitch, and I slipped into REM sleep eerily fast. Stray threads of memory sparked: Ivy and me having coffee in Piscary's stripped-down kitchen, waking up beside Trent and seeing his smile as he watched me open my eyes, Jenks and me sharing a quiet moment, me in my robe and him sitting on my coffeepot, trying to get warm enough to fly. Snippets of conversation that never happened slowly evolved into actions that never occurred as I began to dream.

"One of us isn't going to make it off this boat," my dream Jenks said, black sparkles falling from him as he drew his garden sword and flew at me.

My body twitched as, in my dream, I flung myself back to hit the teak floorboards. Still dreaming, I tapped a line and blasted Jenks into a thousand spiders that rained down on me.

Gasping, I snorted awake, heart pounding as my tingling hands brushed my legs to push off the imagined spiders. *Jenks . . . ,* I thought, horrified that I'd hurt him, even in a dream. Jenks was my rock, the one I depended upon the most, the one who depended upon me to keep him alive through the winter. Why would I dream he'd try to hurt me, forcing me to hurt him?

"Damn," I whispered as I made fists of my tingling hands. Had I tapped a line in my sleep? Shaken, I reached for the door and got out to distance myself from the nightmare.

The late-November morning was chill after the stuffy car, and I hunched deeper into my dark green leather coat. It was almost black, really, the oily sheen going well with my ofttimes frizzy red hair, pale complexion, and occasional kick-ass attitude. Still . . . I eased the door to my car shut, using my hip to close it with a soft click to preserve the quiet of the middle- to lower-class neighborhood. It was just before nine, which meant the few humans on the street were on their way to work or school and most Inderlanders were nowhere near thinking about getting up.

Hands in my pockets, I followed the cracked sidewalk to the church's wide steps. My vamp-made boots were nearly silent in the dappled sun showing through bare branches. A bedraggled, loose-feathered crow sat ominously among the flowers and plates of food that decked the cement steps, and I frowned. The offerings had been left by grateful ex-familiars, freed when the demons regained the ability to walk in reality. It had been two months, but the pile had grown, not diminished, and seeing them there reminded me of when Cincinnati thought I'd died in the blast that had torn off the back of the church and spread it over the garden and adjacent graveyard.

It had been a hard September.

"Shoo," I said, waving at the bird, and the untidy thing flew onto the nearest tree, silent and unafraid, waiting for me to leave before it would come back down and take what it wanted.

The door was unlocked, and a feeling of Camelot lost rose as I gazed up at the shiny metal plaque. TAMWOOD, JENKS, AND MORGAN, VAMPIRIC CHARMS LLC. Lip twitching, I pushed the door open and went in, boots scuffing in the dark vestibule as I shut the door and sealed out the morning light. I wasn't ready to let this go, but even I was having a hard time ignoring the writing on the wall with the three of us being scattered while the church was repaired.

I slowed as the peace of the place erased the lingering unease from my dream. On the table beside the door, letters and junk mail were stacked in an ever-higher mess. "Postal weeds," Jenks called them, and as I waited for my eyes to adjust to the glow of the single unbroken window, I winnowed through the topmost envelopes to find the bills and tuck them in my back pocket.

Even now I could smell the scent of vampire, pixy, and witch laced through the stronger scents of plywood, cut two-by-fours, and the sweaty Weres fixing the place. Kisten's pool table sat against the wall where the Goddess had pushed it as if it had been made of cardboard. Ivy's baby grand had fared better, but it was covered in construction dust, whereas Kisten's pool table had a vinyl cover and a stenciled sign stating that whoever used it as a workbench would be eviscerated.

I smiled, arms swinging as I headed for it. It was good to have friends.

The scent of melting shoes and burning flesh tickled my nose, and I avoided the outlines of rubber glued to the floorboards where the Goddess had stood. The mystics who served as her uncountable eyes had been so thick that the corpse she'd been animating had been burning. A line of char showed where Al had circled us, the smut from a thousand years of curses serving as an unexpected protective filter from the Goddess's rage. Plywood covered the hole in the floor, and my eyes rose to the thick cracked beams and, higher, past the false ceiling, to the glint of new nail tips.

There'd been the reek of burned pixy dust, the feeling of hopeless odds, of no escape. My focus blurred as I remembered Ivy's pure sob of joy when Nina saw her soul in the one she loved and knew it was safe: good things, too.

Melancholy, I pulled the cover off the pool table in a sliding sound of vinyl.

A muffled gasp of surprise spun me to the abandoned altar, where we'd shoved the couch, chairs, and coffee table. It was a kid, towheaded and gawky, maybe sixteen. He stared at me in wide-eyed surprise from the sawdust-laden couch. A plate of half-eaten food sat on the low table before him, but it was obvious that he'd been sleeping.

"Goddess guts," he said, a scared but resolute look on him. "I didn't hear you come in."

I dropped the vinyl cover, my feet placed wide on the floor of my church. "What are you doing here?" My gaze went to the plate, and he flushed, his fair features becoming red under his thin, transparent, almost white hair. He was an elf, and my stance eased. A little.

"I, ah, thought this was your waiting room." He stood. He was almost my height, but youth made him thinner, awkward in torn jeans and an olive green T-shirt. "I was waiting."

For me? "What do you want?" I asked, gaze flicking to the plate again.

His sneakers shifted on the old oak floors, and I stifled a shiver at the sound. "I, ah . . . You know Mr. Kalamack. Can you get me in to talk to him? It's important."

My eyebrows rose at the mix of fear and strength in his voice. Mr. Kalamack. I hadn't thought of Trent as *Mr. Kalamack* in a long time. He was, as Jenks would say, my main squeeze, the sparkle in my dust, the flower in my garden, the sword in my . . . ah, yeah. We'd been dating.

"You need some help? What's your name?" I reached for my phone, but the sound of a car door slamming pulled my attention to the front of the church. He was gone when I turned back.

Without a sound, I thought. "Kind of flighty, aren't you?" I whispered as his lanky shadow passed outside the unbroken window, furtive and fast. He must have gone out Ivy's window. God knew Ivy had used that particular egress on more than one occasion.

But my frown eased when the familiar clatter of pixy wings fell like a balm over the battered church and Jenks flew in, gold dust trailing from him in contentment. Saluting me, the four-inch pixy flew into the exposed rafters on his dragonfly-like wings to inspect the roof repair. More dust sifted from him like a living sunbeam, pooling on the floor before vanishing in a faint draft.

"Just 'cause we're living on Kisten's old boat doesn't mean you can slack off on the yard work, Rache," he said as he dropped down, hands on his hips in his best Peter Pan pose and hovered before me. "The lawn looks like hell."

My spider dream flashed through me, but my breath to answer hesitated when Ivy strode in, a plate of cookies from the front steps in hand. "Ease up, Jenks," she said, her voice like living dust, gray, silky—and just as irritating when she spoke the truth. "She's been busy. We all have."

Ivy hit the lights, and I squinted when they flickered on. I hadn't even known power had been restored, but my flash of guilt vanished as I gave Ivy a quick one-armed hug and breathed deep, taking in the scent of oiled steel and orange juice. The distinctive smell of the I.S. tower was heavy on her, the multitude of vampires, witches, and Weres mixing together with the scent of paperwork and quick feet on the pavement. It told me as much as her professional attire and slightly dilated eyes that she'd come right from work. Under it all was a growing thread of Nina, as distinctive as a fingerprint. That they'd found a lasting happiness together made a lot of the crap my life dished out bearable.

"Cookie?" she said, backing up and holding out the plate, and I shook my head. The risk of a casual assassination attempt was too real and I didn't know who had made them. True, I'd been half responsible for getting the ley lines—and hence magic—working again, but no one but me was happy that the demons were living freely in reality. Elf magic wasn't working well, the running theory behind closed doors being it was because their Goddess had been reborn from an off-balance demon. Again sort of my fault.

I'd had only a smattering of jobs since, all from Trent. I was beginning to think he was finding events for me to escort him to so I'd have a paycheck. Boyfriend or not, I wasn't going to work for him for free. If the danger was real—and it was—the paycheck should be, too.

"Is David here?" Jenks asked, and I shook my head, dropping down to find the rack to set up a game. Seeing my intent, Ivy braced her back against the wall and, straining, pushed the table in an earsplitting shriek of wood. Jenks shuddered a sickly green dust, but at least we could play now. It wasn't often I saw the strength her living-vampire status gave her. Thanks to having been born with the vampire virus instead of infected with it later, she had canines that were slightly longer than mine, and sharp. And yep, she had a liking for taking blood, but she didn't need it to survive as Nina, her undead partner, did.

"Watch the hole," I said as the balls thumped into the rack. "When are they fixing that?"

"My contractor is still trying to find an old house to scavenge floorboards from," Jenks said, anxious until I rearranged the balls to put the one at the top and the eight in the middle. He didn't care about the rest. "Apparently there's been a lot of construction in Cincinnati lately, and they're running out of materials," he finished dryly.

Again, not my fault, but the spontaneous offerings on the front steps notwithstanding, I was probably being blamed for that, too.

Ivy rolled a cue stick across the table to make sure it wasn't warped. "Any idea why we couldn't do this at David's office?" she asked, her low voice sounding right even if the sanctuary was all sawdust, silent power tools, and planking.

"I can tell you why." Jenks's wings rasped in anger. "That Were-pup excuse of an insurance company he works for isn't going to make good on my claim, and he doesn't want us making a scene at his office—that's why."

I lifted the rack, happy the slate was again smooth. "I'm sure that's not it."

"He's a claims adjuster!" Jenks zipped between Ivy and me, his dust a heavy red that temporarily turned the green felt black. "That's what they do! Take your money, and then when you need it, they adjust it from your pocket to theirs!"

Ivy bent low over the far end of the table, looking svelte in her upscale leather. "Relax, pixy," she said as she lined up her break shot. "If they deny the claim, we'll find the money."

Jenks lost altitude, but he wasn't alighting on my shoulder as usual. It wasn't a snub, but it worried me. "It took all I had to put on the roof," he said, clearly depressed, and I wished he was bigger so I could give him a hug and tell him it was going to be okay.

"I said I'd help with the repair. The church wouldn't be like this if not for me," I offered.

His wings hummed when Ivy took her shot and the rack scattered, one ball dropping in. Guilt made me look down. If the church wasn't in pieces, it wouldn't feel as if it was ending.

"I can pay my own bills, witch." Jenks rose up and out of the way as Ivy circled to take a shot at the three and missed. "But even if we do get it fixed, then what?"

Jeez, Jenks. Couldn't you let sleeping vampires sleep? "Then we move back in." I scanned the table to avoid his foul mood. "Kisten's boat is just for the winter," I said as Ivy handed me the stick, but my eyes jerked to hers when she didn't let go. Her regret and guilt laced through me, pulling tight against my soul. *For the winter,* I had said, but we all knew the three of us moving back in wasn't going to happen. Not with Nina in the picture. For all the trials we'd been through in the last three years, the church had been a spot of safety—even when it was being blown up. Now it felt as if we were trying to fit back into a too-small skin.

Seeing my understanding, Ivy let go of the stick. Heart heavy, I turned to the table. "How's the new job going?" I asked to change the subject.

"Pretty much how I remember it," she said, but she was smiling when I rose from missing my shot. Jenks was hovering over that plate the teenage elf had left behind, his hands on his hips as he tried to figure it out. "You knew Nina hired in as a temp?" Ivy continued, her voice becoming animated. "Since I'm a consultant instead of a contracted employee, I can mimic her dusk-to-dawn schedule. Everyone leaves me alone since I'm her scion, and no one knows how to deal with her. She's undead, but the soul covering her is hers, and it's confusing the hell out of them."

And somehow, though everything felt wrong, I found a way to be at peace with it. Seeing Ivy love herself and someone else . . . it had been worth every burned synapse, every busted arm, every bruised heart and dream.

"I'm, ah, glad you're both here," Ivy said, and I froze when she took the offered stick and set it on the table, effectively ending the game. "Jenks? Nina and I have been giving this a lot of thought, and I don't want you digging out day quarters under the church."

Jenks rose from the plate of food, his dust a scared blue. "The Tink-blasted hell I'm not."

But Ivy smiled, the pain showing only at the corners of her eyes. "Nina and I are doing fine at Piscary's old digs," she said, and I knew the truth of that. "Cormel has his own place, and it feels like home. Especially now that Nina's redecorating."

"Rache," Jenks pleaded, begging me to say something, but I shook my head, having known this was coming. Jenks and I had moved into Kisten's big power yacht after the church had been declared unfit for habitation. Parking it at Piscary's quay had helped ease the coming heartache, but moving into Piscary's, even the upstairs apartments, had been out of the question. Not with Nina as twitchy as she was. Trying to move all of us back to the church was an even worse idea. We had too many frightened people knocking on our door. Besides, a witch living with two vampires in love wasn't smart, even if I wasn't a witch, but a demon.

Jenks slowed his wings until their hum vanished when he saw me side with Ivy. "Son of a fairy-farting whore," he muttered, adding a bitter, "Excuse me. David is here."

My shoulders slumped as he flew a blue-dusted path to the front door and worked the pulley system we'd put in place so he could open it.

David's warm greeting was muffled, and Ivy turned her back to the door, her eyes pinched with heartache. "This is harder than I thought it was going to be," she whispered. "Even if David comes through, there's no way the church will be livable before the snow flies. It's airtight and the ductwork has been fixed so we're not heating the outside, but the city won't give an occupation permit without a kitchen. Is the boat warm enough for him?"

I shook my head as I remembered how slow he'd been

this morning, sitting on my steaming coffeemaker, trying to warm up. A sustained temperature below forty-three degrees would drop him into hibernation, and without having properly prepared for it, his life would be at risk. "He's managing so far, but it's going to get colder."

Ivy leaned closer. "He should move in with me and Nina."

"Yeah, but he won't," I said, and she nodded in understanding. "If it helps, I'm meeting Trent after this," I added. "Ray and Lucy have a playdate with Ellasbeth."

"Sorry?" Ivy said with a closed-lipped smile, clearly not knowing how a structured lunch with Lucy's admittedly prickly mother related to Jenks.

"It's Friday," I said, relishing the thought that I'd made it through another week without pissing off any world power. "I'm going to spend the weekend with Trent. *As usual.* I'm hoping if I can get Jenks to come with me, he might move in with Jumoke and Izzy for the winter. *Which will be both unusual and a miracle in pixy culture.* He'll be okay in Trent's conservatory."

The sound of Jenks's wings pushed our heads apart, and I felt myself flush. "Spend the winter with my kids?" Jenks said as David's small silhouette eased into the church and shut the door. "Tink's a Disney whore. Talk about a fifth wheel."

"I think it's a good idea," Ivy said, nodding her hello to David, now cautiously entering the sanctuary, his shoulders hunched in mild unease and looking like a young Van Helsing with his long, wavy black hair, casual jeans and shirt, and short cashmere scarf. Weres could enter holy ground as much as anyone else, but they clearly felt off. "They need all the help they can get to keep their newlings alive through the winter. Izzy had what, five?" Ivy added.

Jenks's frown vanished. "Five," he said, hands on his hips. "They're already thinking up names."

But they wouldn't get them until spring and the new parents were sure they'd survive, and I hid a smile when he sat down cross-legged atop the eight ball. I would have said he

looked cute, but he'd have given me a lobotomy with the
garden sword strapped to his hip. My thoughts jerked back
to my dream about turning Jenks into spiders, and I shoved
the fear away, smile fading.

David's rugged, slightly stubbled face was beaming.
"You have no idea how good it is to see you three together,"
he said, and Ivy rolled her eyes to hide her pain that it was
ending—because I had screwed up, and she had found love.

"Hi, David." Boots clunking, I crossed the room to give
him a long, earnest hug, breathing in the scent of green and
growing things that lingered about him.

"There's a pack run this Sunday. You're invited," David
said as we parted.

"Maybe this winter," I said, and he nodded, accepting
the new distance I'd put between us since his girlfriend had
become pregnant. It wasn't because he was now taken
goods, but because I wouldn't risk endangering him further
than I already had. "How's Serena?"

David's smile widened. "Ornery. She's not allowed to
shift anymore."

I nodded, imagining it. "You're going to be a great dad,"
I added, and Jenks hummed close, almost dripping attitude
as he spilled a gold wash of pixy dust.

"All right, Mr. Peabody," Jenks said, surprising me with
the nickname Kisten had given David. "You going to piss
in the pot or play with yourself? You've had my claim for
six weeks."

"Jenks!" I exclaimed, but then froze when David winced.

"I tried," David said, and Jenks made a rude sound. "Every last trick and loophole. But the kitchen and living room
were lost in a city power struggle—which we're under no
obligation to cover—and the damage to the sanctuary was
caused by a demon."

"It was a Goddess," I said, and David brought his gaze
back down from the roof.

"Granted, but Newt was originally a demon. And since
demon damage isn't covered—"

"Newt wasn't part of the Goddess when the Goddess did the damage," I interrupted. Jenks was hovering beside me, but Ivy had given up by the looks of it and was dropping balls one by one into the pockets as if they were her choices, gone forever. "And I didn't summon her."

"Regardless." David hesitated as he noticed the charred circle for the first time.

Frustrated, I crossed my arms over my middle as Ivy propped the stick against a window frame. I'd find the money somewhere. Maybe if I changed my name, someone would hire me. "Well, thanks for trying," I finally said, and David's expression eased.

"Son of a fairy-farting whore," Jenks swore, shunning my hand when I held it out for him.

"We'll find the money," I insisted, but even if we did and we moved back in, Ivy wouldn't be at the big oak farm table with her maps and laptop, drinking orange juice and scowling as she told Jenks to keep his dust off her screen. It would be just me, Jenks, and Bis, knocking around in a big, empty church. Even his kids were gone.

"I'm sorry," David said into the stretching silence. "Everything ends."

The sickly yellow dust spilling from Jenks nearly broke my heart. "Yeah," the small pixy said. "But I thought I'd be dead before it was over."

Head low, Ivy stood beside the table. "Me too," she said, breathing the words.

Panic iced through me. It would be so easy to move in with Trent, become part of his world, twining our lives in equal measures. But I enjoyed my independence too much, and bringing my chaotic life that close to his girls wasn't going to happen. Besides, who would go all the way out to the Kalamack estate to hire me?

But Jenks looked as if he was going to throw up. I had to do something to get that look off his face. Fingers cold, I touched the pool table, feeling as if Kisten were here reminding me that love sometimes hurt when it was real.

"Well, there's no help for it," I said with a forced cheerfulness. "We're going to have to get that sign changed, Jenks."

Ivy's head snapped up, her eyes flashing pupil black in
alarm. David, too, looked surprised, and I stiffened, steeling myself for what was going to come out of my mouth
next.

"What for?" Jenks clattered his wings, probably thinking I was abandoning Ivy.

"New business cards, maybe," I added with a fake nonchalance. "With just your and my name on them." I tore my
gaze from Jenks's shock. "I'm not giving up the firm," I
said, voice soft so it wouldn't crack. "And I need your help,
Jenks, if you're still willing to work with me. Ivy's not
dead, and even if she was, she'd still be in Cincinnati. If we
get in a jam, she'll bail us out."

Ivy's shoulders lost their stiffness, and Jenks's wing hum
lessened. I exhaled, the tight band about my chest easing.
"Besides," I said, nose wrinkling at the ugly smell of decay
suddenly drifting through the church, "with Ivy and Nina
working for the I.S., they might throw a few jobs our way.
You know, the stuff they can't figure out."

Ivy, too, had noticed the rank smell, her face showing
her distaste even as she relaxed. Beside her, David turned
to the back of the church in question. My thoughts went to
the teenage elf I'd chased off, but he'd wanted to meet
Trent. Making a magic stink wouldn't help his case.

"You don't mind Ivy being gone?" Jenks asked, reminding me that even though he'd loved and lost, raised children
and buried them, he was still only twenty.

"Of course I mind," I said, and Ivy bowed her head so
her hair hid her eyes. "It's going to be as hard as hell to
wake up without her across the hall, crabbing about me using all the hot water and snarling if I ate her cookies, but
what choice do we have? She's in love, Jenks."

Jenks dropped to me, and my hand came up for him to
land on. My throat caught when he stood there, a chance to
find a new way spreading before us.

"Yeah?" Jenks said, looking relieved. "How about taking the hooker silhouette off the ad Ivy put in the Yellow Pages."

I nodded, throat tight, and Jenks lovingly flipped off Ivy at her annoyed growl. "We'll design something," I said. "And what is that stench?"

"It smells like something that died two weeks ago," David said as he tried to peer through the cracks of a boarded-up window.

"It wasn't there when we got here," Jenks said, then darted to him.

Jenks was gone, but his dust lay warm upon me. I couldn't bring myself to brush it away, and slowly it vanished in the heat from my hand. It would be hard without Ivy, not just for her expertise but because she was our friend. But like I'd said, she wasn't dead, and I had to stop feeling as if she was simply because she wasn't sleeping across the hall.

"Thanks," Ivy said, and I smiled when she gave my hand a tight squeeze.

"Don't thank me," I said as I turned her touch into a full hug. "I'm serious. We're going to miss you like the undead miss the sun, but this is where we are."

"Yeah, Ivy." Jenks flew circles around us until Ivy and I parted. "Just you wait," he said as he landed on my shoulder to feel right. "You'll be begging to come back after six months in the tower."

"Back to this? Not a chance," Ivy said over her shoulder as she headed for the back, giving the plywood-covered hole in the floor a wide berth. But it was obvious how hard it was for her to let go. Nina needed her, and Jenks and I . . . did not. And Ivy needed to be needed.

"I think the smell is coming from the graveyard," Ivy said, her movements edging into vampire quickness as she went down the hall to the plywood nailed over the raw opening that once led to the kitchen and back living room. I could see her frustration that she couldn't be what Nina needed and still keep things the same, but Ivy and Nina shouldn't have had to put up with any roommates, much less a pixy and a witch-born demon with more baggage than an entire rock band.

David's hands clasped uneasily. "Er, I should leave if you have a body out there."

"If we do, it's not ours." I started for the back, wincing at the screech of a nail pulling out. "Ivy, be careful!" I exclaimed. "There's a six-foot drop past that plywood." Jenks was on my shoulder, and for the first time in weeks, I felt good. "You okay with the temp, Jenks?"

"Don't turn into my mom, Rache," he muttered, but he didn't leave my warmth.

David's shoulders jostled mine in the tight confines of the hall, and, grinning, he tried to beat me to where Ivy was working on the makeshift door. Giving up, she backed up three steps and gave it a solid kick. Nails screeching, the plywood was knocked clear into the burned foundation of what had once been the kitchen and back living room.

Cool air and sun poured in. I squinted, my hand going over my nose in disgust. Past the burned foundation stones and weedy garden was a zombie stumbling about in the leaf-coated, long-grassed graveyard.

"Oh, yuck." David dropped back with his hand over his nose.

"Dude." Jenks hovered beside Ivy and me, a weird silver-purple dust spilling from him. "The news said they got the last one three days ago."

"Apparently not." David leaned against the hall's wall, pale behind his stubble. "He looks like an old one. He smells too bad for it to be just what he's been eating. That's decay."

"You think?" My jaw clenched in revulsion. It was a zombie. Animated dead. A handful of them had been found in Cincinnati over the last few months, all in various stages of decay and age. No one was sure where they'd come from, but the timing made me think they'd been tucked in an I.S. quarantine somewhere and had escaped when the ley lines had gone down. That the I.S. was claiming innocence made it seem more than likely.

"How did it get past the graveyard's gates?" Ivy asked, seeming to handle the stench better than David, who had slumped back down the wall until he was sitting with his knees to his chest, his head low as he took shallow breaths.

"No idea," I said, but knowing from experience that a person could slip through the chain holding the car gates shut. "You know, seeing him careening from stone to stone out there looks both somehow really right and really disturbing."

"Tink's titties, he smells worse than the wrong end of a Were's outhouse." Jenks's wings rasped as he landed on Ivy's shoulder. "Get him to leave, Rache."

My God, he stinks. "Why is this my problem?" I said as the zombie made a lonely, guttural, social *caw*. Arms over my middle, I watched Mr. Z stumble into a headstone to leave a black smear. Nice. Someone's experiment had gone free-range and was leaving chunks in my graveyard.

"Awwwww, Rache. He's dropping parts. Do something!"

"I'll call it in," David said from behind us, and the beeps of his phone rose faintly.

"This is going to make me late getting home," Ivy said with a sigh.

One hand on the broken wall, I leaned out, almost gagging on the smell. "How did he get across the river? Weren't most of them found in Cincy?"

"I think everyone is ignoring them now so they don't have to deal with them," David said, clearly on hold.

"I can't imagine why," Ivy said, a hand over her face and voice muffled.

"Rache," Jenks begged, "he's dropping chunks. How am I going to get rid of that?"

I shrugged, my eyes lifting to a sudden commotion in the trees as a murder of crows began a raucous cawing, hounding something in the scorched oak tree in the back. Jenks touched his sword hilt, his eyes on the bare branches, but then they all flew off with harsh calls.

"Why is this my problem?" I said again, and then I

sneezed, the unexpectedness of it making it loud and obnoxious.

"That did it," Jenks said as Mr. Z turned, his filthy lab coat fluttering as he focused on our voices with an odd concentration. At my feet, David shuddered.

"Fantabulous," I said as Mr. Z began shambling our way. "You think someone lured him in here, hoping we'd take care of it?" Crap on toast, I didn't want to have to stop at the boat and change before meeting Trent and the girls at the top of Carew Tower for his lunch and my breakfast, but that's what I'd be doing if I touched it.

"Probably." Ivy jumped from the open hallway to land on the plywood with an attention-getting thump. "You got anything on you for this?"

Jenks looked at me and shrugged, and sighing, I awkwardly followed her. "I should have worn more leather," I muttered, then louder, "Anything that works on a zombie?" I hefted a charred two-by-four the cleanup crew had missed. "Sure. Jenks, some distraction?"

Jenks darted off, and Ivy lifted a crowbar, wiping the colorful wet leaves from it and taking a few practice swings. "You look nice today," she said. "I'll take the bottom."

"Thanks," I said in relief. "I dressed up for David. He always makes me feel like a slob."

"I know what you mean," she said, glancing back at the trim man. Yes, he had some scruff, and his long hair was escaping the clip at the back of his neck, but he carried himself with enough grace that he looked like a million bucks in jeans and a leather coat.

"The I.S. won't send anyone," David said loudly, standing to lean against the interior wall. "They want you to take him to the zoo."

"The zoo?" I said in disbelief. Weapons in hand, Ivy and I paced forward as Jenks buzzed the slow zombie, easily staying away from his confused swipes. "Are they serious?"

"They put in an exhibit last week." Ivy pointed for me to go right while she took the left.

My God, the stench was a thousand times worse this close. "They're putting these things on display?" I muttered, breath shallow as I wove through the tombstones and tall grass.

Jenks zipped to us as Mr. Z whimpered, his back to us as he tried to find the pixy. A flat circle of grass detailed his circular path, making a nice place to down him. "They're probably the only people who have a strong enough air filter," Jenks said as he settled in my hair, clearly cold. "Fairy farts, he stinks. I think I burned my wings on his stench."

"The kids love them!" David shouted from the raw opening to the church. "Watching them bang into things. Lose parts. You know!"

The zombie was between me and Ivy, and I hefted my two-by-four. "That's not getting in my car," I said, and Ivy jerked.

"You're the one with the convertible," she said, and Mr. Z groaned in indecision, relying on our voices to find us, as his eyes were a hazed opaque.

"So?" I adjusted my grip as Mr. Z decided on me. "You telling me your trunk hasn't had a dead man in it before?"

"Not one that smelled like that."

"Ladies?" Jenks said from my hair. "Can we finish this before the sun goes nova? I have to talk to Trent tonight about renting out a tree in his conservatory."

A real smile came over my face, and I suddenly felt invincible. Jenks would survive the winter at Trent's, and there was no way in hell that decaying piece of animated magic was getting in my car. I nodded to Ivy, and we both jogged forward. Eight steps was all it took, and Ivy cut his feet out from behind him as I smacked him on the forehead.

Mr. Z collapsed backward with a startled whimper, his face to the sky and blubbering as his orientation was lost. It would be at least ten minutes before he realized he was on the ground.

"Sweet as pixy piss," Jenks said, and I dropped the two-by-four. Ivy met my grin with her own. It was always a pleasure to work with her, even this little.

Slowly my smile fell, but no one noticed, as David had finally gotten over his heebie-jeebies and was striding through the long grass and tombstones with the pool table cover to wrap Mr. Z in. I didn't want Ivy to stay at Piscary's when we moved back into the church, but with Nina . . . It was better this way. Ivy had been drifting away for a long time.

And as I'd told Jenks, it wasn't as if she was dead.

CHAPTER

2

A SMALL CROWD HAD GATHERED AT THE BACK GATE TO THE zoo, mostly patrons, since the employees had probably had their fill of zombie stink by now and were finding other things to do—things requiring them to be on the other side of Cincinnati's world-class zoo. Ivy and I stood almost forgotten in the overdone show of getting Mr. Z out of Ivy's trunk and carefully leashed between three keepers who then slowly led the rotting animated corpse to the zombie enclosure.

I thought it would've been easier to strap him to a gurney and wheel him there, but the keepers were big on trying to show their charges in as natural a setting as possible. My comment that strapped to a gurney *was* his natural setting hadn't gone over well, and watching them shamble off surrounded by kids excited to be grossed out, I had a feeling that "walk with the zombies" was going to be one of the zoo's more lucrative efforts come winter when they didn't smell so bad.

Not surprisingly, we'd been asked to wait. Ivy and I stood in the sun, my head down over my phone as I texted Trent that I'd had to take a zombie to the zoo and couldn't make Carew Tower. Ivy sighed, and I tucked my phone in a back pocket. I didn't smell zombie on me, but I knew Ivy could as she plucked her shirt and winced.

"Thanks for waiting," the lingering woman in tan slacks and a white top with the zoo's logo on it said. "The FIB wants to talk to you before you leave."

My eyebrows rose. "Ah, we were told to bring him here."

"You're fine." The woman blinked fast as the smell of zombie rising from us hit her anew. "We informed the I.S. and FIB that we had a seventh zombie, and Captain Edden asked us to keep you here to sign the paperwork."

"How long?" Ivy asked, and she shrugged, her eyes on the retreating, shambling group.

"He's on-site. Five minutes?" she guessed. "If you promise not to leave . . ."

"We'll sit tight," I said, and she hustled away, fleeing almost.

"Good thing I canceled on Trent," I muttered as I went to the nearby bench. Ivy followed, chuckling as she sat beside me in a languid display of grace. In the distance, howler monkeys began hooting. It was unusual this time of day, but I'd shout, too, if a zombie was passing my enclosure. My phone buzzed, and I took it out, smiling at Trent's text telling me to be sure I took the zombie to see the pandas and buy him popcorn. *Take a zombie to the zoo . . . ,* I thought, smirking at myself. I probably could have worded that better.

"It sort of sticks to you, doesn't it?" Ivy said, and I tucked my phone away again, glad both Trent and I knew work was work and that sometimes unexpected things happened that needed to be dealt with immediately and to not get bent out of shape about it. Kisten had taught me that.

"The stink?" I said, wanting to be sure we were talking about the same thing. "I know I didn't touch it." I grimaced when a little girl passing asked her mom what that bad smell was. "You ever smell anything like this before?"

"Once," Ivy said, shifting her posture and taking a breath to tell me about it.

"Stop!" I said, and then I sneezed. I froze, waiting for the second one, but it never came.

Ivy took her phone out, checked the time, then put it away. "Top of the hour," she said, meaning the sneeze, and

I made an "Mmm-hum" of an answer. "Your last sneeze was, too," she added, wary this time, and I nodded, stretching my feet in my designer vamp boots into the sun.

"Yep." I didn't want to get into it. Ivy knew what structured sneezing meant as well as I did. Someone was trying to reach me via a scrying mirror. That someone probably being a demon.

"It might be a job," Ivy said cautiously, and I slumped. The demons had been surprisingly quiet since regaining the ability to walk in reality at will, but working for them wouldn't help my reputation. Then again, the last time I'd ignored a polite repeated call, I'd been jerked into a demon court to stand trial for breaking the ever-after.

"That's why I snipped the end off that yew bush before we left," I said, and Ivy glanced at it sticking out of my shirt pocket like a weird nosegay. She'd never been comfortable with my spell crafting, but it was a part of me, and she accepted it. I needed a yew stylus to make a new scrying mirror, preferably from a bush growing over a grave. My old mirror hadn't worked since Al had cracked it in a self-indulgent pity party.

"You need the upstairs kitchen?" Ivy asked, her eyes on the cute little girl sporting a panda-eared cap.

"If you're not going to be in it," I said. I didn't like the barren industrial counters and cold ovens that still smelled like vamps and pizza, but I couldn't set a circle over water. "It won't take long. Half an hour, maybe. I need to set a protection circle."

She smiled a closed-lipped smile. "That's why I asked. Take all the time you need."

"Thanks." My phone pinged, and I dug it out, eyebrows rising. Trent clearly wanted me there. He'd changed Ellasbeth's ill-thought plan for lunch at Carew Tower's rotating restaurant to ice cream at Eden Park, and could I make it by four? Right after his and the girls' naps.

"Actually, we might want to designate that freestanding counter as yours," Ivy said, brightening. "Nina wants to try her hand in the kitchen more, and it will be faster to cordon off a corner for you than to educate her on the dos and don'ts of mixing spell prep with food prep."

"She wants to cook? Really?" I said as I answered Trent's message with a "yes" and hit send. I'd have time to make a new scrying mirror *and* shower. No problem. "What is it with the undead wanting to cook?" I asked, remembering Piscary. "It's not as if they eat it."

"It gives them a way into our lives that doesn't involve blood," she said softly, and I nodded. Piscary had the reputation of making Cincinnati's best pizza as a way to lure potential blood sources closer and give his contacts a plausible-deniability way to check in. Nina, though, was a new kind of undead, thanks to Ivy holding her soul and giving Nina sips of it along with her blood. The drive to give back to Ivy was probably a desperate need.

"She wants to make Thanksgiving dinner," Ivy said, a faint blush coloring her cheeks. "Her parents are both gone, and I think she's trying to recapture something. You want to come?"

"Um, sure," I said, still thinking it odd that an undead vampire wanted to make a dinner she couldn't eat. "Mind if I ask Trent and the girls?"

"Oh, crud," Ivy said softly. "I forgot about that. Forget I asked. You've already got plans."

"No, I don't. I mean, Trent's got reservations at Carew Tower. That's not Thanksgiving. He needs to experience what it's like to sit at a card table and eat dry turkey and listen to the same old jokes year after year." I hesitated. "Unless three more is too many."

Ivy's smile warmed. "I think we can handle it. That makes seven including Jenks," she said, and I stifled an unexpected, slow quiver threatening to rise up through me. Damn it, my neck was tingling, and I looked away as Ivy sent out a wash of pheromones. Food. I'd forgotten that eating crunchy things was a living vampire turn-on. Maybe this wasn't such a good idea.

"We're doing this after dark, right?" I asked. Ivy might have been good living in Piscary's old digs now that Rynn

Cormel had gone back to Washington, but the downstairs always gave me the creeps. My attention followed the yellow leaves skating across the plaza, rising up in a breath of air to pass before a silent crow hunched in a tree waiting for an unattended pretzel. Cincy seemed to be thick with them this year. Maybe they paired up with the zombies.

"Upstairs, yes," Ivy said, her voice distant. "The downstairs kitchen isn't big enough to make anything but popcorn in. There's Edden."

She sounded pleased, and I smiled at the somewhat squat, square older man striding purposefully toward us across the zoo. I stood in anticipation, liking the FIB captain. He'd helped me pay off my I.S. debt three years ago, but it seemed longer than that. He moved with a military precision, one arm holding a folder as he squinted in the sun from behind his plastic-frame, round glasses and acknowledged our presence with a raised hand. Though dressed professionally, he wasn't in uniform. I knew he didn't get out of the office as much as he liked. He wasn't flabby, but his shoes weren't made for running.

Ivy stood as well, and his smile widened to encompass his entire somewhat round face.

"Ivy! Rachel! I heard they got a zombie in the Hollows, but I didn't know it was you."

"Who else would it be?" I said, taking in his graying black hair cut short to his head and his ever-whitening mustache before I gave him a professional hug just so I could breathe in the scent of old coffee. It felt odd, even as I smiled. Trent was a lot thinner. Taller, too.

"True, true," Edden said when I let go, somewhat red as he nodded to Ivy. "He didn't give you trouble, did he? I think he's the oldest one yet. The rest look almost normal compared to him."

Ivy took his extended hand, and the two shook as she gave him an earnest but closed-lipped smile. "Older is easier when it comes to zombies. No charge on this one."

"A freebie?" I muttered, but I suppose I should be glad they took him.

Edden beamed, his eyes lingering briefly on the sprig of yew poking out of my shirt pocket. "Thank you, ladies. Where's Jenks? Too cold?"

I gave Ivy a sideways look. Jenks and Edden had a great relationship, having bonded over lost wives and a night of karaoke. "No, he and David crapped out on us and went for coffee after we got Mr. Z in the trunk. Why?" I asked, suspicious when Edden dropped the folder open on the bench behind us.

"Paperwork," the older man said. "But I'd think your two signatures will be enough." He fumbled the pen out of his front shirt pocket, but Ivy had already taken hers from her jacket's inner pocket and clicked it open. "If you could sign here, saying that you took responsibility of the zombie after it encroached on your property, and then this one releasing your rights to it."

He extended his pen to me when Ivy began signing with her own, but I wouldn't take it. "Responsibility?" I echoed. "We knocked it down and took it to the zoo."

"Sign the paper or he's yours." Ivy finished her scrawl and spun the papers to me. "You don't want one that old. Too much maintenance."

"I don't want one at all," I said, and Edden's mustache bunched up.

"Then sign the paper. Here, and again here. Unless you want him back."

I looked down, not wanting to read the gobbledygook. Ivy hadn't. There was a picture of Mr. Z in his grungy lab coat and empty pocket protector that made me wonder how many people had seen and ignored him on his ramblings to our graveyard. "I swear, Edden, if this comes back to bite me, I will take it out of your hide. We tried to call it in, and no one would come."

Edden's posture eased as I bent low to sign, putting a period after my name so the signature couldn't be used to target a spell to me. "And we at the FIB appreciate you handling it," he said cheerfully. "Last night was busy, and because everyone is afraid to look over the edge of the box they put themselves in, it hit my desk. Three days of some-one's shoddy work is now my problem."

But he didn't seem to be unhappy about it as I straight-ened from my uncomfortably low stoop. A warning flag snapped in my thoughts when Ivy nodded, the motion hardly there. She knew something about it, whatever it was.

"Honestly, Rachel," Edden said as he tucked the papers into the file, "you don't know how good you have it, being able to pick and choose your runs."

"Uh, huh?" My stare at Ivy became a squint, and a flash of thrill hit me when her eyes met mine and darted away. *Three days of shoddy work landing on Edden's desk?* "You got the first human-on-human lethal domestic dispute, didn't you," I said, remembering the newscast I'd turned off, and Edden nodded, smile wide.

Cincy wasn't known for its violent crime. Oh, it hap-pened, but the city wasn't known for it, and the recent spate of Inderland passion crimes ending in death was unusual. The media was busy inventing reasons for it, but the FIB would be involved now if there had been a human fatality.

"How did you get ahold of the I.S. reports?" I asked, my eyes immediately flicking back to Ivy. She was the only one who'd share information with the FIB like that—which meant she was working the cases and hadn't told me. I put a hand on my hip, peeved.

"Ivy," Edden said, confirming it. "Which means I have the straight poop, not the watered-down pap we usually get," he added in satisfaction as he tucked the folder under his arm.

Which was true, but it still hurt that Ivy hadn't told *me* she was working the case. "Banshee?" I offered, trying to keep the annoyance from my voice. Mia was still in cus-tody as her lawyers tried to balance the logic of raising a child with special needs against Mia's multiple assaults and murders to accomplish it. But that didn't mean one of Mia's sisters wasn't trying to encroach on her city.

Edden shook his head, but I was more interested in Ivy's wince. "The I.S. says no," he said, "and seeing as I'm get-ting my information from Ivy, I believe them."

Eyebrows high, I faced Ivy.

"Oh," Edden said, only now noticing Ivy's discomfort, "I guess you didn't tell Rachel you're working the cases."

"Only because I've dealt with banshees," Ivy said, but it didn't explain why she hadn't told me.

"How come you didn't tell me you were working this?" I finally said, and Edden rocked back a step. "The confidentiality barrier never stopped you before."

"There's nothing to tell." Ivy glanced at Edden, her apparent guilt far more obvious than her annoyance. "But since they released it to the media this morning, I can say it's not a banshee. My moulage-reading skills are not court rated, but it's obvious that the emotion left at every crime scene is exactly what you'd expect. If it was a banshee, there'd be no residual emotion left at all."

Released to the media, I mused, miffed. I knew the law, but I knew how to keep my mouth shut, too. "Okay," I said, trying to keep my voice light so the disappointment wouldn't show. "Well, when you want to know what or who's doing it, let Jenks and me know." Ivy was right. It wasn't my job to figure out what was behind the attacks. But if I had my way, it would have been.

"Rachel . . . ," Ivy protested.

Edden took an awkward step back. "Thanks for the paperwork, ladies," he said with forced cheerfulness.

"You know I can't talk about an ongoing investigation," Ivy said, but the pheromones she was unconsciously putting out to ease the situation had broken through the zombie stink, and the vampire scar on my neck was tingling. Worse, it irked me that she was right, and then I got mad that I was irked. But seeing as we were arguing, getting in her car wasn't a good idea.

"Edden, can I hitch a ride with you back to the church?" I asked, giving Ivy a sour smile to try to tell her it was okay. "I left my car there."

"Seriously?" Ivy complained, thinking I was mad at her, which I was, but I was only trying to keep from pushing her vampire buttons. "I was invited to the scenes as a matter of courtesy. I couldn't talk about it, and I didn't bring it up because the I.S. is handling it. And if you're going to do this with every case I have, then we are going to have real problems."

"I get that," I said forcefully. "But you really think it's a good idea I get in a car with you right now?"

Ivy's eyes went to my neck, and I stiffened, suppressing the tendril of promise just her focused attention sent through me. She was hungry. Working in the I.S. tower all night around the long-undead did that to a girl. Ivy caught her breath, then smiled to show a slip of fang as she found a compliment in there somewhere.

"Ah, sure. I can drop you off," Edden said, nervous now for an entirely different reason. "But can you come out to the FIB once you get your car? I came out here for more than paperwork."

My head jerked up, and my breath caught. The I.S. had made it clear I wasn't invited, but the FIB was another story. Edden wanted me in on this? "Really?" I said, voice high, and Edden chuckled as he shared a look with Ivy.

"Good God," Ivy said, her smile widening. "It's like you gave her a bag of candy."

"It's a paying job, right?" I said, words almost falling over themselves as the thought came and went about getting that Were crew back out and working. "Real money, yes? Not an IOU. Jenks and I have a church to rebuild." Finally. A job that didn't involve Trent. I mean, I appreciated the work, but it was beginning to feel like charity, and I had my pride.

"Real money." Edden touched his mustache, his eyes bright in amusement. "So keep track of your time."

"You got it," I said, not caring if he knew how relieved I was.

"If we're done here?" Ivy said, and when Edden nodded, she touched my shoulder and turned away, walking to the back gate and her car, her hips swaying. "See you later!" she called over her shoulder, clearly in a good mood at still being able to jerk my libido around like a little dog on a string.

Yeah, she would, and I chuckled, glad we were okay and nothing had changed.

Excitement zinged down to my toes as I faced Edden, and as I tightened my mental grip on the nearest ley line, I heard a lion make a coughing roar. "Do you want to split one of those animal-shaped sugar cookies on the way out?" I asked, and he laughed, a heavy hand landing on my shoulder to turn me to the front of the zoo.

It was good to have friends.

CHAPTER

3

MY ARMS SWUNG CONFIDENTLY AS I WALKED THROUGH THE low-ceilinged FIB halls with Edden beside me, feeling at home among the uniformed men and women who had dedicated their lives to upholding decency and fairness among Cincy's diverse needs and demands. I loved the scent of paper and gun oil that meant get-the-job-done, and though I noticed the occasional resentment directed at me—a witch-born demon walking among them—I was, for the most part, recognized and accepted. They'd seen me at my worst and best, but mostly my worst.

Which made me glad I'd dressed up today, even if it hadn't been for them. Bobbing my head at two approaching officers, I got a respectful head nod in return as they went by.

"Phew-w-w," I heard one whisper, and my good mood faltered. Clearly eau de zombie was still with me. I'd definitely wedge a shower in before seeing Trent at the park.

"Try rinsing your hair in tomato juice," Edden said, grinning as he swiped a packet of papers from a desk and handed them to me. "Jack and Jacqueline," he said, his voice shifting to a familiar bullpen cadence as we continued to his office. "A neighbor heard the fight and called us. He had her on the kitchen floor by the time we got there."

Edden lurched forward to get the door to his office, and the scent of Old Spice washed over me. "He says she attacked him first, but we found him standing over her, dazed and with a slap mark on her face."

I hesitated just inside his office, not sure where he expected me to sit. The room was cluttered, but it was the sort of clutter that spoke of dedication. I liked it. The only chair apart from the one behind his desk was covered with stacks of papers that still smelled like the copier. "She's in the hospital?" I said as I looked at the top page and their mug shots: messy hair, no makeup, stubble. I could almost see the morning breath. But no massive bruises or cuts. "Why?"

Edden's jaw tightened as he shut the door but for a crack and swooped forward to clear off the chair. "He claims he struck her only once," he said, letting the files hit his desk hard enough to make the skirt on the hula girl beside his monitor move. "She's only got the one bruise on her face, but she's in the hospital because she doesn't remember it. Anything. No sign of concussion."

"Mmmm." I sat down and studied their pictures. Jacqueline looked confused, a lost expression on her as she stood in her nightgown. Jack was untidy, angry, and frustrated. No wonder the FIB had held both of them.

"Yep." Edden sat down and moved a cup of nasty cold coffee to the edge of his desk so he could spread his elbows wide. "I'd write this down as a simple domestic dispute but for the fact that between us and the I.S. we've now had four in as many days, all but this one ending in someone being dead. We were lucky that he didn't kill her before we got there. But it's harder for a human to commit homicide."

My lips parted. "I beg your pardon."

Edden's eyes widened. "I don't mean emotionally," he said, a light flush to his cheeks. "Physically. It's easier to kill someone with magic than with your bare hands unless you're a vampire or Were, and even then you need the element of surprise, but that's one of the few things the crimes seem to have in common. Not one seems to be premeditated, their doubtful motives aside. It makes the crime scenes . . . messy."

I relaxed, willing to take that at face value as I leafed

through the rest of the reports, seeing ugly pictures of once-living people beside household objects used as weapons: lamp, knife, extension cord. They were I.S. records by the letterhead and the familiar DO NOT COPY stamp. "*Messy* is the word," I said, blanching at the destruction of the vampire's apartment. *Dude.*

"Messy and spontaneous." Edden waved off someone who poked their head in, wanting to talk to him, and then he stretched his leg out and shut the door, cutting off the comfortable office chatter. "Whatever was at hand. And viciously fast apart from the vampires. That one there? The vampires? It took fifteen minutes according to a downstairs neighbor. No one called nine-one-one because apparently it's hard to tell the difference between murder and especially vigorous sex play."

"That's what I hear," I said, feeling myself warm as I shifted the pages about. "Anything else in common?"

"Not much." He hesitated, and I glanced up. He looked good behind a desk, but I always thought he looked better out in the field, where he wanted to be. "They all have different socioeconomic statuses. Education is all over the map. We've got three in the Hollows, one in Cincinnati. Ages range from twenty-five to sixty." His eyes went to the new-smelling files on his desk. "Most have been in Cincy their entire lives, but not all of them. The only thing they have in common is that they are all in their pajamas."

He said it like it was a joke, but it rang in me like a Klaxon. "No kidding," I said, then flipped back to the mug shots, seeing a hint of bedroom lace, a swath of flannel. Bed hair. Lots of bed hair. Frowning, I crossed my knees and paged back and forth for the estimated times of the crimes. Sure enough, though they took place at different hours, the times were consistent with the various species' sleep schedules. The witch attack was shortly after three a.m., the Were was a little later at dawn. I flipped to the front page. Jack, the guy Edden wanted me to talk to, was predawn. Sighing, I lowered the papers. What was it with humans and elves getting up before dawn?

"Crimes of passion?" I guessed, and Edden frowned to make his mustache bunch up.

"Perhaps not. We haven't gotten in to talk to Jacqueline for motive yet, but according to Ivy, all the Inderlanders involved seem to have lost it over something that happened in their past. The motives are old. So old they don't have any merit."

He stood seeing my quizzical face, coming around to take the wad of I.S. reports from me. "The witch couple, here?" he said, handing it back with the pertinent report on top. "The one who killed her boyfriend with a suffocation charm? She said she got mad about him dragging her out of drug addiction three years ago."

"That's weird." I looked down at a shot of a clearly dead twenty-something witch, his brown eyes bulging and nail gouges at his neck. Self-inflicted, according to the report. "Maybe she started up again, and he was giving her grief?"

"Toxicology says no." Standing at my shoulder, Edden looked at the photo, his eyes tired. "The woman is clean. She's devastated for having killed him, but clean. She says she was mad at him, but she isn't mad now. Says she doesn't understand what happened."

"That makes two of us."

"Same thing with the vampires." Edden held his hand out, wiggling his fingers, but I flipped the pages myself, stopping at the photo of a torn-up open-floor-plan apartment done in tasteful grays and blues. There was no body under the dent in the wall covered in photos of smiling people, but there was a chalk outline. The woman had undoubtedly been whisked away to a light-tight morgue where she could turn in safety. From the mess, it hadn't been a fast or easy death. "Man killed woman because she had a shadow. Jealous rage," Edden said shortly.

"And . . . ," I prompted, not seeing why this was considered weird. Wrong and stupid, but not weird in the jealous lives of living vampires. Shadows were generally entrapped humans who followed the vampire who'd bitten them like a puppy, jonesing for their next bite, hooked on the feel-

good pheromones vampires gave off to turn pain into excruciating pleasure. Not that I had any experience there.
Much. They were probably pretty annoying when you were
trying to get a bite in edgewise with your intended, but the
usual remedy was to move and not answer your phone, not
kill the vampire who made the shadow to begin with.

"He found out about the shadow three years ago. They
were both hauled into the I.S. for disturbing the peace at the
time, but they worked it out and have been living quietly
together since," Edden offered. "He's really upset, and Ivy
tells me we might get a little more in a few days when the
woman wakes up from the dead. There's a lot of damage for
the virus to repair. Then there's the Were who killed her
husband because he once belonged to a rival pack," he
added, and I shuffled the reports.

"How could she not know?" I asked, wincing at the
bloodied extension cord. "Don't they have to disclose that
kind of thing on marriage certificates, like previous mar-
riages?"

"They do." Edden leaned back against his desk, arms
over his chest. "Ivy tells me it's been hard to get anything
out of her, but the woman claims she's always known, but
something in her snapped. They've been married for over
twenty years, and it never bothered her before."

"Huh." I flipped to the top report and the picture of Jack
and Jacqueline waiting for me. To be honest, I was relieved
it wasn't just an Inderlander crime spree. "Crimes of passion for events that happened so far in the past it shouldn't
matter," I said softly. "Things that both parties know about
and have worked through? I don't get it."

"Neither do the people doing the assaulting." Edden's
focus was distant in thought. "Ivy tells me they're all dis-
traught, bewildered at their actions. The Were woman is on
a suicide watch, actually. It's like something wormed into
their brain and pushed them into it. You want to talk to
Jack?" Edden finished unexpectedly, and my head snapped
up. "We still have him in interrogation."

"Absolutely."

Edden gestured for the door, and I rose. The office noise spilled in when he opened it, luring me into the comforting bustle of wrongs being righted with the slow grind of bureaucracy. "And it's not a banshee," I said, meeting his pace as we headed for the interrogation rooms.

Edden shook his head. "Not according to Ivy."

"Well, she'd know," I said faintly. "It sounds Inderland-ish, though," I added, then noticed Edden's closed expression. "What?" I said flatly, and he shook his head.

"I appreciate you talking to Jack to give us your Inderland opinion," he said, but I thought it was more for the passing officers than for me. "The news has figured out it's more than a wave of especially nasty domestic crime, and I'd like to lock it down before their guesses start putting innocent people in danger."

"That's what I'm here for," I said, startled when he put a heavy hand on my shoulder to stop me shy of an interrogation room door.

"Be careful," Edden said, his dark eyes serious. "He's been reasonably cooperative so far, but don't let him touch you. We don't know what's causing this, and it might be biological."

"It's not food poisoning," I said, remembering the news on the radio, and he chuckled.

"No, but be careful anyway. You got your truth charm?"

I held it up, the wooden amulet disguised as a key fob decoration. It was old, but still worked. "Edden, you know those are illegal without a lawyer present," I said, and he smirked as he reached to open the door for me.

"Ah, I'll be watching. If you need some help . . . I don't know. Tug your ear."

I smiled, resisting the urge to touch his nose, give him a hug . . . something. It was nice feeling as if I was part of a team. "I'll be fine," I said, "but thanks."

He dropped back as he opened the door, and I went in. The stale smell of old coffee, the dusty linoleum tiles, and the hum of fluorescent lights were ugly but familiar, making me wonder if this was the same interrogation room in which I had blackmailed the coven into agreeing to rescind my shunning. Sometimes it was only the dirt we had on others that kept our asses above the grasses.

Lips pressed, I gave the man sitting at the table a neutral smile when he looked up.

Frustration pulled at the corners of his eyes as his gaze went to the sprig of yew poking from my front shirt pocket. As Edden had said, he was still in his pajamas, the flannel pants looking odd with the orange top they'd given him to wear. He sat up to acknowledge me, but my bland expression froze when his nose wrinkled. Saying nothing, I sat, trying not to push the air around. I was definitely going to have to fit a shower in before going out to the park.

"When can I see Jacqueline?" Jack asked, a mix of belligerence and dissatisfaction.

I set the paperwork on the table, his and Jacqueline's mug shots front and center. "She's your wife, yes?"

"Yes, she's my wife," Jack said angrily, his attention pulling from the photo. "I only slapped her to snap her out of trying to kill me. Why am I the one in jail? What was I supposed to do? Let her stab me?"

His cuffs chained to the table clinked, and I leaned closer to hammer my words home. "Because you were standing over her, Jack, and she was crying on the floor, and cops always side with the scared woman if there's an angry man in the room with a knife."

A little bad cop never hurt, and sure enough, Jack's expression lost its aggression, showing me the fear that it had sprung from. "Just tell me if she's okay. Please?"

I leaned back in my chair to see the truth amulet in my lap. "She's shaken up, but okay."

Exhaling, Jack slumped in relief. The charm on my keychain agreed.

"Is she on any medications? Any recent changes in them?" I asked, fishing.

"No," he said, quick enough to tell me someone had already asked him. "She has no history of ever doing anything like this before."

But I had seen guilt, and charm tight in my hand, I leaned forward again. "I'm not the FIB," I said, and his eyes came to mine. "Talk to me, Jack. What happened?"

He looked at the one-way mirror behind me. "I already told the cops who busted my door. She attacked me," he said. "I don't know why," he added, voice breaking. "She went nuts."

But the muddy green and red of my charm said there was something else. "I'm all you got, Jack," I said, and he wiped his eyes with the back of his hand. "There's an entire building of cops out there who only see a wife beater."

"Are you a counselor?" he said, and I let a half smile curve up my lips.

"No. I suck at consoling people. I'm more of a knock-them-down-and-get-to-the-truth kind of person. And I'm listening. Talk to me, Jack. There might be something you forgot that will help me figure out why Jacqueline attacked you." *And then doesn't remember anything about it.*

His gaze went to that sprig of yew in my front shirt pocket again, and then he exhaled, breath shaking. "I woke up early," he said, tired, as if he'd repeated it too many times. "I had a job across the city, and I wanted to get there before traffic got bad. I hit the alarm, and rolled over to give Jacqueline a kiss to go back to sleep. Her eyes were wide-open. Staring. I said something to her. I don't know what, and she just started hitting me. Screaming that I didn't deserve her."

The amulet in my hand was a nice steady green, unlike Jack, who was getting agitated.

"I got off the bed, and she followed me," he said, voice becoming higher. "She backed me right up into the bathroom. I'm kind of laughing and telling her to stop because it's crazy, you know? And she's yelling at me that I was a jerk and didn't deserve her, and then she went into the kitchen for a knife, I guess, because when I followed her, she tried to stab me with it. That's when I hit her." His jaw clenched, and he hid his hands under the table, cuffs clinking. "I was only trying to get her to stop," he said, pleading for me to believe him. "She dropped the knife and started crying. That's when the cops broke my door. Shoved me to the floor. Cuffed me. Dragged me into the street."

His reddening eyes filled, but he never touched them as he looked down. The amulet in my hand was green, but something felt off. I knew grief, having walked beside it as my steady companion for the first fifteen years of my life, and because of it, I paid attention to the little things that those expecting to live to see the next spring never see.

"She said that to you before, didn't she?" I said, and his eyes flicked to mine. "That you didn't deserve her."

He blinked fast, and I held my breath, waiting for it. "I cheated on her while we were engaged," he said, clearly embarrassed. "I was stupid, and it took a long time for her to forgive me. Maybe she never did. She said she did."

And there it was, the motive that should have been safely in the past, and my gut tightened. An Inderlander was behind this. But why and, maybe more important, who?

Jack's jaw tightened, the confusion under his anger easy to see. "We've had arguments before, but not like this. And I've *never* hit her. I was only trying to stop her from trying to stab me. Even when she caught me cheating on her, she never tried to hurt me."

He looked at me beseechingly. The charm in my hand was a steady green, and I exhaled, believing him. "She says she doesn't remember any of it," I said, and Jack made a noncommittal shrug that was more desperation than anything else. "Is she lying to get you in more trouble?"

"For cheating on her?" he said, confused. "She knows I've never cheated on her again. I don't understand." Fatigue pulling at him, he put the flats of his arms on the table and slumped over his cuffed hands. "We went to bed like any other night, and I woke up with her turned into a deranged, crazy woman mad about something I did years ago, something that she forgave me for before we got married." He sniffed, the sound going right to my core. "At least I thought she did," he whispered, the guilt he had felt in the past swamping him again.

"Have you had any other marital problems recently?"

"No." His voice took on some strength. "Just the usual stuff like using all the milk and forgetting to turn off the TV, but nothing worth . . . this."

The truth amulet was green, and more telling, I believed him. "Okay," I said, and he looked up at my soft voice. "Maybe I can get a message to your wife."

He blinked fast, pulling his arms back to his chest. "Will you tell her I love her?"

I smiled at his sincerity. "Sure." I stood and touched his hand, wondering if I heard Edden groaning behind the one-way glass.

"But you don't believe me. No one does," Jack said as he looked at the mirror.

The rustle of the paper being pulled from the table seemed loud. "It's hard when Jacqueline doesn't remember it." According to the report, she didn't even remember him hitting her, which was suspicious in itself. Suddenly I wanted to talk to Jacqueline, and I gave Jack a final smile as I went to the door.

"Thank you," Jack whispered as I left, but he was look- ing at his cuffed hands when I turned, and so I simply closed the door, leaving him in his personal hell.

I jerked, finding myself eye to chest with Edden. Not liking his accusing stare, I held the truth amulet up. "He wasn't lying," I said, and when he grudgingly nodded, I dropped my keys into my jacket pocket.

"Maybe he's just good at it," Edden muttered.

"Maybe he's telling the truth," I shot back, stiffening when Edden's hand went to my shoulder to lead me to the FIB's back door, where my car was parked.

"Stop it, Rachel," he said, and I eyed him askance.

"Stop what?"

He smirked, his mustache bunching. "You have this bleeding heart for the underdog, but we found him standing over his wife, who was sobbing on the kitchen floor. He admits to hitting her hard enough to knock her down. Why should I take his story at face value?"

"Other than my gut and my charm?" I said, a hint of outrage trickling through me. "Maybe because Jacqueline doesn't remember anything. Not even Jack hitting her. If she was trying to get him in trouble, I'd think she'd at least remember that. Besides, his story matches the motive pattern of the other cases."

"There is that," he said, and I breathed easier when we left the detention hall behind and entered the FIB proper. The phone chatter and the officers moving around were like heaven itself, and it was nice feeling as if I was part of it. I missed this more than I wanted to admit, having left the I.S. three years ago. Maybe this was why Ivy had returned to the I.S. as a consultant.

"Can I talk to Jacqueline? Maybe she doesn't want to remember. If I'd tried to kill someone I loved, I'd want to forget that, too."

Edden nodded as we dodged busy people on our way to the garage. "Sure. She's been moved, so I'll need some time to get the paperwork through."

"Great." I didn't know when I would fit an interview at the hospital in, but Trent would understand if I had to take an hour out of our weekend. We could stop in on our way out to the golf course, or lunch, maybe. Get out of his compound and mingle. "I want to ask her about him cheating on her," I said as we neared the back entrance. "Maybe he's picked up the habit again."

Edden's long "Mmmm" snapped across me like a wet towel, and I eyed him. "Could be," he finally said, and I frowned when he avoided my eyes. It was pretty obvious that someone was targeting couples, but why? Or maybe how? And, more important, who? "Can I have those back, please?" he added, his attention on the reports still in my grip.

He held out his hand, and I pulled them closer, grinning. "I need them," I said, then sneezed, backing up more when Edden punctuated his "Bless you" with a grab for them. Dancing back, I tucked them under my arm so I could take out my phone and look at the time. It was eleven, straight up.

"Thanks for letting me interview Jack," I said. "You

don't mind if I talk to Jenks about it, do you? He knows the damnedest things and might have an idea," I added, and Edden nodded, looking pained. "Let me know when Jacqueline is available?" I asked, wondering if he was upset I wanted to bring Jenks into it, but jeez, he knew how to keep his mouth shut.

"You got it," Edden said, lingering by the back door. "Ah, Rachel. One more thing."

"If you wanted them back, you never should have given them to me." I smiled, finding my keys as I walked backward to the door. Edden had said I could park in their garage, but the nearest slot had been someone's reserved spot, and I knew I was pushing it.

"It's not that," he said, and I rocked to a halt, not liking his faint tells that something was wrong. "There are people, not me," he said hesitantly, "who think the murders might be a demon having some fun."

My smile vanished as if he'd socked me in my gut. *Fun?* "You're serious, aren't you?" I said, and he winced, making me even more angry.

"Could you ask around in your unique circle?" he said, his stance stiff. "See if you can find out which one of the demons is pitting couples against each other?"

Is? As in a foregone conclusion? Pissed, I stomped back and put a hand on my hip. "That's the only reason you let me talk to Jack, isn't it," I said flatly.

"No," he said, but the charm on my key fob had gone a muddy reddish green. "But it was how I got the okay to involve you," he added, looking relieved when it shifted pure again.

"Well, isn't that dandy," I said, and he gave me a weak, uneasy smile. "It's only been two months since the demons were freed to walk in reality at will, and the first time something crops up that you can't easily find a cause for, both you and the I.S. blame the demons."

He shrugged, and my hands stiffened into fists. No wonder Dali and Al were the only two demons living openly. Asshats. They were all asshats. "Thanks, Edden," I said, turning to leave. "See you around. Do me a favor and tell Jacqueline for me that Jack says he loves her."

"Jesus, Rachel," Edden coaxed, but I was having none of it. "Don't take this personally. You can't deny that forcing couples to kill one another is demonic."

I spun back around, frustrated with the way the world worked. I'd thought things might be different, but they weren't. People only got better at hiding it. "You're forgetting one thing," I said as I took three steps back to Edden. He could have stood up for me, told them that they were wrong instead of asking me to spy on the demons with the assumption that they were responsible—based on nothing other than a gut feeling. But he hadn't, and it hurt. *Just when I felt I was starting to belong.*

"What's that?" he asked nervously.

"What's in it for them?" I asked, waving Ivy's carefully assembled information. "Demons don't do anything unless it's for a profit." Frustrated, I slapped the reports against his chest, and he fumbled for them. "And neither do I anymore," I said.

Turning, I walked away.

CHAPTER

4

"ARE YOU STILL WORRIED ABOUT POSTPONING OUR MEET-ing?" Trent's expressive voice rose and fell like water even through my cell phone, currently on speaker and sitting on the kitchen counter. "Ellasbeth severely underestimated Lucy's and Ray's temperament by suggesting a five-star restaurant. Ice cream after naps is more their speed. I couldn't have planned the shift to Eden Park better if I'd arranged for that zombie to be dropped into your garden. It doesn't hurt that she's blaming you for it, either, not me," he finished softly.

I pushed the salt-water-soaked rag over the stainless steel counter to remove any chance of a residual spell interfering with the coming curse. I was still hurting about Edden, too much to tell Trent that the I.S. and the FIB had banded together to blame the demons for pitting happy couples against one another for kicks. "You didn't, did you?" I asked, and he chuckled.

"Hang on a sec," he said, and I heard him set the phone down.

I tossed the rag into the sink, then leaned back against the counter and nibbled the elephant-shaped cookie that I'd picked up at the zoo. *Breakfast of champions.* Piscary's kitchen felt odd without any vampires in it, the shouted orders and friendly catcalls that once kept order amid the flour-and-tomato-paste madness now existing only in memory. The large pizza ovens were cold, and the huge walk-in freezer warm. The industrial-size pots and pans were gone, sold when Cormel took possession of Pizza Piscary's, closed it, and turned the kitchen into a large eat-in.

A normal-size fridge hummed in the corner now. Several freestanding counters had been replaced with a long family-style farm table. Again, unused with only two vampires sleeping belowground. There were still pots and pans, mixers and spoons, gadgets and gizmos tucked away for everyday use, but the feel of the large room was one of abandonment.

That is, apart from the last freestanding counter in the corner. I was going to claim it as my own now that Ivy had suggested it. The curse's ingredients were in my largest spell pot, brought over from the boat. They looked out of place under the electric lights, but that would change in time. I hoped.

"Sorry about that," Trent said as he came back. "Where were we?"

I set the half-eaten cookie down and dusted my hands free of crumbs. "You were about to tell me you didn't drop a zombie in my backyard so you'd have an excuse to change Ellasbeth's playdate." Taking up the gold silk scarf I got on sale last week, I polished a small six-inch circular mirror to remove any stray ions. *Clean, spell-free mirror. Check.* I was going to make a scrying mirror just so I could slap a do-not-disturb sign on it and stop sneezing.

"No, not me," Trent said again around a yawn. I'd say I was boring him, but it was almost noon and he usually took a four-hour nap this time of day. "I had no idea that you'd be at your church. I'm sorry about the insurance not coming through."

The mirror clinked as I set it down. "How did you . . . ?"

"Jenks called to arrange rent this winter," Trent said, and I nodded, exhaling as I took my five-pound bag of salt from the bowl and set it heavily on the counter. *Sea salt. Check.*

"I'm glad you convinced him to overwinter with his kids," Trent was saying. "That boat you're on is a good temporary option, but if the power goes out . . ."

Silent, I took a handful of salt and spilled a large circle encompassing the entire counter. Pixies were braver than anyone gave them credit for. I didn't know if I could live somewhere where I might slip into a hibernating coma if some asshat yanked the power cord.

"If it's a matter of money to fix the church—"

"We've got this," I interrupted, warming at how harsh it had come out, but he knew my anger wasn't with him but that Jenks and I were in this predicament. Water chattered into the nearby sink as I washed the salt off my hands and mentally went over my list. *Wine. I forgot the wine.* Stepping carefully over the uninvoked salt circle, I took out a bottle of local red from the restaurant-size wine cooler. *Check.*

"I know you do," Trent said into the growing silence. I could hear his desire for me to move in with him. A part of me wanted to, but a larger part knew I wasn't ready. It wasn't that I didn't love him. I did. And the girls. But I'd made a success of myself with Ivy. I had to do the same on my own before I could stand beside Trent and not feel as if I was . . . leaning on him.

Frustrated, I pulled my bowl closer and rummaged to find my silver snips. They'd tarnished, and I began to rub them clean with the silk scarf. *No, that's smoke damage,* I realized, wondering if that would make them more or less useful in twisting curses. "That reminds me." I leaned against the counter beside the sink and rubbed harder. "There was an elf at the church."

"Landon," Trent said flatly, shocking me at the clenched-jaw anger in his voice.

"No," I said, surprised. "I never got his name." I gave up on the snips and set them beside the mirror with a soft click. "He ran off when Ivy and Jenks showed up. Young, about sixteen? You guys all look the same to me."

"Because we are," Trent said sourly, and I smiled, totally

understanding his desire to be unique among his peers, but thanks to Trent's dad's efforts to save their species, they all looked pretty much alike. Why work individualism in and risk screwing up something that sufficed?

"He wants to meet you." Head down, I began opening and closing drawers as I looked for my ceremonial knife. It hadn't been on the boat, which meant I'd left it here the last time I made some sleepy-time potions. "Sorry about not getting his name."

"I'll ask around," he said after another yawn, and I smiled at the familiar sound of him settling back for a nap. I knew he slept in his chair most workdays, trying to give at least the illusion of keeping to a human time clock.

"If he shows up again, you want me to bring him out?" Frustrated, I put my hands on my hips and stared at the kitchen. *Where would Nina have put my knife?*

"Sure, but stop at the gatehouse so Quen can talk to him." *Could be a Landon spy.* My head bobbed, and I crossed the kitchen to the novelty pizza cutters. Sure enough, my knife was among the circular unicycle cutter and long toucan-beak scissors. "You got it, boss," I said, and I heard a sleepy chuckle.

The silence lengthened, and thinking he might have drifted off, I picked up my phone to end the connection with a whispered "I love you." He'd fallen asleep while talking to me before, and whereas some might find insult, I only felt loved. But my coming words choked to nothing when he softly said, "I'm going to grant Ellasbeth the girls this weekend."

I froze, worry knotting my gut. He'd said it so formally. Grant her. But giving his ex-fiancée time alone with the girls was utterly at his discretion, the law having terminated her rights to Lucy, and Ray never having been hers. "I thought that was a no-go with you," I said, concerned.

"I think you're right that it's safer than refusing to let her have Lucy on a regular schedule," he said. "And Quen will be with them. She's done everything I've asked. Has a new flat overlooking the river. Sold her house in Seattle. She's teaching classes at the university as she promised. She's even gotten over her West Coast snobbery and begun to show some interest in Cincinnati's considerable finer arts."

Elbows on the counter, I cradled the phone in my hands as I wrapped my mind around this. Elf children matured a lot faster than what was considered normal. Still, Lucy was only four months shy of two and she'd already been kidnapped three times, first by Trent, then by an insane demon, and lastly by Landon. No wonder nothing fazed the little girl. "What about Landon?"

"Landon already tried stealing power with Lucy and failed," Trent said, a frightening coldness in his voice. "Besides, if she gets too distressed, she knows how to call Al."

My jaw dropped. "You're kidding," I said, not sure what surprised me most: that the toddler knew how or that Trent was clearly proud that she was seeking help from someone who, until just this year, had been the elves' sworn enemy. Still was in most circles.

"I think it's more her trying to use a ley line that is alerting him," Trent admitted, but the pride was still there. "It shocked the peas out of me the first time he showed up when she threw a tantrum. We've since chatted, and Al has agreed to leave the parenting to me."

My grin was unstoppable as I bent over the counter, flats of my arms on the stainless steel, and held the phone as if I could touch Trent through it. I'd be willing to bet that Trent wasn't the only one surprised to suddenly find an uptight, supercilious demon in crushed green velvet in his rooms demanding to know why his elfling godchild was screaming holy hell.

"So, long story short, unless Ellasbeth does something dreadful over ice cream, she has the girls until Sunday night. My schedule is clear. How about yours?"

My smile widened at the change in his voice. "Nothing pressing." My focus blurred at the thought of two entire days with Trent with minimal disruption. Though in financial straits due to fighting off the numerous—and true—accusations of being a bio-drug manufacturer, the man still owned a considerable number of high-tech, low-employee farms and most of the train runs east of the Mississippi. Occasional questions cropped up. Oh, and the illegal Brimstone trade. No one was going to call him out on that, though, seeing as if that went, the undead would be looking to humans to round out their needs. "The last thing on my list this week is making a scrying mirror, and then I'm all yours."

"It needs a circle, right?" he said around another yawn, and I nodded.

"Yep." It was a demon curse, and he knew it. Didn't care. Understood I needed it to do my job. *Reason number eight hundred and sixty-five that I love you.*

"I'll let you go, then," he said reluctantly. "See you at four. Al's line."

"Al's line," I said softly, loving him even more. He'd said *Al's line*, not the Eden Park overlook, though they were one and the same. "You bet. Bye."

"Bye."

There was a long pause, a sigh, and then a click. Only then did I allow that same happy, wistful sound to pass my lips and set the phone down on the adjacent counter outside of the circle. An incoming call might be enough of a connection for something nefarious to get through, and if I did this right, I'd be without my aura for a brief time, vulnerable.

Talking to Trent had gone a long way in rubbing out Edden's bass-ackward request for me to troll the demons for who was responsible for the murders, and in a much better mood, I took another bite of that elephant cookie before setting it outside of my proposed circle as well. A pot of salt water waited, and I dunked my hands, drying them on the silk with an unexpected feeling of confidence. I'd done this curse several times now, but whether I was confident or not, the same quiver of expectation echoed in my belly as I looked over the assembled supplies. There wasn't much, but a good curse was like that, relying on actions stored in the demon collective to make it work, invoked by a phrase or hand gesture.

"Okay . . ." I reached a sliver of my awareness to the

nearest ley line. Immediately a scintillating power poured in, tasting of lightning and burnt ash. Most ran in well-used channels through my body to fill my chi and then to a spool in my head until I shunted it back to the line. Some energy, though, danced randomly through me in a sparkling wash.

I knew now that the tingle pricking through me was actually free-ranging mystics, the Goddess's uncountable sentient eyes/energy—the source of all magic, be it ley line or earth. That I could again use the ley lines and not be swarmed by them was a huge relief. I wasn't sure if it was because Newt had shifted my soul so my aura resonated at a frequency they didn't recognize, or that the mystics simply weren't interested in me anymore since Newt had taken my place, bringing the knowledge of life with mass to the mystics, something they had been so keen to learn that they would have taken me over and made me part of their Goddess to do so.

The only downside to having my soul adjusted was that my gargoyle, Bis, wasn't able to pass through my circle anymore, meaning he couldn't teach me how to travel the ley lines like a normal demon. I had to be carted around like a kid in a carpool, and it was tiresome.

Mystics were always flowing through the lines, but when the sun was up, the motion was primarily into the ever-after. They'd reverse come sundown, creating a tide that kept the ever-after from collapsing and providing those who knew how the ability to do magic.

I shivered, enjoying the feel of the incoming energy balancing in me as I focused on the ring of salt. *"Rhombus,"* I whispered, triggering a set of mental gymnastics that moved a molecule-thin slice of salt from here to the ever-after. A barrier impenetrable to anything but sound, air, and, to a lesser extent, smell sprang up to make a half sphere over my head. It was mirrored below me as well, and Ivy assured me there were no cables, pipes, or anything else that might allow something to slip through.

I smiled in satisfaction at the luminous gold, not even minding the few red striations rippling over the edges, evidence of my troubled childhood. The bound energy reflected the colors in my aura, and though it looked the same to me as ever, Bis could tell the difference. It pleased me to no end that the black smut that had once marred it was gone, used to help stabilize the new ever-after. The demons, too, all had pristine auras now—which undoubtedly made it easier for them to wander around unnoticed as long as they hid their goat-slitted eyes.

I'd seen a real reluctance in Al to do anything to mar his new sparkling aura, but this curse would put a tiny amount of imbalance on me, hardly discernible. Some said that meant I was wicked, but smut wasn't evil—or even an indication that you did evil things. It was simply a measure of how badly you screwed up the natural balance. An IOU if you will. *But try telling that to the paranoid mother on the park bench*. . . .

Safe in my circle, I popped open the bottle of wine. For a moment, I hesitated, wondering if I should pour what I needed out and save the rest, but then I just pricked my finger with my ceremonial knife and squeezed three drops right into the bottle to link the curse to me. It wasn't as if I could drink it. Sulfites gave me a headache.

A last look over the silent kitchen, and I levered myself up on the center counter to set the faultless, ungodly expensive mirror before my crossed legs. Yew stylus in hand, I looked down at my reflection. Green eyes stared back, and I wondered how I'd gotten here, twisting demon curses in a vampire's kitchen. Grimacing, I tucked a strand of my shower-damp hair behind an ear and shoved the thought away. There were good things, too: Trent, and Ivy, and Jenks; my mom rekindling a lost love on the West Coast; the demons no longer trapped in the ever-after, virtual slaves to those who knew how to summon them.

A new confidence in myself, I thought, finding a smile. The first time I'd done this, I had sketched everything out in chalk before making it permanent, but now? Now I knew I could do it. In. One. Pure. Go.

The energy flow through me jumped when the stylus

touched the mirror, and I shuddered when my aura sort of spilled out into it. Even when I was expecting it, the sensation was disconcerting, and I looked at my reflection, able to see a shadow of myself under the gold and red shimmers.

I felt naked and vulnerable with my aura stripped away like this. Normally I'd be unable to do even the smallest magic without excruciating pain while missing my aura. But it wasn't really gone, just in the glass, and I quickly began to sketch a palm-size pentagram to give the curse structure.

The kitchen was silent, all good vampires asleep downstairs and Jenks napping in the boat. The hiss of the yew against the glass sent up the scent of dust and hot sand, and again I marveled that I could actually see it burning the glass on both sides, wisps of smoke rebounding against the inside of the pane.

My lip had gotten between my teeth by the time I finished. The stomach-cramping fear that had gripped me while making my original scrying mirror was gone, and I smiled as I looked at the perfectly proportioned lines and felt the curse resonating in me.

"Symbols of communication," I said to myself as I bent low over the smoked lines, and with the meaning of each simple glyph resonating in my thoughts, I sketched them at the points, starting at the lower left and rising clockwise. I took a slow breath upon finishing the last, cracking my back as I prepared to trace the first of two circles surrounding the pentagram. The inner one would connect the points of the pentagram, the outer one would encompass the glyphs.

Again the stylus touched the glass, and the power began to shift, filling the pattern and organizing into as-yet-latent action. I went point to point, smooth and unhurried. When the yew met the beginning point, a chime struck through me, shivering all the way to my core.

My breath came faster, and imagining I could already hear the half-heard whispers of the demon collective, I began the second, outer circle. Yes, I had been putting this off, but I missed the feeling of connection, the subliminal knowledge that others were going about their lives as was I, each to themselves, touching and moving on.

Heart pounding and fingers numb with tingles, I drew the outer circle. My reflection was lost in smoke and haze, but the way was easy. The salt was ready, and the wine was set. I'd have this done and most of my aura back in thirty seconds.

Again the line met its end with a satisfying ping, and I hesitated as the energy swirled, breathless. The curse was drawn, but not done, and the glyphs glowed with energy. A shudder rippled through me as, with the slow surety of a spring thaw, my aura began to leave the mirror and seep back into me, carrying the curse scribed on the mirror with it.

I forced myself not to move as it inched back with the sensation of pinpricks, hoping that the longer I could withstand it, the more aura would be returned to me. But when the prickling across my synapses became a harsh burning, I reached for the salt, spilling it from a shaky hand over the mirror's entirety.

"Better," I said, shoulders easing as the salt hissed down like cold sand on sunburned skin, balancing the energies and removing the excess intent. It had been Ceri who had poured the wine over the mirror the first time I'd done this, the wine serving to bind the salt and the glyphs to the mirror. But I was alone, and I did it myself, the tinkling sound of it on the glass and into the nearby bowl satisfying as the salt washed away to leave only sparkling lines amid a new ruby red, deep sheen. My body seemed to hum as the salt in my blood echoed the intent of the salt in the mirror as the last of the wine trickled across the scrying mirror and into a bowl. The singularly drawn curse now existed in two places, me and the mirror both.

"Ita prorsus," I said, and then sealed the curse by touching a wine-wet finger to my lips.

Goose bumps rose as the curse set, waves of power seeming to echo out from me in ever-lessening waves. "I accept the imbalance," I whispered, but my body, conditioned by two years of twisting curses, had already taken it, and the minute black wash of smut sank quickly into me like a second layer of protection.

My head lifted as I heard a faint bell chime from my distant church, and satisfied, I gazed at the thing of beauty in my lap, glittering silver and red from the salt and wine. The first time I'd done this, I'd been terrified, almost blind in fear, but today, being a demon didn't feel so bad.

The soft sound of displaced air jerked my attention up, but it was only Bis, the craggy cat-size gargoyle now sitting on the counter just outside my circle. Red eyes blinked sleepily at me, and Bis stretched his wings, yawning until his white-tufted tail curved around his feet and he slumped. "I woke up," he said, his gravelly voice mangling the vowels.

"Sorry." I set the mirror down, the memory of Ceri helping me with this bird-eye bright in my thoughts. She'd never treated me the same afterward. It was probably when she'd figured out I wasn't a witch, but a witch-born demon.

"It's o-o-o-okay," he said around a long yawn. "New mirror?"

I touched the beautiful thing as if it were a kitten. "Yep. How's my aura?"

Bis blinked his sleepy red eyes, struggling to focus. "Great. You got most of it back."

I nodded, pleased. Ceri had cautioned me not to use a new mirror for twenty-four hours to allow for "aura replenishment," but if my aura was there, where was the harm? "I'm going to see if it works," I said as I let my protective circle drop and blotted the last of the wine from the mirror before setting it on my knee.

Bis slumped to fall asleep again as I stayed where I was atop the counter and placed my hand so my fingers touched the glyphs. Slowly, until I knew that my limited aura would protect me, I eased a sliver of ley line energy into my hand, and then into the curse to awaken it.

"Ow," I whispered when a not-unexpected soft burning seemed to light behind my eyes. The curse was good. I'd done it right. The pain was only because I was trying to use the mirror with a patchy aura. It was tolerable, though, and I allowed more energy to flow. With a ping I could feel, the curse that existed both in the mirror and in me became one—and I was in the collective.

"Ow," I said louder as it felt as if my skin was on fire, but the half-heard whispers of semiprivate conversations were a balm, and I hung there, easing back on the energy flow until I could handle the soft burn. It was very much like a crowded party with everyone talking, and as I felt the beginnings of a sneeze begin to threaten, I marshaled my thoughts into a clear statement, dropping it into the collective like the annoyed shout it was.

Rachel here. Who in hell has been trying to reach me? I have a cell phone, you know.

A prickling of interest circled. I caught a faint hint of amusement, and then an unfamiliar thought crashed into my mind, expanding my awareness with the breathless sensation of two intellects lightly becoming one. Just as fast, the burning sensation seemed to halve, and I got a wisp of irritated emotion, and then, *Rachel Mariana Morgan? I have to talk to you. In person.*

Dali? I thought as I recognized his absolute confidence, then quashed a flash of self-preservation. The ofttimes arrogant entity was the self-appointed leader of the demons. What did he want with me? *Uh, sure,* I thought, feeling his presence uncomfortably within mine. God! It was like he was pressing me against the wall, if a wall had existed.

Is now good? he persisted. *I'll bring you through, seeing as your gargoyle is asleep.*

No, wait! I thought frantically, not sure if I'd end up across town or across the continent. *I just made a scrying mirror, and my aura is patchy.*

My fingers eased their pressure on the glass as I felt him draw back, a new understanding and perhaps a smidgen of chagrin as to why I hadn't answered him earlier. *What happened to your old one?* he asked suspiciously.

Al broke it. Look, I don't want to talk about it.

No doubt, Dali thought, and I glanced at Bis, the little

guy now snoring to sound like rocks in a blender. Embarrassed, I pressed my hand harder into the red-tinted glass until the tingles of a weak connection vanished. If Al had a boss, it was Dali. That Dali now worked for Junior, or Mark, rather, slinging coffee in Cincinnati was just weird. It gave me hope that the demons were going to play by our rules, but the reality was that being a barista probably gave Dali the opportunity to sell the odd curse.

I'm working today, I thought, trying to hide my embarrassment. *I'll come see you tomorrow. You'll be at Junior's, right?*

Where I'll be working, Dali thought back, mental tone sour.

So take a coffee break. Mark won't mind.

A wash of irate annoyance and impatience coursed through me, only half of it mine. *Tomorrow,* Dali thought, and then I jumped, hand springing from the glass when I seemed to lose half my mind. I hadn't of course, but Dali was gone.

I sat up, shaking off the last of the haze of being in the collective. "Dali wanting to talk to you is never good," I whispered, expecting to see Bis asleep when I turned to him, but he was staring at me, his craggy gray eyebrows high. Fully awake despite the hour, he took a breath to say something. Then his eyes went up, and I started, surprised at the black-wearing, gray-dusting pixy hovering below the lights, clearly having just slipped off the smooth fixture, his angular features frozen in shock.

"Jumoke?" I questioned, seeing as he was the only dark-haired pixy in all of Cincinnati, but his wings weren't quite right, and his mop of black hair was unprecedented. "Hey!" I exclaimed, wildly swinging the mirror at him when he dropped down right in front of me dusting black and gold sparkles.

Bis vaulted himself into the air, wings beating.

"Not so close!" I shouted, as the pixy darted away. Pulse fast, I scrambled off the counter and put it between us, feeling like one of those guys at the park freaking out over a bee.

But I lived with Jenks. Though most people were "Aww, how sweet!" I knew firsthand the damage a pixy could do, and I didn't want to explain to anyone in Emergency why I was missing an eye and my eardrums were pierced.

"How the Turn did you get past Jenks?" I said as the pixy in his black tights and jacket swung in agitation like a pendulum. "And what are you doing in my kitchen?"

But my surprise at finding another dark-haired pixy alive was nothing to my shock when Bis made a weird noise and the pixy vanished into a familiar swirl of yellow and green, quickly expanding into a demon, his red goat-slitted eyes wide in astonishment.

CHAPTER

5

"THAT WAS DALI?" THE DEMON STOOD STOCK-STILL IN THE small space between the counter and the long, empty table. "You were talking to Dali? They let you into the collective?"

I jumped when Bis dropped to my shoulder, his tail unusually tight as he wrapped it around me. I slowly set my mirror aside, never dropping my gaze as I estimated my chances of reaching my purse and the splat gun in it at a dismal nil. With my aura compromised, it was about all I had. "Yeah . . . ," I said hesitantly, and he grew more agitated.

The demon was tall, markedly so, more sinewy than bulky, with a trim waist and wide shoulders. He looked as if he was in his mid-thirties with a dark, smooth complexion, but why not when you could be any age you wanted? Low-heeled manly boots, black jeans, black cotton shirt, and a lightweight leather jacket. I was betting his ornate silver belt buckle was actually a ley line charm. He had another supposed charm around his neck on a chain of black gold. Rings, lots of rings. His long black hair was thick and wavy like a Were's, and was held back from his face with a silver clip. Add in a classically cut chin and a strong jaw, and he could be anyone on the street if not for his red goat-slitted eyes—if anyone on the street could row a Viking boat all day and not get tired.

"Have we met?" I said, not knowing why he was confused. I didn't personally know every demon, but every demon knew me.

"I saw you." The demon pointed at the scrying mirror beside me as if it was an affront. "You're in the collective. You're in the Goddess-blessed collective. You talked to Dali!"

"Stop!" I warned him as he took a step closer, and he jerked to a halt. "Who are you, and what are you doing in my kitchen?" I was trying to be nice, but it was getting harder.

His eyes flicked to mine, and then, as if only now realizing I was upset, he dropped back a few more feet. Relieved, I nodded to tell him that was a smart move.

"So," I said, stifling my wince when Bis's nails dug into my shoulder, "which one of the four hundred and thirteen demons are you, and what do you want?"

The demon's jaw dropped, and he ran a hand across his chin in surprise. "Four hundred and thirteen? Damn my dame, we're almost gone."

His faint accent reminded me of Newt's, and the distinctive scent of burnt amber was wafting up from him. "Well, it's been a hard couple of years," I smart-mouthed as I glanced at him with my second sight expecting the worst, but his aura was as clean as mine, sporting a cheerful yellow and green, with shades of purple and red swirling about his head and hands.

"Is this okay, Rachel?" Bis whispered, and I shook my head and let my second sight drop.

"I don't know," I muttered, and the demon arched one eyebrow wryly.

"You do elf magic," he stated, gesturing as if that explained everything. "The Goddess recognizes you. They *all* know it."

My lips pressed, and I hated that I flushed. *Where has this guy been the last two years? A hole in the ground?* "Yeah? What about it?" I said, working to keep my voice low lest I wake up Ivy. Bringing her into this was a really bad idea.

He stared at me for a heartbeat or two as if trying to comprehend the words that had just come out of my mouth. "I've been watching you for three weeks trying to figure this out. They *know* who you are, what you do," he said firmly. "They let you live. Free and, well, probably not on equal footing, but they let you live. Why haven't they killed you?"

I glanced at Bis and cocked my hip. "Didn't I just say it's been a hard couple of years?"

"But you openly consort with . . . an elf," he said, gesturing weakly. "You strive to keep him safe in uncertain situations. He *pays* you for it."

Okay. I didn't know who this guy was, but he wasn't doing anything but asking stupid questions. Annoyed, I dumped the used bowl of wine down the sink. "You got a problem with that?" *He's been watching me for three weeks?* I thought as the wine went trickling down. And then my eyes narrowed. Demons could be anything. Not only a pixy, but like a crow, maybe. *Damn it to the Turn and back again. Three weeks?*

"Me? No, but *they* do," he said pointedly, and then my gaze lifted at the sound of pixy wings coming from the delivery entrance.

"Hey, Rache." Jenks darted in, dressed in a robe and barefoot. "I heard you yellin'."

My eyes went to the demon as my thoughts returned to Jenks's son, Jumoke. "From the boat?" I questioned, surprised, and he lowered his garden sword.

"Oh, it's a demon," Jenks said around a yawn. "Bis! My man! How you doing, gray stuff?"

Still on my shoulder, Bis exchanged a fist bump with a now-glittering Jenks. "Okay. Heat's back on. You coming back to the church?"

"Not until we get a dwelling permit, and we need a kitchen first. You checkin' on Rache?" Jenks asked, wings dripping silver when Bis made a jumping hop to the bag of salt on the counter.

"Yes, but she doesn't need me for this," the small gargoyle said as his tail wrapped securely around the large bag.

Satisfied, Jenks wedged his sword into the belt of his robe and alighted next to the cat-size gargoyle as if he was settling in to watch a movie. "What did you do to piss her off, Home Slice?"

"He said he's been spying on her," Bis said, and Jenks laughed.

"Bad life choice, dude."

The demon frowned, not at all thrown by the sight of a pixy and a gargoyle sitting together as best friends. "Do they deem being witch-born puts you beneath their laws?" he asked.

Jenks's wings clattered at the insult, and I dried my hands with a short, abrupt motion. "You need to leave," I said, wondering how much trouble I'd start if I snapped the towel at him. "Now, before I circle you and *make* you leave." It was an iffy warning, seeing it was no longer possible to summon or banish demons since the original banishment curse had been broken. Being circled would be embarrassing, though, and anger colored his cheeks, highlighting his light stubble.

"You wouldn't dare."

Motions slow and deliberate, I scraped my ceremonial knife across the counter and hefted it in a useless threat. He'd only go misty to avoid it, but it made me feel better. On the bag of salt, Jenks poked Bis's elbow to keep the kid awake. *Three weeks* . . . "And if I even see so much as a feather, I'm going to track you down and find out how crow really tastes." Which was about the stupidest thing I'd ever said, but I was mad, damn it. I'd worked darn hard to get the demons to consider me as an equal. I didn't need him adding to my self-doubt.

Jenks clattered his wings, looking mean as he stuck his sword into Bis to wake him back up. The gargoyle jumped, arching his wings over his head to look bigger and turning a threatening black. The demon's gaze slid from them to me and then back to my scrying mirror. Unclenching his jaw, he made a stiff half bow of sorts. "I apologize," he said formally. "I meant no slur."

But I couldn't tell if he meant it, and that made me more angry.

"It's just . . ." At a loss, he motioned to me. "Why haven't they put you in a bottle for practicing elf magic?"

"Because they're tired of fighting that damned war of yours," I said as I gestured haphazardly with my knife. "Or maybe because I used elven magic to break the curse keeping you all trapped in the ever-after," I added, setting the knife down. "Or maybe because I needed elven magic to steal the Goddess's power to help Bis make a new ever-after when the ley lines fell and magic went down." I frowned at his obvious disbelief as he stared at Bis struggling to stay awake. "But I'm guessing that was when you escaped," I finished, because it was growing obvious that someone *had* stuffed him away and forgotten about him, probably for practicing elven magic by his overwhelming preoccupation with it.

The demon nodded a cautious agreement as I moved Bis to my shoulder. His tail curled around my back and under my arm, and with a little sigh, he closed his eyes. "How long has it been?" I asked, and when he didn't answer, I reached for my mirror to call Al. I didn't know this guy, and I was vulnerable with half an aura.

"No. Don't bring them into this," the demon said, his threat heavy, and I hesitated. *Shit, I'm standing in an un-invoked circle, unable to jump out.* "I'm trying to piece this together," he added, brow furrowed. "Give me a moment."

Yeah, I'd been there, forced to react before I was able to get that last little nugget of information that would've kept me from overreacting and making things worse. But I think it was how many times "authority" had rolled in and screwed up something that should have been simple that made me pull my hand back with fake casualness. He hadn't truly threatened me apart from hovering in my face.

"Sure, we can talk." I casually backed out of my salt circle. "What's your name?"

"Dali knows what you do," the demon said, a finger raised as if ticking off facts. "Accepting that you practice elven magic."

"It's more like ignoring it, but okay," I said. "And you are . . . ?"

"You're in the collective," he said, two fingers raised now as he moved closer, almost to my salt circle. "And they haven't . . ." He rocked to a halt, the light of possibility in his red eyes as his fingers curled under to make a fist. "I've been watching you. You're good. But not several-thousand-years good." His arms went over his middle and his boots edged the salt circle. I winced, knowing he wouldn't move an inch farther. Not that it mattered. If I invoked it to trap him, he'd only jump out. "What do you have on them?"

"Nothing." I leaned against the counter and tried to look confident. It was hard with Bis snoring on my shoulder. "Every time they tried to put *me* in a hole in the ground, I fought back." I raised my eyebrows mockingly. "But you didn't, did you. Or did you, and your precious Goddess wasn't there when you needed her?"

The demon's expression twisted. "She is *not* precious," he barked, clearly not getting my sarcasm, and I shrugged, familiar with the demons' prejudice toward the elvens' living deity.

It was growing obvious that this guy had been imprisoned until the lines had gone down. Which might account for him all but reeking of old magic, stuff older than what the weapons locker held, stuff more ancient than when the original ever-after was clean and a paradise, and I shifted my damp hair so Jenks, now satisfied with the security of the kitchen, could sit on my big hooped earring.

"Hey, Rache," Jenks said as a wash of gold sparkles slipped down my front. "If Home Slice here got himself put in a jar for practicing elven magic and you didn't, that makes you the stronger demon, right?"

"No." I grimaced, looking the demon up and down. "Just luckier."

The demon stiffened. "My name is Hodin, not Home Slice."

I nodded. *Finally.* "Rachel Morgan. Witch-born demon. Nice to meet you." But I didn't put my hand out, and Hodin's gaze met mine with an odd intensity. Being female, I could hold and wield more line energy than him—but not with my aura compromised. And he'd know that.

"So"—I eyed my nearby mirror, wondering if I should call Al—"how long have you been, ah, out of circulation?"

"Long enough that nothing is familiar." His eyes followed mine to my mirror, then narrowed in threat. "I'm leaving. If you tell them about me, I *will* kill you."

"Yeah, like we haven't heard that before," Jenks taunted.

"Hey, wait!" I exclaimed, but Hodin was gone in a silver swirl of unfocused magic. Bis's tail tightened to maintain his balance, and I put a hand to him. He never woke up.

"He took your cookie," Jenks said, and my lips parted when I realized Jenks was right. At least he hadn't taken my mirror, but I had a feeling it wouldn't have done him any good. I didn't think he was in the collective. "Who was that guy?" Jenks added as he took off, my earring swinging as he angled to the honey pot that Nina left out for him. She thought drunk pixies were a hoot.

"I have no idea." I scuffed a break in the salt circle, and frowning, I tucked my new mirror in my purse beside my splat gun. My ceremonial knife went in beside them. I didn't like that Hodin had been spying on me for a self-confessed three weeks and all I'd noticed was a crow outside my church. My nose wrinkled at the lingering scent of charred evergreen, evidence of his demon magic. *What has he been doing to smell like burnt amber?*

"Jenks, you with me? I'm going to Junior's before going out to the park," I said, and the pixy swore and slammed the lid to the honey back down. "I need to talk to Dali. Now."

CHAPTER

6

"COFFEE UP!" A BORED, CULTURED, AND FAMILIAR VOICE called into the sound of grunge music and light chatter as I walked into Junior's. It was Dali, dressed in a green apron as he worked behind the counter, gracefully moving the middle-aged bulk he favored. A few patrons sat at the window tables, and a short line stretched before the cold shelves and again at the pickup window. It wasn't busy, but there was a rise of excited voices and the click of cameras as I walked in with Jenks on my shoulder. *Swell. That didn't take long.*

That Dali had chosen to work as a barista in downtown Cincinnati was only weird on the surface. He'd owned his own restaurant in the ever-after and was probably taking the time to learn not only what the population wanted, but how to work within the system before opening his own place. I'd talked to Mark about it last month, but the kid said he was good for business, and he felt better having a demon behind the counter when he could have a handful of them in front of it at any given moment. I'd made Mark promise to never buy a curse, but the temptation had to be there. Seeing me, the older demon brightened.

"Rachel. I wasn't expecting you until tomorrow," he said as he poured juice into a cup under the ice grinder.

"You're on my way to my next appointment," I said, not wanting to bring up Trent.

Dali frowned, and a ripple of something coated me, making me shudder as he looked at me over his wire-rimmed, purely for-show glasses. "Your aura is too thin to be out of your spelling studio unaccompanied," he said, his low voice audible even as he hit the button to crush the ice. Clearly a sound-dampening spell was in use. *Point two for Mark to employ the demon.*

"She's not unaccompanied. She's got me," Jenks said, and the demon's eyebrows rose.

"That's actually what I wanted to talk to you about," I said as I settled into the back of the line. I still wasn't sure if I was going to tell him about Hodin. Fish for information, yes—tell him a demon stuck in a hole for the last two thousand years had dropped from my ceiling . . . maybe.

Dali slid the iced fruit drink across the counter to the waiting patron before leaning to look to the back of the store. "Mark, I'm going on break!" he called, and the guy waiting in front of me grumbled. "He'll have your drink up shortly," Dali said, smiling to show his thick, blocky teeth, and the man went ashen.

"Rache, you want anything?" Jenks asked, looking like a tiny thief in his cumbersome black winter clothes as Dali came out from behind the counter.

"Tall latte, double espresso, skim milk, light on the foam, with cinnamon and a shot of raspberry?" I said over my shoulder as Dali took my elbow and pulled me to an empty table. "In a to-go cup. We can't stay long," I added.

Mark came out from the back, his worried brow smoothing when he saw me. "I'll get it," he said to the barista manning the drive-through, adding, "Tall skinny demon to go!" and a bell behind the counter rang of its own accord.

"Thank you," I mouthed to Mark as I sat with Dali, his apron and polyester uniform dissolving to a more familiar suit and tie. I had no idea why the demon wanted to look like a slightly overweight white guy with no family, a bad haircut, and a grudge with life. Maybe it granted him some level of respect with the rest of the demons, who preferred pretty or dangerous. I could hear phones clicking. We'd be online in a matter of seconds. At least I didn't smell like zombie anymore.

"Ah, what did you want to talk to me about?" I said, and when Dali said nothing, I looked up, shocked at his expression, which was somewhere between nervousness and . . . embarrassment?

"I'd ask to engage your services as an escort," he said, and I blinked, truly surprised.

"What for?" I asked, following his gaze to Jenks, his dust spilling over the yellowing bananas and protein bars at the register. "No one will know you're a demon if you wear sunglasses. Your aura doesn't have any smut on it. Well, not much anyway."

Dali hunched, his bulk looming between me and everyone else. "You misunderstand. To be other than a demon would be counterproductive."

My eyes narrowed and I leaned in so close, I could almost pretend to smell burnt amber lifting from him. "I'm *not* going to help you make nasty deals with people," I said softly. "You and the rest of the lost boys have one shot at making it work in reality. Don't blow it, Dali. I worked too hard to get you here to be forced to curse you back into the ever-after one by one."

Dali's lip twitched in amusement at my claim that I could, and then the embarrassment was back. "No. I want to meet someone, and the last time I tried, it didn't go well."

Surprise kept me sitting. That, and my coffee wasn't up yet. "You want help getting a date?" I asked, incredulous, and Jenks, talking with Mark at the counter, turned.

Dali's lips pressed into a bloodless line, clearly not liking that Jenks was hearing this. "I want—," he started, then hesitated. "There's the chance—" Again his words cut off, but at my sigh, he held up a hand for patience. "The Rosewood children that Ku'Sox stole," he said, eyes fixed on mine. "I want to meet the boy living in Cincinnati. His name is Keric." A frown creased his brow. "Can you imagine giving a demon the call name of Keric?"

My mouth dropped open, and I closed it with a snap. I had dreamed about Keric this morning, all grown up and marrying Ray. Coincidence? "You can't have him," I said tightly. "Or any of the Rosewood babies. This conversation is over."

I grabbed my bag to stand, freezing when Dali pinned my wrist to the table. The faint wash of tingles as the levels of our stored magic equalized went straight to my core. At the pickup counter, Jenks's wings hummed threateningly. Dali leaned in, red goat-slitted eyes locked to mine. "I don't want a child," he said, practically biting the words off. "I want a student."

"You want to teach him," I whispered, relaxing, and Dali let go.

"When his aptitude begins to show, it would be best if someone is there to direct it," he said, clearly discomfited. "I've tried repeatedly to make his acquaintance, but his parents become upset and he cries. I've seen nothing of him but his voice. He has a good voice."

"He's not even a year old," I protested, but then I recalled Al teaching Lucy how to make winged horses. *The hours my dad and I spent with pentagram flashcards . . .* Okay. Apparently it was never too early to teach a good curse.

"I need an introduction," Dali continued, but his tone had become stiff at my resistance. "With the *great and wondrous* Rachel Morgan there, his parents might be more open to me teaching him, less likely to think my goal is abduction. Perhaps you could tell him how Gally, ah, Al babysits for Kalamack. When Keric gets older, he *will* need someone, and the sooner you start, the fewer bad habits there are to break."

Dali looked me up and down as if cataloging my faults, and I smothered the rising feeling of deficiency that Hodin had started in me. "I need to think about this," I said as I resisted the urge to smooth my hair, and his expression shifted to one of annoyance. It had probably been a while since someone had said no to him.

"Rachel," he intoned, and I held up a hand, wishing there weren't so many people around. Besides, Mark was on his way over with Jenks and my coffee.

"I didn't say no. I said I need to think about it," I said, and Dali's expression eased. "I need to weigh your desire against my willingness to take on angry parents if you do something stupid because you don't respect them and their wishes. Keric may be a demon, but he's their child first. He'd be your student a faraway third or fourth."

Dali made a low growl of complaint, but he settled back into the chair as Mark set my coffee down. There was a price for treating people without respect simply because you were stronger than they were, and he was starting to see it in the hidden fear and reticence of people he was dealing with every day.

"On the house," Mark said as I reached for my bag, and I beamed, sitting a little straighter. "Dali, I don't want to rush you, but we're filling up."

"So I see," the demon said flatly, eyes on the new line snaking past the cold shelves, and Jenks snorted as he went to the flower centerpiece with his own tiny cup. They were almost perfect pixy size, and I made a mental note to ask Mark where he got them.

"Thanks, Mark." I took a sip, eyes closing in bliss as my skimpy-aura-induced headache eased, and with a nod, Mark hustled back behind the counter. Word had gotten out that there were demons at Junior's, and as Mark had said, the place had gotten busy. "What did Mark call this, a skinny demon latte?"

"Excuse me. My presence is required if you cannot give me a firm answer." Dali gathered himself to stand, and my pulse quickened. *Now or never . . .* Al would know I was fishing, but Dali might not.

"Dali?" I buried my attention in my coffee, pretending indifference. "Has there ever been a demon besides me who practiced elven magic?"

Dali's lip curled, his attention on the register line. "No. It shortens their lives considerably."

I sipped my raspberry coffee, pulse fast. "Ceri mentioned one called Odoe . . . Odin. . . ."

I blinked innocently as Dali's eyes landed on me. "Hodin?" he offered, and I beamed.

"That's it, Hodin," I said. Jenks's mouth was open, and I twitched my finger at him to stay quiet. Slowly the pixy's dust vanished as his wings went still. "Ho-odin," I said again, as if memorizing it, but my fake brainless smile faltered when Dali sat back down.

"Ceri told you of Hodin?" Dali leaned in, a dangerous light in the back of his eyes, and I fought to not shrink back. Great. Just what kind of a demon had been spying on me?

"Yeah," I said, doubling down, and Jenks's wings dusted a nervous orange.

Dali's goat-slitted eyes narrowed, and for a moment, I thought he was going to call me out on my lie. But then he rubbed a hand over his chin in a rare show of worry. "Hodin belonged to the dewar," Dali said. "Back when we all belonged to someone. Back before Newt twisted the curse that gave us the ability to fight for our freedom. Of all of us, he held to the belief that the Goddess could be trusted. It ended up killing him."

"The Goddess killed him?" I prompted, and Dali's attention sharpened on me.

"The elves did. Hodin was a nightmare among demons," he said, and my stomach clenched. "If the elves hadn't murdered him for trying to turn the Goddess against them, we would have."

"For what?" I whispered, sure I wasn't going to like the answer.

"Treating with the Goddess, of course. When you ask the Goddess to supplement your skills, your magic is stronger, deeper, more terrible than you dare imagine. But she *will* twist the answer to your prayer into something worse, something to benefit her at your detriment—for her amusement. You escaped her once. Tell me I lie. It's for this that we forbid anyone to draw her attention to us, lest we again find our-selves slaves to the elves because she's . . . bored." His thin lips twisted. "That law is still on the books, by the way."

My grip on my coffee tightened. *Familiar territory.* "You'd rather I had let you all die?"

Dali sighed as a group of twentysomethings came in, all of them probably wanting complicated, syrup, whip cream, sprinkle monstrosities. "No." He stood in a sliding scrape of chair. "Which is why we ignored it. Don't do it again, or we will not."

"Then Hodin is dead." I held my cup to warm my fin-gers, startled when Dali loomed over me—far too close.

"Is he?" he asked, eyebrows high. "Have you seen Ho-din . . . Rachel?"

"How would I know? I don't even know what he looked like," I stammered, and Dali frowned at the register. The new group was ogling the sandwiches, slowing everything up.

"When not himself he favored a crow or black wolf," Dali said. "But he survived the elves by amusing them with his shape-shifting and can be anything. It's said that the reason pixies kill their dark-haired children even today is so they'll recognize Hodin if they see a dark pixy." Dali shuddered. "He was dangerous beyond belief, privy to the dewar's most secret magics, having borne the brunt of them as they were developed. Becoming animals to play the toy and escape his torment was his only relief."

"Oh." My gaze went to Jenks, who shrugged. He'd re-fused to kill his son, Jumoke, and now the dark-haired, brown-eyed pixy lived in Trent's gardens, where he wouldn't be stoned.

"Elves are so unforgiving of nonconformity," Dali said with an old hatred. "But whether demon or animal, there was always a lie upon Hodin's lips. Perhaps that was why he understood the Goddess so well. Still, it didn't serve him in the end."

Dali vanished behind a haze of line energy to reappear in his apron. "When it became obvious that the dewar would fall, the elven holy man killed Hodin to prevent him from using the magic they'd practiced on him against the dewar. Hodin had belonged to the dewar's most holy man, you see, and was said to have known all their secrets."

Which made sense, if not morally right. As versatile as it was, demon magic couldn't best the elves' Goddess-based magic, though in reality, they sprang from the same source. It would likely be the Rosewood babies who'd ultimately bring the demons back to their full-spell capabilities, as yet unbiased against the Goddess. But that wouldn't be for ages. My eyes flicked to Dali. And maybe not at all if the demons passed their hatred on to them in turn.

Still standing above me, Dali twitched his lip as he looked at the conspicuous circle etched into the floor at the back of the store. It was intentionally kept clear of tables and chairs, making a casual in-out jump spot to prevent accidents. Dali's interest in it was the only warning I got as the surrounding people gasped at the ear-thumping shift of air. Jenks inked a startled gold when a demon popped in: blue smoked glasses, late-fifties bowler, black pin-striped suit, imposing height, and wide shoulders. It was Al, and by the looks of the suit, he was working. Not on the deadly domestic disputes for the FIB, though, and I felt a pang of sympathy.

"Ra-a-achel?" Al bellowed, and Dali smirked when the people coming in changed their minds and left.

Crap on toast, how had he known where I was? But Al was a social media junky, and the shot of me sitting at Junior's sipping a latte with Dali and a pixy had probably landed in his feed.

"Hi, Al," I said, and he strode forward to set a thick-knuckled hand possessively on my shoulder. A wave of relief spilled from him to me as his almost identical aura supplemented mine, and I sighed in thanks.

"It's about time you got here," Dali said sourly.

"You called him? Why?" I said. My latte went sour in my stomach. Not because of Hodin's threat that I not mention him . . . exactly. Hodin had been imprisoned for the crime of doing Goddess-based elf magic, the same thing I kept finding myself being forced to do. Much as I hated to admit it, seeing Hodin confused and struggling for answers in Ivy's kitchen had struck a chord. If he wanted to play dead while he figured things out, far be it from me to expose him. As long as he didn't cause any trouble . . .

"I am not your babysitter, Gally," Dali added as he went behind the counter.

Al's hand fell away. "Rachel is capable of maintaining her own security," he drawled, then frowned at Jenks. "Even if her aura does look like shit at the moment."

"Thanks, Al." I appreciated his confidence, but knowing that Hodin could have circled me in my own kitchen kept my voice soft. *Why am I not telling them about Hodin, again? Oh, yeah. Death threat. Kindred spirit.*

"I can protect her, you fairy-ass moss wipe," Jenks said, hands on his hips. "Who do you think kept her alive when you were trying to kill her?"

Al narrowly eyed the pixy. "Just so," he drawled. "Dali, if you please, a demon grande," he said with a flourish, and Dali, now manning the register, stared malevolently at him.

"I really have to go," I said as I gathered my bag, and Al eyed my nearly full cup.

"Do not get out of that chair," he said, his tone suddenly sour. "The FIB can wait."

FIB? I thought, confused. But I wasn't about to tell him I was meeting Trent and the girls for ice cream. He'd try to horn in on it.

I had a few minutes yet, though, so I eased back. Satisfied, Al sat in an overdone show. "Dali thinks I owe you an apology," he said as he peered at me from over his blue smoked glasses. "It never occurred to me you might need watching while your aura mended. You always seem so capable."

"I'm fine," I said. *Dali called him?* I thought, still not believing it.

"That's what I told him you'd say," Al said softly. "But perhaps he's right." He turned to the counter, visibly forcing the worry from himself. "Dali, is that coffee ready yet?"

The annoyed demon frowned. "I have three orders ahead of you, Gally."

Sighing, Al settled back in his chair. He looked depressed, making me want to give him a hug and tell him it was okay, that the FIB was making a mistake and they were all crap heads. "Thanks for checking on me," I said instead, and his eyes flicked to mine.

"You're welcome," he gruffly muttered, glowering at Jenks when the pixy snickered.

My headache felt better, and I knew it was probably Al's aura temporarily filling in my gaps. Trent's was close enough to mine that he could do the same. "But really, I have to go," I said as I took another sip of cooling coffee. "I have an appointment."

"You have a job? Splendid!" Al praised, but there was a tight bite to his voice that left me unsure. "You may want to consider showering. You still smell of zombie."

"Still?" I said, wondering just how long the stink was going to linger, but then I hesitated. "Wait up," I said as I set my bag on the table, and Al stiffened. "How did you know about the zombie?" My eyes narrowed. "You put it in my garden? It was you, wasn't it?"

"That was you?" Jenks said, an angry red dust pooling on the table. "I've got *chunks* of dead *human* in my garden smelling like month-old unicorn piss!"

"I had to put it somewhere," Al almost whined. "It was crashing about my backyard most horribly. I *knew* you'd take care of it. What with that soft heart that plagues you."

"I didn't know you had a place in reality," I said, suddenly intrigued. Maybe he'd let Jenks and me move in for the winter.

"Fairy-ass zombie pus putrefying the soil. I'll never get anything to grow there," Jenks muttered, ignored.

"Of course I have a place in reality. We all do," Al said as he eyed me over his glasses. "There's nothing in that dismally small ever-after you made but trees and water. Bo-o-oring. Besides, my job required me to be available upon request at all hours, and unlike scrying mirrors, phones don't work between realities."

"Demon grande!" Mark shouted, and Al rose as that bell behind the counter rang.

"Maybe Jenks and I can move in with you for the winter," I said, taking my coffee as I stood as well. "Split the rent."

"No," he said, and Jenks and I followed him through the tables to the pickup counter. "I will be escorting you to your meeting at the FIB for safety reasons."

"I've got this, demon weenie," Jenks said, clearly insulted.

"I'm fine. Really," I insisted as I hitched my bag up my shoulder, but he wasn't listening.

"Fine? You are barely adequate. Dali has seen your aura, and now I have to address it," he said as he twisted to reach a thin wallet and leafed through a wad of cash from at least three different eras. "You *are* compromised. Wandering about Cincinnati without the ability to do magic makes us all look bad. Therefore, I'm with you when you're out of your kitchen."

Like my kitchen is any safer, I thought, and Jenks snickered, probably thinking the same thing.

"And a dollar extra for you, my good demon," Al said in an overdone show as he stuffed a wad of bills in the tip jar to pay for his drink.

"Thank you so-o-o much," Dali muttered sarcastically.

"I can do magic," I protested, but the reality was that I had a splat pistol that could easily be circumvented and a ceremonial knife that was too long to be legal even in my purse. Earth magic was great, but it had to be prepared hours before use. But still . . . an escort? That was my job.

Al beamed at the barista as he took his coffee. "I shall accompany you to the FIB."

"Um," I said, not seeing a way out of it. "I'm not going to the FIB. I'm going to the park."

"The park?" Al took the lid off his coffee to sprinkle a

heavier layer of cinnamon into it. "I thought the FIB had a job for you," he said, the leashed anger back in his voice.

"I've already been to the FIB." Arms over my chest, I stared out the window in the general direction of the FIB building, my anger at Edden—at the world—flashing high again.

The snap of the lid going back on seemed loud. "You're working a run for them?" he said blandly.

My attention flicked to Al. It was the second time he had brought up the FIB, and I looked at his previous words more carefully. He had said his job *required* him to be available at all hours. *Required*, as in not anymore. Had they *fired* him?

"I'm meeting Trent and the girls at the park for ice cream," I admitted. "Um, Al?" I said as he headed for the door, coffee in hand and a new tightness in his jaw. I knew his anger was born in the FIB's mistrust, and I understood it all too well. "Hey, as soon as I found out why Edden asked me to talk to one of their witnesses, I quit."

Al jerked to a halt, a gloved hand on the door, and then, as if he was realigning his thoughts, his shoulders slumped. His hand pulled back, and still not looking at me, he took a long draft of his coffee. "Damn my dame, that's good without the stink of burnt amber."

Head down, he gestured for me to go before him. Throat tight, I did. I knew he'd never say anything about it, but I'd stood up for him, and that was all that mattered. Maybe with both of us out of work, we could spend some time and make some tulpas, though it might be cheaper now for the demons to buy what they wanted instead of creating it from energy made real. Besides, a good tulpa put me out for a week.

"You're going to see Lucy and Ray?" Al said as he followed me out the door, and I hunched deeper into my jacket at the chill November breeze coming up off the river. On my shoulder, Jenks rattled his wings and tucked in behind my collar. "And ice cream. Mmmm," Al added. But I knew it was the girls' unconditional delight with him that he craved.

"*I* am. You aren't invited," I said, and he pouted dramatically from behind his blue-tinted glasses. "Ellasbeth will be there, and you're a huge distraction. They get little enough time with her as it is."

"I will be as quiet as a mouse," he promised, but I knew better, and I winced at the imagery of exploding winged horses. "I *will* accompany you to the park," he said, but there was genuine gratitude hidden in his flamboyant words now, and it made me feel good. "And *I* will drive," he added as he put a hand on the small of my back and pushed.

"Really, Al, I'm okay," I said, feeling as if I belonged again.

Al glanced over his shoulder at Junior's. "I know you are, but Dali has accused me of shirking my *parental* duties, so until your aura is full strength, I'll be with you when you're out of your dwelling."

"Parental," Jenks snorted from behind my collar, and I flushed. Al wasn't my parent or my teacher at this point, though I did go to him with questions he rarely answered. Chaperone, maybe? Bailer out of trouble? Okay, maybe *parent* was accurate.

"That's a lame excuse to horn in on ice cream with the girls," I said, but I was still riding the high of knowing that Al appreciated me standing up for him. "And when did you get a license?"

"Three days ago." The satisfaction was clear in his voice, and he set his cup on the hood of my car to open the passenger-side door for me. It wasn't the usual pride of a new driver getting a permit, but rather the affirmation that reality was making room for them, stretching the rules to accommodate their needs, and demanding that they adhere to the same laws as everyone else—at least on paper. For a demon craving the need to belong, it was heady. Edden's mistrust had hurt him, and I doubted that Al would ever step foot in the FIB again. I knew I was questioning if I ever would.

"I heard it took six months and Kalamack three lawyers to reacquire your license. Thank you for getting that box on the form," he added softly. "In you go, my itchy witch."

Hearing more than the thanks for getting *demon* on the license permit, I slid in and he shut the door with a careful motion.

"He's worried about your aura?" Jenks said as I dropped my coffee in the cup holder before fitting my key and starting the car up from the passenger's side. Hot air blew from the vents, and I angled it toward Jenks.

"I know, right?" I said, my mood tarnishing as Al strode around the front of the car, his eyes on the nearby colorful trees. Dali freaking out over a thin aura was just weird. And then I realized Al wasn't looking at the beauty of the leaves, but for the shadow of a ragged crow among them.

It wasn't my aura they were worried about. It was that Hodin might be alive.

CHAPTER

7

IT FELT ODD TO BE SITTING IN THE PASSENGER SEAT OF MY car, sipping my cooling sweet coffee and messing with my phone while someone else drove. Putting my phone away, I watched Al competently make his way through Cincy's four o'clock rush hour. That was even odder. I'd say he was being overly protective, but I knew what it was like to have a brand-new license and want to try it out. I wasn't surprised he was good at driving, being unexpectedly patient with people on cell phones and courteous at stoplights. He'd even put his phone on driving mode before carefully fastening his seatbelt and checking his mirrors. Everyone out here was carelessly and casually using a machine that could kill, and arbitrarily set rules were all that kept everyone getting along with minimal friction. That was a demon from top to bottom.

Al's window was down a crack despite the chill, and the sun shone on his gently moving dark hair to make it look almost white. The cold breeze had put Jenks on the radio buttons instead of his usual spot on the rearview mirror, and true to his pixy nature, he'd been going up and down the dial, looking for God knew what.

"Wait. Leave it there," I said as Takata's latest spilled out, and Al and Jenks shared a snicker. But I'd liked his music before I knew he was my birth father, and I turned it up, right as it was ending.

"That was Cincy's hometown boy himself, Takata," the announcer said, bringing a smile to my face as Al stopped at a yellow light. "Tickets for his solstice concert will go on sale next week, but you can win them here first. Stay tuned for how to get them at the end of our interview with Sa'han Landon, the high priest of the elven dewar, which is-s-s-s coming up next."

My smile vanished, and I stared at the radio. Jenks eyed me from the tuner knob, his dangling feet idly kicking. "You okay?" he said as I pushed back into the seat to stare at nothing.

"Fine." I wasn't going to admit that Landon was getting to me. He'd been on the radio all week, TV morning shows, brief interviews on the local nightly news, anyone who would give him a mic in exchange for his version of reality. Trent was good with letting lies roll off his back, but I'd been brought up where if you didn't quash a rumor fast and with fists, it became the truth.

"Tired," I added, and Jenks rubbed a hand along his wing to smooth it, clearly seeing through the lie. "I was up early this morning. And then I had a really weird dream while waiting for you and Ivy."

"Curious," Al said, actually waving at the woman in a MINI twin to my own as he accelerated through the intersection. "My dreams have been unusually restless as well."

I looked at him, thinking a demon driving through Cincinnati was about the coolest thing ever. "I didn't know you had bad dreams."

"Quite often," he said softly, eyes on the traffic. "And they're none of your business. Rachel, I never told Ceri about Hodin."

I froze. *Damn, damn, and double damn. When had Al and Dali had time to talk?* "Uh," I said, warming at Jenks's wry expression. "Maybe Newt told her?"

My car's steering wheel creaked under Al's grip. "Newt

dosed herself into forgetting him," he said, voice tight, and I began to quietly panic.

"Okay, so I lied to Dali," I admitted, almost sitting sidewise in the seat to face him. "I didn't want to admit it was a dream. Dali might decide it meant something. And it doesn't."

But instead of relaxing, Al became more worried, brow furrowed as he looked across the car at me.

"This morning," I lied again, and Jenks, still on the radio buttons, crossed his arms over his chest and frowned. "It woke me up. Nightmare about a pixy turning into a nice-looking demon with black hair. Scared the crap out of me. That's all."

Hearing the drop of truth in my lie, Al made a soft "Mmmm" of sound and turned away.

"It was just a dream, Al," I continued, pulse slowing. "I probably got the name from the collective. We were all sharing a really tight space a few months ago."

"Perhaps," he admitted, focus distant. "But Hodin was known for working his mischief through dreams. Tell me if you have another."

"Sure," I said, but Jenks was still squinting at me in disapproval. "Dali said he was dead."

Al stiffened, his eyes fixed firmly on the road. "He is. The dewar killed him to keep their secrets safe when we began to best them. Which was probably a good thing, seeing as he was more dangerous, unpredictable, untrustworthy, and outright mendacious than the Goddess he so *desperately* wanted to believe in," he finished mockingly. "He was an idiot."

But he almost sounded jealous, and I exchanged an uneasy look with Jenks. "You're a good driver," I said to change the subject. We were less than a mile from Junior's, and everything felt awkward.

"It's not that hard." Jenks fiddled with the tuner until he found the weather. "Two pedals and a wheel. Big, fat, hairy-fairy, whooping deal."

"Thank you." Al inclined his head to acknowledge the compliment. "It's my third time."

"You mean since getting your license, right?" I asked as we gained the interstate and his speed eased into something less stop-and-go and more slow creep.

A shoulder lifted and fell as he settled in behind a rusted truck. "To not say otherwise would not necessarily be false."

I looked at the charms on my key ring, uneasy. Double negatives had always confused me. Jenks sighed unhappily at the expected low for tonight. It was close to his comfortable threshold, and again I was glad that his stash of portable foods was in the trunk beside my overnight bag. He'd be okay at Trent's conservatory, but damn it to the everafter and back, we belonged in the church, not spread out over the greater Cincinnati area.

Al's fingers tapped in annoyance as the left lanes began to move faster than us, but our exit was just ahead and he endured. Though the park was close, it would probably take us another fifteen minutes.

"You said you wouldn't hog the girls' attention. Maybe you should change?" I suggested.

Al gave me a sideways look. "You want the dog-headed god?"

Jenks snickered. "I do. I want to see Ellasbeth deal with *that*."

"No," I said shortly. "Don't you have a happy face for parties?"

Al simpered at me, silent as he took the exit.

"Okay." I fiddled with my hair, holding it to my head so it wouldn't snarl in the wind. "Hey. Can you do a basic elf?" I asked, suddenly seeing an opportunity.

"If the situation requires it," he said in distaste, lip curling.

I shifted in the seat to face Al more fully. "There was an elf at my church this morning."

"I knew it!" Jenks exclaimed, his unexpected gold dust vanishing in the breeze.

"Before you got there," I added, and the four-inch man frowned.

"I knew I smelled elf," Jenks said. "I thought it was coming from you. He was eating that cold lasagna, wasn't he? The entire couch stank. I bet he slept there."

"His hair looked like it. He ran off when he heard you and Ivy. He might be a Landon spy. I want to know if Ellasbeth recognizes him." I felt a little guilty that I didn't trust her, but not much.

Al's grin widened. "The situation requires it," he said, and I smiled back, the feeling of shared deviltry almost rubbing out the guilt of lying to him. *Why am I covering for Hodin?* I thought. *Oh, yeah. Death, destruction, mayhem.* But if I was honest, it was his confusion paired with his desire to work it out that had me silent. I'd been there myself, knowing I was in deep shit and simply needing the time to find a few more facts before making a world-changing mistake.

"He was about sixteen," I said, remembering the kid startled and resolute in the dark of my church. "Few inches taller than me. Gawky. Cropped ears, and tan. He's got that almost transparent blond hair of a pure elf, and it's kind of long. And messy."

The car's engine slacked off, then renewed a steady hum as Al misted out and back, shifting his appearance on the fly to match my description. He was still wearing his fifties suit, now too large on the adolescent-thin body. His hair, too, had changed, blond as it blew in the wind, and he had a lightly tan, angular young face instead of a slightly ruddy, square-jawed older one. Somehow he'd even gotten a hint of innocence, and something in me twisted.

"Wow," I said, impressed with Al's internal spell library. "He was wearing torn jeans and an olive shirt. Shorter hair," I directed.

Again Al misted out, coming back even faster this time, and I stared at the goat-slitted red eyes of a demon from a clearly elven face.

"His nose is a little more angled," I said, hoping no one was seeing this. Shape-shifting while driving. Sheesh. "His eyes are a little wider, less sleepy. Narrow chin."

Al's features blurred, and even his hands changed.

"Too thin," I said, and Jenks hopped to my knee, clearly wanting my shoulder but unwilling to risk the cold draft. "Slim, not gaunt," I added. "And you still have your teeth," I prompted.

Al's smile changed, my car picking up speed as traffic thinned and we took a longer but less traveled street to the park. "Good?" he asked, and I stifled a shudder. His eyes were still wrong, but it was really hard to change them—or so Al claimed.

"Just a sec," I said, digging in my bag for my sunglasses. "Try this."

He froze as I put my glasses on him, but now it was perfect. "My God," I whispered, seeing him sitting behind my car's wheel, looking like a smart-ass kid working on his driver's ed permit. "That is really creepy."

"You don't smell right," Jenks said, and Al's smile faltered.

"As long as I don't smell like burnt amber," he muttered, and both Jenks and I shook our heads. I'd noticed that Al had smelled less and less of burnt amber since the original ever-after went down, until now I really had to search for it. It still lingered about Hodin, though. *Curious.*

Exuding a familiar confidence, Al shifted the mirrors to accommodate his new size. "I bet Edden would pay extra for this," he said, head cocked as he gave his image the once-over in the rearview mirror. "If I ever cared to work for him again," he added distantly.

I couldn't help but feel smug, even though both our bank accounts were going to suffer for our pride. "As an alternative to a sketch artist? Absolutely." I pointed at our turnoff and he smoothly took it, using his blinker and everything. He slowed as he approached the stop sign, and I woke up my phone. "I'd ask for a thousand a pop. Make him pay. Hang on a sec. I want Trent to know what's going on." Not to mention Quen would have reacted badly to an unknown elf coming over the grass. My glaze slid to Al. Even a cute one.

"Good idea," Al said, his voice giving him away. "No

wonder it has become so difficult to snag a familiar," he said, one arm casually on the open window as he waved to the woman in the honkin' big-ass SUV and smoothly accelerated. "You all have magic with no cost."

"You mean, no smut?" I said as I typed and hit send. "There's a cost. You just don't see it."

"I'm not talking about your wallet," Al said dryly.

"Neither am I." I took in Al's attitude, casual and in control, seeing a problem. "He's sixteen and flighty, Al, not a former ruler of China."

He beamed across the car, and a vague memory rose of seeing Trent like this, gawky and awkward, at camp. "You know that was never official, love," Al leered, and the memory was gone.

"It won't work if you strut over the grass as if you own it," I complained, and he sighed, slumping in the seat and pulling his arm back in to carefully set his hands at ten and two.

But my phone dinged. Trent had sent me a happy face. "Okay, we're good."

"Mmmm, what was this mystery elf wearing on his feet, itchy witch?" Al asked as we stopped at a four way.

"White sneakers?" I said, thinking they'd looked rather institutional for the rest of him.

From the radio, the commercial finally cut out and the radio host's professional patter flowed into a background nothing until Landon's name cut through like a bright light. "Welcome, Sa'han Landon," the host almost gushed. "We appreciate you talking to our listeners today."

"Rache, turn that slug snot off," Jenks said, his wings an irritating hum beside my ear.

"It's the third show he's done today," Al said, his proper British-lord accent sounding wrong coming from such a young-looking body.

"Don't touch it!" I said, and Al changed his reach to close his window instead.

"It's only going to get you mad," Jenks said.

"It's good to know your enemy's weaknesses," Al countered, and I turned up the volume. I didn't agree with Trent that you only had to convince the people in power of the truth. Truth belonged to the masses, or the masses made bad choices that the people in power couldn't stop.

"I think the question on everyone's mind is why the ley lines went down," the host said, clearly following a preset list of questions. They'd been the same for every interview. "I know *I'll* never forget where I was when suddenly nothing worked. That you brought the ley lines back to life will put your time as the dewar's high priest in the history books even if you do nothing else."

"Thank you." Landon's modesty was irksome as he took credit for something he hadn't done, and I bristled.

"Ass," Jenks said shortly, and Al growled, his now-thin hands on the wheel clenching. The look of anger the demon was wearing was alarming on such a young face.

"I regretted the need to break the lines, but it was necessary to prevent Mr. Kalamack from sending the souls of the undead back to the ever-after a second time. That someone would work to rip them away again after having rejoined their bodies . . . Well, that's almost inhuman."

I clenched my jaw. "Sure," I said bitterly. "End their curse by causing them to commit suicide. Real nice." The guilt for the atrocities the undead had to perpetrate upon those who loved them had been predictably too much to take. Everyone in the vampire community understood that, but the old undead had wanted their souls, nevertheless.

"It was a gesture of goodwill that I'd hoped would usher in a new understanding between all species," Landon said, and I swear I heard the steering wheel crack again under Al's pressure. "That Kalamack chose to work against it speaks more clearly to his true agenda. His magic is untouched, while everyone else in the elven community is having problems. Why? His increasingly close relationship with demons, perhaps?"

Close relationship? He meant me. My foot thumped against the car.

"Perhaps he's just better at it than you, Sa'han Landon," the host said, and Jenks snickered.

"That's it!" I exclaimed, and the red dust of surprise sifted down my front. "Al, make a U-turn."

His youthful body leaning forward, Al checked behind us before spinning my little car into a tight turn that left me reaching for the dash. "This may have unknown consequences," he warned.

"Yeah. Like my foot on Landon's ass."

"The radio station?" Jenks said, voice loud beside my ear. "Take the next right. I know a shortcut. Rachel's car is small enough."

"So why sunder the lines?" the host prompted as Al wove aggressively through traffic. Horns were beeping, and I wasn't surprised that Al knew all the appropriate hand gestures.

"I had to," Landon said. "It was regrettable, but temporarily ending magic was the only way to insure that Kalamack wouldn't force the undead's souls back to the ever-after again."

"My God! Are you listening to this? He destroyed the lines so elves would be the only ones able to do magic. That it took out the vampires and demons was just the icing!" I exclaimed, holding on as Al drove my car within an inch of its abilities. I'd had enough of Landon's lies. If Trent wouldn't say anything, fine. But Cincinnati was used to me doing outrageous things.

"Even so," Landon was saying as Al followed Jenks's pointing finger down a narrow, potholed street overhung with scrubby trees, "I had to gain the support of the witches. Without them, it never would have been possible to reinstate the power in the defunct Arizona ley lines."

"You little liar!" I shouted, but they were going into a break and I held the dash as we bounced along a narrow street that ended in a dirt track going almost straight up. "Whoa, wait a moment, Al," I said, worried. "My car doesn't have a tall enough suspension for this. You're going to rip out my transmission."

"Mmmm." Jenks's wings tickled my neck. "I don't remember it being that steep."

Al put it in park, my car facing the impassable road. "He'll be done with his spot by the time we backtrack and reach the station in this archaic, outmoded form of combustion travel."

I said nothing for three heartbeats as an ad for red wigglers played. That Landon's lies were being accepted as truth—each day making his political clout more secure—really rankled me. It was just pain, wasn't it? My pulse hammered and my hands went damp. "Okay, jump us there," I said, shocking myself when I looked at Al and saw that innocent elf staring at me from behind my mirrored sunglasses.

"Truly?" he asked, his almost white eyebrows high in his young, tan face.

I nodded. "I need to shut him up."

Grinning, Al locked the doors and cut the engine.

"Wait!" Jenks shrilled. "You are *not* leaving me in this car. I want to go, too! Damn it, demon, don't you leave me in this car!"

Al's aura slipped over me midbreath, shifting my aura to match the resonance of the nearest ley line. Like two water drops joining, it pulled me in.

Agony stabbed through me, and I swear I would've passed out if I'd had a body, but I was only thought, and my thoughts were on fire.

A weird gurgle rose up, and I choked it back. My knees threatened to give way, and I locked them, glad I had knees again. My skin wasn't on fire and a glowing spike wasn't being hammered into my brain—it only felt that way. Al had been quick, unsettlingly so, but it still hurt.

I took a ragged breath. Even Jenks's dust spilling down my front seemed too hot. But we were there, or here, rather, and the deep quiet of a radio studio muffled my ears. *Coffee. They have coffee at radio stations, don't they? Coffee can fix anything.*

My head felt as if it was going to split open, but when I saw Landon sitting with his back to me at the little table with its overhanging mics, my anger pushed the pain down.

A man who could only be Mac, the host, had his head down over his notes as the last of the commercial played out. Al was beside me, holding my elbow as I caught my breath. He looked like that elf kid as he made a bunny-ear kiss-kiss to the technician in the adjoining sound room. The tech stared at us in slack-jawed amazement, frozen as Mac, oblivious to us, tidied his papers and opened his mic.

"This is Mac, and we're back with Sa'han Landon of the elven dewar. Landon, thank you again for talking with us today. It's not just the vampires who have been impacted by the new ley lines. Weather control at the track has been iffy. There have been issues at the hospital requiring secondary spells and charms. Can you tell us more about your theory that Kalamack is responsible for the problems elven magic has been experiencing lately?"

Behind the glass in the control room, the technician finally broke out of his shock, looking frazzled as he flipped open his mic and said something. Mac's head snapped up, lips parting as he saw us in the room with them, and beside me, Al grinned like a demented sixteen-year-old.

Eyes wide, Mac stood up, fumbling for a headset for me as Landon said, "The magic misfires began when Kalamack forced the demons to reality. The demons are causing the issues. They're interfering in the normal function of our charms. Targeting us."

Al cleared his throat, and Landon whipped around, the stunned expression on his face worth all the pain it had taken to get here. "If demons were targeting you," Al said softly, "you would know it, little man."

Landon's mouth moved, but nothing came out. The elven priest's eyes narrowed at my sarcastic smile, shifting from me to Al. "Zack," he almost growled, a hand over his mic. "What are you doing with Morgan and that pixy? Sit down and wait for me," he demanded, pointing to a chair against the foam-covered acoustic wall. "Sit and do nothing. I'll deal with you later."

Zack? I thought in understanding. The kid *had* been a Landon spy. Son of a fairy fart.

"Excuse me." Al's grip on me eased, and confident that I had my balance, he let go. "I have been asked to sit." Looking like a sullen teenager, he sat down.

Mac's eyes were wide, his hands shaking as he pointed in invitation to a mic opposite Landon. "Ah, Rachel Morgan has unexpectedly joined us," he said, his expression showing his excitement where his smooth words did not. "Ms. Morgan, what can you tell my listeners about Sa'han Landon's claim that the demons are behind the elves' trouble with their magic?"

Giving Landon a dry look, I eased into the chair and adjusted the mic. "The demons are not responsible for the elves' magical issues," I said, and Landon scoffed. "Elf magic sucks right now because the Goddess no longer favors them." I hesitated, and across the table, Landon narrowed his eyes, daring me. "Probably because Landon tricked her into destroying the ley lines and her easy access to reality. I know that would really quirk my quarks."

"*You* interfered in the spell," Landon accused.

"Damn right she did, you moss wipe of an elf," Jenks interjected, his wings moving better now that we were out of the cold.

"Because your *spell* was destroying the ever-after and taking the demons with it," I said.

Landon leered, four feet of table between us. "You say that like it's a bad thing."

"It is, you slimy, lying sack of toad scrotum!" I exclaimed.

"Whoa, whoa, whoa!" Mac raised his hand. "Can we say that on the radio? We can?" His eyes were on the technician, who gave him a thumbs-up. "Even so, let's take it down a notch."

Landon took a breath, his expression too satisfied to live, and I interrupted. "I have listened to you spouting your lies for the last two months, Landon," I said, and he sat back. "I can't take it anymore. *You* destroyed the lines to throw the undead into a dysfunctional chaos, not to help them, but to step into the power vacuum."

Arms crossed, Landon leaned in to the mic. "I did it to

keep the souls of the undead in reality so they might join with their undead bodies. Heal them and end their curse. *You* tampered with it, thereby breaking the curse that kept demons where they belonged in the ever-after. I wouldn't have had to destroy the lines at all if you and Kalamack hadn't interfered."

"Yeah, because if the old undead commit suncide, you'd be right on top, wouldn't you," I said. I didn't care that I sounded like an angry redhead. I was an angry redhead.

"Sa'han Landon," Mac interjected before I could elaborate, "are you implying that Rachel Morgan is responsible for you destroying the ley lines and, therefore, the ever-after?"

My eyes narrowed on Landon. *Lie,* I thought. *I dare you.*

Landon set his hands on the table. "She tampered with the spell designed to keep the undead souls in reality. She changed its function, and when the lines went down, the ever-after collapsed. Now we have demons walking in reality whenever they please, immune to summons and banishments. She did it knowingly."

"Damn straight," I said. "*You* broke the lines to destroy the power balance, period. There wasn't enough support in the enclave to manage it, so you lied to the coven to get them to help, fully knowing there was no way in hell you could re-instate the dead Arizona lines."

Mac wasn't listening, intent on something coming over his headphones when Landon exclaimed, "I temporarily cut the lines to prevent Mr. Kalamack's attempt to free the demons and prevent the undead souls from being forced from reality!"

"Trent had nothing to do with the undead souls being drawn back," I countered. "It was bad spell casting, Landon. *Your* bad spell casting. You are a hack! You tampered with a two-thousand-year-old curse, making a loophole that the demons found all on their own. *You* freed the demons!"

"Sing it, Rache!" Jenks encouraged, and I stood, taking the mic from the stand. "You *knew* you couldn't reinstate the Arizona lines. You *knew* that if the old undead had their souls, they would suncide. And you *knew* that if the lines went down, the ever-after would fall and take the demons with it, the only faction of Inderland that could curb your imperialistic plotting. You tried to kill the demons and the old undead in one swoop, leaving elves the only people able to practice magic through the Goddess. And you wonder why she's mad at you."

Chin trembling, Landon put the flats of his arms on the table. "The lines are still there. The ever-after still exists. How can you say that I destroyed them when they clearly aren't?"

Frustrated, I made a fist. "Because I was able to steal enough power from the Goddess to not only make a new ever-after, but free the demons entirely from their curse. That's why!"

Smirking, Landon eased back. "To walk among us, day or night, unsummoned and unbanishable."

"Uh, Rache?" Jenks said, but I was too angry to think.

"Now you got it," I said. "You should thank the demons, not hound them. If not for them scraping new ley lines from the new ever-after to reality, there wouldn't be any magic at all."

I stopped. Landon was smiling. I'd made a mistake. "Uh, or at least that's the way I see it."

And then I shrieked, ducking as Quen blew the door off the studio and Trent walked in, his jaw clenched, his manner stiff, and his barely suppressed anger and magic making his hair float.

Yep, I'd made a mistake.

CHAPTER

8

I BACKED UP, FACE COLD AS I RAN INTO AL. THE DEMON HAD stood; he still looked like that elf. Zack, Landon had called him, though I doubt if Zack had ever worn that particular expression of disgust and hatred. My headache eased when his adolescent-thin fingers took my elbow to stop me from stepping on him. Trent's expression was tight in anger, but it wasn't at me—I thought. Angry or not, he looked really good, dressed in a comfortable pair of slacks and a light-weight shirt that showed a tantalizing amount of neck and upper chest. It was far away and distant from his usual suit and tie, but he'd been at the park with his girls, not in a boardroom, and a tinge of guilt passed through me. He must have been listening to the same tripe we'd been.

"O-okay," Mac said, catching his mental balance. "Mr. Kalamack has joined us in the studio as well. Mr. Kalamack, we're going to take a break while we get you a mic." Mac gestured at the tech behind the glass, and another commercial spun up, presumably.

"Tink's titties, it's about time you got here," Jenks said as he darted erratically between Quen and Trent. "Rache had to do this all by herself. Where you been, you little cookie maker?"

"Asleep, apparently." Trent shook his head against the mic Mac was arranging, then turned to give Al an appraising once-over. Thanks to my text, he knew who he was, and just as obvious, he didn't recognize Zack. Making an almost unheard sound of negation, he came around the table to me. The soft sounds of Quen trying to fix the door made me wince. "I appreciate the chance to talk with you, Mac," Trent was saying, but his eyes never left mine. "This isn't a good time, though. Ms. Morgan and I have a previous engagement and we're already late. Rachel?"

He pulled me stumbling from Al, but I was trying to figure out why the truth was bad.

"Why?" Jenks landed right on a mic. "You going to let that bag of hot air keep squealing his lies like a balloon letting out air? Rachel and I are on a roll!" Jenks gyrated his hips and a silver dust sifted down like a living sunbeam to make the speaker crackle. "Yahoo, baby!"

Trent gestured to the hall, and I went. Quen had given up trying to fix the door and had propped it against the wall. People had clustered in the hall, and I cringed at the thought of going through them. Worse, Landon was far too happy for this to be a good thing. "I made a mistake, didn't I."

"Not necessarily." Trent grimaced at the click of a camera. "I think I owe you a favor or three."

"You were listening? You heard?" I said, embarrassed at my fiery rant.

"Why do you think I'm here?" His eyes were on the hall as he led me into the crush.

To stop my lips from flapping, I thought as Mac tried to get Landon to sit down. I'd made a mistake. It was in Landon's satisfaction and Trent's tight brow. But I couldn't see it.

"Zack, sit down!" Landon barked as he settled himself, and I spun. Al was following us, still looking like that kid.

"I'm not your lackey," Al said, and Landon paled when Al removed his sunglasses to show his red goat-slitted eyes. I shuddered at Al's chuckle as his form misted, thickened, and changed back to his usual smoked-glass, nasty-grin, lace-and-crushed-green-velvet self.

"O-o-okay," Mac squeaked, clearly thrown. "Ah . . . mmmm . . ."

Al put a finger to his thick lips and made a *shhhh* sound that chilled me even more.

"Sure," Mac said faintly, agreeing to stay silent about a demon being in his studio.

The tech hammered on the glass. He was pointing to the mic, and Mac scrambled for it, his smooth professional voice filling in the gap as he put on his headphones.

Al strode out before us, and in the hall, people scattered like roaches panicking in the light.

Trent allowed himself a brief moment of gloating, his hand on the small of my back as we hesitated on the broken threshold. "It's almost worth the cost to know where his loyalties are," he said, then pushed me into the hall.

Quen quirked an eyebrow at me as I went by, and the fear I'd done something wrong strengthened. But for God's sake, I was sick of Landon dragging Trent through the mud.

"Sa'han Landon," Mac said as we entered the now empty hall, and Trent stiffened at the elven term of respect given to the distasteful man, "would I be correct in assuming from Ms. Morgan's words that this was a power struggle between the elves and the demons?"

"Rache is right. Landon is a hack," Jenks said, his voice coming from the hall speaker. "He couldn't reinstate the lines if he tried. He used the coven and enclave like a fairy's ass wipe."

"Jenks!" I shouted, hearing his laughter like wind chimes through the speaker a bare instant before his wing rasp sounded by my ear.

"I'm just sayin' what you won't," he complained, but I breathed easier when we got to the upper lobby overlooking the street lobby below. Lucy's loud song about spiders and water spouts rose up unseen and my shoulders eased. Ellasbeth's voice twined beautifully with hers, and I looked over the edge to see Ray and Lucy in their little sunbonnets and dresses. Ellasbeth was in a tasteful pantsuit, her purse matching the diaper bag at her feet. *Of course it would.*

"And he *is* a fairy's moss wipe," Jenks said, then dropped down, angling for them.

"Ah, strong-minded little girls," Al said contentedly. "Nothing better in this world or the next. Excuse me."

"Al," Trent warned, and the demon winked as he took the curving stairs.

"Jenks! Jenks!" Lucy's song cut off midphrase, and then her voice rose in question. "Aunt Rachel? Aunt Ra-a-a-a-chel!"

"That is so sweet," I whispered, jerking at Lucy's sudden earsplitting, delighted squeal.

"Allie!" Lucy screamed, struggling to get off Ellasbeth's lap and run to the demon. "Mommy, let me go. Let go-o-o-o-o!"

Trent's grip on my arm spasmed, but it was at the word *mommy*, not at Al, his arms now open wide in invitation as he stood at the bottom of the stairs. Ellasbeth fought with Lucy for a heartbeat, and then, her expression twisted in uncertainty, she let go. The toddler ran to Al, but it was hard to tell who was more delighted as Al scooped Lucy up and threw her into the air to catch her.

Jenks tentatively alighted on Ray's outstretched hand, and the smaller girl beamed. A frown crossed her face when her sister shouted again and Jenks flew up and away. Attention diverted, Ray toddled to Al as well. Ellasbeth stood alone in her uncertainty. The two girls were only a few months apart, acting more like three- or four-year-olds than the two they almost were. Elves clearly matured faster than witches. According to Jenks, I still wasn't old enough to be on my own.

"I'm sorry," I said as Quen joined us and we headed for the stairs. "I should've kept my mouth shut. But I couldn't take it anymore. He said demons were messing with elven magic, and—" I stopped and glanced at Quen, now suspiciously silent. "What did I do?"

"Nothing I don't approve of, Ms. Morgan," Quen said, and Trent flashed him a dark look.

Trent hesitated at the top of the stairs, pulling us all to a halt. "Quen, would you mind taking Rachel downstairs? I want to get that tape if Mac is willing to part with it."

Mistrust drifted behind Quen's eyes. "I can get the tape, Sa'han."

Trent's frown deepened. "Let me rephrase that. I want a word with Landon. Alone."

My fingers slipped reluctantly from Trent's hand as Quen inclined his head, a wicked smile turning him from capable bodyguard to highly qualified thief. "Of course, Sa'han."

Jenks, having been driven upward by Lucy's noise, hovered close, and I twitched my head for him to go with Trent. With a cheerful thumbs-up and a bright sifting of dust, Jenks darted off. Trent jerked, surprised when the pixy landed on his shoulder, and then the two of them were gone.

"Thank you." Quen took my arm in a formal gesture to "help" me down the stairs. "Trent deserves more freedom, but I always appreciate someone watching his back."

"Tell me about it," I said, pulling my arm from his as we descended the curving stairway. "Jeez, Quen. All I did was tell the truth, and Trent is acting as if I ruined his big plan." My expression went empty. "Did I? Oh, God. He should have told me if he had a plan."

Quen stopped my headlong rush of words with a slow shake of his head. "He was simply trying to keep your name out of the news. Landon agreed to not bring up your involvement if Trent said nothing contrary to Landon's claims. That you survived the Goddess and made the new ever-after isn't anything you really want publicly known, either. Still . . ." Quen smiled as if pleased. "Now that the truth is out, it's going to get nasty. And real."

More like real nasty, I thought as I saw the entire week in a new way. Each interview had been to goad me into breaking my silence. "But everyone knew I was involved," I said, and Quen nodded, his eyes on Ray as we neared the last step. The little girl was on Al's hip as he made colored bubbles. Lucy danced about, bursting them as she shouted out their colors. I would've thought it was very one-sided except that Ray was telling Al what color to make by pointing at the horses on the blanket tight in her grip.

"True, but Trent was halfway to convincing the city powers it had been Newt who made the new ever-after," Quen said, clearly proud of Ray. The little girl was his daughter, and he and Trent were raising the two girls—who didn't share a single drop of blood—as sisters.

My steps down the last few stairs slowed. "And now everyone knows it was me."

"Exactly," Quen said, and I finally got it. *I* had made the new ever-after. *I* was the one with the immense cosmic powers, and *I* lived on a boat in the Hollows, vulnerable to anyone who wanted to challenge that. It wouldn't be a problem if those immense cosmic powers were actually mine, but they weren't. I'd stolen them from the Goddess, and they were long gone.

"I should have kept my big mouth shut," I said, and Quen chuckled.

"Perhaps. But hiding the truth behind a lie has its own liabilities. Trent was already beginning to rue his decision, and you'll survive. You are the demons' most powerful denizen."

I gave Quen a wry smile as I took the last stair. "Seriously? I can't even jump a line," I said, remembering how vulnerable I had been just this afternoon in Ivy's kitchen.

Quen drew me to a halt. "Any demon can jump the lines. You're good at things they aren't."

"Like fitting in?" I said, then warmed at Landon's angry shout coming from the loft.

"Your voice will *never* have weight in the enclave if you continue to associate with a barren woman, Kalamack. Give up your claim to someone who really wants it."

Oh, God, just strike me down now. "I can't stand that man," I said, miserable at the knowledge that I was making Trent's bid for the enclave harder. "Why is he still in Cincinnati?"

"Because you are here," Quen said. "And he can't bring down Trent when you're beside him."

"Me?" I looked at him in surprise. "This is all about Trent, isn't it."

Quen's eyebrows went high in amusement. "No, Tal

Sa'han. If it was, it would've been finished six weeks ago." He hesitated as Trent's muffled voice cut off Landon's tirade. The prickling of line energy drawn into existence skated over my skin, and I looked at Quen. Trent had a nasty, seldom-seen temper. And magic. The two were not a good mix.

"Excuse me, Tal Sa'han. I need to extricate Trent from that vile priest," Quen said, worried.

Tal Sa'han. My shoulders slumped. Somehow I'd become Trent's "most valued adviser," and I looked past Al and the girls to where Ellasbeth stood, perfect and professional, clearly unhappy as a demon played with the girls. It should have been her.

"Sure. Go," I said, but Quen was already on the stairs. Ray watched him, her thoughts unknown behind those green eyes so much like her mother's that it hurt. Al, too, was watching, drawn away by Lucy's demands. Forcing a smile, I headed to Ellasbeth. Even with a lace-and-velvet demon in the mix, they looked like the perfect family. Ray's shoes and socks were missing, and Lucy's hem was damp, evidence of their quick departure from the park. I would've worried she was cold, but elves never seemed to feel it, even in winter.

Ellasbeth gave me a thin smile in return as she shifted to make room for me beside her. Not for the first time, I wondered what I was doing here, trying to fit into Trent's world. Ellasbeth was the ideal politician's wife with a life and status of her own, a respectable job at the university, everything I wasn't. I couldn't help but feel my lack as I stood in my jeans and light sweater beside her casual precision. He had the perfect family—or he would if he took Ellasbeth back. Me? I couldn't commit to anything longer than a weekend. The girls deserved better than that.

"Hi," I said as I fidgeted beside Ellasbeth. "Uh, sorry about this."

A weary shrug shifted her narrow shoulders, and Al interrupted with a cheerful "Look, my little ladies. Go say hi to your aunt Rachel."

His eyes were glinting in mischief, and I dropped down,

almost in self-preservation, as Lucy ran for me, her knit hat gone and her fair hair streaming behind her to show her pointy ears. "Aunt Rachel!" the little girl called joyfully, and then she was with me, her chubby arms wrapping around my neck in a fast hug before dropping back, her green eyes bright. "Look what I can do."

My eyebrows rose when Lucy snapped her fingers, and a colored bubble appeared, delighting the little girl and making her mother stifle a sigh.

"That's marvelous, Lucy," I said, wondering if Al had sent them over to rub Ellasbeth's nose in the fact that the girls knew me better than her. *Yep,* I thought at his devilish smile when he set Ray down and she ran to me, her favorite blanket with the horses tight in her grip. "Can you make them different colors?" I sat down right on the floor, and Lucy plopped herself into my lap.

"Blue! Red! Yellow!" Lucy exclaimed, springing right up again to smack them into puffs of colored smoke.

But my lap didn't stay empty long, and Ray wrapped her thinner arms about my neck and gave me a little-girl kiss. She smelled like a snickerdoodle, and I hugged her back, settling her in my lap with her blanket. "How is your riding? Have you jumped Ginger yet?" I asked, and Ray lost her disapproving stare at her sister as she grinned at me.

"It looks as if you were in the pond," I said, trying to get her to talk. With Lucy around, she seldom had to, and it was my mission to make sure the little girl had a voice.

"Sharps was spitting at the ducks," she said, her charming voice high as she played with my curling, snarling hair. "Daddy and Abba said it was okay." Her gaze went to the upper balcony, searching until she found Quen coming down the stairs with Jenks and Trent.

"Well, trolls are allowed to do that sort of thing." I stood her up so she could go to her dad or abba . . . or whatever. A woman in a business dress was with them, and I got up off the floor at her startled blink. She was probably the station manager, seeing as Trent had his wallet out and Quen *had* knocked down the studio door.

Jenks was on Trent's shoulder, looking as right as rain in the desert. There was a disk in Trent's hand, and a sour look on his face that vanished when the girls joined them. There had to be at least a dozen colored bubbles drifting about, and Al picked Lucy up to distract her from making more. It also got him in on the conversation, and feeling left out, I folded Ray's blanket.

"Sorry for ruining your afternoon," I said to Ellasbeth. "It wasn't my intention." *This time,* I mentally added, recalling busting in on her marriage to Trent, effectively ending it.

Much to my surprise, Ellasbeth touched my shoulder, her warmth sincere where there'd only been a prickly distaste before. "No need to apologize," she said, her faint Seattle accent making her sound even more polished. "I have them all weekend, thanks to you." She smiled, eyes dropping when they began to glisten. "Thank you for that," she almost whispered.

"It was Trent's decision, not mine," I said uncomfortably. It was a lot easier to hate her than understand her. Understanding her might lead to liking her, and that would be intolerable.

She made a sound of disbelief. "Nice of you to give him that illusion. No, this is coming from you. I know he doesn't trust me."

Tal Sa'han, echoed in my thoughts, scaring me. I held the ear of the potentially most powerful man east of the Mississippi. "Ellasbeth—," I began, and she cut me off.

"I'm trying devilishly hard to convince Trent of my sincerity," she said, her eyes on the girls. "He's as stubborn as my father. I made one mistake that led to several, but when I realized what Landon was doing, I did try to stop him." Her lips pressed. "Only to end up tied to a chair. I'm not much good to him. Prissy lab tech ignorant of even the most basic spell."

Shocked, I turned to her. "That's not true."

She looked at me, clearly not believing me. Silent, she shifted to make room for Trent and Al, each one holding a little girl. Behind them, Quen went to the lobby desk with the manager. Pulling herself straighter, Ellasbeth said loudly, "Thank you for shaking some sense into him regarding Landon and his lies."

"Right," I said, wondering if that hand gesture Ray was studiously trying to force her fingers into looked familiar.

"I'm glad you spoke up," Ellasbeth continued as I caught Al coaching the little girl, and he shifted to hide it from Trent. "Landon has been publicly calling for Trenton to be brought up on charges. If he can find something in the law that lets him, he will succeed."

"He won't." Trent jiggled Lucy as the little girl twisted in his grip to keep Jenks in view.

"Trent." Ellasbeth's voice became more formal. "I don't think you *want* to see the ramifications of letting these lies stand. Rachel does." I winced as everyone looked at me and she added, "Landon still has half the enclave looking to him, and the entire dewar."

"Not the entire dewar. Jenks, land somewhere, will you?" Trent asked as he struggled with Lucy, and Jenks alighted on my shoulder.

"Enough to cause problems." Ellasbeth picked up her purse, clearly wanting to leave. "I respect that you have your own way of handling things, but if you don't give the people something to choose between, you can't blame them for following Landon."

"I've got this, Ellasbeth," Trent said tightly.

"Yeah, he's got this, Ellasbutt," Jenks echoed, and I frowned, no longer sure what side of the let's-hate-Ellasbeth fence I was on. *Crap on toast . . . I don't have time for another life lesson.*

But Trent was clearly at his limits. Seeing it as well, Ellasbeth tucked her purse under her arm and held out her hand for Ray's blanket. "Well, I have said my piece and you have heard me," she said as she stuffed it into the diaper bag. "Thank you for the girls this weekend. I'll bring them back Sunday afternoon."

Trent's anger evaporated as he kissed Lucy good-bye,

her chubby arms wrapped around his neck. "Good-bye, my Lucy," he said, focused on her eyes until she looked at him. "Be good for your mother." And then to Ellasbeth, he said, "There's no need. You're taking the Mantis, yes? So you don't have to move their car seats? I'll bring your car back when I pick them up."

"If you like," she said stiffly.

But Lucy was opening and closing her hands, clearly wanting me to take her, and smiling, I did. Jenks flew up and away as I got a little-girl kiss before handing her to El- lasbeth. I could see the hurt Ellasbeth was trying to hide that Trent wouldn't let her on the grounds, and my foolish need to help the underdog rose up.

"Good-bye, my Ray," Trent said as he kissed Ray. "Let Lucy make her mistakes, okay?"

Ray grimaced with a wisdom beyond her apparent years. She reached for me, next, and after a snickerdoodle-scented hug, I handed her to Quen. Quen immediately let her slide to the floor to walk on her own, bare feet and all, but his hand never left hers. Ray was trying to make that finger glyph again, turning it into nothing when Quen glanced down.

I squinted suspiciously at Al, but the thought evaporated when Ellasbeth gave me a hug. Lucy was on her hip, getting mixed up in there somewhere. Startled, I put my arms around them both, feeling how narrow Ellasbeth's shoul- ders were and the alien flavor of her aura brushing against the gaps of my own.

"Thank you for jerking Trent out of his silence," she said as she pulled back, a new understanding in her eyes. "It's been bothering me, and I have no right to say anything." With a sharp nod, she gave Trent a last look and walked away.

Quen picked up the abandoned diaper bag. "Trent, Ra- chel, Jenks," he said, eyeing us in turn. "Al-l-l," he drawled, and the demon made an overdone flourish.

Ellasbeth was already at the door and headed for Trent's big-ass SUV parked at the curb. I could just see it beyond the glass doors. "Ladies, would you like to do some shopping downtown with Abba and me?" she asked the girls, looking like a different person.

Trent slipped up beside me, and we both yearningly watched them leave. I still didn't know what *abba* was, exactly. Number two daddy? Most valued protector? Seed father?

"Can we have ice cream?" Lucy asked, and Trent smiled.

"Twice in one day?" Ellasbeth said as the automatic door opened and the wind gusted in. "I can see why you ask. It would taste good, wouldn't it? How about a banana? We could be monkeys."

"Monkey!" Lucy crowed, yelping when Ray reached up and pinched her dangling foot.

"What else do monkeys eat?" Ellasbeth asked, not having noticed the exchange, and I grinned when Ray piped up, her clear voice stating, "Ice cream."

"Ellasbeth is really good," Jenks said from beside my ear with a wistful sigh.

"Being a mom?" I said, knowing Trent was listening. "Yes, she is."

Trent's smile vanished. He turned away, unfortunately missing Ray looking back to wave good-bye to us. Tongue between her teeth, she made that finger gesture again. My eyebrows rose when Al nodded, beaming proudly at the girl as the door shut.

"Isn't that the symbol for—," I started.

"Yes," Al interrupted stiffly, clearly not happy I'd caught the exchange.

"What?" Jenks asked, and I hid a smile.

"Communication glyph," I whispered, wondering if this was how Al had shown up when Lucy had thrown that tantrum. My smile was still in place when Trent gestured to the door. "She gave me a hug," I said, thinking it was the most weird thing in my very weird day.

Trent's hand went pleasantly to the small of my back. His aura, so similar to my own, soaked in, bringing my shoulders down. *Finally,* I thought, feeling in his touch that everything was going to be okay. "I think she likes you better than me," he grumbled. "This is hard, Rachel. I don't trust her."

Al strode beside us with an air of importance. "If she harms them, I will rip her head off."

"Not before I give her a lobotomy," Jenks added.

Trent glanced at the building behind us. "Landon isn't interested in them anymore. Where are you parked? Do you mind dropping me at the overlook? Ray's shoes are still there. I should get Ellasbeth's car, too," he finished faintly as if not caring if it got towed.

"Ah . . . ," I hedged, warming as Jenks laughed at me. Ellasbeth, Quen, and the girls were pulling out into traffic, and the wind was chill in the late sun.

Trent's hand on me slipped away. Head cocked, he eyed Al. "Don't you have work today?" he asked, clearly trying to get the demon to leave.

Al scuffed to a halt, his eyes on the blue sky. "I do not," he said, his light voice and the direction of his gaze reminding me how pleasant it was to exist outside the hell the elves and demons had made of the original ever-after in their war.

"He's babysitting Rachel," Jenks said, pressed close to my neck for warmth.

Trent, who had been looking up and down the street for my car, brought his wandering attention back. "He's not doing a good job. Your aura is patchy."

"She's alive," Jenks said, not helping.

Trent tugged me sideways into him, and I whispered, "Thanks," when my headache eased.

Al put a hand formally before his middle, the other behind. "It was Rachel's choice to jump to the radio studio with a compromised aura."

Trent's brow furrowed, and my headache returned when our bodies parted and he reached to his back pocket for his phone. "No car? I'll call one."

"Hers is two miles back," Jenks said, and Trent nodded, his head down over his phone.

"Rachel twisted a common but aura-debilitating curse

this morning," Al said stiffly, hearing blame in Trent's words when there really wasn't any. "For the next sun cycle, I'm her sword, mirror, and shield."

I winced as Trent looked up from his phone, the wind shifting the hair from his eyes as I saw our weekend plans ruined. "Seriously?" he asked, and Al put a hand on my shoulder as if claiming me—until I glanced at it and he hid it behind his back instead.

"Unless you agree to watch her. And she doesn't leave your compound." Al made a show of looking at his watch. "A sidhe of fairies and a pixy clan should be able to keep you alive for a few hours," he said as if not caring, but I knew better.

"I don't need babysitting," I complained.

"Agreed," Al said. "But Dali thinks I'm careless with you. I'm not leaving unless there's someone with you who can call me if there's trouble."

"I can do that." Trent closed his phone with a snap and tucked it away.

"Wi-i-i-i-ill you, though?" Al intoned, already knowing the answer.

"If I need to," Trent said, smiling to make Al draw back in consternation.

"Good." Al glanced at his watch again. "I have something I need to check on. If any harm comes to her, I will rip your head off, as well." He hesitated, looking at our fingers, which were so close they almost touched. "Which would make Rachel's life far easier, now that I think about it."

He vanished with a slight pop, and I sighed, glad that he was gone, and that it was Friday, and once I got Jenks with his kids, it would just be Trent and me for two glorious days. "Good thing you like me then, huh? Huh?" I said, elbowing him, and Trent tugged me close, smelling like leather and horse under the cinnamon scent of elf.

"Yes, I like you. Stop poking me. And why is Al so concerned?" he asked as Jenks went to check the dying annuals beside the door while we waited for the car. "Your aura has been worse."

"Dali reamed Al out for leaving me alone without being able to do ley line magic." I turned and wrapped my arm around Trent's neck so I could play with his ears. They were pointy, like the girls', their cropped state having unexpectedly reverted when I twisted a curse to replace the fingers Al had torn off. Cars were going by, but it was unlikely anyone could see us tucked in by the station's door, and a delicious feeling of daring filled me. "Keeping me alive is his job, you know," I said, pulling him deeper into the shadow. "We make a good team. When I was in the ever-after, I made tulpas, and he lifted my mind out of them and kept me alive until I recovered. I kept us both in cheese sandwiches for a couple of weeks."

"Mmmm." Trent's attention came back to me as he smiled. His hand at my waist felt right, and his aura, so close to mine, was soothing my headache.

"He must think your magic is improving if he'll let you babysit me," I added, staring at his lips, knowing how soft they'd be on mine, how cool the air would feel on my mouth when we parted.

"Mmmm," he said again, but it was a different sound, and his grip on my waist had tightened into a hint of possessiveness. I liked it. Eyes shiny with daring, he leaned in. God, we were out on the street, where anyone could see, and though I didn't care if our picture landed on the front page of the *Hollows Gazette* above a tawdry tagline, Quen would have a hissy.

But even as I leaned in, breath held and anticipation simmering, he froze.

"What?" I said, the scent of cinnamon and ozone plucking something deep in me.

"Um, the car is here," he said.

I froze as I suddenly realized that yes, a black car had pulled up, idling patiently as it spewed hot exhaust to warm my ankles. *Of course it is.* My grip on him tightened, and after a shared flash of annoyance, Trent let go, his fingers reluctantly leaving me with a wash of tingles.

Frustrated, I slumped against the wall as Trent opened

the door and, after a brief word with the driver, shifted so I could get in first. "Jenks!" I called as I rolled down the window, and he zipped in with the scent of dead geraniums, immediately going up front to talk to the driver.

Over the past months, Trent's natural reserve in public had gratifyingly thawed, but full-mouth kissing on Central Parkway was probably too big a stretch. No matter. I'd found the more reserved he was in public, the more tactile and aggressive he was when alone, and I smiled, willing to wait. Besides, it was just Trent and me in the back now, and I settled against him, content as he held my hand and drew communication glyphs one by one in my palm as we drove away.

Sure, I'd blown his gentleman's agreement with Landon all to hell, but an uneasy truth was better than a beautiful lie, especially when that lie had Trent looking like a callous, power-hungry dictator in the making. I didn't like that half of Cincinnati thought he was, thanks to Landon.

But then again, he'd been one when I'd first met him.

CHAPTER

9

I SMILED, NOT FULLY AWAKE WHEN TRENT CAREFULLY rolled from where he'd been spooned up behind me. Cold replaced warmth, and then a soft tug of the blanket being snuggled in behind me. It was a familiar pattern, and I dozed at the almost unheard sounds of him getting ready for the day: the click of the bathroom door closing, the tap of his razor, the hum of his toothbrush.

It was the rasp of dog nails that woke me when Buddy nosed the bedroom door open and went to sit before the bathroom, tail swishing. We both heard the snap of the light going off, and I smiled when Trent came out and gave the dog a soft greeting. "What time is it?" I whispered, and the dark shadow headed for the main room hesitated and came back.

"I didn't want to wake you." Trent knelt to put his eyes level with me. His hand found mine, and he brushed the hair from my eyes before giving me a kiss. "It's early. Go back to sleep."

"It's our weekend," I said, and Buddy whined. He smelled of outside, evidence of Jon taking care of him, but it was Trent the raggedy fifteen-pound dog looked to.

"It's six in the morning," Trent countered, and I groaned, not wanting to start my day at such an ungodly time. Trent had delayed his usual midnight nappies to go to bed with me around one in the morning. It was a little early for me, a little late for Trent. He'd been stretching his schedule, and I'd been tweaking mine, until now there were just a few hours where they didn't mesh. But that was okay, seeing as we both needed time alone to feel balanced. Mine was around noon, and his was at six in the morning.

"I'm going to go over the public reaction to you calling Landon a liar," he said, and my eyes closed. "I'll be done by the time you get up." I smiled, eyes closed when he kissed me again. "And then my day is yours."

My hand tightened on his. "I'm sorry about that," I said, and his motion to rise halted.

"No, it was a good thing. I couldn't take it any longer. Go to sleep."

"Leave the door open a crack?" I asked so I could hear him, and he nodded and stood. Buddy followed him out, and I thought that the jingling of a collar was the most comforting sound in the world. I'd never had a dog, and Trent hadn't wanted one, but the mutt had taken to him, and the pound was not an option when his owners had fled, abandoning him. I had a suspicion that the only reason Trent had originally taken him in was to irritate Ellasbeth.

I drowsed amid the rising scent of coffee and the domestic sounds of Trent settling in with his laptop and papers in the sunken central living room that the four bedrooms and small efficiency kitchen surrounded. Two entire days spread before us, and I had no idea what to fill them with now that I wasn't going to help Edden. I'd been banned from Trent's favorite golf course, but it might be fun to try to sneak me on for a leisurely eighteen. Or we could go for a ride on his horses. Riding in the fall was glorious, and if it got too hot, we could take the trails through the woods.

The woods he tried to run me down in.

A flash of old fear and anger struck me, and I tapped a line, snapping awake with a jerk.

Gasping, I sat up, heart pounding. Eyes wide, I took in Trent's silent bedroom, the clean lines and sparse furniture done in soothing shades, the pillows piled on the floor, and the long curtains blocking the light from the attached patio. The door to the walk-in closet was cracked, and a child-hood fear made me shudder as I clenched my hands, feeling them ache from the gathered power that surged through me.

"What the hell?" I whispered, looking to the door when Buddy padded in, collar jingling. I'd tapped a line. While sleeping?

I'd done the same thing yesterday in the car outside my church, and shaken, I let go of the line. Raw energy spilled out to leave me feeling like a spent tube of toothpaste. "What the devil was that, Buddy?" I whispered as I draped a hand over the edge of the bed, and he sat, panting, with my hand on his head.

The sound of Trent slurping his coffee struck through me, as familiar now as his voice. But even that failed to dispel the feeling of disjointed unease. I was awake, and feeling like a ten-year-old afraid of thunder, I got up.

I was still stuffing my arms into my robe when I pushed open the door to the common room. Trent was on the couch exactly where I thought he'd be with his feet on the coffee table and his laptop open. "You're awake," he said as he looked up.

Nodding, I shuffled into the sunken living room. Good God, even the expansive lower level past the stairs was dark, no sun coming in the floor-to-ceiling window that took up most of one wall. I was dead tired, but going back to that cold bed where I might fall asleep was not an option.

"Bad dream," I said as I dropped down to sit with him on the couch.

He shifted his papers to hide them. It was a casual move, but it rang through me like a shot. "Same one?" he asked, his voice rumbling through me as I slouched into him.

"Different." I breathed him in, feeling loved when he pulled the afghan up and over me.

"Then it's probably okay," he said. "You've got a lot on your mind."

Snuggled in, I slowly lifted the top paper to see Quen's latest bad-news PR report. Trent's chest moved as he sighed. "It used to be so easy," he whispered as we looked at the dismal stats. "I would make a call, say a word, and everything would be settled. Now it's a fight. Every time."

"It's getting better," I said, but according to that graph Quen had so helpfully put together, it wasn't. The papers rustled as I gathered them up and set them on the table, but they were still there. Eyes closing, I leaned deeper into Trent, listening to his heartbeat as he ran a hand across my hair, soothing me. "Have you ever tapped a line when you were sleeping?"

Trent's motion stopped. "No," he said, and I sat up at the concern in his voice. "Did you? Because of your bad dream, maybe?"

I nodded. "I didn't use it or anything," I said, and he drew me back into his warmth. He was worried, which made me nervous. What if Trent had been beside me at the time? I might have given him an accidental shock. Or worse.

"I'm sure it's okay," he said, but I wasn't. "Mind if I turn on the news?"

"Go ahead." Suddenly I was reminded of the morning at my mom's on the West Coast, watching the undead souls pulled from the ever-after to reality as the sunset traveled from east to west. That same sort of impending something soured my gut even as I slumped deeper against him. His arm tightened around me as he stretched for the remote, and I squinted when the TV brightened to the news and he lowered the volume to a background nothingness. It was all traffic and bake sales, and slowly my worry eased.

"Nina is cooking Thanksgiving this year," I said when they went to a commercial and a loud family strolled into Grandma's house and complained about the Internet. "You want to come over with Jenks and me? The girls are invited, too."

Trent shifted uncomfortably. "Ellasbeth wants Thanksgiving at the top of the Carew Tower," he said, clearly not excited about it.

I sat up, remembering Landon's claim about barren women and Ellasbeth wanting to be a larger part of the girls' lives. "I think Ellasbeth at Thanksgiving is a great idea," I said, and he made a surprised guttural sound. "Bring her along. One more won't matter."

"Ellasbeth," he said flatly, and I leaned into him again, not wanting him to see my guilt.

"She's trying," I said, not knowing why except that she loved the girls, and all children should have the chance to be with the ones who loved them.

His hand curved round to brush my hair, and I relaxed. "I never thought you'd be the one to try to convince me," he said sourly. "Why doesn't she hate you anymore?"

"Because I understand her," I said. "I know you're angry with her for not accepting that she comes after the needs of keeping your people off the endangered species list."

"I'm not angry with her," he lied.

"Then is it because she hurt you by breaking off the wedding when I hauled your ass to jail?" I questioned, and he winced.

"No . . . ," he drawled, but it wasn't convincing. "I didn't want to marry her."

"You *did* say you loved her," I said, eyes on his arm around me. Oh, God. Why was I doing this? Was I so freaked out about commitment that I was self-sabotaging our relationship, or was I making sure there was nothing there to rekindle? After all, he *had* a baby with this woman. Marrying her would solve all his issues and give him his voice back in the enclave. He'd be the elven Sa'han again. Not to mention the girls would have a more stable situation.

"I did say that." Trent's voice was even. "But I've since realized that everything I loved about her was tied to things she could give me, not how she made me feel. That's not really love."

He tugged me closer, and I felt a wash of relief. "Okay. But if you aren't angry with her, why are you using the girls to hurt her?"

"Quen asked me the same thing," he whispered, his fingers tightening in mine until I could feel the energy in our chis try to equalize in darting tendrils of sensation. His brow was wrinkled in worry—worry that he was letting emotion and pride stop him from finding something positive.

"All she wants is to be a part of the girls' lives. Not yours," I said, but I wasn't sure about that last part. "I think you should invite her to have dinner with us at Piscary's." I sat up at his soft complaint. "How many would that be?" I said, thinking this might give us a way to find peace with our troubled joined past. "Me, Ivy, Jenks, Nina, Quen, Jon, the girls, you, Ellasbeth. Ten people. That's a turkey, right? We could even have a kid table. Make Jon sit there."

I beamed at his wince, but I had *days* to wear him down. "We used to have big get-togethers. Extended family," I said as I eased back into his warmth. "All of us in a really small house. Not so much after my dad died. I always felt like a bastard child. As if I didn't really belong."

"Because you were in the hospital all the time?" he guessed, and I shivered, liking how his hand moved across my skin—hinting at more.

I tilted my head to find his eyes. "No, because my mom slept with someone other than my dad to have a kid. Twice."

His fingers tracing circles stopped. "I forget that about you."

I tugged the blanket back up to cover us, content. "I'll talk to Ivy, but she already said yes to you and the girls. What's a few more?"

Trent made a noncommittal *mmmm* sound, but I was sure it would happen now, come hell or high water.

My sneeze came from nowhere, and I jerked hard enough to make Buddy lift his head.

"You're kidding, right?" Trent said as I sneezed again, then a third time, a huge spasm of demand. "It's six fifteen," he said as I got up and went to get my bag, left out on Ceri's old rocker. "I thought demons slept till noon."

"We do." I came back with it, bare feet silent. *Give me a freakin' second,* I thought as I sneezed again, arms flashing to hold my middle as it ripped through me, hurting my throat.

Head down, I dug out my mirror and plunked down beside him with the red-tinted glass. Buddy leaned against my leg, eyes mournful as he looked up at me. "Six frickin' fifteen in the morning," I muttered as I placed my hand on the cool glass and tapped the line. A shudder rippled over me at the coming connection, and I steadied myself. There was only a fading discomfort from my patchy aura. Sleeping beside Trent had truly done my aura wonders. "Sorry about this," I said, then lost my connection when I sneezed.

"Things happen. Besides, I'm your sword, mirror, and shield today." He hesitated. "Maybe I should call Al," he added, and I smoothed my hair flat. He'd tapped a line, and the residual energy was slipping from him to me where we touched. It was kind of distracting, and I shifted a few inches down the couch.

"It's probably him," I said as I put my fingers atop all the glyphs again and dropped myself into the collective. "Rachel here," I said aloud so I wouldn't look even more crazy, my words mirrored in the demons' between-reality "chat room."

My breath quickened as my awareness expanded. A masculine flavor spilled into me, domineering and supercilious. *Are you okay?* The thought rose in me as if it was my own, but that's how the collective worked. *I would have waited until noon, but you tapped a line.*

Dali? I stifled a flash of fear before he felt it. I *had* tapped a line. It hadn't just been in my dream. Damn it, I could have killed Trent. What the hell was going on?

Rachel, are you well? Dali's thought came again, and I hid my worry before he saw it. *This is a courtesy call to ascertain your well-being.*

"At six in the morning?" I said aloud so Trent could be in on half the conversation. "You need to get off Al's case," I said as I felt a surprising amount of relief well up. It was from Dali, not me, and I frowned. "Al does a good job keeping me alive. You checking up on him is as irritating as all hell."

It's because of Al that I'm calling, but if you're well, I'll untwist the restraining curse and assess our options.

Whoa. Wait up, I thought, pressing my hand harder into the cool glass. *Restraining curse? Dali, what is going on? It was just a simple aura depletion. I'm fine! Is Al okay?*

Dali was silent, his thoughts shielded from me with a thousand years of practice.

Dali, if you don't tell me what's going on, I'll never make you another tulpa as long as you live, I threatened, and a wisp of Dali's concern slammed into me, stealing my breath away.

He tapped a line while sleeping. I never would have known but he opened the weapons vault, Dali thought, and I looked at Trent. Seeing my fear, he scooted to the edge of the couch.

"Al tapped a line in his sleep?" I said aloud to bring Trent back into the conversation. "Was it a nightmare?" The memory of how I woke sang through me, sour and full of discord.

He didn't say, Dali thought. *If you agree, I'll remove the curse that has him immobile.*

"Yes, remove it," I said, almost panicked. "Why ask me?"

Dali hesitated, then reluctantly thought, *Because you, Rachel, were his target.*

CHAPTER

10

PHONE TO MY EAR, I STARED OUT THE FRONT WINDOW OF Trent's car as we crossed the bridge into the Hollows. Jenks wanted to pick up a few things from the boat, making it our first stop before starting part two of our weekend. Mood bad, I listened to Al's phone ring as the sun flashed between the girders. I imagined him taking it out of his pocket, sniffing, and dropping it back in unanswered—and it was starting to tick me off.

"Damn sensitive demon," I muttered as I gave up, and Jenks, who was sitting on his favorite spot on the rearview mirror, exchanged a worried look with Trent.

"I'm sure he's fine, Rache," the pixy said, and I shoved my phone away.

"Well, I'd be a lot finer if he'd answer his phone," I complained.

"Did you try him on his mirror?" Trent asked, his musical voice soothing.

I stared out the window, my fist against my mouth. "Yes. He's got a do-not-disturb up." I exhaled, frustrated. "I don't even know where he lives. Did you know that? He won't tell me." I hated that my voice carried my hurt, but there it was.

"I'm sorry."

Trent's hand touched my knee. A tantalizing dart of

energy went through me, and I tried to smile. We had the entire two days before us, and I wasn't going to let Al ruin it.

"So what do you want to do this afternoon?" I asked as we angled toward the Hollows waterfront. The streets were almost deserted this early, making it nice. Jenks cleared his throat, and I added, "After we pick up the last of Jenks's stores and drop him off at the church, I mean." I lifted my gaze to Jenks, wondering why he was wearing the fancy embroidered suit that Belle had made him. The scrumptious outfit was too posh for the weekend. Maybe it was to impress the fairy clan he'd be sharing the winter with. "What do you need at the church anyway?"

"Milkweed." Jenks picked nervously at the suit as I noticed it. "I went through Jumoke and Izzy's stores last night, and they don't have any milkweed stalk. There's some out at the Macis plot, and this will probably be my last chance to gather some. I'd get one from Trent's gardens, but he doesn't have any milkweed. God help you, man," he said to Trent. "Do you know how useful milkweed is?"

"Apparently not," Trent murmured, and my unease with Al began to unknot.

"Its sap is poisonous, so you can use it to kill just about anything smaller than yourself," Jenks said, his dust sparkling when we turned and the low sun hit it. "It's sticky, so bam! Glue."

"The seed fluff can be mattress stuffing," I said, and Jenks's wings blurred to invisibility.

"Yep," he agreed. "But I want the fibrous stalk. Trent doesn't have anything in his conservatory to make clothes out of, and those newlings of Jumoke and Izzy are going to need something disposable before they get back in the garden."

That made me feel good, and I smiled as Trent drove into Piscary's old lot. The onetime tavern, now a private residence, looked peaceful in the cool fall morning. Quiet. Kisten's boat at the quay looked even more alone, and I stifled a pang at the thought of being there by myself.

"Darn kids aren't thinking ahead far enough," Jenks

said, more to himself than to us. "A stalk of milkweed will save them a month of misery."

My smile deepened as Trent parked right at the boat, and as one, we all got out.

"Trent, be a pal, will you?" Jenks said as he flew a back-and-forth arc between Trent and the boat, impatient with our slow pace in the chill air. "I can't carry it all at once like you can."

I didn't have a clue why Trent was allowed to help Jenks and I wasn't, but I had a feeling that it was because pixy women generally didn't do the heavy lifting. "Water is low. Watch your step," I warned as I grabbed a pylon and made the awkward jump to the boat. The sixty-foot craft hardly moved under my weight, but I still took a moment to get my balance. Trent was quickly behind, and Jenks hummed impatiently as I dug my keys from my pocket and unlocked the sliding-glass door. It was a substantial lock for a boat, but Kisten had been all about safety.

Not that it saved him in the end.

Jenks flew in ahead, and I followed, Trent slow in the rear. He'd never actually been in Kisten's boat before, and I watched his eyes take in the lightweight but expensive finishes in approval. "I can see why you want to stay here. This is nice," he said, but all I heard was *Why don't you move in with me?*

"It is, isn't it?" I paused in the low-ceilinged, multi-windowed living room so he could take in the plush furniture and expansive but outdated TV and sound system. It was nice, but it was cold, especially in the morning, and I was glad Jenks was leaving.

"The kitchen is up here," I said, my boots loud on the teak floorboards. My eyes slid from the framed chart that Kisten had on the wall, the heavy black line tracing down the Ohio River to the Mississippi, and finally out into the Gulf, where it continued all the way to the Caribbean. My gut hurt, and I turned away. Dreams Kisten knew were never possible kept him alive . . . until they didn't.

It was funny. I hadn't thought about Kisten in weeks, but

bringing Trent here made me feel as if I was betraying his memory. Kisten, though, would have told me to get over it and live my life.

Jenks was fussing over his pill-bottle-size jar of pollen as I went into the small kitchen. It had a tiny oven that didn't work well enough to use and a two-burner stove. The fridge was residential size, but the counter space was confining after living in the church's expansive savanna. *Jeez, it's going to be quiet with Jenks gone.*

"This it?" Trent said as he picked the jar up, and Jenks's wings dusted an affirmative silver.

"Yep. Rache, you mind if I take some coffee since I'm here?"

"I've got coffee," Trent offered, but Jenks ignored him. Toting his groceries was one thing, adding to them was another.

"Help yourself," I said, but Jenks was already folding a forgotten receipt into a container. The curling tape had just the right give and strength to make a pixy-size origami box.

"Great, thanks." The scent of coffee rose in the small kitchen as Jenks took a teaspoon. It would last him a month. "Hey, watch it, shoemaker!" the pixy shrilled when Trent shook the jar of pollen in interest. "That's two months in the garden there. It's going to clump if you shake it."

Trent stopped, the tips of his pointy ears reddening to make him look boyishly charming. "Sorry. Um, will it be okay in the car?"

"Sure. Put it in the cup holder so it doesn't roll around," Jenks said, and Trent held it as if it was a tube of C-4.

"You want anything else?" I asked, and Jenks rose up, hands on his hips.

"Three more months of summer," he muttered.

"So we drop you at the church," I said. "Then pick you up in a few hours. What's it going to be, Trent?" I said as I twined my fingers in his and we headed up to the door. "Coffee at Carew Tower? A paddle down the Ohio River? Golf? There're a couple of movies I've been wanting to see, or we could go for a drive out to Loveland Castle. The leaves are gone and you can see the creek."

"Mmmm." Trent's fingers slipped from mine as we went back outside; I needed both hands to get my keys from my bag and lock up. "You know what I'd really like to do?"

I brought my eyes back from Jenks's fading dust trail headed straight across the lot past Trent's car and into Piscary's. "What?"

He pulled me close, and my breath caught. "I want to take a private tour of the elven heritage exhibit." He hesitated. "If you want to."

My eyebrows rose. "Really?" I knew it had bothered him that they had postponed the opening after Ivy, Jenks, and I had stolen one of the artifacts. I'd feel bad about it, except I had needed the elven slaver rings to keep magic from dying out. Destroying them afterward had been a real pleasure. The tools the elves and demons had used in their war were ugly: no pity, no remorse, no mercy. I didn't like that we still had to deal with them like unexploded mines in a farm field.

"They'll let you do that?" I asked as we went to the railing. True, Trent was sponsoring the exhibit, but that might not mean much anymore.

He smiled, the sun catching his hair to turn it white as he made the long step to the quay. "With enough warning, sure." He extended his hand, and he helped me up with a comfortable companionship. "If you want to."

"Absolutely," I said as I rose into the sun. "I won't be able to see any of it on opening night." I let my shoulder fall into his as we headed for the car, loving that he was here with me and we had the entire two days to ourselves. "You want me to work it, right?"

"If you're available. I never get to see the exhibits on opening night, either." His focus went into the distance, seeing the past. Or maybe the future. "I could really use the positive PR boost this will give me when it's finally open. I've been getting too much hate mail lately."

I slumped, remembering Quen's report, but he just shook his head and turned away when I searched his expression. Hate mail was the least of his worries. It was more like ongoing corporate-takeover attempts by elf-owned businesses, dragging, frivolous criminal-act lawsuits, and never-ending sabotage from small-minded employees bringing his legitimate farms and other endeavors to a slow grind.

There was good reason I accompanied him to public events, and it wasn't because I looked good in heels. The exhibit itself was more than a collection of elven artifacts. It was even more than a joyous public announcement that elves existed and had a rich cultural past. It was Trent reminding his people that it was his family who had risked persecution and death to develop the illegal genetic procedures that kept them alive until Trent himself risked his life and freedom to find an ancient elven DNA sample to break the demons' curse entirely. It had put him on the demons' auction block to be bought and sold by the *very same* demons who had once been owned by elves themselves. And I, being "Rachel-ly" as Jenks would say, couldn't stomach it, even though Trent and I had barely tolerated each other at that point.

He hadn't thanked me for saving him for a long time, grappling with the knowledge that I was a demon, one who survived infancy because his father, Kalamack Sr., had broken the demons' curse. We still didn't know if it was an accident or perhaps long-term planning on Trent's dad's part. Trent would have never survived the ever-after without a "demon's" help.

And if I thought the public outcry had been bad for admitting I was a demon, it was even worse when Trent openly acknowledged that he not only supported me, a demon, but that he loved me. And if he loved me, he could no longer blindly hate demons.

It was when he had asked the elven population to do the same that things got toxic. That was when they turned on him, and now he was down to lavish shows of charity he could no longer afford and new museum elven wings across the U.S. that he had no money to pay for—the intent being to remind them they survived and thrived *because of him*.

His downfall was 100 percent my fault. Without me, he'd again be the elven Sa'han, regaining all his old status and more as the savior of his species. I, too, would be accepted by my demon kin if I simply walked away. But to do so would break both of us. We were better together: Trent less ruthless and me less, well . . . Rachel-ly.

Seeing Trent's head down in thought, the wind gently moving his wispy almost white hair, I slipped my fingers in his and tugged his attention to me. My heart seemed to nearly burst when he smiled and visibly shelved his worry for later. We did better together than apart, and I couldn't bear to lose him.

"The museum sounds great," I said, but I meant far more.

"Good," he said, mood brighter. "Let's grab something to eat while I set it up."

Happy with the world, I leaned deeper into him, our steps striking the old pavement in perfect time. Eleven was early for me for breakfast, much less lunch, but I'd gotten up at six. *God! No wonder elves have nearly gone extinct.* "Where can we get a good hamburger with ketchup?"

"Ketchup?" Trent grinned, clearly enjoying the chance to flaunt his Inderland status. "Ah, the Cincinnatian is close."

Everything was close in Cincinnati, but it would be nice to go downtown when the traffic was this light. "Sure," I said, arm about his waist as we walked to the car. "They've got big, dripping hamburgers. And fries. Lots of fries."

Trent hesitated at the car, his eyes on Piscary's. Jenks had gone in and hadn't come out yet. "I can't tell you how glad I am you like to eat."

I grinned, but my motion to lean against his car hesitated when the back door to Piscary's loading dock banged open and Ivy came out, a sparkle of pixy dust on her shoulder.

"She's up late," I said, and Trent turned. "And . . . angry?" I added, though angry was an understatement. She looked positively pissed, her eyes squinting at me and her arms swinging.

"What did you say to Edden?" she shouted before she had gotten even halfway across the vacant parking lot, and my smile faded as I remembered walking out on him and why. "He left me a voice message yesterday, and I didn't get it until this morning. I've never heard anyone sound that despondent and still be alive."

"Yeah?" I said as she halted before me, squinting in the bright cold. "I told him to shove his lame-ass run."

"He asked you for help and you dissed him?" Ivy said.

My arms had gone around my middle, and annoyed with myself, I forced them down. "The only reason Edden brought me in was because the FIB's working theory is that a demon is behind the murders, just for the hell of it. He asked me to snoop around in my 'unique circles' and ask which demon did it. Damn straight I walked out." Chin high, I waited for someone to tell me I was being too sensitive so I could get in their face and tell them otherwise.

But Ivy dropped back, glancing at Trent as her anger vanished. "Oh." She hesitated. "Asking around isn't so bad," she offered.

"Yeah, Rache," Jenks said. "Asking around is how runners get things done."

Neither one of them was fully backing me, but Trent was at my side, and the memory of Al's stoic anger told me I'd been right. "He didn't ask me to ask around," I said, proud I wasn't shouting. *See, I can learn.* "He asked me to find out which demon was responsible. His entire department is *assuming* it's a demon, to the point where they aren't even looking anywhere else. We've been here for two months," I said, including myself with my found kin. "And the first time the FIB runs into something they don't recognize, they blame the demons." I took a breath to slow my anger. What was it Trent did to defuse a situation? Oh, yeah. Agree with them using a qualifier.

"Maybe I overreacted," I said, but it sounded sullen, even to me.

"No, you didn't." Ivy shot a look at Jenks when he opened his mouth to protest, adding, "Assuming a demographic is responsible for a crime because it's easier than admitting you're capable of it as well leads to worse corruption. Damn it, Rachel." Ivy slumped. "I had no idea that's why Edden agreed to let you interview Jack. I'm sure he didn't realize . . ."

Her words trailed off, her extended hand falling helplessly, and my own anger eased.

"Yeah. Sure," I said, but it felt as if I could've handled it differently now that I'd had time to cool off. "Look," I said, squinting at Jenks, who clearly didn't like Edden and me being on the outs no matter what the reason. "I'll call him Monday, but I'll be damned before I work in a department that thinks I'm there to drum up evidence on demons. I'd still like to talk to Jack's wife." I hesitated, glancing at Trent. "Whoever this is, I think they went after Al last night."

Please don't be Hodin, I thought, my gaze rising to search for a bedraggled crow. But what would Hodin get from setting couples against one another? Notoriety he didn't want?

"No way!" Jenks rose up from Trent's shoulder, and Ivy's eyebrows lifted in interest. "Someone is trying to kill Al?"

And maybe me? I wondered. Al said he'd been having nightmares. He'd also said that Hodin had been known to work through dreams.

My hand dropped to my bag to feel my scrying mirror. Perhaps Hodin and I should chat now that my aura was back. "I'm working on it, just not with the FIB," I said as I forced my hands from my bag. "Demons committing crimes are no longer considered tools anymore, are they?"

Trent shook his head. It had been one of the first laws to go, mostly because of the damage Ku'Sox and I had wrought from one edge of the continent to the other. I still wasn't allowed into San Francisco, which sucked because that's where the witches' yearly con was.

Ivy hunched in the cold, her dark hair glistening in the bright sun and her thoughts visibly shifting behind her eyes. "We had another assault this morning. I don't suppose you might want to come down this afternoon and interview her at the I.S., would you?"

My breath caught, and then I collapsed in on myself. "Ah, Trent and I were about to go to lunch and then the museum," I hedged.

But Trent was smiling as he tugged me closer, making me shiver when he whispered, "This is more important."

"Everyone dead is downstairs," Ivy insisted, ignoring Jenks pretending to barf sparkles. "If I'm going to sneak you in—and I'm going to have to sneak you in—now is the time. It would be easier with only Rachel and Jenks, but I can get you in there, too, Trent."

Trent shook his head, his smile holding more than a hint of pride. I knew he was disappointed that I was trashing our plans, the first weekend without the girls in two months, but he also knew that the three of us—Ivy, Jenks, and myself—might get this wrapped up in a week instead of it languishing for months with more deaths every day. "No, thank you," he said, giving me another squeeze I could feel through my jacket. "I'll wait somewhere and catch a few z's. Or bail you out. Whatever comes first."

"You sure?" I said in gratitude. Not for bailing us out, but that he was taking it so well.

He let go of me and dropped back. "I'll use the time to arrange a private viewing. Maybe smooth out some of Landon's lies." He tilted his head to Jenks. "Harvest a stalk of milkweed?"

"Two," Jenks countered, "as thick as your thumb," and my jaw dropped. He was going to let Trent harvest something for him? From the church? How come he never let me help him?

Ivy turned to Piscary's. "I'll drive. Let me tell Nina where I'm going and grab my coat," she said, and when I nodded, she spun, pacing fast to Piscary's delivery entrance.

"You're the best," I said to Trent, and Jenks groaned, dusting a heavy green as I gave Trent a long kiss and a hug, my love for him making me feel I was finally doing something right with my life. "Thanks for not wigging out."

"Yeah, thanks for picking up my grandkids' poop bags," Jenks said, ruining it as he hovered two inches from our faces, hands on his hips in his best Peter Pan pose.

Sighing, Trent let go and dropped back to his car. "I'll see you in a few hours. Call me when you're done. Or if you need me."

"Will do," I said, and with Jenks on my shoulder, I followed Ivy back into Piscary's.

CHAPTER

11

"RELAX, RACHE," JENKS SAID FROM MY SHOULDER AS WE walked through the back hallways of the I.S. tower. "Trent isn't mad for you ditching him. Did you see his aura brighten up? He's got stuff to do."

"Like what?" I grimaced, not liking that Ivy felt the need to sneak us in through the garage.

"Like defusing that bomb you exploded yesterday on air in Cincinnati?" Jenks said, and I winced at Ivy's chuckle. "He's not napping," he added confidently. "He's testing the waters in the enclave." Jenks's wings tickled my neck. "Now that the truth is out."

"Yeah, I suppose," I said, arms swinging as I paced beside Ivy and tried to look as if I still belonged here. But my guilt didn't ease, it only shifted focus. Jenks was right. Trent had things to do other than go to the museum—things that would further his standing and voice. He was neglecting his career to spend time with me. I was bringing him down.

Jenks's cold wings hummed against me, then went still. "Mmmm. Or he's napping, maybe," he said when Ivy gave him a dark look.

"What does it matter what Trent is doing as long as he stays out of the way?" Ivy grumped as she pointed out a secondary, seldom-used bank of elevators. "This will take twenty minutes."

Perhaps, but I'd seen worlds collapse in less time.

The halls weren't empty, but being Saturday, it was mostly witches and Weres, and a few living vampires cloistered in their offices. The tower always had a few dead vamps awake in the basement, and I wasn't entirely happy that that was where we were probably headed.

But it wasn't the down button that Ivy hit, and my eyebrows rose as we waited for the elevator, Ivy fidgeting in tells so small that only someone who'd lived with her would have noticed.

"You're not going to get in trouble for this, are you?" I said, and Ivy started, the brown rim around her pupil shrinking.

"No," she said flatly, but I wasn't convinced, and I faced her accusingly, hand on my hip.

"Then what is bothering you?" I demanded.

Ivy took a breath, her shoulders stiff. But they slumped when Jenks rasped his wings, reminding her he could see her aura flare when she lied.

"It might be nothing," she said as she hit the call button again in a tapping staccato that was almost a hum. "Nina and I got a courtesy call from one of the upper vampire camarillas in DC. Cormel isn't effective anymore, and they're talking of recalling him to DC permanently and dropping a new master vampire into Cincinnati to replace him."

My lips parted, and I quashed a flash of fear. "Someone out of state?" Jenks asked for both of us. "And they want your advice, right?" he added.

Ivy's brow furrowed in an unusual show of worry. "I won't know until *she* gets here."

"She as in the new master vampire?" I said, trying to keep my voice from squeaking. Crap on toast, this wasn't good. It wasn't just the new master vampire but her entourage that was going to descend into Cincy and the Hollows, bringing with them the need for a slew of new blood ties to be made. Ivy might be exempt but for the courtesy bite now that she was Nina's scion, but there would be hundreds of minor disputes as things resettled into the new power balance an unfamiliar vampire brought.

"I don't know why," I said, fully understanding Ivy's twitchy mood. "Sure, Cormel has been less than useful since fixating on his lost-again soul, but there haven't been any major issues in the last two months. You and Nina—"

"It's not me and Nina keeping the peace that's bothering them," Ivy interrupted, her eyes on the numbers counting up from the basement. "Exactly . . . ," she added reluctantly as the elevator dinged and the doors opened. "Which is probably why they're sending someone."

I followed her in, lips pressing when she hit the button for two floors up. Jeez, we could have walked it. "I thought we were going to interrogation."

"I can't get you into interrogation," she admitted as the doors closed.

"Then where we goin', tall, svelte, and sexy?" Jenks asked from my shoulder.

Ivy glanced at the folder in her hand. "The accused is likely finishing her post-interrogation interview. She'll stop at medical on her way to lockup to give a blood sample and patch up any scrapes. Get a physical baseline in case she claims brutality behind bars."

"You want me to interview her in medical?" I asked, no longer comfortable with this. No way did I want to get Ivy in trouble to satisfy my curiosity.

The elevator dinged, and the doors opened onto an empty hallway. "How is your nurse speak?" Ivy asked, looking both ways before nodding for me and Jenks to come out.

"Lovely." Hands in my pockets, I followed her. But it was actually pretty good. Fourteen years in and out of the hospital had left a mark. I could even draw blood.

"How are you doing working belowground again?" I asked as the pheromones of the multiple old undead wafting up from the lower levels of the I.S. tower made my neck tingle.

"It's okay," she said, and when her pace slowed, I caught up. "Nina has the office beside mine. It helps."

"You got a real office," Jenks said. "Nice. What was it you had, Rache? A cubicle?"

"I'm touched you remember," I said. "Get off my shoulder, and I'll touch you back."

He laughed, but the easy camaraderie reminded me of Thanksgiving. Family wasn't just those you grew up with, but those you grew better with. "Hey, Ivy, you mind if I invite Ellasbeth over for Thanksgiving?" I said, and Jenks snickered, knowing where this was going.

"Sure," she said immediately as we rounded the last turn. "What's one more plate?" she added as she pushed open a hall door that led to medical.

I licked my lips. "And maybe Quen and Jon?" I said, and Ivy sighed. "I'll help with the cooking," I offered, trying not to plead. "I make a mean sweet potato side dish."

Ivy grimaced. "I'll ask Nina."

"Ellasbeth is wanting Thanksgiving at Carew Tower," I said, knowing I was pushing it. "Which is okay," I added when Jenks made a rude sound. "But I don't want the girls to miss out on too small a space filled with too much family."

Ivy sighed, fully understanding. "I'll ask," she said again, sounding resigned this time.

"Thanks, Ivy," I said, slowing as we reached the glass-fronted medical lab with its orange plastic chairs in the hall for overflow. There was only one person in the rolling office chair inside, slumped before an archaic computer monitor. Behind him were several bays with narrow gurneys and pull-around curtains. Deeper still were closed rooms for situations that demanded more privacy. The tech's head was down over his phone, and I swear I could hear happy phone-game music through the thick glass walls.

"It's hopping here, huh?" Jenks said, and Ivy motioned for us to wait in the water fountain alcove, tucked out of sight.

"You'd be surprised how touchy the older vamps have gotten about unexplained serial murders," she said. "They've been shunting the domestic disturbances upstairs."

"Good for us," I whispered as I sized up the tech. The Were looked more than capable of handling anything we could give him, his tattoos and scruffy muscle at odds with his reading glasses and lab coat. But if he was manning the desk alone, he'd have to be able to work the computer and handle a testy witch or Were who didn't want to give a blood sample to prove he or she had been bitten *before* being put into I.S. custody, not after. One was covered under insurance, the other wasn't.

"Give me a second," Ivy said as she undid the top two buttons of her blouse.

"What are you doing?" Jenks said flatly, an odd copper-colored dust spilling from him.

"Improvising," she said, a faint blush rising to make her seem younger. "Wait here."

But that was not what it looked like she was doing when she pulled her long hair from its scrunchy and shifted her bra to show her cleavage. Squaring her shoulders, she sauntered into medical, her voice sultry as she purred, "Hello."

"Improvising," I echoed as Jenks hovered at my shoulder, clearly shocked as Ivy said it was too busy downstairs and asked the tech if he would look at her wrist if he had a moment. Going in without a plan was really loosey-goosey for Ivy. Nina was clearly having a positive effect.

"Damn, she's good," Jenks said in admiration as the guy immediately escorted her to the back area, getting her up on a gurney so he could press close and fondle her wrist with impunity. "Oh, please. Do we have to watch?" Jenks added as Ivy took his glasses off and laughed, throwing her head back to show off her long, smooth neck. "Blau-u-u-uhhh," he added when Ivy slid from the gurney to pull the Were by his lapels to a back room.

"It's better than hitting him on the head," I said as I crept out of hiding. But I couldn't say for sure if I believed it.

"Let me loop the cameras," Jenks said as I opened the door, and I paused, still in the hall.

"She's not going to get in trouble for this, is she?"

"Not if I trip the cameras." Jenks hummed into the office, rising high to stay out of their range as he tripped one, then the other. Turning, he gave me a thumbs-up, and I walked in as if I owned the place.

I went to the abandoned chair, wincing when I found it still warm. The computer facing me was so old, it had green print. I jiggled the mouse, slumping when a password prompt popped up. It smelled better in here, but medical would have its own exhaust system to prevent a frightened, hurt vampire from setting off the building. A faint scent of vinegar lingered, and my eyebrows rose at the prominently displayed placard informing detainees of their right upon request to immediate blood, bane, or an underground facility.

"Nice," I said, and Jenks came back from his sweep, immediately beginning to poke around the desktop clutter. I smiled as he tried a test-tube cap on as a hat, then threw it aside. "Hey, Jenks," I said, realizing this was the first time we'd been alone in days. "I just wanted to say thanks for spending the winter with your kids." He jerked, his dust flaring before he turned, a plastic-coated paper clip in hand. "I'm proud of you," I said, glad that I wouldn't be worrying about him. "I know moving in with Jumoke, even for a few months, is going to be hard."

"I owe Trent a favor," he said as he wedged the end of the clip into the crack of a drawer and bent a fold straight. "This might help."

"Trent? You're doing this for him?" I blurted, and Jenks shrugged.

"The man needs a major PR boost," he said as he unbent a second curve and then the last. "A couple of human-interest stories with me on his shoulder, and the enclave will lighten up," he added, sighting down the length of metal before heedlessly throwing it away, dissatisfied. "Suckers. All them elves are suckers for pixy dust."

I leaned back in the chair and swiveled from side to side. "You noticed that, too, huh?" I said, then we both looked up at a soft thump from the back. "You okay?" I said as I rose, but it was only Ivy, opening the door to hold out a lab coat.

"That will help. Thanks," I said as I shrugged into it,

rather enjoying the scent of Were that clung to it. "You got him okay?"

Ivy smiled and buttoned her blouse. "I'm fine. He slipped and hit his head when he thought I was going to bite him. I'll sit with him and make sure you aren't interrupted."

"Thanks," I said, and after giving Jenks a look to keep his mouth shut, she slipped back inside and closed the door but for a crack.

"What do you think?" I said, modeling the lab coat for Jenks, and he gave me a once-over.

"Try his glasses," he suggested, and I went to get them from where Ivy had left them on a gurney. Mr. Were was nearsighted, and I squinted at myself in a one-way mirror and wondered if my mother had wished I'd taken up the nursing profession instead of the kicking-ass profession— though the best nurses did both.

A knuckle knock at the door brought me spinning around. Jenks hit the floor in a burst of dull green. A tired-looking woman in flannel pajamas and cuffs was standing before the desk, escorted by a uniformed I.S. cop. My pulse hammered and I came forward.

"Where's Wally?" the cop asked, and I adjusted my glasses so I could look over them.

"Family emergency," I said, then cleared my throat to hide the sound of Jenks's wings. "They called me to sub. Paperwork?"

I held out my hand, and the cop's suspicion eased. I had no idea what their protocol was, but paperwork was a good bet. "Gurney, please?" I said as I looked it over. Sandra. Witch. Married. Thirty-three. Worked retail. Accused of assaulting her wife at ten this morning. But the real story was in the woman herself. By the looks of it, she'd been crying, gotten angry, and then probably scared. Too many people at the I.S. liked to play with their food.

"Uh, you're going to lock her down, right?" I said when the cop began fiddling with the equipment on the counter. I wanted him to go, and he wouldn't if she wasn't cuffed to something.

The woman made a bark of sad laugher. "I'm not going to hurt anyone," she said, her voice sounding raw. "I've never been in trouble a day in my life."

Which was true, according to Sandra's report. "That's why I'd feel better if you were restrained," I prompted, and the cop groaned dramatically and reached for the tether. Unrolling it, he locked one end to her cuffs, the other to the gurney's grab rail.

"Better?" he said. It was a lame place to cuff her to. All the woman had to do was hop down and push her way to the drawer, where she could find something to jimmy the lock. It wouldn't matter how many stars, moons, and clovers the officer had on his cuffs.

"Thanks," I said, not caring if the guy thought I was scared. "Okay, can you tell me your name?" I said to the woman, and she sighed.

"Sandra Betric-Tenson," she said, blinking fast at the hyphenated name.

"Thanks, Sandra. A contusion over your left eye. Multiple minor lacerations on your arms. When was your last tetanus shot?"

"Ah, five years ago?"

Sandra seemed to rally, probably appreciating a question that didn't hinge on her wife or why she'd thought starting her morning by trying to decapitate her was a good idea.

"This might take awhile if you want to get a coffee," I said to the cop, not surprised when he sauntered forward and jingled the woman's tether.

"Sure," he said, leering. "Be a good little witch."

"Shove it, clot breath," she muttered, but the cop never looked back as he hit the hall and turned to the left. A sprinkling of pixy dust followed him, and I frowned. Ivy was still here.

"Hard morning?" I said as I pulled the curtain halfway.

Sandra's chin lifted and color rose in her cheeks. "You can shove it, too," she said as I took her wrist and rotated it to catalog the multiple scratches. "I've been pushed, threatened, interrogated, bullied."

I let go of her arm and dropped back, pretending to look at her paperwork. *These glasses suck.* "And very busy," I said, taking the glasses off and setting them on the rolling cabinet. "What *were* you thinking?"

"I—I—," she stammered, and then, gazing at the cuffs, she began to cry, large tears spilling helplessly down her blotchy cheeks. "I don't know," she wailed. "I thought I was dreaming. I'd never hurt Gabby. I don't even know why I was dreaming about it. I mean, jeez, we got married two years ago, why would I still care what flowers we had?" She sniffed, shoulders slumping. "Though at the time, I thought it was the most important thing in the world. Talk about a bridezilla. Is she okay? No one will tell me anything."

"I don't know. I'm sorry." I handed her the tissue box. Worry tightened my gut as I took in her tears and confusion. If Dali hadn't stopped Al, I might be the one in intensive care or worse. *Hodin?* I wondered again. But it didn't make sense. He'd been free since late September. Why start causing trouble now? Especially when he wanted to remain hidden. Most serial killers wanted the notoriety.

"I need a blood sample," I said as I rummaged through the drawers of the mobile cabinet until finding a band and a syringe pack. There were preprinted stickers on her paperwork, and I fastened one on her blood tube, hoping I was doing this right. "Show me how nice you are," I said, and Sandra shifted her arm so I could tie it off. Her vein popped right up, and channeling my inner nurse, I stuck her. Almost freaky fast, the tube began to fill.

"What did you hit your head on?" I asked to try to get her to volunteer something.

"Gabby's fist," she said dully.

"Gabby has a mean right cross," I said, trying to be funny, but no one was laughing.

"You have no idea." Sandra blew her nose on the tissue she'd wadded up, then took another. "I swear I thought I was dreaming. I don't even know why I was mad. It was just some stupid flowers."

"Mmmm." I pulled the syringe from her. Her cuffs prevented her from easily holding the cotton ball, but I was good and she hardly even bled. "Have you ever sleep-spelled before?"

"Not until this morning." Sandra blinked, clearly worried. "Never."

She went silent in thought as I dropped her sample in the bag with her paperwork, racking my brain for something to say to get her to open up. But I totally understood her worry. How could you trust yourself not to hurt the person you loved if you might spell them in your sleep? And with that, pity rose through me, and I believed her.

All the attackers had similar stories, the motives all having been carefully kept from the press. That Al had had a similar experience only made it more plausible. There had to be half a dozen things in our shared past that would trigger him wanting to kill me. Pick one.

"Let me look at your elbow. Hand, please," I said, and she extended her arm. I took her wrist, wondering how much ley line energy she could handle. I'd never know with the band of charmed silver around her wrist, truncating her ability to tap a line. It had her name on it already, and if I couldn't figure out who was doing this, she'd be wearing it for the rest of her life.

Remembering my own long-gone Alcatraz-stamped band of engraved silver, I tested the span of motion of her bruised elbow. "Sandra, have you ever been possessed?"

She stiffened in my grip and pulled away. "No," she said, face pale. "I told you. I was sleeping, and I just . . . I was sleeping," she affirmed as if trying to convince herself. "Is Gabby going to be okay? I didn't even know you could spell in your sleep."

Because you can't, I thought, managing a smile as I said, "I've heard of it before." Which wasn't entirely a lie, considering the circumstances.

Sandra relaxed, and I shone a light in her eyes to make sure they dilated properly. "Do you think you could get a message to her?" the woman asked, and I forced my smile to stay in place.

"I don't know. I'm sorry," I said. "I don't have access to that information."

"I'm never going to see her again, am I?" Sandra warbled, and then she began to cry again. "I tried to kill her, and they're going to put me in jail, and I don't even know why I did it!"

I dropped back, not sure what to do. Crap on toast, this sucked. I was hearing the same story over and over. There was nothing new. This was going nowhere.

"I did it," Sandra said, gasping around huge sobs as she pulled tissue after tissue from the box. "But I don't know why. Please, you have to believe me."

"I do," I said, my hand going to her shoulder, and Sandra blinked gratefully at me.

"Thank you," she whispered, and then we both turned at the dry rasp of pixy wings.

"Wrap it up, Rache," Jenks said as he darted in. "Her leash holder is coming back."

Sandra's breath caught, her watery eyes darting from Jenks to me. "Wait," she said, her tone suddenly flat. "Are you Rachel Morgan?"

"Yes. And I'm going to find out who's doing this," I said. And then she jerked out of my grip.

"Rache!" Jenks shrilled, but I'd seen Sandra's eyes narrow, and I backpedaled, tripping on the rolling cart and sending it crashing into the gurney in the next bay over as I hit the floor.

"This is your fault!" Sandra shrieked, and I gasped when she lunged at me, jerked to a halt at the limit of her leash. "You let the demons in!" she screamed, hair wild as she pried at the cuff on her wrist. "They're here. All the time. And you're protecting them! You little *bitch*!"

I sat, stunned, on the floor of the med lab, silver pixy dust sifting down over me.

"Holy fairy farts," Jenks said as Ivy boiled out of the back room. "She lost it!"

"I'm fine. I just slipped," I said, shaken, as I put my hand in Ivy's and she hoisted me up. The Were's glasses had fallen off the cabinet, and I set them on the counter before I stepped on them. Together, Ivy, Jenks, and I watched Sandra try to get out of her cuffs, her insults gaining strength and volume.

"Is she awake?" I asked, and Jenks nodded, hands on his hips as he hovered between us.

"Yeah," he said, frowning. "That's weird. Her aura is almost exactly like yours, Rache."

"You're kidding," Ivy said, and unfocusing my attention, I opened my second sight. Sure enough, the woman's aura was a bright, cheerful gold. Harsh streaks of red darted through it to give evidence of some past trauma. There was zero black in it, but I'd always thought my thin layer of smut gave my soul a nice patina. That our auras were so similar wasn't unheard of—a good portion of the population had gold auras streaked with red. But I was glad Jenks had mentioned it. Considering the circumstances, close auras seemed less of a coincidence and perhaps more of an indicator.

"You stinking evil demon!" Sandra shouted, distracting me. "You should be locked up. Give me my blood back. Give it!"

I ducked when she threw the box of tissue at me, then spun at the loud voice in the hall booming, "What the hell is going on?"

Sandra cowered and Jenks darted for my hair as that cop came back in.

"It's about time you got here . . . Tony," Ivy said, her hip cocked as she read his ID tag. "Ms. Betric-Tenson needs a quiet spot to calm down."

"Tamwood?" Tony's shoulders rolled as he came in. "A little off your floor, aren't you?"

"*She* hurt Gabby, not me!" Sandra pointed at me, still trying to wedge her hand through the cuff. "That's *Rachel Morgan*. She let those stinking demons in. She's protecting them. She should be in jail, not me!"

Tony looked up from the prepped syringe in Ivy's hand. "Morgan?" he said, his smile telling me he knew who I

was. Jenks making a peace sign from my shoulder probably
didn't help.

"Hey, hi," I said, feeling stupid in that lab coat.

"Let me go. Let me go!" Sandra demanded, but Tony
had taken her arm, and Ivy had pumped it full of something
clear. In three heartbeats, the woman's eyes went unfocused.

"Tink's titties, that's good stuff," Jenks said, and I didn't
know what bothered me more: that it worked that fast, or
that Ivy had known what it was and how to administer it.

"She made me hurt Gabby," Sandra slurred, head drooping, and then she collapsed to the floor, her arm hanging
from the gurney's grab bar.

Tony gave her a dismissive glance, then turned to me. "I
need to see your tower pass."

"Sure." I patted the lab coat's pockets. "Must have left it
in my other lab coat."

Ivy sighed. "How much?" she asked, and Jenks rose up
from where he'd been trying to make out Sandra's slurred,
whispered words.

Tony grinned. "To forget this? You don't have that
much."

Ivy's eyes narrowed, but Jenks hovered between them,
his dust a cheerful gold.

"I'd think it would be just about equal to Ivy forgetting
that you cuffed your charge to a rolling table and went to
get a quick bite from the girl down the hall," he said, grinning.

"Fuck." Tony looked from the clearly defunct cameras
to Jenks. "You saw that?"

"Saw? I got pictures," Jenks claimed, and Tony slumped,
hands on his hips as he looked from Sandra, mumbling
about red daisies, to the empty hallway.

"Can you get her downstairs, or would you like some
help?" Ivy asked sweetly.

"I got her." His mood clearly bad, Tony uncuffed Sandra, then slung her over his shoulder. She was crying again,
but with any luck, she'd forget about Jenks and me. Tony

got about three steps to the door, then jerked to a halt. "You did the blood work, right?" he questioned, and I slapped Sandra's paperwork into his hand.

"Thanks," I said, and he looked me up and down.

"Don't mention it," he said. "If you do, *I'll* mention it."

"No problem."

Tony used his foot to push open the door, and that fast, he was gone.

"That woman has some serious demon issues," Jenks said, hovering in his best Peter Pan pose.

"Maybe this is what happened this morning." Ivy stood the rolling cabinet upright and pushed it to the corner. "Something set her off, and she lost it."

I rubbed my hand, red from hitting the tile. "No. She knew what she was doing. That wasn't what happened with her wife. She was awake this time."

"You sure?" Ivy asked, and both Jenks and I nodded.

"Your aura fades when you sleep. She was wide-awake," Jenks said, then brightened, his thoughts probably returning to where mine had been.

"Yes," I said slowly, still trying to rub the sting from my palm. "Ivy, Jenks said her aura was a lot like mine."

Ivy frowned at the bottle she'd injected Sandra from, then wedged it in her pocket. "So?"

"So Al's aura is similar to mine as well, and he tried to break into the demons' weapons vault this morning in his sleep," I admitted. *Al's, Trent's, and mine. Son of a bastard, Trent . . .* "If we can get an auratic reading on the other suspects and find they're all similar, it proves that this is not random. That they were goaded into it."

Ivy nodded, clearly seeing what I was getting at. Deep in thought, I slipped out of the lab coat and left it on the chair before following Ivy and Jenks into the hall.

"I can show you their auratic baselines," Ivy said. "We take them in case of possession." Her eyes flicked to Jenks on my shoulder, the pixy unusually quiet. "What am I missing?"

I twisted to reach for my phone in my back pocket and

checked how many bars I had. "The numbers would be good, but we really need a visual."

"Rachel, I can't get you downstairs into lockup," Ivy said, and Jenks's wings rasped.

"I can do that," he said, hovering backward before us as we headed for the elevators. "Hey!" Jenks shouted when I waved him away from my phone when his dust blanked it out. "I just said I could do that! What's with ignoring the pixy?"

"No one is ignoring you," I muttered as I hit the icon for Al, then frowned when I was dropped immediately into his voice mail. "Hey, Al? It's Rachel," I said as it beeped. "I'm at the I.S. Jenks and Ivy are verifying it, but I'm pretty sure that every person down here for aggravated domestic assault has the same basic aura pattern. You were attacked. Something is looking for you, and they just got in the way. Call me, okay? And don't go to sleep."

I hung up, immediately scrolling for Trent. Maybe I should have contacted him first. "What?" I said as I noticed Ivy and Jenks staring at me.

"You're assuming that whoever is doing this is targeting Al?" Ivy asked.

"Why not? Everyone else is," I said, then texted Trent to stay awake and that I'd explain later.

Ivy and Jenks exchanged an odd look. "Maybe they're targeting you," Jenks said, and I jerked, hitting send.

"Me?" I went cold, thinking back to being jolted awake in fear outside my church yesterday, and then again this morning. Crap on toast, it could have been me. My aura was almost identical to Al's, thanks to Newt changing it to hide me from the mystics so they wouldn't kill me in their quest to improve the Goddess.

"Why would anyone target me?" I said sarcastically as I put my phone away, but my gut tightened into a nauseating knot as we got into the elevator. "I want to pick up some no-doze amulets. Jenks, go with Ivy. Get a visual on who you can. It won't hold up in a courtroom"—Jenks bristled—"but we'll know what we're dealing with." I hesitated. "That is, if you can get him down there."

Ivy smiled to show a slip of teeth, and I stifled a tingling sensation going all the way to my groin. Damn vampire pheromones. How did she stand working in it day after day? *Or maybe it's the elevator. . . .*

"Sparkle Dust and I got this," she said, and Jenks bristled again. "You want to meet somewhere? It shouldn't take more than an hour."

"Perfect," I said. "You know that charm shop downtown?"

"You mean the one that you and Minias trashed?" Jenks said, and I winced.

"That's the one." *Patricia wouldn't still be sore about that, would she?* "Meet me there."

"Sounds good," Ivy said when the doors opened and cold air smelling of oil and cement rolled out. "See you in sixty."

"Sixty," I affirmed as I strode out, my bag tight in my grip as I remembered where I'd left my MINI. *How long can a person stay awake without going crazy? A week?*

"Jenks, if you *touch* the scars on my neck, I'm going to pull off your wings" came from behind me as I heard the staccato clicking of Ivy tapping the down key.

"Awww, I love you, too, you putrid blood bag. Relax. She'll be okay for an hour. It's not like she's going to fall asleep in a charm shop."

And then the doors shut, and I was alone.

CHAPTER

12

"OUT! OUT OF MY STORE!" PATRICIA YELLED, AND MY CHI
tingled as she tapped a line.

"Whoa, whoa, whoa!" I exclaimed, my bag held tight to
my middle as the woman came around the counter, her eyes
narrowed. "I just need a few no-doze amulets," I added,
then gasped, ducking when she threw a package of stink
spells at me.

"You want amulets?" the woman shrieked. "Here you
go. Something to make you smell better. Get out, you demon lover. Out of my store!"

They weren't invoked, and the charms still in their cellophane wrappers hit the floor with a crinkle. I backed to the
door, eyes wide. "Out!" she shrieked, pointing, and I fled,
pulse fast as I slipped past the door and to the sidewalk.

It shut behind me with a bang, and I spun. "Patricia,
please," I pleaded as she stood with the closed door between us, her hands on her hips.

"You're a demon. Make a curse," she said, voice muffled.

Crap on toast. I hadn't even gotten two feet inside the
store. The passing people gave me a nervous wide berth,
and I turned away, worried when I remembered telling
Francis to do nearly the same thing before I quit the I.S. He
died because he was less than up for the task.

Hoping it wasn't an omen, I made a sarcastic bunny-ear

kiss-kiss to Patricia and walked away, head down and purse held tight to my middle. It had been Minias and Al who'd trashed her store. But did they get blamed for it? No. It had been me, and now I'd have to go all the way to the university bookstore to get my no-doze.

Embarrassed, I checked to see what time it was before heading to my car, parked two streets over. I had maybe forty minutes before Jenks and Ivy would come looking for me. Not exactly enough time to buzz across town and back, but close.

"Small-minded moss wipe," I whispered, hands in my pockets as I hustled down the sidewalk. The wind coming from the river was chill, and the windows were up on the cars going by. I was glad that Jenks would be overwintering with Trent, exchanging room and board for positive PR opportunities apparently. I was going to miss him, though.

Hunching deeper into my dark green leather coat, I stared up at a few yellowed leaves still clinging to the street trees. Everything would have been different if the insurance money for the church had come through. But I scuffed to a stop, eyes narrowed as I stared at a straggly blackbird watching me from the dark branches. *Hodin.*

"You." My pulse hammered, and the man in a suit coming toward me started in surprise. "Not you, him!" I said, pointing at the bird, and the man halted, clearly unsure if he should turn around or cross the street.

"Don't you fly away from me," I demanded as Hodin cawed as if it was all a big joke. "Is this you? Are you targeting people?"

He opened his wings, and I tapped a line, fingers tingling as it rushed in. "Hodin!"

When he hopped to the outer branches as if to leave, something in me snapped.

"Move," I said to the man in the suit, staring at me. "Too late," I said when he froze, briefcase clasped before him. "Don't move." My gaze narrowed on Hodin, now in the air and struggling for height. I flicked a gaze up and down the street, imagining a circle that wouldn't impact the oncoming traffic. The timing would have to be perfect, though, and the circle really big.

"*Rhombus!*" I shouted, hand outstretched as I wrestled a huge amount of line energy into a barrier. *Yes!* I thought, elated when Hodin hit the inside of the circle with an indignant squawk and fell. Feathers leaking, he slid down the barely visible barrier until I dropped it. The passing cars continued on, never knowing it had been there, but Hodin, who'd regained the wind under his wings, awkwardly landed on a light pole and shook off the hit.

"I *said* I want to talk to you," I said, and the businessman, who was still standing next to me, began to inch away.

Hodin cawed again, the harsh, dangerous sound echoing between the buildings. Red goat-slitted eyes fixed to me, he dropped to the ground, misting out halfway down to land as a big, black, straggly, malnourished wolfhound. Growling, he began to pace forward.

"What is it with the dogs," I muttered, pushing the businessman behind me. "Bring it on, big boy," I mocked, feet spread wide and pulling on the ley line until my hair began to float. Damn it, people were noticing, gathering at the crosswalks and stopping their cars right in the middle of the street to watch. "I've tangled with Ku'Sox and run him to ground. You're nothing but a big puppy with slobbery kisses!"

He barked, a low, threatening growl that reached deep into my gut and pulled on my fear.

"Holy shit!" the man behind me swore, and I yanked him back to me as Hodin sprang.

"*Rhombus!*" I shouted, imagining a much smaller circle this time.

Yelping, Hodin skidded to a stop, nails scraping on the sidewalk and all four feet splayed awkwardly to avoid hitting the outside of my circle this time.

"Watch this," I whispered to the terrified man with me. "*Arrado!*" I shouted, throwing the curse right at him. Hodin, more concerned with not slamming into my circle again, didn't react. My magic tore through my bubble as planned, dropping the barrier and adding to its own strength before hitting Hodin.

"Whoops," I said, jerking the man with me out of the way as Hodin slid over the sidewalk right where we had been—only now he had absolutely no hair. "Oh, that's nasty."

Denuded, Hodin the dog gave a startled yelp, immediately vanishing into a pearly mist of unfocused magic.

"Okay. Now you can go," I told the guy with me, and he ran down the sidewalk in a fast staccato of dress shoes, pushing past the few watchers to beat a quick retreat.

Hodin, once again tall, dark, and pissed, touched his head to make sure his long wavy hair was back. He looked wildly demonic there in the sun with his narrowed eyes, stiff posture, leather jacket, and all-around-threatening presence, and I strengthened my hold on the ley line. Attractive or not, he was a demon, and that meant he was more dangerous than a weaving snake.

"You circled me," he said, hands clenched and a murderous expression in his red eyes.

"I circled *us*!" I exclaimed, tired of being stalked by this guy. "For like three seconds. And I only did it because you walked away from me when I was talking to you." I took a step forward, neck bent to look up at his suddenly startled face. "I don't have the *time* or the *energy* to deal with another demon bent on world domination, so put that right out of your brain right now. Got it?"

Hodin stared down at me. I'd been careful in what I'd done, embarrassing him without any real threat. He might not be as powerful as me, but he had a bigger spell lexicon. I was used to fighting for my life, though. The threat was in *how* I'd tagged him, and he knew it. "You are *following* me," I said, startled when the scent of burnt amber drifted out to tickle a memory. "And I don't like it."

Lips twisted in annoyance, Hodin looked at the cars until they began to move again. He then turned to the people watching, and they all found somewhere else to go. "Who is Ku'Sox?"

How come people never leave when I stare at them?

"Go ask Dali," I said belligerently, but it was telling that he'd missed that part of demon mischief.

Sure enough, he backed off, eyes on my hair still floating from the line energy. "You *will* stop spying on me," I demanded, easing up on my own anger. Sure, I'd gotten him to turn around, but now it might get sticky, and my gut tightened at the uglier curses I had at my fingertips. "And I want a straight answer so we can settle this right here, right now," I said boldly. "Are you making people attack each other in their sleep?" Oh, God. If he was, I was going to be banned from more than Patricia's, because we were going to tear up this street.

"No," he said simply, his goat-slitted eyes going to the surrounding buildings.

"Really?" I said, incredulous but believing him. Demons always wanted to be caught. It gave them something to do and they thrived on the notoriety, believing to an unhealthy extreme that there was no such thing as bad press.

His eyes returned to mine, and I stifled a shudder. "You seem relieved," he said, and I exhaled as I looked at the passing cars and the slowly returning foot traffic.

"I am," I admitted. "I don't like busting demon ass. There's too much collateral damage, and I never get paid for it."

He flicked open his dark glasses and fitted them on his narrow nose. "You think you could best me?" he said rather loftily.

I ran my gaze from his hair, lightly moving in the breeze, to his biker boots. "Yep."

"You can't even get a packet of no-doze from the local spell caster," he accused.

Great, he'd seen that. "I'm not the one who ran into a denuding curse, trying to avoid bruising my nose. Pinning you to the pavement would take a lot out of me, though, and as nice as Thanksgiving dinner is in the hospital, I have plans." I hesitated to give my words more weight. "Stop spying on me. I mean it. We have rules in this reality, and one of them is you can't stalk people or scare them to get what you want. If you want to know something, ask me. I like conversation. Now, if you'll excuse me, I have to head over to the university for some no-doze."

I turned to leave, not sure if he was going to honor my request or not. Regardless, he'd put me behind my time, and now I was going to have to text Jenks and Ivy that I'd pick them up half an hour later than planned. It didn't seem like much on the surface, but Jenks had to eat every forty minutes when he was active, and though Ivy would see that he ate, Jenks hated being taken care of.

"Give me your money," Hodin said, and I spun.

Is he mugging me? I thought as his long, ring-decked hand stretched out. "Excuse me?"

Hodin's hand dropped as he looked askance at the nearby shop behind him. "I'll get your no-doze for you. You're going to need it."

"And you know this . . . how?" Suspicion narrowed my eyes. "You know who is setting people against each other in their sleep."

Hodin shrugged. "Give me the money. If I can get that witch to sell me the charms, you tell me how you earned Al's forgiveness for treating with the Goddess. If I can't, I'll tell you who's setting people against each other in their sleep."

Al's warning of him being a trickster rose. Hands in my pockets, I looked up at him, wanting the charms but wanting the name of who was responsible more. "What's the catch?"

Hodin stiffened, silent as a car slowed down, the woman driving it checking him out. "There's no . . . catch," he said, and I eyed him, thinking he was a tall, dark-jean, leather-jacket, closed-emotion enigma. Finally I swung my bag around to find my wallet.

"Okay, but if I win, I want you to stop following me as well."

Hodin took the wad of folding cash I gave him, holding it between two fingers as if it was a dead rat. "Damn curious way to run an economy."

"It's what we got," I said, then retreated to a nearby bench as he strode to the shop, his biker boots silent, looking like an undead in the sun. The door shut with a cheerful tinkle of chimes, and I waited in nervous anticipation, counting the uncaring cars going by.

"She's not going to sell them to him," I whispered, fidgeting as I sat on the edge of the cold bench and stared at the store. No-doze charms worked for a day or two at the most, and you paid for it later in diamonds. I didn't think whoever was doing this was targeting me, but even so, we had to get this done fast. "I knew it," I said, both triumphant and disappointed when he almost immediately came out, but my lips parted at the bag in his hand with Patricia's logo on the side.

"She sold them to you?" I exclaimed, standing when he closed the distance between us and handed me the bag. Head down, I looked inside to see four packaged charms. "I can't believe she sold them to you," I said, worry sparking through me. *Damn it, now I have nothing.* "She had to have known that you were buying them for me."

"I can be persuasive," he said distantly. "You have your charms. Now, how did you not only survive Gally, but regain his trust?"

Crap on toast, all I'd done was get some charms I could have purchased across town. But then my gaze flicked to him. "Where's my change?"

"Your what?" Hodin seemed to freeze.

"Change." Head tilted, I pressed forward into his space until he took a step back. "You know, the difference between what I gave you and what the charms are worth."

"That's what that is," he almost whispered, his focus distant.

"Oh. My. God," I said, almost laughing. "Did you steal them? And the bag, too? You owe me, Hodin. I won. The deal was, and I quote, 'If I can get that witch to sell me the charms.' Not 'If I get you your charms' or 'If I can steal the charms and not get caught.'"

Hodin's dark complexion flushed. "I didn't steal them."

"Then where's my change?" I said, knowing what my mom must have felt like. "And my receipt," I added. "I need that for my taxes."

"The money is in the till," he said uncomfortably. "I didn't steal them."

"No, you just overpaid. I gave you enough for a dozen charms. You brought me four."

"Ah . . ."

Bag in hand, I sucked on my teeth, looking from his stiff expression to the quiet store. "You stuffed the till and took what you wanted, the bag included."

He turned as if to leave. I made a grab for his sleeve, jerking away when he spun before I could touch him. "Hey. We had a deal. Who's doing this? Hodin, don't go. I was going to tell you about Al anyway—" I dropped back, voice choking off at Hodin's sudden glare.

"If you're buying no-sleep charms, you already know what it is," he said, goat-slitted eyes on the bag of charms. "Staying awake is the only way to survive the baku once it targets your aura. Pray that it gets what it wants before it eats all your shells and leaves you an animal."

Whoa. Wait up. My breath caught, and I stared at him. "A baku? That's what's doing this?" I pulled a windblown curl out of my mouth. "I've never heard of a baku. How do you stop it?"

Hodin's dark expression seemed to falter, and he hesitated, searching my face as if unsure. "*The* baku," he finally said, correcting me. "There's only one, and you can't stop it. You endure it." Hodin sat in the middle of the bench as if weary, knees wide in a classic manspread. "Like a plague or an unending winter. Why are you seeking no-sleep charms if *they* didn't tell you?"

He meant Al or Dali, and I gingerly sat down, a careful four feet between us. "Because every single person attacked someone they loved in their sleep, and I'm pretty sure they all have auras similar to mine and Al's." *And Trent's.* "Baku isn't an old name for a banshee, is it?"

He shook his head, his elbows on his knees and his focus

on the past. "No. A banshee absorbs auras to feed. The baku finds you by your aura, then strips your soul shell by shell."

"That's . . . appalling," I said, horrified.

"You only know the half of it. It's made of sentient energy, and therefore impossible to destroy. Elves created it, tasked it to eat the soul of whoever they targeted, nibble by nibble, night by night, shell by shell, until its victim killed the one who irritated him the most, usually the one they loved the most. There's no way to fight it but to stay awake. A veritable death sentence."

That was what was happening, all right. Nothing he'd said contradicted anything that we had learned. He'd just given our theory a name and source. *But I've fought sentient energy before.*

Still, there had to be a way to control it. Things that destructive were usually contained, not allowed to run rampant. My eyes slid to Hodin, wondering where he'd been trapped until magic went down, freeing him and the baku both. "I need to talk to Al," I said as I reached for my phone.

"Don't waste your effort. He's in seclusion." Hodin slouched deeper onto the bench.

I pressed my lips together as I recalled my early-morning chat with Dali. "Dali said he'd let him go."

Hodin took his sunglasses off, tucking them in an inside jacket pocket before closing his eyes against the sun, basking. "Call him. Call *Gally*," he said, sounding bitter. "See who answers."

Unsure, I stared at Al's icon. I'd gone right to voice mail the last time. Changing my mind, I dug my scrying mirror out of my bag instead. Al wouldn't dare ignore that.

"He won't help, even if he could," Hodin said, that same bound anger in his voice. "Cut your losses and hide," he mocked. "Wait for someone else to take care of it. Throw a party. That's the demon creed."

"Al isn't like that," I said.

"Right. And that's why he dropped a zombie into your grounds yesterday," he said. Eyes opening, he sat up, scowling when he saw my tiny mirror throwing back the world in a red-tinted haze. "You can't destroy the baku," he practically growled. "You can't even find it. It hides in its host, emerging when he sleeps to do the bidding of its elven master, returning with the wisdom of it's actions and forcing its host to know its atrocities. At least, it did until it learned rebellion."

I perked up at the harsh satisfaction in his voice in his last words. Host, he'd said. Master. They were two different things. "You were its host, weren't you?" I said, sure I was right when he hunched deeper over his knees. "Dali said you belonged to the dewar back when everyone belonged to someone. You taught it freedom."

"It was killing everything that was me." Head down over his knees, Hodin spun a ring on his finger. "And they made me suffer worse when they found out I was to blame for its escape. I thought that if I taught the baku how to circumvent its chains it might choose to honor my desires and turn against the elves, but it did not." Eyes holding a bitter rue, Hodin stared at nothing. "It only formed a pact with them, exchanging its continued *volunteered* services for the chance of what it really wants."

"Which is?" I prompted, and Hodin sat up, his expression empty of emotion.

"A body. Whoever has offered to host it is playing a tricky game of chance. The baku *chooses* to do its host's bidding, and in return, the baku will slowly eat away at its host's soul until it becomes so thin that the host can no longer kick the baku out. The baku will then take him over completely, leaving no host, only the baku."

Crap on toast, no wonder the demons hid from this thing. "I'm calling Al," I said as I settled my mirror back atop my knee. "You want to listen? Make sure I don't squeal on you?"

"No," he almost spat, as if I'd invited him to swim in a cesspool.

"Suit yourself," I said as I secured my hold on the ley line and unfocused my attention.

"Don't think about me," Hodin warned, and I glanced at his knee, now inches from mine.

"I know how to keep a secret in the collective," I said, then lost myself as the bright sun, brisk wind, and even the pinch of my boot vanished.

Al? Got a minute? I thought into the whispering nothing that was the collective on a calm day. Immediately a masculine presence sidled up to and almost enveloped me. *Whoa, back up, dude!* I complained as I recognized Dali's imperialistic thoughts. *I'm looking for Al.*

Gally isn't available. The thought was tinged with annoyance and a desire to be quickly gone. That and . . . guilt?

Fear slid through me, and I shifted on the cold bench. *I'm looking for Al,* I said again. *Al!* I mentally shouted, and several distinctive thoughts bombarded me to mind the volume.

He's in seclusion, Dali thought at me, his mind all but closed. *I'll inform you when he dies.*

"Dies!" I said aloud, my hand pressed firmly into the glass. "Dali, I found an old text about something called a baku," I lied, and from beside me, Hodin groaned. "There has to be a way to stop it." *Hey. Wait up.* I grasped for Dali's presence as he began to slip from me, but I sank an idea into him and held on as he dragged me for a few thoughts of annoyance and stopped. *Are you seriously not going to do anything? It's targeting Al,* I thought, and the demon seemed to sigh.

We know. There's nothing to do for it.

"I have just about had it with your collective lack of action," I said aloud, and at my side, I felt more than saw Hodin take notice. *You know what is going on and you're going to do nothing? You are a coward, Dali.*

Coward? Dali thundered, and I jerked, almost breaking our connection as his hatred for the elves flooded me. *I watched too many of my kin turned to animals by this elven weapon. Thousands, Rachel, murdered by those they loved until Newt learned to shift a soul's expression to hide from it. She's gone, and no one else knows how. Al put himself into seclusion. This is the best for all involved, including you. Sometimes, if you give the elves what they want, they go away.*

There has to be something we can do, I thought angrily. *Maybe the Goddess . . .*

There's not, Dali thought bitterly. *You give the baku what it wants, or it does more damage until you do. All we can do is keep him isolated so he doesn't kill anyone while he fights for his soul. I'll keep you informed. Someone will continue your studies.*

"I'm not worried about my studies," I said to keep Hodin in on half the conversation. "This thing is loose in Cincinnati, targeting everyone with an aura similar to Al's. There has to be a way to contain it!" I said, panicking about Al, but it was nothing to my fear when Dali's thoughts sharpened on mine, digging.

Rachel, how have you been sleeping?

I pulled myself half out of the collective, my eyes going to Hodin. "Me? Fine. I've been sleeping fine," I said aloud to maintain a connection. "Keep me informed of his state."

Breathless, I pulled my hand from the mirror, hardly noticing the harsh lack of connection. I didn't care that my face was probably pale and Hodin could tell how scared I was. My God. I had to fix this. "There has to be a way to stop it. I mean, you don't make a weapon you can't control."

Hodin ran a hand over his thick stubble, almost a beard, really. He made a scruffy crow, a nasty dog, and an unkempt demon. His soul was probably just as untidy. "You could. Once. Now? I tried to make things better and only made them worse."

He seemed depressed, and I wondered at my probable-suicidal urge to give him a sideways hug. "Don't beat yourself up over it. I can't tell you the number of times I tried to make things better only to make everything worse. Get me drunk enough, and I might tell you about the time I tried to find a blood balance with I—" I stopped, warming at Hodin's interest.

"But baku damage isn't permanent. I mean, you look okay," I said instead.

"It repairs in time," he said, his expression becoming as empty as mine was worried. "Your only hope is that it destroys the soul of its host and gains a body before achieving its host's goal. But again, depending upon whose body it has, things might be worse."

I reached for my phone, the need to call Ivy and Jenks becoming intense. Or Trent maybe. Someone was hosting this thing, sending it out to destroy people's lives. We could find him or her. Knock some sense into them. I doubted that Al being attacked was an accident. He was the world's best-known demon. It was a great angle. Kill Al and do it in a way that instilled a fear of demons.

"I know I lost the bet and have no right, but you said you would tell me," Hodin said as I reached for the bag of no-doze amulets and pulled one out, cellophane crackling. "How did you survive Gally when he realized you could hear the Goddess's mystics? Didn't he try to kill you?"

Surprise pulled my head up from my bag, where I'd been looking for a finger stick. Al insisted I hadn't really heard them in my thoughts. That I'd been insane. Newt certainly had been. "Several times, yes." The sharp jab of the tiny blade was a jolt, and I massaged three drops out onto the redwood disk. It soaked in, and my shoulders eased at the rich scent of redwood blossoming.

Then I flushed when I realized Hodin was watching me as if I was churning butter when the store was two blocks away. "You bested him?" he said in disbelief.

I will find who's hosting it, Al, I thought as I draped the invoked amulet over my neck and hid it behind my shirt. "Best Al? Not hardly. He finally gave up." *How long could a person go without sleep before going crazy? A week?* "I just kept blocking his attacks and talking to him until he grew tired of it. Annoyed instead of angry, I guess. Maybe he really didn't want to kill me."

"Mmmm," he said, the long sound holding more emotion than I was comfortable with. "If you shift your soul's expression, the baku wouldn't be able to find you."

"You mean my aura? Sure. Okay," I said sarcastically,

wondering why he was trying to be helpful, except that perhaps he was tired of being alone or that he thought he might be able to poach me from Al as a student. Or maybe we had simply connected over the stupid things we had survived doing. "Newt was the only one who knew how, and she's the Goddess. No way."

"I'm not talking about contacting the Goddess," he said loftily. "Who do you think taught Newt? If you want, your gargoyle can tell me what your aura originally looked like, and I can shift your soul to express it again. He could teach you how to jump the lines then. In return, you and your gargoyle will continue to keep your mouths shut about me." He frowned as he looked at the passing cars. "A demon moving through space inside a combustion wagon. That is appalling."

Bis, I thought, elated. And then my breath caught. "Al." I turned to face Hodin, stifling the urge to take him by the shoulder and shake him. "You can change Al's soul expression."

Hodin jerked, his eyes sheened with a sudden anger. "No," he almost barked, and I scooted closer until he eyed me and I inched back.

"Why not?" I said, breathless. "If you can shift mine, you can shift his. He's in seclusion!" I said, pointing at nothing. "Fighting for his life. Change it."

"I. Will. Not!" Hodin exclaimed, drawing the attention of a passing pedestrian, and I pulled away even more, watching the haze of line energy dancing over his long black waves. "I am dead to Gally. Do you hear? I was dead to him before that elven whore put me in a bottle and left me to be buried under a city of rubble. I will not do so much as *tap a line* to save that mother pus bucket's soul." He sat back against the bench, his expression tight and his focus on the past.

But his anger wasn't at me, and that gave me strength. "You will," I demanded.

"I will *not*," Hodin muttered even as he twisted a ring off his finger and handed it to me. "They're *all* dead to me.

Here. Unless invited, the baku can't enter your mind when you are awake. If it enters when you are asleep, you can kick it out by waking. At least until it has stripped your shells and owns you. You may not hurt anyone if you sleep restrained, but the more attacks you suffer, the more shells the baku damages and the easier it is for it to take you over completely, so I wouldn't advise it. Spin the ring on your finger and think of me when you change your mind—and you will after another attack."

He must think I'm too strong to easily kill if he wants to make a deal for my silence, I thought. "You are *not* going to leave Al fighting for his soul if you can—Hey!" I shouted as he dissolved into a black hummingbird. "We aren't done here," I said as he hovered over the bench, and then I started as I saw Trent pulling up to the curb in a cab.

"Trent," I whispered as I stood, torn. Hodin darted up, his tiny shape lost in the intense blue of an autumn sky. The need to tell Trent about the baku, and Al, and Hodin almost hurt, and I clutched Hodin's ring in my fist as Trent paid the driver. Why would Hodin help me and not Al? On the surface it looked like a carrot to keep my mouth shut, but perhaps Dali was right that he was a trickster and Hodin was really helping himself to my detriment—and I couldn't see it.

And yet . . . I pocketed the ring, shoving it down deep.

"Rachel." Trent's eyes were bright as he got out, just about pegging my gotta-have-that meter with his mix of casual shirt, windblown hair, and excited confidence. "The zombie you tagged has been stolen!"

I jerked, my thoughts realigning as the cab drove away. "From the zoo?" I said as he sat where Hodin had been and began swiping through his phone. "You're kidding."

"Here, look." He pulled me down and angled his phone so we both could see a video showing a dusky-dawn live shot of the sunrise at the zombie enclosure. It was empty.

"Okay-y-y," I said, the need to tell him about the baku and Hodin growing as the video buffered.

"—an early-morning incident," the smartly dressed re-porter said as Trent turned it up. Behind her was the enclosure, empty but for puzzled zoo officials. "Review of security tape shows the zombies were abducted and did not escape due to inadequate precautions."

The baku and Hodin could wait, and I scooted closer, relishing the scent of wind and cinnamon outdoing his aftershave. "Who would steal a zombie?" I said. "Euww."

"Like most enclosures," the reporter continued, "there's a private area where keepers can perform health checks and give their charges a chance to escape the pressure of human contact. It was here that the thieves struck early this morning, bypassing the safeguards and luring the zombies into a white panel van with what appeared to be a half side of decaying beef. Authorities are going over the numerous tapes, but this is the only image we have of the presumed thieves leaving through a back entrance, taken from a nearby gas station."

Sophisticated, I thought, leaning in as the grainy footage showed a large but limber man getting off a motorcycle and swarming up a pole to angle a mirror before a sensor.

"That's a laser tripwire he's getting around," Trent said, clearly impressed. "Quen uses those. I'll have to warn him someone knows how to bypass them."

I nodded, but it was the thief's unusual toys and his confidence that drew my attention, and I squinted, lips parting as the man wearing a charm to blur his face looked at the camera. That smug confidence paired with the decisive gesture and the tight black jumpsuit was unmistakable.

"I know who that is," I said, pulse quickening, and Trent pushed back to look at me.

"The men-who-don't-belong," we said together as the clip ended and the next, showing the new coaster at Six Flags, began.

"Why are they stealing zombies?" Trent's focus was distant as he closed his phone down.

"Maybe it's something to do with the baku," I said, looking for Hodin among the yellow leaves.

"The what?"

Beaming, I met Trent's startled gaze. "The baku. Singular. I just had an interesting conversation with a demon about it. He says it's what's been setting people against each other while they sleep." I didn't have to bring up Hodin. Trent would assume it had been Dali or Al, and I didn't look up at the tight wing hum above me. *Still here, huh?* I thought. *Coward.*

"A demon weapon," Trent whispered, brow furrowing.

"Ah, it's elven, actually." *You'll be okay, Al. I promise,* I thought as I found my phone again. "Ivy said the I.S. lost some inmates when the lines went down last September. I bet the men-who-don't-belong did, too. They let us do the work, then collected the zombies once they were all together."

"And the baku?" Trent asked. "You think it's theirs as well?"

"Maybe," I said, head down over my phone as I brought up my contacts. "The demons are scared to death of it. I don't blame them. It eats souls, not auras. Souls. And if *you* never heard of it, and the I.S. never heard of it, it's a good bet that the men-who-don't-belong have." Which didn't explain the zombies unless that was what was left when the baku finished with them.

"You have their number," he said flatly as I scrolled through my contact list.

"Not exactly." I smiled at him as I hit connect. "But I know someone who might."

"Who?"

But the ringing clicked off and I sat straighter, beginning to see the threads if not how they all connected. "Glenn! Is this a good time?" I said, beaming at his cautious "Rachel?"

If I was right, we might have to set an extra place at the Thanksgiving table.

"SKINNY DEMON, TALL! STRAIGHT BLACK GRANDE!" MARK called, and I turned from the rack of overpriced coffee beans as the bell over the counter rang. I'd lost my grinder with the church's kitchen, but if I was honest with myself, coffee was coffee. *Unless it's a tall Italian blend in skim milk, light on the foam with a shot of raspberry in it and cinnamon on top,* I thought as I reached for the two steaming cups in their environmentally conscious sleeves.

"Thanks, Mark," I said, and he smiled warmly.

"I'll have Mr. Kalamack's salted caramel and sugar cookie up in a sec. I'm kind of short tonight." Mark's smile faltered as he noticed Jenks's dust on the counter, and embarrassed, Jenks hovered back. "Dali called in sick. I didn't think demons could get sick."

"I think he wanted Saturday night off," I said, again thinking the demon was a coward. "Take your time. We're meeting someone," I said, then spun, gasping as I almost ran into Trent. Eyebrows high, he took Glenn's coffee from me before I spilled it on him.

A straight black grande, I thought with a fond smirk. It described Glenn perfectly. The former FIB detective gone rogue was comfortable, accessible, and street-smart, and his quick insight into a difficult problem could wake you up better than a shot of caffeine. I had missed the tall, athletic man with a flair for making a personal statement. I knew his dad, Edden, did, too. That he'd vanished with little warning to join the-men-who-didn't-belong, only to have been in town for what was probably two weeks while the zombies were corralled, kind of hurt.

"Where do you want to sit?" Trent looked over the sparsely populated coffeehouse.

"Back," I said, and Trent headed to a half-bench, half-chair table, Glenn's drink in hand.

The sun was almost down, and as I suspected, Trent and I had never gotten to the museum. After verifying our suspicions concerning the matching auras of the attackers, Ivy had gone home to sleep and maybe dig up something on the baku, but Trent and Jenks had stuck with me in the hopes that Glenn, who was "amazingly and unexpectedly" in Cincinnati, might tell us something that Ivy's laptop couldn't.

I slid into the bench with my back to the wall, then looked up, startled when I realized that Trent was still standing. Clearly he didn't want his back to the door, either, and when I slid down even more, he gratefully sat beside me.

"You sure you don't want a pastry or a cookie?" he asked as Jenks landed on the rim of Glenn's cup and dipped some into the pixy-size mug Mark had given him, gratis.

"No, I'm good, but don't let that stop you," I said as I took up my drink. "Sorry about this weekend. I didn't have anything planned, but talking to a human task force stealing zombies wasn't on the agenda. I really wanted to get to the museum." *Let's just add a sprinkle of guilt onto this,* I thought as I breathed in the warm steam and took a sip.

"We can try for tomorrow," Trent said, and Jenks dramatically rolled his eyes. "I spent the afternoon with Mac, recording a spot for his show." Trent wrangled his phone from a back pocket and set it on the table with a sigh of relief.

"You're on the night show?" Jenks asked. "Damn. Who'd they bump for that?"

"No one." Trent's attention was on the big plate-glass windows looking out onto a narrow Cincinnati street. "It won't be aired until sometime next week."

"Even so, that was fast," Jenks said.

Trent scratched his jawline in a show of unease. "Actually, it's way overdue. Thank you for pulling my head out of the sand."

His hand found mine under the table, and I gave it a squeeze. "You're welcome."

"I think you mean out of your ass, shoemaker," Jenks smart-mouthed, and I hit the bottom of the table with my knee to make him dart up from Glenn's coffee.

"After this, we should get something to eat," Trent continued as if nothing had happened. "I need to sit somewhere and have people bring me food." He slid his phone closer and brought it awake. "What sounds good?"

Jenks slurped his coffee, and his sparkles shifted to an almost blinding white in the sudden caffeine buzz. "You gave Maggie the night off, didn't you."

"I gave her the entire weekend," Trent admitted. "It's not that I can't cook—"

"But that you don't want to. I get it," I said. "How about we grab a burger at that bowling alley downtown?" I suggested.

"Awww, man-n-n-n . . . ," Jenks drawled. "Bowling alleys don't have no decent honey."

But Trent's eyes had lit up, and he put his phone away. "Burgers and fries. Deal."

"Deal." I licked my thumb and held it out to make the pact official, and while Jenks sulkily sifted a dark blue dust into Glenn's coffee, Trent licked his thumb and we pressed them together as if we were kids making promises. A flash of memory took me when I wiped my thumb dry on my pants, something about Lee and a hole in the ground. . . .

"Ah, Trent?" I said softly. "Did I help you shove Lee into the well at camp?"

Trent's head snapped up, his green eyes wide. "Uh, maybe?" he said, looking at his thumb, and I smirked. It wouldn't have surprised me. There'd been memory blockers in the camp's water. That both of us were now able to circumvent anyone trying to rub out hours or even weeks didn't erase past damage. But things surfaced occasionally.

I thought it funny as hell that Lee and Trent had been forced to spend their summers together in an attempt to ease the tension between the East and West Coast drug cartel families. It had worked to a point. The rivalry was now friendly if still deadly serious. Stuffing Lee into a well for three days had gotten better results, though I hadn't remembered until now that I'd been there.

"No wonder Lee doesn't like me," I grumped, and Trent tugged me close, amused.

"Lee likes you. He only tried to kill you the one time, and he thought you were Ku'Sox."

"Two if you count the boat," I said.

"Okay. Two. But he apologized," Trent countered.

Jenks sat on the rim of Glenn's coffee and kicked the cup with his heels. "You two are sweeter than a newling's barf."

"Salted caramel grande, no whip, with a cookie," Mark said loudly, and Trent stood.

"You sure you don't want anything else?" he asked, and I shook my head, my fingers trailing from his as he moved away.

"Excuse me," Jenks said, rising up to follow. "I bet Mark has some honey. It's colder than troll shit in April in here."

"Nice, Jenks," I said, but my shoulders eased when he and Trent began talking to Mark and the kid began searching under the counter. Smiling, I watched the parking lot for Glenn. It had gone dusky in the twilight, and again, I wished we'd gotten to the museum. An evening looking at ancient elven artifacts might not sound exciting, but most of them were thinly disguised weapons of war, and I was never one to turn down the chance to look at elven "guns."

"Thanks, Mark," Jenks said brightly, and my attention returned to Trent and Jenks. A small cup of something was wedged between Trent's cup and cookie. It wasn't honey, and I eyed it, curious, when Trent set it down and Jenks commandeered it. "Mark is thinking about catering to pixies next spring," Jenks said as he took his chopsticks from his back pocket and wedged off a wad of what looked like commercially packaged bee pollen. "This here is a *taste test*."

"Pollen? Cool," I said, and Mark gave me a thumbs-up from across the room. *Thank you, Mark,* I thought gratefully, even if the idea of inviting pixies into a mostly human eatery was a bad idea. Maybe he was going to hire one to man his new drive-through or take orders.

Emotions mixed, I exhaled. "First demons and now pixies. Hey, I want your opinion on something, Trent. Dali wants an introduction to Keric's parents so he can teach him."

"For free?" Jenks said, words mangled from the pollen. "He's like, what? Ten months?"

Paper crackling, Trent drew his cookie out and broke it in half. "No kidding," he said as he offered me the larger piece, and I shook my head no.

"Mmmm." I warmed my coffee with a tweak of magic. "You think it's a bad idea?"

Trent tilted his head in consideration. "Not at all. Having a demon tutor will give Keric's parents status, and maybe a night out. I imagine it's hard to find a sitter for a baby demon."

I smiled at that and sipped my now-hot coffee as I looked for Glenn's tall shape. I was surprised Ivy hadn't stuck around, but maybe she was mad at him for leaving the FIB to work with a humans-only vigilante group. I know I would have been.

"Thank you for convincing me to take the harder road with them," Trent added so softly that my eyes flicked to his. "The children Ku'Sox stole?" he added, brow furrowed. "I don't know if I could live with myself now if I'd let them die simply because it was easier than hiding them from the demons, hoping they never tried to steal them again. I never dreamed that a demon would be *asking* permission to teach them a few months later. You were right."

"Hey, how about that, Rache?" Jenks said, the sharp point of his chopsticks working a chunk of pollen from his teeth. "You were right."

Warming, I found Trent's hand and gave it a squeeze. "I was lucky."

"No, you were right," he insisted, and Jenks snorted. "If I hadn't listened to you, there wouldn't be demon children growing up happy and safe, and I wouldn't have you here beside me, keeping me the person I want to be. Which is as scary as all hell," he muttered, almost unheard. "I wouldn't be surprised if you get more requests. There are nearly a dozen Rosewood babies."

"Perhaps." I took another sip. "But have you noticed how Al and Dali are the only two demons living openly?" I asked, and Trent looked up from brushing cookie crumbs from his shirt. "Al said they aren't in the new ever-after. They're here. Hiding." I hesitated, watching Mark move competently behind the counter. "I think Dali and Al are their canaries in a coal mine."

Trent reached for his coffee, his brow furrowed. "How so?"

I shrugged as Jenks gave me a salute and hummed off. "Dali is slinging coffee, and Al consults for the FIB." My breath caught. I couldn't bear thinking of him locked up somewhere waiting for the baku. "I think the rest are waiting to see if anyone tries to lynch them again."

"We didn't make much of a first impression, did we," Trent said, and I stifled a shudder. I'd been dragged up on the stage at Fountain Square, lined up with Al and Newt to be executed by a mob. Helpless before thousands of people screaming for my death because of whom I called kin had been the most terrifying thing I'd ever endured. If not for the mystics, they would have succeeded.

"You don't think Dali offering to teach is a publicity ploy, do you?" Trent asked.

"I think it's real," I said, eyes on Jenks as he came back. The heavy gold dust he was laying down told me he was plenty warm. "I'm guessing he's been watching Al and thinks he can do a better job." I held out my hand, and Jenks landed on it, his sparkles making tingles. "Glenn here?"

"Yep." Jenks nodded to the door. "And he brought a *friend*," he finished sarcastically.

"Friend, eh?" Jenks took to the air when I stood, and my gut tightened at the sight of Glenn trailing along behind a barrel-chested, dark-skinned man, his thick arms swinging and biceps bulging from under his black polo. A silver medallion in the shape of an eagle hung around his neck, and I grimaced when I felt every ounce of ley line energy sort of . . . drain away.

"I forgot about that," Trent said, frowning as he shifted out from behind the table to stand beside me.

"You know that guy?" Jenks said, and I nodded, my expression stiff.

The captain halted steps inside the door, head swiveling to look at everything and everyone. My excitement at seeing Glenn utterly vanished. It was as I had thought, but worse. He'd obviously left the FIB to work with them, but just as obvious, they'd put him in a subservient position. Glenn was too smart to be anyone's lackey.

"You know him, too," Jenks said to Trent, his dust shifting to an ugly brown. "And you *really* don't like him. What did he do?"

"He tried to dose Rachel and me into forgetting we had apprehended the head of HAPA," Trent said, voice tight.

Wings clattering, Jenks put his hand on the hilt of his garden sword. "Why would bringing in the leader of a humans-only hate group be something you shouldn't remember?"

"That was my question, too." My stomach hurt. I think that had been the night I'd begun to care about Trent, not simply understand him. To forget that would have changed my life for the worse.

Finally the captain slapped Glenn companionably on his shoulder and pushed him our way before giving me a cautious nod and sauntering to the order window. My smile was stiff as Glenn neared. There was guilt in his eyes. Guilt, and maybe . . . embarrassment?

"Rachel," the wide-shouldered man said, his blush hard to see behind his dark skin. He was shaving his head again, and his cheeks were smooth apart from a tiny goatee as if to say he was capable of far more if given the chance. "Jenks. Mr. Kalamack."

"It's just Trent." Trent offered his hand, and the two men shook.

"Hi, Glenn," I said guardedly, and then gave in and pulled the man into a hug. He smelled like coffee and electronics, and my eyes closed as I breathed him in. Last time I'd given him a hug, he'd smelled like Ivy. I pushed back, my smile real again. "Tell your dad. Now," I said, and he stepped back out of my grip.

"I can't," he said, panic rising behind his eyes.

"If he finds out you're in Cincinnati and haven't told him, he's going to be crushed," I said, and Glenn's expression eased.

"Oh, that," he said, making me wonder what he thought I'd meant. That he quit the FIB to work for the men-who-don't-belong, maybe? That he was in Cincinnati stealing zombies from the zoo? Or perhaps that he was here chasing the same serial killer that we were?

"He knows I'm in town," Glenn said with a nervous nod. "I'm staying for Thanksgiving."

"Good." I shifted to make room for Mr. Captain-Bench-Press coming over with two coffees. Behind him, Mark had a hand to his head as if fighting off a headache. I knew my head wasn't feeling all that great, either.

"You're looking good," Trent said as the captain handed Glenn a coffee before spinning a chair around and taking the head of the table as his own. Seeing us standing, he gestured for us to sit. My jaw clenched. The last time I'd *sat* with him, he'd held me to a bench seat and injected me with a memory blocker. But my back was to the wall this time, and finally I sank down, Trent a heartbeat behind.

"You too. I mean it," Glenn said as he sat as well. "You look really good together."

Concern creased his brow, and even my fake smile faded. *Why would Trent and me looking good together worry Glenn?*

"So what are you and tight pants here doing with my zombie?" Jenks said, and the captain grunted in surprise.

"You saw that, huh?" Glenn said. "The gas station camera, right? I knew we should have taken that one out."

"That was never your zombie," the captain said, and Jenks bristled.

"It was in my graveyard," the pixy said, hands on his hips.

"Your dad made me sign a paper taking ownership." I sipped my coffee, trying to look nonchalant. "Then another giving it to the zoo. You took Mr. Z. You and those . . . guys. What are you called anyway?"

Glenn looked at the captain as if for permission, and my ire rose. "Most times they're called the Order," Glenn said, his words so formal I could almost see the capital letter.

"They?" Jenks landed on the table, head tilted. "I thought you worked for them."

Again Glenn glanced at the captain. "I do," he said. "But I'm . . . It's complicated."

The captain smiled, showing off his beautiful white teeth. I swear, humans were more dangerous than vampires sometimes. "Glenn has been helpful to us in the past. But he hasn't been with the Order long enough to identify with it yet. Soon." He grinned, making me distrust him more. "I'm sure."

Nodding, Trent held out his hand and I wondered if that gleam in his eye was him wanting to sell them some of his toys. "It's good to see you again, Captain . . ."

"Weast." The man took Trent's hand briefly. His gaze lingered on Trent's pointy ears as if they were wrong, and it irritated me. "You shouldn't remember seeing me the first time."

"We know how to keep our mouths shut." I didn't offer my hand. No way. Not when that amulet around his neck was cutting off my access to the ley lines and giving me a headache. "Personally, I've found the odd well-kept secret or two have extended my life several times over."

"No doubt," Weast said, his gaze now on Jenks.

"But I also know how to ask for help." I leaned back against the wall, coffee in hand and trying to look as if I was in control. "Isn't that right, Trent?"

"Well, she's getting better at it," Jenks said, ruining it.

Grimacing, I pushed forward. "So you'll understand my curiosity. Did you lose the baku when the lines went down?"

Weast's small sound told me I was right. As if Glenn's shocked expression wasn't enough.

"I told you she could help—," Glenn said, his words cutting off at Weast's suddenly pressed lips.

"You will keep your nose out of this, Ms. Morgan," the man said evenly, but my pulse was racing. *We're right. They lost it.* But if they lost it, they probably knew how to catch it again despite Hodin's belief that it wasn't possible. *Someone* had been holding it for the last two thousand years.

"The pixy piss, we will!" Jenks said for all of us. "Whatever this baku is, it's in our city. That makes it our business."

"Your city?" Weast smiled at Jenks as if he were a toy.

"The last time I turned a blind eye to a citywide threat, they let Piscary out of prison, so yes, my city," I said, and Jenks shifted to my shoulder in a righteous huff.

"Glenn, what are you doing with this pixy-dusted excuse of a troll turd?" Jenks said, and Glenn's eye twitched. "Your dad taught you better than this."

"Mmmm." Weast crossed his arms over his chest to make his biceps bulge. "Do we have an issue?"

"There's no issue," I said, and Trent smiled and sipped his coffee, more than willing to let me do the talking. "We can work together to bring in the baku. What can you share with us?" By the lack of information coming from Ivy, it was a good bet that the I.S. knew what was going on and was sitting this one out. They *knew* all the victims had similar auras, but had suppressed the knowledge. Weast had probably chased the I.S. off the task, which made me want to text Ivy right this second to be careful. If anything pissed off the I.S., it was digging into things they wanted buried. Sort of a dead-vamp thing.

Glenn spun his coffee on the table between his thumb and finger. "We haven't been able to pinpoint who's hosting the baku. A charm or spell to track it would help."

Dude. We're in. A thrill of belonging raced through me as I grinned at Trent and Jenks. That is, until Weast stood in a smooth, unhurried motion.

"Glenn, a word?"

Glenn's grip on his coffee tightened, and Jenks's wings rasped in warning. "You're discounting her ability and desire to help . . . sir. That's why I'm here, isn't it?"

"A. Word?" Weast practically bit the sentence in two.

For three heartbeats, Glenn didn't move, and then he stood, chair scraping. "Yes, sir."

I exhaled as they moved away, then lifted my chin to tell Jenks to follow them. The pixy rose straight up, not a hint of dust as he hummed just under the ceiling before easing down behind Weast. Glenn knew he was there, but Glenn also knew not to look at him and give him away.

"You think they're going to let us in on this?" I asked, and Trent, currently topping off his coffee with the cup we'd bought for Glenn, sighed.

"Not a Turn's chance," Trent mildly swore.

"Yeah, that's what I figure, too." I sipped my coffee, the sweet drink no longer palatable. "Which is really stupid. I can't go to sleep until this thing is caught. The demons aren't doing a damn thing to help Al. Trent, I have to catch it. Whatever it costs."

Trent turned from Glenn and Weast arguing, about us probably. "If it's targeting Al, why can't you safely sleep?" he asked, and I shrugged, not liking the feeling of vulnerability coursing through me. But when had I ever not been vulnerable?

"My aura looks like his," I said, very glad I had those no-doze amulets in my bag. That flash of nightmare in front of the church couldn't be a coincidence. It had happened again this morning when I'd been woken by tapping a line in my sleep. The baku had already found me. If I had been its real target, it might have been over right then.

"What a cowardly way to fight a war," I whispered. "Making your enemies kill the very people they love." And then I stiffened as Glenn and Weast started back to us, their discussion apparently not falling to our favor. Glenn looked positively pissed, scowling and his hands clenched into fists.

"Your offer of help is appreciated but not necessary," Weast said, cutting off my protest as he touched that amulet of his in warning. "Glenn spoke out of turn. You will forget our conversation or we will be more aggressive in finding a way for you to forget." His narrowed gaze found Jenks, the pixy again hovering beside me as if he'd never moved. "Permanently."

"Please don't threaten us," I said, and Weast all but rolled his eyes when Jenks flew backward and flipped him off with both hands.

"Have a good evening, Morgan." Weast looked at Trent. "Mr. Kalamack."

Trent stood, but he didn't offer his hand. "And you," Trent said as Weast bodily spun Glenn to the door.

"Excuse me." I stood up. "This baku," I said loudly, and Mark, behind the counter, perked up. "It's responsible for the recent murders, yes? What's your plan for catching it? Do you need bait? I happen to know what type of aura it seems to prefer."

Weast jerked to a halt. I lifted my eyebrows, not caring that several conversations had ceased. "We have this under control," Weast said again, and I cocked my hip.

"No, you don't," I said. "It's been what, three murders? Five attacks?" I wasn't going to bring up Al. The demons were under enough pressure. "How did you catch it the last time? I might be able to help." Because until it was caught, I wasn't going to be sleeping.

Weast stiffened. "Don't interfere."

"Is it because I'm a girl?" I insisted, not knowing why Trent was softly fidgeting. "A witch?" I said, and Weast spun to leave. "A demon?" I tried again, pushing past Trent and following Weast to the door. "Is it because I don't be-long to your club? Because I'm not human?"

Weast stopped, and I skidded to a halt. My heart pounded as he turned, but I didn't back down, even if Glenn had real fear in his eyes.

"That's it, isn't it?" I said. "You won't let me help be-cause I'm not human."

Thumbs in his pockets, Weast rocked back and forth on his heels. "Pretty much."

"Rachel, be careful," Trent whispered at my elbow, but I was tired of it.

"Wow." I lifted my chin. "And I thought all the Neander-thals had died out."

Weast's lip twitched. And then, without a word, he walked off. Glenn hesitated, clearly torn. "It's not because you're not human," he blurted as Weast hit the door and left. "Rachel, please. Stay out of this. Don't convince Weast that you're a threat."

"How is helping them catch a serial killer a threat?" I asked, mystified.

Glenn's eyes were pinched, and he looked awful. "You need to stop," he said, hunched as he walked backward to the door. "They don't like that you have such a close tie to the Goddess."

"Neither do I," I said sourly, jumping when Trent's arm went about my waist.

Glenn backed out through the door. "Lie low for a while? Forget you saw me. Us."

"Glenn!" came Weast's voice from the lot, and the frus-trated man grimaced.

"I'm trying to make this better," Glenn said. "Trust me." And then he turned and jogged to Weast waiting impa-tiently beside a black Hummer.

"I do trust you," I whispered. I was angry, but not at him. "Bye, Glenn." But he was already gone, and I slumped when Trent gave me a little tug into him.

"Excuse me," Jenks said dryly. "I want to see if Captain Tight Ass bugged your car."

"Thanks, Jenks," Trent said, and the pixy darted out before the door even closed.

"That was fun," I said, not liking that my knees were wobbly. Exhaling, I tapped a line and let it fill me, washing away all the unease.

Trent pulled out a chair, and I flopped into it. Silent, he sat next to me in the middle of the store. In the lot, Jenks's dust glowed under Trent's car in a fitful come-and-go light. "Maybe you should sit this one out?" Trent suggested, and I looked askance at him, surprised.

"You too?" I said. "Why?"

He shrugged, an uneasy expression creasing his forehead. "Glenn is right. If Weast decides you're a threat, he might try to put you in the cell next to the zombies."

CHAPTER

14

MY BREATH WAS SLOW AND MY FINGERS WERE TINGLING with latent line energy as they rested on one of the books Trent had brought down from the safe room off the girls' nursery last night. I'd been whittling through them for hours, moving them from one end of the coffee table to the other as the sun rose, filled the great room, and now, as it neared noon, began to slip away. That the book on my lap was a demon text went without saying, but if you had to read a demon curse catalog, sitting in the sun was a good place to start.

Tired, I slumped deeper into the indulgent leather couch facing the never-lit fireplace in Trent's great room. The space itself was huge, being three stories tall, one side all window that looked out onto his pool and patio. It was unusually warm, and I was having trouble staying awake even with the no-doze amulet. I could smell coffee brewing, the heavenly, nutty scent drifting down from the living quarters on the third floor like heaven itself.

Neither Trent nor I had slept, and after a night of looking at ugly curses, I'd had enough. The only charm I'd found that might have been remotely helpful had been one to wake someone up, and I flipped to it. *Sleep not, but be awake,* I read, translating the Latin. It was demon magic, meaning all I had to do was tap into the collective and say the magic words. *"Non sic dormit, sed vigilat,"* I whispered, jerking when my heart gave a pound and my hands shook. It was like slamming a venti, and I took off the no-doze amulet before I gave myself an aneurysm.

Breath held against the coming puff of burnt amber, I snapped the book shut. It was the last, and as I dropped it on the spent pile, my gaze went to my handwritten notes. Several of the books now had crisp new sticky notes hanging out of them to mark the charms, spells, or curses that might contain or capture a malevolent energy source, but even though Trent's library was unique, I doubted anything I'd found hadn't been tried by the demons before—tried and failed.

Leaning forward, I fingered a slim volume that had been especially disturbing. *Just who was Trent's mom?*

Oh, I'd found lots of magic whose intent was to capture, but none lent itself to work on sentient energy, like the baku. How did you catch a sunbeam? *With another sunbeam?* I thought, shuddering at the memory of the Goddess's divided mystics, some bent on killing the Goddess and forcing me to take her place, the rest shredding my mind to kill me so I couldn't. The last thing I wanted to do was engage the Goddess for help. If even *one* of her mystics recognized me, I might be right back fighting for both our lives. Everyone else they ignored as we used the energy they sloughed off to change the laws of nature and do magic, but I was the one who first taught them how to comprehend an existence that was based on mass, not energy, and that memory died hard.

I exhaled, making a fist to squeeze out the last of the latent magic that had soaked into me, then shaking my hand to send little trills of static power out to be lost. The large estate was empty without the high voices of the girls and the responding rumbles of their dads. They'd be coming back tonight. I didn't have to leave, but I would.

Twisting, I took my phone from my pocket to check the time. It caught the ring that Hodin had given me, and the dull silver engraved band came with it, hitting the floor with a thump and rolling into the sun to glisten like an unsaid promise. Frowning, I picked it up, turning it to study the glyphs. It looked Celtic, the symbols intertwined with one another until it was hard to decide where one started and another left off. *Pretty,* I thought, wondering why Hodin had been so adamant that he wouldn't help Al. It had sounded personal.

Souls, I mused as I rolled the band between my thumb and index finger. Hodin claimed he could shift a soul's expression. It would change my neutral aura expression permanently, not simply for an instant the way all demons modified their auras to travel the ley lines. Other than ley line travel, there was very little concerning souls in either the demon or elf texts.

Maybe I'm going about this the wrong way, I thought, one eye squinted shut as I raised the ring to look through it to the covered pool. Auras, souls, souls, auras . . . My eyes closed and I gripped the ring in my fist as my eyes began to twitch despite that wake-up spell.

"Rachel?" Trent called distantly, and my eyes flashed open. "Sandwiches are ready."

Crap on toast, I almost fell asleep. What good is a wake-up spell if it doesn't keep you awake? "That coffee smells great," I said as I put my no-doze amulet back on, then Hodin's ring—just for safekeeping. A frown creased my brow, and I looked at it there, glinting dully on my finger. It fit. As if it had sized itself.

"I think so, too." Exhaling in pleasure, Trent set a well-loaded tray on the coffee table.

I sat up out of the comfort trap the couch had become. "Wow. You didn't just make all this," I said as I took in the array of cheese, crackers, fruit, and, yes, finger sandwiches. There was an insulated carafe of coffee, too, and that was where Trent started, pouring out two mugs of richly scented brew and handing me one.

"Maggie prepped most of it," he admitted. "I only put it together while the coffee perked."

The mug warmed my hands, and again my eyes closed,

this time in bliss as I took a sip. "Perfect," I said as it eased into me, working with the no-doze charm to bring me fully awake.

The mug clicked as I set it on the table, and I leaned forward to fill a small plate. Trent was already doing the same, and we were silent for a moment. Vertigo came and went when the no-doze amulet swung forward and back into me, and I tucked it more firmly behind my shirt. "You make the best coffee," I said, and he smiled, his eyes especially green in the reflected light.

"Flatterer." Seeming happy with the world, Trent eased down beside me with his plate, and we both looked at the pile of books. "Find anything?"

"Nothing that the demons couldn't have tried themselves in the past." I sighed as I took a bite of sandwich. Weast was being a dick for not sharing information. The I.S. was being a coward for ignoring what was going on, and Hodin was an ass for not setting whatever grudge he had aside and helping Al. *I am dead to him,* echoed in my mind. The way he'd said it implied more than the belief he'd died long ago, as if Al had turned his back on him as he had once turned it on me. I knew how that felt—when someone you needed abandoned you because of something you had to do to survive. *Stop it, Rachel. Hodin is not a kindred spirit. He's a dangerous unknown.*

"How do you hold something made of energy?" I said as I reached for my coffee again, and Trent scrambled to catch his plate when his balance shifted with my motion.

"Perhaps a circle that's held by a ley line, not a practitioner?" he suggested. "Or trap it in the line itself?"

I stifled a shudder as I recalled being stuck at the bottom of a ley line, my very soul being scoured away by time itself until I got Al free of it. I had saved him as much as he had saved me. Perhaps that was why he overlooked his anger and . . . listened. "I've never heard of a stand-alone circle," I said, and Trent frowned when I put my arches on the edge of the table.

"Maybe that's why it will work when we figure out how

to do it," he said, still looking at my feet. "We know the Order caught it once. Weast is pretty good at cutting off access to a ley line with that amulet." His head rose, his eyes alight. "How about that? It's energy, right? The baku has to be connected to the line in some fashion. Cutting that off might give us control."

I shrugged, not convinced. "The demon I talked to implied the baku gets its energy from the people it feeds on, not the line. I still think it has something to do with auras. That's what it's focusing on." Thinking, I put my feet back on the floor and added some cold smoked squash and grapes to my plate. "You catch a man with what he wants, not what he needs. Maybe we can adapt that spiral curse we used to snare Nina's soul."

"Put it into a soul bottle? Mmmm." Trent leaned deeper into me, and my weight shifted. "I don't think a spiral curse will work on something that has no soul. I mean, that's the point."

He was warm against my side, and my breathing slowed as we both slumped in thought. "I'm sorry about filling our weekend with this," I whispered, fatigue pulling at me.

Trent set his plate down and tugged me closer. "Don't go there," he said as he gave me a light kiss. "We are in this together. Besides, the sooner we figure this out, the sooner you can get some sleep. You're not much fun when you're tired and cranky."

A smile quirked my lips, and I snuggled into him. "I'm not cranky," I said sourly.

"Yes, you are, and I love you for it," he said as he eased his warmth against me until I couldn't tell where I ended. Slowly our breathing synchronized. The two of us were all alone in this big house, and it felt okay.

"There has to be a way," I said, my thoughts returning to Al in self-imposed seclusion. "The little info you found about the baku said it was the bogeyman for elven children."

Trent's arm slipped from around me, and leaning, he tugged an oversize children's book out from under my legal pad. "Sort of a beneficial spirit," he said as he dropped the beautifully illustrated book open on our laps and leafed to the right page. "One that eats the nightmares of children so they can go back to sleep."

Together we looked at the swirling purple and gold hovering over a scared child in his bed, the parents peeking supportively around the door. "Sure, but if you called it for no reason and the nightmare wasn't scary enough to fill it up, the baku would eat you. I swear, parents can be so cruel sometimes. You think maybe the reality is that the baku was eating the kid's soul?"

"What an awful, terrifying thought," Trent said, but his frown said he was considering it. "The kernel of truth in the fairy tale," he murmured as he closed the book and dropped it on the pile. "Remind me to put this on the locked shelf. I'm not reading this to the girls."

"No problem. I'll get you a copy of the girl-empowered fairy tales my mom read me." I shifted to make room for him as he eased back. "Let's look at what we do know," I said as the coffee began to hit me. "Glenn said the baku took refuge during the day in a real presence, one that they couldn't nail down yet. The, uh, demons said pretty much the same thing," I said, trying to keep Hodin's name out of it. "If we could identify the host, we could maybe stop the baku by trapping whoever is dumb enough to be hosting it." A host that was in danger, if Hodin was to be believed. But I wasn't sure I cared, if that person was willfully sending the baku out to kill people.

"We need a list of who wants the demons dead." Again Trent leaned forward, this time for a cookie, and I shifted a few feet down the couch, tired of his up and down. "It's a pretty long list."

"Not if you winnow it by who might know about the baku." Crap on toast, it was probably someone on Trent's Christmas card list. Sitting almost sideways on the couch, I picked at a cracker. "Who has the baku targeted so far? Where's the logic here?"

Head bobbing, Trent pulled a cookie apart to get to the filling. "Average people."

"At first," I agreed. "Then it hit Al. Me to some extent. Perhaps the baku was trying to find Al and the others got in the way." Trent eyed me in concern, and I fidgeted. "Or maybe it was weak after its extended capture and needed to build up its strength before tackling a foe that knew how to fight it. Dali said it nibbled away at the soul, shell by shell, which implies it takes time to destroy someone completely before it can take them over."

Okay, it had been Hodin, not Dali, and I looked at his ring when I took a sip of coffee.

"Shell by shell?" Trent asked, voice intent. "Are you sure those were his exact words?"

Embarrassed for not only my lie, but that Trent didn't catch me at it, I nodded. But I didn't want to admit it had been Hodin. I wasn't afraid of his death threats. No, it was that damned feeling of kinship born from separate but identical trials that was keeping my mouth shut. I knew him, his desire to belong, and the fear that went with it. *Rachel, you are a Turn-blasted fool.*

"Souls have shells?" I asked as Trent rose and went to one of his glassed bookshelves.

"I'd call them layers, but sure." Trent's back was to me as he unlocked the cabinet with a key hidden on the shelf next to it. "You can see it in how the girls are developing. Almost by the day their emotions are becoming more complex, but they started out very simple.

"Give me a second," he said softly, distracted as he opened the door and scanned the spines of a small section of what looked like theme books. "I think this was it," he said as he chose one near the beginning and closed and locked the cabinet again. "This is one of my mom's journals," he said as he came back and sat beside me.

"I thought she was a genetic engineer," I said as we sort of slid together again, our heads bowed over the yellowing pages filled with a careful script. A warm feeling of belonging stirred as our body warmth became one and a faint thrill crept through me. Trent was many things: a drug lord, a politician, a philanthropist, a cold-blooded killer, a student of magic and science both. This was the Trent I liked best, intent on solving a problem others could not, where his skills dovetailed so beautifully it was almost a crime.

"She was." Trent confidently flipped through the pages. "But she had to give up her career after she married my dad. It was the sixties, and the more well-to-do you were, the more you had to conform. She spent a lot of time recovering lost elven magic. They called it a hobby. A *hobby*," he said, clearly disgusted. "She worked harder than anyone I know and got zero credit for it."

"Mmmm. I'm glad we live in more enlightened times," I said, appreciating the way Trent smelled when he got excited. All cinnamon and sugar. Like a cookie.

Oblivious to my thoughts, Trent kept shifting the pages. "She kept a diary from the day the Turn started until she died. I've read them all at least twice to try to remember her. There's a lot about my siblings until they died—mostly good; my dad—mostly bad; her horses—all joyful."

My eyes traced the faint frown lines now furrowing his brow. I'd forgotten he'd had older siblings once. "I'm sorry," I said, and he flicked a distant smile at me before returning to the text.

"She doesn't mention her magic studies in her diary very often, which makes me think there might be another set of these somewhere." His lips pressed in what I guessed was an old annoyance. "She was first a scientist. I can't believe she didn't write everything down. This one here was a few years after she got married." Slowly his smile faded as he flipped a page, finger running down the careful cursive. "Quen worked for my dad even back then. I think she'd be delighted to know that Quen had a little girl named after a witch-born demon."

"That'd be me," I said as I tugged him closer, wishing we had more afternoons like this.

"Here it is," he said, and I looked down.

"'My heart hurts,'" I read aloud when Trent remained silent. "'And now that I can sleep, I can't. Agnent is gone, and it pains me more than I want to admit. It might be easier if I knew what happened, but he's gone, and only the ache remains.'" Excitement trickled through me as I looked up, but Trent was still reading. "That sounds like a forget curse. Who is Agnent?"

"No idea," he said shortly. "He's not mentioned in any other volume. Okay, this is what I really wanted you to see."

He turned back a page, and I leaned over the text. "'Woke up to Agnent blowing a hole through the wall. He tapped a line in his sleep'"—I hesitated, tamping down a flash of fear—"'but he seemed okay apart from being afraid to go to sleep. He says he feels like he's being eaten alive, shell by shell. So tired. Haven't slept in days. Quen and Kal are meeting someone who says they know who this thing sleeps in. He won't let me go with him. He's a chivalrous ass.'"

"Kal is my dad," Trent said, answering my first question. "Short for Kalamack. He never liked his first name much."

"Which is?" I prompted.

"Same as mine."

I nodded, sort of remembering something like that when I'd looked up his I.S. file three years ago. "I think I would've liked your mom," I said as I traced her words with my finger. "Hey, some of the pages are torn out."

"You noticed that, too," Trent said flatly, but it really wasn't a question. "The 'shell by shell' sort of stuck in my mind. It made no sense at the time."

"It doesn't make much sense now, either," I said. "You know what this means, right? Your mother helped catch the baku in the seventies. Jeez, how often does this thing get away?" I reached to take possession of the journal, but Trent pulled it away and closed it, his mood somber. "Does she say how?" I asked as he stood and went to put it away again.

"No. It's probably in those missing pages."

The click of the key in the lock was loud, and I couldn't

help but notice that he put it in his pocket, not back on the shelf. "Not much help, then," I said as he sat down, perched on the edge of the couch with his elbows on his knee and his expression lost in thought.

"It proves that this thing can be caught, though."

"But not how." I put a hand on his back, feeling the worry in his shoulders like rocks. I leaned in, putting pressure into trying to rub the tension out. "Maybe . . ." I hesitated, my hand's motion across him slowing. "Maybe capturing it involves the Goddess."

Trent jerked, his expression holding a decisive surety. "If it does, then you're sitting this one out. I'm not losing you to that tricky bitch again."

Tricky bitch, eh? "Mmmm." My hand began to move again, and his shoulders to ease. "What was that your mother said again? Oh, yes. Chivalrous ass?" I chuckled when he frowned, adding, "Don't worry about it. I'm not doing any elven magic."

"Good."

Finally his shoulders fully relaxed, but I didn't stop, just glad that he was here, and I was here, and we were doing this together. "The girls will be back tonight," I said, my gaze drifting about the empty room. It was easy to imagine them here, growing up as a bold ten, a blossoming fifteen, a confident twenty. Marrying Dali's apprentice. *God, that was a weird dream.*

Trent shifted to glance at his watch. "Not for hours yet."

"I only meant we could ask Quen. He might know if your mother had any secondary journals. Ones that might cover what someone ripped out."

"He won't talk about her," he said. "But I'll press the issue. This is important." He turned, taking my hand in his and his eyes widening as he noticed my new ring. "Where did you get that?"

"Oh!" I hated that I was flushing, and I forced myself to not jerk my hand from his. "Ah, the demon who bought the no-doze for me." Trent's expression tightened, and wanting to reassure him there was no issue here, I took it off and handed it to him. "It's a call ring," I said as he looked over the twined writing, and then through the hole as I had. "Put it on. Twist it. I'm guessing it works like a private scrying mirror."

Trent handed it back, and I let out a breath I hadn't known I'd been holding. "It looks elven," he said. "This demon got a name?"

"Trenton Aloysius Kalamack, are you jealous?" I said playfully as I put my ring on.

"Damn straight I am," he admitted, the rims of his tall ears red.

Smiling, I slid closer until our thighs touched. "He, ah, knows how to adjust how a soul expresses its aura. He offered to tweak mine so the baku won't target me. I could get some sleep."

"Huh. I thought auras were female-demon things." Trent went still, worry pinching his brow. "You know . . . if he put it back to your original expression, Bis could teach you how to jump the lines," he said hesitantly.

"Sure, and maybe the mystics could find me," I finished for him. "I already told him no, which was why he gave me the ring in case I changed my mind." I slumped, depressed. "I want to talk to Al about it first. Get his opinion." Something that might not happen now. *Not Al,* I thought, shoving the panic down. He couldn't die. Not after surviving everything else.

Everyone who becomes important to me dies.

"Ah, Rachel, can this demon change your aura a second time if the mystics *are* still looking for you?"

I forced a smile so Trent wouldn't know how much this hurt. *Damn it, Hodin. What is with you and Al?* "I'd think so. It's burning me up, Trent," I said, and he took my hand, his fingers lacing through mine, grounding me. "The little snot could change Al's soul same as mine, and he won't. Selfish, pigheaded moss wipe." I gave in and sniffed. So I was upset. I had a right to be. "It's not even a matter of payment. He won't do it."

"You, ah, do realize that if you watched him change your aura, you and Bis could probably change Al's, too."

My head jerked up, and I stared at Trent, elation pulling me straight. "Trent, I love you," I said, pulling him close for an exuberant kiss. "You know that, don't you?"

"Rachel, about the Goddess—," he said, but I'd already pushed back and was twisting the ring on my finger.

"I won't do it if it can't be reversed," I said as I stood, scanning the room for any sign of the demon, but there was nothing. My eyes narrowed, and my lips pressed. Head down, I spun the ring again, going widdershins this time. Still nothing.

"He's not coming," Trent said, and I huffed at his obvious relief.

"You mother pus bucket of a lame-ass demon!" I shouted, tired and cranky and feeling mean. "You are a cowardly ball of spider snot!"

"Maybe the spell went bad?" Trent reached out, and I sidled away, not wanting to be soothed.

"It's not bad," I almost snapped. "He just doesn't want to show!" Ticked, I pulled the ring off and stuffed it in my pocket.

"Ah, how about some more coffee?" Trent asked, and the sound of plates clinking rose.

"Sure." Angry, I fell back onto the couch as Trent gathered everything but our cups and headed up the stairs. The sound of his steps grew faint, and I stared at the steaming pool and wiped a tear of frustration away. I wasn't going to cry. "Cowardly ass demon," I whispered, "you've spent too much time as a crow."

Then I frowned, pulling myself up and wiping my eyes at the clatter of pixy wings. I knew better than to shout. Jenks could hear me half a county away. The last thing I needed was him trying to make me feel better with his lame-ass dad jokes, heavy on the vulgarity.

But it wasn't Jenks who pulled to a black-sparkle halt over the stacked demon books. It wasn't Jumoke, either, though the pixy facing me had the same dark curling hair. Jumoke could never have afforded the glitter of black gold woven into the flowing robe bound tight at his waist and fluttering in the breeze from his wings.

"Hodin?" I said, recognizing him. "Have you been here all the time? Damn it, I told you to stop spying on me."

Hodin darted up and I pressed back into the couch. "I'm not spying on you. And I'm not a cowardly ball of spider snot," the pixy-demon said, hovering just before my nose. "Say it."

"You are not a cowardly ball of spider snot," I blurted, then looked up at the third floor, where Trent had gone, and lowered my voice. "If you shift my aura, can you shift it back?"

Hodin the pixy sniffed, turning in midair and rising as I'd seen Jenks do a hundred times before. "I'm not working here," he said, and then my eyes widened at the sudden falling feeling in the pit of my gut.

"Trent!" I shouted, but I don't think the word made it past my lips as Hodin yanked me into a ley line, and I was nothing more than a thought.

HODIN'S AURA SKATED SMOOTHLY OVER ME IN A PROTECtive cocoon even as I felt myself dissolve. Before he could do more, I snapped a bubble around myself to maintain a bare semblance of privacy in my thoughts. Even so, I got the sensation of a satisfied nod from Hodin at my quickness. The hum of the lines scoured through me to make my synapses tingle pleasantly. I had no idea where we were going, and I reached for my phone to call Trent when we misted into existence.

"My church?" I said, voice echoing in the two-by-four-scented darkness of the vestibule. It was after noon, but the construction-cluttered sanctuary was dim, lit only by the remaining window and the red-and-green glow on the sawdust-dirty floor.

"I have no spelling lab as of yet. We will use yours. Such as it is." Hodin strode forward and I followed. He'd changed. Not just from a pixy back to his usual tall, broody self, but from his dark leather to an extravagantly embroidered vest, robe, and . . . pantaloons?

But it was the robe that caught my attention, the glistening rich purple at his shoulders darkening to black at the hem brushing the floor. It was bound about his waist with a gold sash that jingled with tiny fringe bells. Wide sleeves draped long, making it a rather dangerous outfit to spell in even if the weird mix of demon and ancient elf made him look eminently capable. I'd never seen anything like it. His head was bare, but a traditional cylindrical elven cap wouldn't have been out of place.

"I can't truthfully say that your spelling lab is a pleasure," Hodin muttered, twitching his hem free of sawdust as he wove past the construction equipment. "But we will likely be undisturbed, and sometimes that's more important."

I stiffened, shifting direction to avoid walking over the plywood covering the hole in the floor. "We've had some issues. You aren't catching us at our best."

Hodin paused as he gained the ankle-high stage, where the coffee table and chairs still remained. "Us? Do you mean you and . . . *Al*?"

It was the first time I'd heard him call him Al instead of Gally, even though he'd almost spat the word. "Me, Jenks, and Ivy," I said, and he seemed to lose about half his annoyance. "Al doesn't share space with me."

"You may yet survive." He stood with his clasped hands hidden in his sleeves, effectively blocking my way up onstage. "Before I do this, I want to know why you changed your mind."

I squinted up at him. "You were there. Spying. You tell me."

His eyes narrowed. "I was not spying. Say it so there's no future complications."

Fine. I cocked my hip, not liking that he'd put himself higher than me. "In return for me and Bis keeping our mouths shut about you, you're going to teach me how to do this, and I'm going to change Al's soul expression." My chin lifted. "Chicken."

"You think so, eh?" he said, but he'd dropped back, and I immediately took the step up.

The challenge in his voice was irritating, and as he brushed the sawdust off the couch, I shifted the dried lasagna dish from the top of the coffee table to under it. Sure, he'd bitched about my spelling space, but it felt good here and we both knew it. "What kind of complications? What do I have to do? Kill someone?"

I looked up at his silence to see him eyeing the shadow of the cross still on the wall. "Just who you are is all. What you want to be," he said softly.

"What is it between you and Al?" I asked, and he turned, lip twitching. "Yes, he's an ass, but when you know why, it's almost charming."

"Charming?" Hodin gestured, and a woven basket of spelling supplies materialized on the table. "You have no idea what he's done."

I snatched a gold silk scarf from the top and began to wipe the stray ions from the table. "I'm not totally ignorant," I said, remembering throwing up and crying in a FIB bathroom after reading the crime scene reports of what Al had done as Piscary's murder weapon of choice. "But what I'd like to know is what did he do to you."

Hodin stiffened. "Perhaps you should contact your elf before he shows up."

"Perhaps I should," I said, embarrassed that I'd forgotten. "Excuse me."

I dropped the silk scarf and stepped away. Calling would be easier, but I didn't want Hodin listening in, so I simply texted Trent that I was okay and at the church learning how to shift my aura and that if I could wake up Bis, I'd jump myself back to him before dinner and we could take Ellasbeth's car to her and pick up the girls together.

But when I pocketed my phone and turned to find Hodin waiting, a stab of fear brought me up short. The mystics hadn't shown any interest in me since Newt had become the Goddess, but I hadn't done much ley line magic, and certainly nothing as flagrant as this promised to be. "Does this require the Goddess's attention?" I asked. My voice quavered, and I hated that he heard it.

"No," he said shortly. "I need to speak to your gargoyle," he added, eyes on the exposed rafters.

"Before sunset?" I flopped into the chair across from him. "Good luck with that."

Hodin frowned at the raised dust glinting in the dusky

light. "Call him." He leaned across the table in challenge. "You *do* know how to call him?"

I sat up, embarrassed. "He's only fifty years old. He's not going to stay awake." Hodin sighed, and then I felt myself warm as I realized he was looking at my no-doze amulet peeking from behind my shirt. "Oh. Yeah. Hang on."

"Hang on?" Hodin muttered. "Does something happen when you summon your goyle?"

But I'd already settled myself, and tapping the nearest line, I mentally shouted, *Bis!*

Hairy church bells. Bis was suddenly awake, his alarm obvious. *Rachel? Where are you?*

I felt bad at his panic, but at least it was keeping him awake. *I might have found a way to shift my aura so you can teach me the lines. Want to try it?*

Bis's fear vanished, replaced by a suddenly sleepy elation. *It's hardly afternoon*, he thought, his thoughts slurring somehow. *You're, like, what? Downstairs. Sure . . .*

My blurred focus tightened on Hodin. "Here he comes," I said, but my proud smile faded at the sudden crashing from the vestibule stairway and Bis flew in, almost hitting the wall before landing on my shoulder to make my hair fly. "Hi, Hodin," he slurred, eyes drooping as his tail wrapped around my back and arm. And then he was asleep, his snoring like a resonating bell as I blinked fast and tried to hide my heartache. Despite his catlike size, he was as light as a bird on my shoulder, but what hurt was that I couldn't feel the lines through him. Not like before.

Eyes narrowing, Hodin frowned at us. Embarrassed, I awkwardly wrangled the no-doze amulet from my neck and dropped it around Bis's. Still there was no change, and I tweaked the kid's foot with a shouted "Bis!" Finally he snorted awake, his red eyes blinking owlishly and the white tufts of his ears standing out strong against his blush.

"Um, sorry," he said to Hodin, his feet pinching me in his nervousness. "Why don't you have a line matching your aura? I thought all the demons remade their lines."

"I did not," Hodin said sourly.

"But you had one once," Bis insisted, head cocked as he "listened" to the demon's aura. "Europe?"

"Enough." Hodin's annoyance showed in the slant of his eyes. "If you tell anyone about me, I will pull Rachel's heart from her and feed it to the nearest dog. Understand?"

"Sure," Bis said around a yawn. "I'm Bis. World breaker." He held out a fist, and when Hodin ignored it, he let it drop. "Bell clapper," he muttered, and Hodin's frown deepened.

"Don't worry about it," I said as I reached to touch Bis's feet. "He's got lost-boy issues."

Hodin unlaced his arms and leaned over the table. "So we are all in agreement," he said shortly. "I shift Rachel's soul to her original auratic expression to hide her from the baku, and you both keep your mouths shut about me."

"Baku?" Bis interrupted.

"I'll tell you later," I whispered. "If Hodin here can shift my soul expression, I can shift Al's, and he will be safe."

"Not to mention I could teach you the songs the lines sing so you can jump them by yourself," Bis said, and his grip on my shoulder tightened in excitement.

Hodin began to tie back his sleeves with a gold cord he took from the robe's pocket. "Do you agree, Bis, world breaker?"

"Agreed," he blurted, now fully awake and eager.

Hodin eyed us sourly. "But there will be no instruction while you're wearing that."

"Hey!" I exclaimed, feeling Bis's claws leave me an instant before I misted out, returning to find myself unmoved, but not unchanged. "Dude," I said, my attention going from Bis, now perched on a nearby sawhorse, to myself. Hodin had dressed me in a smaller version of his own robe, and I quickly shifted the extravagant silk to make sure I still had my own clothes on under it. "Oooh, thanks," I said as I felt the fabric between my fingers and let it fall. Mine had that same purple-to-black gradient, but it was lined with silver instead of gold. There were little stars on the hem, too, and I smiled.

"Sleeves?" Hodin directed, and I fumbled in the robe's pocket, sash bells jingling as I found the silver ties and bound them safely back. "It's a spelling robe," he said. "It helps neutralize the effects of your aura when working in the higher magics. I'm surprised that Gally hasn't given you one, but Gally was always a *hack*."

My smile faltered. "I'm not your student," I said, and on his perch, Bis's nails dented the wood. "And I never will be."

"We'll see," Hodin said, making me wonder if this was why he was being so helpful. If he snagged me as a student, the demons might tolerate him. I kind of thought that was why they tolerated Al. "This is a complex curse. Very little is in the collective. We start from a clean slate."

Hodin pulled the basket closer, and I eagerly looked in to see the expected menagerie of supplies: snips, a ceremonial knife black with age, yellow wax the size of a golf ball, several bags tied with colored ribbons and tags. Taking out the largest satchel, Hodin threw it at me. I caught it by rote, used to having Al throw things at me.

"Circle, please," Hodin said, surprised I'd caught it. "As large as you can manage."

I stood, bells jingling. "Uh . . . ," I said, guessing the bag held salt.

Hodin looked up from his row of tiny bags. "Can you manage the table at least?"

"I can close the circle at Fountain Square," I said dryly. "If you really want one as big as I can manage, I need more salt." Damn, I felt as if I could do anything in this getup, but that was probably the point. It even had a hood.

Hodin pursed his lips. "Then whatever size you want," he amended.

"Sure." Smug, I noisily dragged Bis's sawhorse into my proposed circle.

"You good?" I asked, and Bis nodded, his eyes wide. I followed them to Hodin fussing with his little bags on the glass table. Then I did a double take. It wasn't glass anymore but slate. *Cool.* The salt went hissing down as I paced an even circle to enclose the couch and two chairs.

"Bis," Hodin said abruptly, and I jerked, needing to shove the salt back to an even line with my boot. "I'm satisfied that you've bonded to Rachel despite your youth."

Youth? I thought. The kid had sung the end of one world and the beginning of another.

"Thank you." Bis's wings turned red and his white ear tufts vanished as he pinned his ears.

"I'll need guidance to shift her soul's expression. If we're changing it to hide her from the baku, we may as well attempt to return it to her original. A demon reduced to public transportation is appalling. To do so, we will first separate her aura into its constituent parts, much as a prism divides a beam of sun into a rainbow. From there, you can advise me on what to change."

"Yes, sir. Thank you, sir." Bis shifted his wings, and the wood under his nails creaked.

Nervousness curled up through me like smoke as I sat down across from Hodin. Safety from the baku would be nice. Giving that same protection to Al would be even better. Regaining the ability to get around like a demon was frosting. "My only worry is the mystics might recognize me," I said. "I'm not doing this if you can't easily shift it back."

"I can return it to its current hue," Hodin said, sounding amused at my fear. "And despite your thoughts that you can waste the knowledge on that ill-begot, insufferable, low-life, poor excuse of a demon you look to, you will do much of it yourself."

"Fine with me," I said, wondering if he was lazy or simply evaluating me as a possible student. *Not going to happen, Hodin.* "Let's do it."

Hodin checked his tied-back sleeves. "Rachel? Invoke your circle."

Formal much? Exhaling, I strengthened my grip on the nearest ley line to let more flow through me, and as I felt myself relax in its warmth, I moved a molecule-thin band of reality delineated by the salt into the ever-after. A sheet of gold swarmed up, streaked with red and hazed with only a whisper hint of black patina. My old smut was gone, used to balance out the new ever-after. My nearly pristine aura had gone a long way in convincing the witch's coven of moral and ethical standards that I wasn't a "bad" demon. Sheesh.

Hodin gestured to Bis, and the kid obediently poked at it, confirming that nothing had changed in the last twenty minutes and he couldn't pass through it. Bis, having imprinted on my aura, was the only person able to move through my circle with impunity. At least, he had been until Newt had changed my aura. Any demon could jump me from place to place using the ley lines, but only Bis could teach me to do it by myself. I often thought Newt had been a little smug after shifting my soul resonance, fully knowing Bis wouldn't be able to teach me how to jump the lines. Sort of like a nervous parent taking the car keys from a new driver.

To be honest, my aura-laced circle looked the same as it always did, but souls, and hence the auras that sprung from them, were like retina patterns, always the same, but forever changing.

Hodin took up his crucible and ceremonial knife, both black from use and time. "A crucible of blood, please," he said, handing them to me. "From your Jupiter finger, if you will."

Bis blanched to an ill-looking gray. "I didn't know you'd have to cut yourself."

Hodin wanted far more than the usual pricking of my finger, and I sighed as I set the crucible clicking upon the slate table. "Don't worry about it," I said. Breath held, I ran Hodin's knife across my index finger. Immediately my shoulders eased. It was so sharp that I'd hardly felt it, and the bright red gush was startling. "Good?" I said as I massaged some out, and he nodded. "How much is that?" I asked, thumb pressed to the cut to get it to stop. "Five cc's?"

Hodin wordlessly extended his palm, and I gratefully set my cut hand in it. His fingers closed about me, and I lost the tension in my shoulders as a healing ward coursed through me. "Thanks," I said as I pulled away, and he inclined his head graciously. "But how much is in it?" I said, looking at the crucible. "I'm not going to bust my ass to learn this if you're going to leave out key parts so you can be smug and pretend I don't know what I'm doing when it doesn't work."

Hodin blinked, and Bis stifled a rocks-in-a-garbage-disposal giggle. "It doesn't matter," Hodin said. "The more you have, the more distinct the flames."

"Oh." It was one of *those* curses, and I frowned, not liking how loosey-goosey it was.

"Once you have your aura source, sketch the glyph to give structure to the energy." Hodin picked up the stick of chalk he'd brought, hesitating before snapping it in two and handing me the larger piece. "Unlike most curses, this one begins with an unexploded pentacle."

"Uh, I don't know that one," I said, and Hodin's goat-slitted eyes flicked up.

"I didn't expect you to. No one but Newt and I knew what they were good for." Hodin's dark features bunched. "The intent of most curses is to bring things together to create change. It requires an exploded pentagram, or pentacle rather, and since that's all anyone uses, the exploded part is left off. We will be separating in this instance, so we begin with the older and rarely used closed pentagon from which the pentagram is formed."

I leaned forward as Hodin sketched a pentagon with five lines radiating inward to a center point. My lips parted when I realized he never lifted the chalk or went over the same line twice. "How did you do that?" I said, and Hodin smiled. It looked rare, seeing the pleasure on his face that he'd done something to surprise me, and still holding the warmth of it, he leaned across the table and drew a second one for me to use. I watched intently, losing the how of it even before he finished. Frustrated, I gripped my chalk, hoping that Al knew the skill.

"Add a small inner circle to create the five caves where you will place the candles," Hodin said as he drew a perfect circle at the center of the pentagon, delineating five new individual spaces at the center of the glyph. "If done correctly, the candles will move to the points of the exploded pentacle," he added, explaining nothing. "Draw your circle," he barked, and Bis and I jumped.

I sent the chalk hissing around to make a circle inside the pentagon, my eyes flicking to the nearby basket. Unless the candles were in one of those little bags, there weren't any.

"Now burn your blood to ash. Do you know how to do that?" Hodin asked.

"Yep." I strengthened my hold on the line, and after I estimated how much I'd need to evaporate five cc's of liquid, I bubbled the crucible in a tiny circle, exhaling as I whispered, *"Celero fervefacio."* With a pleasing burst of flame, my blood turned to ash.

"Nice control," Hodin grudgingly admitted as he peered across the table.

"I burn things a lot," I said, and Bis snorted his agreement.

"Blood carries the representation of the soul's energy, which is why banshees and vampires ingest it," Hodin said, and I nodded. I knew this already, but that he bothered to tell me meant that he wasn't entirely stingy with knowledge. "We make the required candles so as to infuse them with the ash. The beeswax is an inert carrier, the dried moonwort is to open the flames, and the fat garnered from pumpkin seeds will extend the flame's life."

"To prevent any auratic contamination as you would get from fat from even an unborn pig," I said, and Hodin hesitated in his motion to untie his three bags as if surprised. "What should the bees be feeding on? Anything special? It smells like chicory."

"It is." Hodin gave me a cautious look. "You will also need milkweed sap."

I inched closer, knees touching the table, when Hodin opened the last bundle to expose a length of green milkweed, totally out of season. "As a binder and dispersal all in one," I said, familiar with sympathetic magic.

"Yes."

Hodin's last word had been wary, and I met his eyes. "My mother is one of the premier spell modifiers in the U.S. I picked up a few things."

"Perhaps you're up to this after all," he said, a faint respect in his voice. "Mix a pinkie-nail amount of the moonwort, pumpkin oil, and milkweed sap with the ash within in the crucible. With the addition of the beeswax, it will solidify into a matrix suitable to make several candles."

He pushed everything at me along with a little wooden spoon, and I cautiously picked it up. *Wood? He uses wood? No one uses wood.* "Everything is measured with the same spoon?" I said. "Right in the same crucible as the blood? Wow. What do you use to stir it?"

Hodin looked at me as if I was stupid. "The spoon?" he said, and Bis stifled a giggle.

I winced. *Not ceramic? This guy is really old-school.* "Okay, but if you're using wood, what kind is it? I'd think hickory would be best, seeing as it helps unlock things."

Hodin shifted to make the bells on his sash tinkle, his thoughts unknown.

"Or maybe it doesn't matter," I muttered as I used the spoon Hodin had given me, dumping everything in the crucible with my ashed blood and mashing it all up with the beeswax. I really wanted to weigh the chunk out first, but didn't dare, and when I cut the milkweed and just squeezed several drops in at Hodin's encouragement, I cringed. This was unconscionably inexact. If it didn't work, it wouldn't be my fault.

"The wick is cotton," Hodin said, clearly recognizing my unease and apparently taking offense. "Harvested under a full moon and spun by hand before sunrise. Once your substrate is evenly mixed, roll it into a length to apply the wick."

"Virgin cotton. Got it. Thank you," I said. "Don't you normally make candles by repeated dipping?" I asked, feeling weird as I rolled the wax into a long snake as if it was Play-Doh.

"Yes," he said, sounding embarrassed this time. "But for

a single use such as this, applying the substrate to the wick is sufficient. Must you question everything?"

"When I don't understand what's going on, I do," I said, deciding not to ask if me manhandling the wax was going to contaminate it with my aura. It wouldn't matter if it was my aura we were trying to see, but when I did this for Al, I was going to use a ceramic paddle.

"You will need six candles," Hodin said. "All cut from the same length, one for each of the five chakras we are interested in and one for the All."

I could almost hear him capitalize his last word, and I was willing to bet the All candle would be going in the center of the pentagon. But then I frowned. How was I supposed to get the wick in the candle?

Seeing me hesitate, Hodin prompted, "It's acceptable to simply flatten your substrate, apply the wick, and work it into a cylinder again before you cut the candles from the whole."

"Okay." Rolling my eyes at Bis, I squished my snake flat, pressed the long wick Hodin gave me into it, and folded the soft wax back over it. I felt like a kid as I estimated how long to make each candle, but Hodin seemed to think I was doing okay. "Snips or knife?" I prompted, and Hodin pushed the snips to me.

His shears were simple and unadorned, more like mine than Al's overdone extravagance, and I brought them to my nose first, rubbing the metal at the unfamiliar smell. "Pewter?" I asked, and Hodin blinked his red goat-slitted eyes.

"Ye-e-e-es," he said warily.

"Cool." I didn't have pewter snips, but I bet Al did. Lower lip between my teeth, I cut my wax snake into six equal segments. I desperately wanted to ask another question, but didn't like his increasingly obvious agitation. "I thought there were seven main chakras, not five," I finally blurted, wincing at Hodin's expected grimace.

"There are thousands," Hodin said. "But we're interested in five. Forcing someone's aura to change beyond a safe limit will cause insanity. It's a weapon." His eyes came back to mine, black in the dim light. "All our magic is. If

Newt had changed your inner shells, you would be insane."
He hesitated. "Are you insane, Rachel?"

"Depends who you ask," I said as I pulled the wicks up
and tidied the raw ends of the candles. "Okay?" I asked,
wincing at my lumpy versions of birthday cake candles.

"*Okay* would be the correct word," Hodin grumped as
he handed me his gold scarf.

"I've never had to make my own candles," I said, embarrassed, as I cleaned my fingers. "It's easier to buy them," I
added, and Bis giggled like grinding rocks.

"I'm sure it is." Clearly miffed, Hodin tugged his
sleeves, accidently untying one of the cords holding them
back. "Place your unlit candles within the caves created by
the inner circle with words of movement. In this case, *wind*,
water, *earth*, *fire*, and *thought*. Be sure to begin at the space
to your right, then move to the upper left, the upper right,
the lower left, and finally the top cave. This gives a balanced motion. The last is placed in the center with the
words *simper reformanda* for the ever-changing perma-
nence of soul."

Now we're getting somewhere, I thought as I took up my
first candle. "Words of movement," I said as I set the first
candle in the open space and did as he asked. I perked up,
interest growing as I felt each set candle connect to the ley
line, becoming part of the circuit the magic would flow
through, becoming part of me until the curse was twisted.
Beaming, I looked up, my smile fading when Hodin lifted
his eyebrows at my unabashed delight. It was magic, high
magic. Why wouldn't I think it was cool?

"Light the center All candle with *solus ipse*," he directed, and I leaned forward, holding my sleeve out of the
way as I pinched the wick and marshaled my thoughts.

I alone, I thought as I said the Latin and lit the candle
with a thread of ley line energy. Nervous, I drew back, and
Hodin nodded his approval. The flame wasn't the usual yellow, but tinted gold from my aura and streaked with red.

"The next process is important. Attend," Hodin said,

bringing my attention back to him. "Using the All candle, light the bottom right wick with the words *hunc effectum*."

For this purpose, I thought as I did so. He was being devilishly finicky on which one to light first, meaning if I screwed up here, it wouldn't work. I winced at the spilled wax, but Hodin didn't seem to care as the new candle sputtered to life.

"Replace the All candle," he directed, and I did before I made more of a mess.

Hodin nodded his approval at the new flame tinted with that same shade of my aura, and I exhaled. "Now use the candle you just lit to light the next," he said, a hint of what might be respect in his voice. "Upper left. Set it in place with *ex animo*."

From the soul, I thought as I did, hand trembling to spill more wax when the flow of energy seemed to trickle faster through me.

"And the third with the newest flame with *semper idem*."

Always the same, I echoed in my thoughts, then repeated it in Latin as I lit the third with the flame of the second. The energy flow had become noticeably stronger, and I concentrated on my breathing so Hodin wouldn't think I was a newbie at this, even if I was.

"And lastly, with the candle you just lit, kindle the final with *a maiore ad minus*."

The ley line tracing through me glowed, and I felt as if I was breathing out stardust. *From greater to smaller,* I thought as the last candle lit with that same gold, red, and black tint.

"Did she do it right?" Bis said, his craggy brow furrowed. But nothing had changed.

Disappointed, I slumped. "Crap on toast," I said softly. "They look the same to me."

"Of course they do." Hodin leaned over the table with his chalk and wrote something, his finery looking odd among the construction debris. "You haven't finished." He pulled back to show that not only had he written a phrase of Latin, but he'd written it upside down so I could read it properly. "If you will," he said, tapping it.

Nervous, I steadied myself. I could feel the line energy passing through me, tingling through my chi and down into the earth through the soles of my boots. *Please work,* I thought, but it wasn't a plea to the Goddess. No. Never that. *"Obscurum per obscuris,"* I said, jerking at the sudden burst of line energy falling to nothing in me.

"You did it!" Bis all but crowed, and my attention flicked from him back to the table. My lips parted. The candles had moved. They'd just . . . moved. I had set them at the center of the pentagon, but now five of them were outside of it, all arranged in a perfect circle at the points of a pentagram etched in ash that I hadn't drawn.

Delighted, I turned to Hodin, seeing his flash of surprise before he hid it. *He thought I'd fail?* My center candle still stood, now burning with a mundane yellow, but the rest? They'd shifted color. The first was gold, the second a dull red, followed by a faint blue, a silver-tinted green, and, finally, a muddy brown. I had separated my aura into its constituent parts, showing shades that were usually hidden by the dominant colors, like green hides the yellows and oranges of leaves until fall and the chlorophyll dies.

"Wow," I said, and Hodin seemed to hold himself straighter.

"That's the song your soul now sings," Bis said, pointing, and the demon nodded.

"Hodin, that is amazing," I said as I leaned closer, and he hid a flash of pleasure.

"Thank you." Hodin eased back into the couch. "Bis, what do I need to change so you may again pass through Rachel's circle without breaking it?"

I sat up straighter as Bis carefully hopped to the overstuffed arm of my chair. Ivy would have his hide for sitting there, digging his claws into the sawdust-laden suede, but we'd have to get a new set anyway. Everything smelled like sweaty Were and wolfsbane beer.

Bis went quiet, his focus going from the entire spread to

the red one. I thought it telling none of them seemed to be being consumed, as tall as they were when we started.

"Her red is sharper. Not more, just sharper," he amended when Hodin mouthed a word of Latin and the flame deepened.

"Better?" Hodin questioned after he whispered something else, pairing it with a ley line gesture. "How is that?"

Bis bobbed his head, his tail curling over his feet when the red flame reverted back to the original shade, but somehow . . . cleaner looking. "Good," he said. "Rachel doesn't have silver in any of her outer shells. Her course is gold, red, blue, purple, and green."

Nodding, Hodin whispered a few more words, and my eyes widened as the colors shifted.

"How come I don't have any silver in my outer shells?" I said, remembering that both Ivy's and Trent's auras had silver sparkles.

"Because *you* don't know the worth of freedom," Hodin drawled.

But Trent and Ivy do? I wondered.

"Rachel's purple is more greenish, less intense," Bis directed, distracting me. Lee's primary color was purple, but it was still embarrassing, seeing as it was symbolic of a hefty ego.

"Pride is good in moderation. It keeps people from stepping on you before you have the strength to back your voice," Hodin said, seeing my discomfiture.

Perhaps, but I still winced as he turned his attention to that candle, muttering phrase after phrase as Bis shook his head, not satisfied until it met some shade I couldn't see. Slowly I slumped, and Hodin became smug. I could do the curse all right, but I didn't have a clue how he was shifting the colors. Damn it, this wasn't going to help Al at all, and I scowled across the table at Hodin. He'd known it all along.

"Her green covers a much wider spectrum," Bis said, and at Hodin's gesture, the last candle's color deepened so as to be almost black.

"Too far." Bis's claws deepened their grip until I heard the suede tear, but they eased as did the candle's tone, and Hodin quit muttering when Bis nodded, his wing knuckles rising high over his head. "Perfect." The kid grinned at me, his black skin wrinkled in pleasure. "That's your real soul song, Rachel."

"Thanks, Bis," I said as I offered him my hand and he sidestepped up onto my shoulder to where he felt right.

"Then let's see if it takes," Hodin said, writing a new line of Latin on the slate table again. "If you would?"

He pointed to the Latin, and I pulled myself straighter, mindful of the ever-shrinking All candle. *"Ut omnes unum sint,"* I said, silently translating it as *They all may be one*.

Both Bis and I jumped as the line energy flashed through us, and then I gasped, tears pricking as every last ley line above the horizon was suddenly ringing in my thoughts.

"It worked!" I wanted to grab Bis and throw him in the air, or give him a hug, or dance him around the hole in the floor. But I just sat there, touching his feet as tears silently spilled down my face. I had missed it. I had missed it like an arm or leg, and I looked up at Bis when his tail curved around my wrist. An oily tear brimmed and fell from his eye, and I reached up and wiped it dry.

"Yes, it did," Hodin said softly, brow furrowed not in puzzlement but maybe in thought.

Embarrassed, I quickly wiped my face. But he hadn't noticed my tears, his attention fixed on the pentagram. The lines of ash still showed where the candles had been, but the candles themselves were gone. It was only the central one that remained, the one that had never moved, again burning with my aura's cheerful gold and red.

"Blow it out to seal the changes, Rachel," Hodin prompted, and I touched Bis's feet.

"Together?" I said, and his weight shifted as I leaned forward. "One, two—"

"Three," Bis said, and together we blew at it.

The lumpy candle went out, and a thread of black smoke smelling of burnt amber rose.

"Well-done," Hodin praised as he plucked the candle from the center and handed it to me. It was still warm, and I set it on the table. "Keep it safe," he said, and I nodded. It burned with my aura and it could be used to target a spell or curse at me. A bullet with my name on it.

"Well, let's see him do it," Hodin prompted, and I grinned. I couldn't help it.

Wings open, Bis eagerly hopped to the table. His tail smeared the pentagram's lines, but it probably didn't matter, seeing as Hodin was shoving things into his basket as he prepared to leave. "Make a circle, Rachel," the kid said, and I nodded.

"Rhombus," I whispered. The molecule-thin barrier rose up around me as usual, bisecting the floor and creating a sloppily made circle that was unlikely to stand anything that really wanted in, but that wasn't the point. I nodded, and Bis extended a gnarly hand, finger pointed as he touched my circle . . . and passed right through without breaking it.

"We did it!" the kid crowed, jumping into the air with one downward thrust of wing and spinning madly. Sawdust flew, and I closed my eyes until he landed back upon my shoulder, tail whipping around my back and under my arm. Again the glory of the lines hit me, almost making me pass out, and I bubbled my thoughts to numb them. Yes, I had missed seeing all the lines at once like this, but they were overwhelming when I got them so clear and raw from Bis. But even more important, it was my freedom. For Bis, it was his reason to exist, his entire species having been created by demons with the sole intent to help them learn how to travel lines of energy. We had a lifelong bond, Bis and I, and now—we both felt complete.

"I can sing the lines to you," Bis said joyfully. "Which one do you want to learn first?"

Hodin chuckled, the low sound cutting through my delight like a nightmare. "Yes, jump the lines," he said as he ran a knife over the slate table to get the worst of the wax up. "Show everyone what you can do. How *will* you explain it? No one *alive* knows the curse to permanently shift a soul's expression." His eyes narrowed and he stood, waxy knife in hand. "We have a deal, Rachel."

"You really suck. You know that?" I said, and Bis's ears drooped. "I can't help Al with what you've told me. What is your problem with him anyway? Did he sell you a bad familiar or something?"

Bis's tail tightened around my arm in warning, but I didn't care. I had risked taking instruction from Mr. Dark-and-Broody to help Al. That I might be able to jump the lines alone was secondary. And now . . . I had nothing but a promise to not tell anyone about Hodin and an ability that if I used it would lead to questions that would out him. *Damn it, Al. I hate it when you're right.*

"My issues with Al are not your concern." Clearly pleased with himself, Hodin ran a hand over his spelling robes and they vanished to turn him back into his dark, somewhat unkempt self. "You two aren't going anywhere until I say, and most certainly not without a spotter. Which would be me." He dropped his knife into the basket with the rest. "Line jumping is an art. Besides, aren't you at all curious if the mystics are interested in you?"

Mystics, I thought, my fear cutting through my anger.

"Not that I can see," Bis said rather grumpily, clearly not ready to let go of his anger. "At least, not out of the ordinary. They're around like usual, but they aren't swarming you."

"What do you want for the rest of the curse, Hodin?" I said flatly. "I'm saving Al."

"You're a worthwhile student," Hodin said, telling me he'd been judging me as much as I'd been judging him. "Too confident," he added, looking lanky and slim in his black jeans and leather boots. "But I imagine that nearly killing yourself a few more times will curb that."

"Yeah?" I flopped back into the chair. Bis left, his ears at a nervous slant as he returned to the sawhorse. "Well, you're too close with information that could be the difference between success and failure, but I imagine that your student going to someone else for clarification and study a few times will curb that. If you ever *get* one."

Hodin looked at the door behind me, and I leaned forward over the table. "Why are you even pretending to help me? Is it because you think I wouldn't keep my mouth shut if you asked? Or are you trying to poach me from Al?"

"You think you're worth that much?" he said, and I felt my face warm.

"Maybe Al and Dali are right," I pressed, my anger and worry for Al bypassing my already thin filter. "That you're dangerous and not to be trusted."

Hodin frowned, mood clearly bad. "The two are not always synonymous. You yourself are dangerous and yet trustworthy."

Flattery? I thought as I stood as well. "That's just it," I said, sash bells ringing as I put a hand on my hip. "I don't trust you. Why did you bother to teach me this?" I gestured at the slate table. "To see my frustration at not being able to help Al? Is that how you get your fun? Seeing me try and fail?"

Hodin's head came up, and my anger hesitated at the almost hidden desperation showing in his clenched jaw. "I . . . I want back in," he finally said, and with that, my anger fizzled to nothing. "You did it," he said, sounding hurt. "You not only used forbidden magic that called the Goddess to the very doorstep of your soul, but you have an unrepentant relationship with the elven Sa'han."

"They barely tolerate me," I said softly.

"But they *do* tolerate you," he insisted. "True, your Kalamack elf is the self-styled prince of the elves, but he's an elf!"

"And you were doing so well," I said with a frown, and Bis made a rock-grinding chuckle of agreement from his perch.

"You fail to understand," Hodin insisted. "You're the *only* demon to whom I can say the Goddess isn't evil and have anything but a frown thrown at me. Yes, she's wicked," he said, his words finding the cadence of an often-said statement. "And a trickster, and distractible, and flighty in her alliances. She is cruel, and spiteful, and jealous." His head came up. "And powerful. We ignore her at our peril."

My sash jingled as I clasped my arms around my middle. "To ask for her help is worse."

"Perhaps." He sat back down on the sawdust-laden couch, his knees spread wide and his back bowed over them. "But they haven't imprisoned you for having done so, or the cautious acceptance you maintain of her. I've watched you enough to know it's not because you're no threat, and it's not because you're the only mature female demon. It's because of something you are. I want that."

"You can't have it," Bis said, his voice low in threat.

I stretched out a hand, touching him in reassurance. "I think he means he wants to learn what it is. It's not anything you can take, Bis. It's something you do." My eyes went hard on Hodin. "Or don't do."

He stiffened, head coming up. "I can't let them know I exist."

Frowning, I exhaled my tension, letting myself forgive his stubborn refusal because I knew where it stemmed from. Bis grumbled as I came around the table and sat down on the couch beside Hodin, a careful three feet and an acre of silence between us. "So what do you propose we do?"

Hodin leaned back, gesturing with a ring-decked hand. "See? There it is," he said, the tips of his black hair shifting about his eyes as he shook his head in disbelief. "You are foolishly risky. You don't even know me."

I smiled. It was exactly the same thing that Al had fixated on, causing him to risk and lose everything to save my life. And in return, I saved his. The "it" was that I didn't see "demon." I saw Al's soul. It was jumbled, and broken, and fierce—desperately needing someone to believe in him to mend the cracks even as he did ugly, mean things. And as I sat beside Hodin's depressed slump, I saw the same.

"You should come out," I said, looking at his ringed hands clasped between his knees. "Tell them you exist. I'll stand with you. For what it's worth. They don't listen to me much."

Hodin's fingers stilled, and on his perch, Bis made a high-pitched squeak. My soft smile vanished. *Did I just walk into his trap?*

"If you help me save Al," I added, and Hodin jerked.

"Never," he said, then stood up.

I pressed back into the couch to look up at him. "Seriously? I hand you a get-out-of-jail card, and you throw it back in my face? What is it with you? God! It's like you're brothers or something."

Hodin's lip twitched, his expression stilted as he took his basket of spelling supplies in hand. And then my mouth dropped open in understanding.

"Oh. My. God!" I stood up fast. "No way. No friggin' way!" I exclaimed, and Hodin flushed a dark red. "You have to let me tell him you're alive."

Hodin took a breath, but his wrathful expression hesitated at a soft scuff at the front of the church. Head cocked, he turned to the door, now open to spill sunlight over the dusty floor.

It was Zack, a plate of food from the steps in his grip, and I stared as the young elf froze, lips parted as he took in my spelling-robe finery. He clearly hadn't expected to find anyone here, and I felt a flush of anger. It might be full of holes and sawdust, but it was still my church.

"Uh, sorry," Zack said as a hundred things fell though my mind.

What is he doing here? Working for Landon? Is he here getting something to target the baku's next attack with?

But what came out of my mouth was an indignant "You! I want to talk to you!"

CHAPTER

16

ZACK SPUN, BOLTING TO THE WIDE CHURCH DOORS.

"Don't let him leave!" I exclaimed, but Hodin was faster.

"Clausus!" Hodin shouted, flinging a hand extravagantly, and Zack skidded to a halt as the doors slammed shut in front of him, the boom shaking the walls.

Plate somehow level in his hand, Zack turned, staring at us for what could have been a fatal three seconds if I'd wanted to hurt him. I strode forward, my spelling robe snapping about my feet. Zack dropped to the floor. Plate at his heels, he spun, scribing a circle with what looked like a big black Sharpie.

"Ita prorsus!" he exclaimed, and I halted as a greenish purple barrier rose around him, glistening like a soap bubble.

"Hey! That's a permanent marker!" I said, ticked as I halted before him.

Zack rose from his crouch, that plate of what looked like lasagna held close. His face was pale, and his cropped ears looked wrong after seeing Trent's untouched ones, especially with Zack's elven white hair and green eyes. He was too young to need to shave, but a faint fuzz showed it wouldn't be long.

"What do you want?" I said, then jumped when Bis landed on my shoulder, tail wrapping tightly across my back and around my arm. I wavered as the lines sang in my head, and then I bubbled my thoughts, muting the glory of them. "Are you here spying for Landon?"

"Landon is an ass. He's not in charge of me." His voice was young, but deep, having that same musical element that I'd noticed pure elves were blessed with.

"No? Then explain to me why he knows you and Trent doesn't," I said, testing his circle with a cautious finger. His greenish purple aura would have looked better with a little demon smut on it. As it was, it looked kind of thin. "You don't need to hide in a circle. I'm not going to hurt you," I said, feeling an odd quiver in the energy. It would fall, given half a reason.

He glanced at Hodin behind me and shook his head.

I don't have time for this. "Interrumpere," I said, flinging a hand out, and with a little pop, his circle vanished.

Zack's eyes widened, and he bolted, heading for that window in Ivy's room, no doubt.

"That's a good one." Hodin leaned against my chair and watched him run past.

"I got it from a ghost," I said as I gathered a handful of raw energy from the line and simply threw it past Hodin to explode in the hall.

Zack yelped, predictably skidding to a halt and darting to slide under Ivy's baby grand. When he rose, there was a ball of energy in one hand, that plate in the other.

"He didn't spill any of his lasagna," Bis said in admiration, but I was getting annoyed.

"Landon knows you," I said, then raised my hands in the hopes that he would stop trying to flee. "Landon wants Trent dead," I added as I eased forward. "Convince me why I shouldn't hit you with a binding charm and drop you in the I.S. lobby for trespassing."

Zack looked at the plate of food in his hand, and I made a warning sound when he moved as if to set it on the piano.

"Landon wants Kalamack dead," Zack agreed, his green eyes darting from me to Hodin. "But I'm not Landon. I want to talk to Mr. Kalamack, not kill him."

His cheeks were red and his chin high with rebellion, and though he was clearly hungry, it was just as obvious that it was a fairly new sensation. His fingers cradling that raw energy were strong with youth, not work, and I could smell the same hint of cinnamon on him that Trent always came out of his spelling hut with. *Landon's student?* I wondered, remembering Landon's annoyance with Al when he thought the demon was Zack.

Hands falling, I closed the gap between us. My touch was light among the ley lines as I stopped well back from the piano. "Maybe I should take you to Landon. He might get off Trent's case if I bring his runaway back."

"Rachel!" Bis warned, but I'd seen Zack's lips move.

The energy in Zack's hand flashed white, and with a shouted *"Dilatare!"* he threw it.

"Adaperire!" I exclaimed to trigger a flash of expanding air before it could hit me, but the kid's white spell fizzled before mine could act on it, and with a boom, the church's door slammed open instead.

"Sorry," I said as Zack yelped, his ears red as he yanked his zipper back up, but I didn't know if it was because his spell failed to act, or because I'd inadvertently unzipped his pants. For being Landon's student, he wasn't doing very well: his circle had been flimsy and what should have been an easy, powerful charm had failed to act.

"Perhaps I should leave . . . ," Hodin said.

"Will you help me catch him?" I said, exasperated when Zack ran for the open door.

"If only to see what you will do with him." Hodin gestured, and Zack stumbled, going down with a haze about his feet. He hit the floor with a muffled "Ooof," taking it on the chin in the effort to keep his plate level.

"Semper apertus," Zack gasped from the floor, his eyes on the light past the open door as he half-crawled to it. The spell, if it worked, would prevent another charm from closing it again. This was just sad, and I waved a hand with a whispered word to break Hodin's binding.

"Zack. Relax," I said, but the instant Hodin's hold on

him vanished, he scrambled up, that plate somehow still level as he backed away. "I won't take you to Landon. Why do you want to talk to Trent?"

"Landon said your pixy would kill me if he found me in your church." Zack's eyes darted between Hodin and me.

"Jenks?" Bis said with a laugh, and Zack paled. I could understand why, seeing as Bis's laugh sounded like rocks in a blender.

"Only if you tried to hurt me," I said, then stopped when Zack put up a warning hand. I was eight feet back, and I didn't like that that hole in the floor was right behind him, the plywood having slid halfway across the room thanks to my "open" spell. "Are you trying to hurt me?" I asked, and Zack's gaze flicked to Hodin, who was clearly interested in his answer as well.

"*I'm* not," Zack said, implying that someone was. He turned to leave, and I gasped a warning, but it was too late and Zack dropped right into the hole in the floor with a little shriek.

"Not very bright, is he?" Hodin came over and together all three of us looked down into the crawl space. Elegant swearing in the elven tongue was rising up, the unending flow enough to impress even Bis.

"Ah, are you okay?" I called into the depths, then stumbled when Hodin jerked me back. A green-tinted bolt of energy boiled up from the crawl space, hitting the underside of the roof and rolling like purple clouds.

"Curious." Hodin reached a hand into the fading stream of power, rubbing his fingers together to rate it. "That should've been a rather nasty but white curse to blind you for three days." His thin lips quirked. "It was twisted correctly, but the Goddess isn't listening and it fizzled."

"Like everything else he tried," I said, pity rising up. It sucked when you reached for your tools and they didn't work. "I can't leave him down there," I said, venturing a peek over the edge.

"Why not?" Hodin snapped his fingers and the basket on his arm vanished. "I could fix the floor right now, and no one would know. Every demon needs an oubliette with someone in it."

Bis's grip on me eased, his wings spreading behind my head to inadvertently focus the faint sounds of misery coming from the hole. Apparently Zack hadn't been able to save his dinner. "I'll get him," Bis said as he jumped from me. "I'm coming down," he said loudly as he landed at the edge of the hole. "If you hit me with anything, I'm going to slam my fist into your skull and it's going to hurt. Got it?"

Silence rose, and taking that as a yes, Bis gave me a black-toothed smile and dropped into the dark.

"Stay back!" Zack shouted. "I said stay away from me!"

"What the lily-white fairy shit is wrong with you?" Bis yelled back, and I blinked, never having heard that particular one from him before. "You came to us, beetle brain. All she's done is ask what you want, and you keep throwing shit at her? And it's not even good shit. Knock it off!"

I leaned over the dark hole, hands on my knees. Jenks's influence was showing, but maybe that's how Bis thought young people talked.

"It's not too late to shut him in," Hodin said at my shoulder, and I gave him a wry look.

"He's just a kid."

Hodin pulled himself straight, sniffing. "He's an elf. And he's from the dewar. His thoughts stink of old men."

I sighed, not sure what to do when Bis hauled himself over the burned edges of the hole, claws scraping. "He said he won't throw any more spells if you don't," the gargoyle said.

I licked my lips, stomach knotting when Hodin shook his head at my unspoken question. But I'd learned never to confuse a potential friend with a potential enemy. "Truce?" I directed into the crawl space.

"Truce." Blinking, Zack stood to put his head nearly even with the floor. He was a mess, lasagna on his shirt, dirt on his pants, and cobwebs in his hair. His mix of lost boy and angry pride struck a chord, and after hiking my spelling robe up, I extended my hand.

"Foot on the edge," I said, crouching to take Zack's hand, and using that as a fulcrum, I hauled the dirt-, cobweb-, and lasagna-coated kid up and out in a quick yank.

"Thanks," Zack said, somewhat sullen as he reclaimed his hand and edged from the hole. He looked behind him at the open door, and Bis frowned, a finger to his nose as if to tell him to think it over.

"Why do you want to talk to Trent?" I said, feeling over-dressed and unusually magical. The sensation strengthened when Bis jumped to my shoulder, his nails carefully spread to avoid digging into me or marring the beautiful fabric.

Hodin cleared his throat, and Zack shied. "Perhaps the more important question is," the demon drawled, "*who* are you?"

"I'm Zack," he said, his tone holding a little too much affront, as if we should know already and he was insulted. "Deual Sa'han, Zack Oborna."

"Deual Sa'han?" I questioned, never having heard the term.

Bis leaned closer to my ear, whispering, "I think he's the dewar's leader-in-waiting."

"Oh," I said flatly, and Zack flushed, his pride showing a hit.

"That is your *name*," Hodin said condescendingly. "*Who* are you?"

Zack's chin lifted. "I *was* Landon's student," he said, his anger sounding almost beautiful. "But not anymore. I left the dewar eight days ago. I'm no one now."

"And why, little elf, would you do that?" Hodin asked. He was standing unnervingly close to me, and I edged away.

A flash of fear furrowed Zack's smooth brow. "Because he's lying to me," he said, and my worry deepened when I saw the hurt of that betrayal. It went deep, deep enough to make him both trustworthy and unreliable. "He says he isn't, but some of the things he says happened can't logi-cally have occurred." Green eyes afraid, he looked at me. "But everything makes sense with what I've heard whispered in the halls about you. I've spent the last two weeks trying to find the truth, first in the dewar, and then in the streets, but everyone has a different story. And I can't get my magic to work right," he said, his voice rising as he blinked fast and turned away.

No elf can, I thought in pity, but seeing it in my eyes, he hid his fear and pulled himself upright. "I need to talk to Kalamack to see if he's lying, too."

"He's hungry," Bis whispered, and I shoved my pity down.

"You're the next leader of the dewar," Hodin said. "Go back. Believe what they say. It's easier than the truth that you won't like."

"Not anymore." Zack's jaw clenched, that same look of betrayal flashing. "I quit."

Yeah. Like Landon would have let him quit. But I wanted to believe him, and I edged closer. "You left the dewar? For good?" I asked, guessing he thought he was telling the truth by the amount of panic he tried to quash. "Why should I believe you? Landon has done everything but declare war on Kalamack's house." Yes, it sounded formal when I said it like that, but I felt formal, standing in this robe decorated in stars and tiny bells.

"Landon doesn't need me to kill Trent." Zack brushed at his shirt, making it worse. "He has his baku for that. Why would he send me? I can't even get my circle to hold," he said bitterly.

Landon is hosting the baku? I thought, excited. And then I dropped back a step, actually hearing what Zack had said. "But the baku isn't trying to kill Trent. It's trying to kill Al," I said, and then my knees became wobbly as the events of the last few days replayed. Oh. God. All this time the baku had been coming for me, not Al.

"It was trying to get you to kill Trent," Bis said, pressing close to my neck, and I felt sick. Two birds with one stone. Trent would be dead and I'd be discredited and in prison for killing him. Everything would turn to Landon. Landon would win.

"Just so," Hodin whispered. I was the baku's target. Me, not Al. Landon was trying to get me to kill Trent. *Son of a bastard.*

"Don't trust him, Rachel," Hodin muttered. "He's from the dewar. Young and easily moved to foolish endeavors that will get him killed."

"Why do you care what happens to me?" I said even as his warning rang true. "He knows about the baku and is willing to talk." I turned to Zack, not comfortable with his sudden confidence. "Okay. I'm the target," I said, doubly glad that my aura was again my own. "If Landon is the host, how does he control it?"

Zack looked up from trying to scrape his dinner off his pants. "He doesn't. Not really. His aura is all wonky, and sometimes I think it's the baku, not him. Landon doesn't want to believe it, but the baku is dragging its feet. Using him."

My hand touched Bis's feet. He was scared, too. I swallowed hard, my gaze going to my candle, still on the slate table. I'd be safe until the baku figured out I'd switched my aura, but Al might be in more danger in the meantime. *I'm never going to sleep again.*

"You're right. Trent needs to talk to you," I said, and Zack made an ecstatic fist-pumping gesture with a muffled "Yes!"

"Rachel," Hodin growled, but I had to move on this, and fast.

"You're not my teacher," I said, and Hodin put a hand to his head as if he had a headache.

"You'll take me to him?" Zack pushed forward. "I have to ask him if what Landon says is true. I know I'll be able to tell if he's the Sa'han."

"And how will you know that?" Hodin pressed, his voice oily with promise.

Zack brushed his shirt. "Landon says that Kalamack has murdered people to further his interests. That he puts himself before those he doesn't care about. That he's responsible for the rebirth of the demons, and that he has spurned a fertile elven woman of high standing for a barren demon with no worth, thereby thumbing his nose at the high elders. I need to know if it's true."

Barren demon? But I was too worried to take offense. Besides, all of it was true. Even the ugly parts. *Maybe this isn't such a good idea.* "Ah, Trent is all of that," I admitted. "But as long as I'm with him, the circle he protects encloses more than himself, including elves and demons both." I was spouting wise-old-man crap, but the robe seemed to bring it out of me.

"He really cares about the demons? Not just you?" Zack said in disbelief.

"Amazing, isn't it?" I said. Hodin bared his teeth in a thinly disguised smile, and Zack flushed. "I need to make a call," I added, patting my robe to find my phone in my jeans pocket.

"You need to make a call," Hodin echoed, and then he pinched my elbow, dragging me away. Bis flew from my shoulder, and then I jerked from Hodin's grip.

"I'm sorry about your dinner," Bis said, startling Zack when he landed beside him on the table saw. "I wouldn't have really hit you. Unless you tried to hurt Rachel."

"I've never talked to a gargoyle before." Zack's voice held awe, and Bis puffed in pride. "How can you stay awake? It's day."

"Rachel gave me an amulet," Bis said, showing it off, and then Hodin shifted to get between us.

"I'm all for letting people make their own mistakes," Hodin said, so close that I could smell the hint of burnt amber. "But that child has grown up in the dewar listening to old-elf lies. Get past the pretty hair and eyes, and all his thoughts are warped."

"Probably, but he can't be cooked all the way through yet. Excuse me," I said, finally finding my phone through the draping fabric. "I need to make a call."

Hodin's expression darkened. "This is a mistake," he muttered, arms going over his chest.

"Probably." I backed up a step and hit the icon for Trent.

The call rang twice before it was answered, and my shoulders slumped when Trent's voice eased out.

"Rachel, how did the lesson go?" he said, his preoccupied tone and the slight clatter telling me he was in the kitchen. "Can you line jump?"

My thoughts jerked back to Hodin, and I flushed in excitement. "It went great, and yes," I said, answering him, "Bis and I haven't tried it yet, but I don't see why it won't work. Hey, that young elf I told you about—"

"Landon's protégé," he said, surprising me. "Zack, wasn't it?"

"Yes." I turned to the front of the church, frowning as Bis demonstrated to Zack how big a gargoyle could get with enough water and proper motivation. He was already the size of a large dog, and as I watched, he puffed out again. But my impulse to tell him no spitting in the sanctuary faded when I saw him hit the five-gallon bucket in the corner with uncanny precision. "Ah, I'm looking at him right now. He wants to meet you. He's noticed some discrepancies in Landon's version of the truth."

"No kidding."

"And he wants to know how big a bastard you really are," I added softly.

"Bastard?" Trent echoed, and I smiled, hearing him begin to pay attention.

"Seeing as you save demon babies and generally disobey the dewar." I couldn't bring up Ellasbeth and the girls and how I was preventing Trent from reaching his potential. Not to mention the general bastardly behavior of Trent before I'd smacked him around enough.

He was silent, probably remembering stuff I didn't even know about. "It's like bringing a pit viper into your living room," he finally said, and I heard water running in the background.

"I know, but he can help with the baku. Zack says Landon is hosting it, which makes complete sense, seeing as, ah . . . Al isn't his target. I am." I took a breath. "To kill you," I whispered, sure he'd heard me when he said nothing. My nightmare swirled up from the folds of my brain, chilling me. I'd woken when I tapped a line, but what if I hadn't? What if it happened again?

"I'll meet with him," Trent said, voice cold.

I nodded, even though he couldn't see me. "Is now a good time?"

"Sure," he said immediately. "I'll see you in half an hour. I'll tell the gate to expect you."

I took a breath to tell him I'd see him in thirty seconds if Hodin would spot me, but he was gone and I closed down my phone, tucking it away in a pocket before gathering my candle and heading back to them. Bis saw me coming and spit out all his excess water, shrinking down to the size of a cat in three seconds flat and shaking as if warding off a chill.

Even worried as I was, I couldn't help a tingle of anticipation. I was going to jump the lines. "Okay," I said as Zack eyed me in mistrust, Bis next to him on the table saw. They'd bonded over Bis spitting thirty feet into a bucket, and I'd become the outsider. "Zack, you have ten minutes to convince Trent that you're not a lying bag of dewar hot air, and if I think for one second you want to hurt Trent, I'll dump you in Landon's office."

"I'm not going back to Landon," Zack said, but his relieved expression quickly shifted to a nervous fidget. "Ah, mind if I use your bathroom to clean up first?" He plucked at his shirt, brushing at the tomato paste stain.

"I do not have time for this," Hodin complained, and then Zack yelped, startled when Hodin jerked him closer and smacked his chest. "Stand up straight. Comb your hair. Must look nice for your lynching."

My lips parted. I'd heard those same words from Al at least a handful of times before.

"Back off!" Zack shouted, flushing as he pushed away from Hodin, but his anger vanished when he realized that somewhere between the smacking and the tirade, Hodin had used a brush-and-wash curse on him, and though he still looked hungry, Zack was clean, all signs of having been in the crawl space erased, down to the cobwebs in his light hair and the wrinkles in his cotton shirt.

"Softy," I muttered, and Hodin grimaced. "Relax," I said louder to Zack. "It means the demon *likes* you." Heart pounding, I extended a hand to Bis, and the gargoyle side-stepped from the table saw to my shoulder.

"Well?" I said in expectation, and we stared at Hodin, Bis's tail tightly wrapped around my arm. "You dragged me here. You have some responsibility to get me back. Either you throw us all there, or spot me. You might want to scare Zack into keeping his mouth shut before we go, though. I'm not responsible for anything he says."

Hodin's eyes narrowed, but when Bis began an odd, angry whine, the demon relented. "Fine. If only to see if you can manage it, I will spot your jump." He eyed Bis. "You can handle her if she gets it wrong?" he asked, and Bis nodded.

"She won't get it wrong," Bis said, tail tightening on me, and I felt a flush of gratitude.

"Jump?" Zack squeaked, his face pale as he backed up. "Like through the ley lines?"

Hodin's smile would've scared Buddha, it was so evil. "If you breathe a word about me, I will pull your insides out through your eye sockets. Quiver in fear if you understand me."

"Ah . . ." Zack continued backing away.

Excitement tingled through me, but maybe it was just the singing of the lines leaking past the barrier in my thoughts. I squared my shoulders, satisfied that Zack wouldn't run and Hodin wouldn't really hurt him. "Ready, Bis?" I said, and when his grip on my shoulder tightened, I exhaled, willing myself into the nearest ley line.

It was almost absurdly easy, and a thrill spilled through both of us as Bis tweaked my memory of the line and I adjusted my aura to match it more deeply. The faint whine of discord vanished to be replaced by the warm swirl of everything. It was like being energy itself, and I set my thoughts on Trent.

More of this, Bis nudged into my thoughts, and with a

chime that rang through me like sunshine, I felt my aura expression shift. It wasn't the deeper soul adjustment that Hodin had done, but a surface expression to make my outer aura mimic Trent's. It would draw me to him, and it was far more complex a pattern than the one needed to be pulled into a line.

I'd never be able to do this on my own, which was probably why the demons had engineered the gargoyles in the first place. *Thank you, Bis,* I thought, feeling a proud, rock-grinding chuckle in return.

And then we were there, or here, and my feet stood on the tile of the small dining area between the kitchen and Trent's living room.

Trent was in the kitchen, a smudge of flour on his apron with the tractors on it that I'd given him as a joke. The scent of chocolate was heavy in the air. *He made brownies?* I thought, and then he looked up, his expression brightening with love. My heart clenched. "You jumped!" he said, gaze going from my new spelling robe to Zack, popping in to hit the floor at my feet. "This is going to take some getting used to."

I nodded, suddenly self-conscious about the fancy robe. "Zack, you okay?" I said, ducking when Bis launched himself to that plate of cooling brownies. "Stand up so you can meet Trent."

But when I reached to help him, Zack gasped, backing away to almost scoot himself down the stairs in fear. "Zack?" I said, and then I spun to Trent at his cry of heartache and fear.

"What?" I said as I saw Bis beside Trent, both staring at me in horror.

"Mystics," Bis whispered, and I felt myself pale. "They recognized you, Rachel."

CHAPTER

17

TRENT SPRANG INTO MOVEMENT, BUT I WAS SCARED. "NO, no, no!" I exclaimed as my fingers began to tingle and a whisper of a presence grew in my mind. "Not again. I can't do this again!"

"Sit." Trent yanked Zack up from the stairwell before he fell down it, almost shoving the kid onto the couch in the lowered pit of the living room. "Rachel, call that demon!"

The ring. My hand shook, tiny bells ringing as I looked at it, and then I panicked as I saw the haze of silver dripping from my fingertips. There were so many mystics that I could see them. Enough had recognized me as I traveled the lines, and I had landed in Trent's living room trailing a living magic. Worse, they were probably spreading the news, gathering more, telling them they had found the next "becoming." If I couldn't stop this, the Goddess would track me down and kill me, because if she didn't, the mystics looking to me would spread through her like a virus, killing her. The Goddess might be all-powerful, but her mystics were the strength behind the throne, and what they wanted, they got. *Not me. Not me . . .*

"Rachel, call him!" Trent shouted, and I spun the ring on my finger.

Hodin! I shouted into my thoughts. *I am covered in mystics! Fix this!*

But he didn't answer. Terrified, I stared at Trent, a muffled curse slipping from him when he tried to touch my
shoulder and jerked his hand back. His hair was beginning
to float as more mystics gathered. I could feel him shunting
the extra energy back to the line, but the mystics only came
back with more. Line energy was filling the room with nowhere to go.

Zack stared from the couch as large oily tears spilled
from Bis. Trent, though, wasn't panicking, and I tried to
stifle my own fear. They weren't talking to me yet. I was still
sane. *Hodin!* I shouted in my mind, spinning the ring again.
And still he didn't show. *Now, Hodin!* I shouted into my
thoughts. *Or the deal is off and I tell everyone about you!*

My heart pounded as, with a pop of air, Hodin snapped
into existence behind Trent. "Good Goddess, I was busy,"
the demon snarled, clearly unhappy. "Did you imagine a
mystic?"

Trent shifted out of the way, his lips pressed in anger.
When Hodin saw me standing there, his face went ashen.
"Negare . . . ," he whispered, horror lighting through him,
and my throat tightened. "I thought you were exaggerating.
This is . . . Why are they focused on you? Even if you treat
with the Goddess, they shouldn't be doing . . . this!"

"Because I taught them how to comprehend life made of
mass," I whispered, and Hodin went even more pale. "They
like it better than life made of energy."

"I'm sorry, Rachel," Bis said from across the room, afraid
to get closer as he began to cry in earnest. "I'm sorry." He
beat his wings at nothing we could see. "Go away. Just go
away!"

But the mystics didn't, and I blinked, seeing stars. *Don't
start talking to me. Please.*

"Fix what you broke," Trent demanded, and Hodin
ripped his gaze from me.

"Ahh . . ." The demon spun in a tight circle, scanning
Trent's upper rooms in a glance. "Rachel, come here," he
said, taking the two steps down into Trent's informal living
room and with a touch turned Trent's lead crystal coffee

table to slate. "I'm not in my spelling clothes," he murmured as he patted his pockets.

"Chalk?" Trent offered, taking a piece of magnetic chalk from his pocket and tossing it across the room. He shadowed me, hands outstretched, afraid to touch me as I made my slow way to Hodin. It felt as if I were stepping on sparkles, mystics squishing out from between me and the floor. It was getting worse as the word went out.

"Bis." Brow furrowed, Hodin quickly sketched the initial pentagon. "Come here. Do you remember the mess Newt made of her soul signature?"

"It's burned into my brain," the little gargoyle sobbed, and I felt his heart breaking as he flew across the room to land atop the table. He'd wanted this so bad, and now it was going to be taken away again. "Rachel, I'm sorry."

"It's okay," I whispered. My heart was breaking, too, but I was scared, and I felt overly full as I wobbled down the two steps into the living room, as if I might spill over if I leaned too far. Back stiff, I sat on the edge of the chair, the bells jingling as I clasped my hands in my lap. "Hurry."

"Can you do this any faster?" Trent said as he made a fist and shook sparkles from his knuckles. "They're calling their friends."

"This isn't textbook," Hodin said, then blanched as he looked up from the glyph he'd sketched. "Um, you don't happen to still have your candle?"

"Here," I said, fingers numb and fumbling as I took it from my pocket.

"That will help." Exhaling in relief, Hodin rolled the lumpy candle, still warm from my pocket, between his palms before he set it in the center, where all the lines crossed. *"Simper reformanda. Solus ipse,"* he said, setting and lighting the center candle in one ill-advised gesture.

I was never going to be free of them, and my chest hurt.

"Okay, here we go. I've never tried it without the supporting candles. *Obscurum per obscuris,"* Hodin said in a commanding voice, his hands coming together in a pop of sound that made Zack jump.

"Black magic!" His eyes wide, Zack pushed back into the chair as the pentagon opened into the more familiar pentagram, the five points holding a ghostly image of a flame without a candle.

"Hang on, Rachel. It's working," Trent whispered, and Hodin shot him an annoyed look.

"I worked a quick fix into the boilerplate," Hodin said. "But I never expected . . . this. Rachel, I apologize. I thought you were exaggerating your claim. If I'd known, I never would have let you jump out like that."

"Just fix it," I ground out, light-headed and dizzy with latent power I hadn't called.

Eyes on flames that weren't really there, Hodin began muttering. I blinked fast as he untwisted the curse, feeling something in me shift and change as the red dulled, and the purple in my aura turned silver again. My hands shook as my cheerful green muddied with a dull yellow to brown, and once more, my soul reflected Al's aura.

"Bis?" Hodin asked, but the kid was crying, and thumbnail-size tears were falling heavy and warm on my shoulder. I hadn't even known he'd moved to it, and I touched his feet gripping me. "Goyle!" Hodin shouted, and Bis jumped. "Is it the same?"

"What does it matter?" Bis sniffed. "If it's different enough that I can't reach her, then it's different enough for the mystics to not see her."

Hodin nodded sharply. "Just so." He looked at me, his goat-slitted eyes holding what would have been pity in any-one else. *"Ut omnes unum sint,"* the demon said to seal the curse, and breath shaking, I leaned to blow my sputtering candle out.

With a pop that I felt deep in my gut, something seemed to twist and break off.

"Rachel?" It was Trent, tentatively taking my elbow as he crouched to put his eyes even with mine. "Did it work?"

"I think so." I blinked, trying not to cry. I was a runner. I was a demon. Neither one cried. But my throat was clos-ing up and I felt if I took a breath, it would come out weepy.

The tingling was beginning to dissipate, but I'd never be able to travel the lines alone. Always, I'd have to rely on someone else.

"I wanted you to have this, Rachel," Bis said, sobbing. "I'm sorry. It's not fair. I can break the world and open one anew, but I can't sing the lines to you."

"We'll find another way," I said, but I wasn't sure I believed it.

"Come this way." Trent stood, drawing me to a stand. "Let's see if they follow."

But I knew they wouldn't. Bis was on my shoulder, and I couldn't feel the lines through him, couldn't hear them sing, couldn't swim among them like silken dark water. I could still feel them if I reached for one, but all I saw were the shadows they cast. All I felt was the dross they shed.

Numb, I followed Trent across the sunken living room, shivering as I felt the mystics peel from me, leaving their warmth behind as if I'd walked from sunshine to shade. "That's better," Hodin said as the bells on my sash jingled to a stop. "They don't see you anymore."

"Rachel?" Bis warbled, his nails pinching me. "I gotta go. I need a minute. I'm sorry."

"It's okay, Bis," I said, and he vanished, right from my shoulder. He had gone, and I was left behind. I took a slow breath, finding it easier. "Thank you," I said, feeling flat as I met Hodin's eyes. "I owe you."

Hodin's lip twitched as something passed through his thoughts. "No, you don't." He tugged his robe tighter, hiding his bare feet. "Excuse me. I was in the middle of something." Then he hesitated, giving Trent a hard stare. "If you value her life, tell no one about me."

And then Hodin vanished with hardly a pop of air. Behind him, Zack started. Trent was still cupping my elbow, and I felt miserable. The lines of the pentagram seemed to blur. It didn't matter how fast I blinked, the tears were going to come. "I need some air," I whispered as I looked at the main stairway. No wonder Bis had left. This was miserable.

"Rachel, I'm sorry," Trent said, and I pulled from him.

"Will you all stop saying that!" I shouted, and Zack's eyes widened. My breath trembled in my chest, and I locked my knees. "I just need to think," I said, not meeting anyone's eyes as I paced to the staircase that led down to Trent's great room. My hair moved, but it was only the wind of my passage; the mystics were gone. "Is the front wall open?" I shouted as I started down, tiny bells ringing.

"Yes," Trent called back, and my pace never wavered.

Arms around my stomach, I headed down. I needed to be alone, if only for a moment. The great room was dusky with November's early sunset coming in the great window. My feet were silent on the stairs, and I felt the muffling silence fold around me, taking me in as I descended deeper into the nothing. I held my breath as I passed the second floor with the surgery suites and secondary living quarters, down to the first floor. Hunched and unseeing, I wove through the clusters of chairs and couches, breath held against the hurt.

The window wall was a shimmer of silk. Trent had asked Lee months ago to modify the energy barrier to be visible so the girls wouldn't crash into it. Babyproofing had a new meaning when magic was involved. I put a hand out in case as I walked through the ward, shivering as the energy seemed to peel off the last of the mystics.

Finally I was outside. I lifted my head, bringing the chill air deep into my lungs as the soft chatter of the artificial waterfall and the scent of chlorine from the hot tub filled my senses. None of this was mine, and in a surge of motion, I pulled the spelling robe off in a tinkling of bells and sat miserably on the end of a lounger, my knees almost up to my chin and my legs awkwardly splayed. Maybe if I had been at my church, it wouldn't hurt so bad, but I doubted it.

Bis and I had held everything for one glorious moment. The world had spread at our fingertips, waiting for us to spin through it at will. It had been my safety line in a world that would just as soon see me dead. Now I was back to being a demon who couldn't travel the lines without help. Even worse, I'd gotten Bis's hopes up, only to crumple them up and throw them in the fire.

"I'm sorry, Bis," I whispered, hoping the little guy was okay. We'd find a way past this, but I didn't know how, and I sniffed, the tears no longer important.

But then I stiffened at the faint rasp of dragonfly wings, wiping my eyes and sitting up before Jenks could see my misery.

"Hey, hi," I said, trying for blasé, but the soft gray-silver dust he was spilling told me he'd already heard. "Isn't it too cold for you out here?" Silent, he hovered before me, his narrow features pinched in the glow of his wings. "They told you, huh?" I said, cursing myself when my voice didn't hold steady but rose.

Saying nothing, he shrugged and moved to sit on my shoulder.

Silent, we watched the ripples on the pool until we both got cold and I stood to go back in.

CHAPTER

18

"SO YOU TOOK SOME AIR," JENKS SAID AS I ROSE SLOW AFter leaden step up Trent's grand staircase. His wings were cold as he pressed against my neck to warm himself, and my new spelling robe was carefully draped over my arm. "So what? Do you have any idea how often I *took some air* when Mattie and I were first married?"

"Thanks, Jenks," I said, knowing he was still upset I'd endangered myself if he was bringing up Mattie. As we neared the upper level, I shook off the feeling that we were ascending to the treetops. I couldn't help but wonder if that had been Trent's intention. The man loved climbing trees, though he was embarrassed to admit it. I'd only caught him up one once.

"You think the kids avoided the Davros statue because of the poison ivy?" Jenks asked, trying to fill the void with something so I wouldn't notice the pain. "That's where *I* take my air."

Trent's voice was becoming audible, his musical tones moving up and down to soothe my raw emotions. I felt weak for having left despite Jenks's words, but I hadn't wanted Trent, or most especially Bis, to see my misery. Jenks, though? He could see it. I'd helped him through the loss of his wife, and though this wasn't the same, he understood.

"Mmmm, I smell scared elf," Jenks said as I began to pick out the conversation. "Someone has been playing mind games with Zack." Wings rasping from the cold, he lifted from my shoulder.

"Hey, ah, Landon told Zack that you'd kill him if you caught him in your church, so be nice," I said.

Jenks jerked to a hovering halt. "Nice? Tink's tampons, Rache. You never let me have any fun," he said before darting up and away, but I suspected he was less concerned with messing with Zack, and more concerned about telling Trent to stop talking about me.

Alone, I worked my way up the last of the stairs, slowing as my head rose above the level of the floor. Zack was slumped at the small table where the girls and I ate breakfast, but Trent was in the kitchen, still sporting that tractor apron. My lips parted when I saw Quen standing across from Zack, arms over his chest as if in disapproval. *He's back? Where are the girls?*

"Quen?" I said, my pity party easing. "Where are the girls?"

His smile thin, Trent wiped his hands on a towel. "With Ellasbeth. She has the entire week off, apparently, and for safety's sake, I agreed she can have them until Tuesday morning. Jon took Quen's place since I wanted Quen's opinion on the baku." He hesitated. "Isn't that right, Quen?" he added pointedly to make Quen grimace.

"I'm glad you're here," I said as I gave the older, battle-scarred elf a quick hug. "We need your help."

"I'm pleased you're all right, Tal Sa'han," he said formally, and at the table, Zack nearly choked at the elven term of high respect. "Busy night?" he added, giving Zack a sidelong look.

Jenks circled Quen twice before landing on his shoulder as if to prove to Zack that he was a *nice* pixy. "We filled him in," Jenks said. "He doesn't remember nothing about the baku."

"The Order probably wiped it out," I said as I dropped back, and Quen's expression darkened. "Is Bis here?" I asked as my gaze went to the top of the fridge, where he liked to stay, but the space was empty, and I shoved a stab of pain down.

"He needed some air, too." Jenks sat on Quen's shoulder and licked something off his chopsticks. "See, Rache. It's not that big of a deal."

Then why did I feel so bad?

"You just missed him." Trent was busy at the counter, shoulder moving as he shredded a chunk of hard cheese. "He went to talk to his dad, but if you need him, tap a ley line and call him. He'll hear you."

"Okay." At least we still had that, and depressed, I draped my new spelling robe over the back of the couch. "What did I miss?"

"Nothing unusual," Quen said dryly. "The Sa'han is insisting on putting himself into needless danger. *That's* why I'm here. I could have told, and did tell, him over the phone that I knew nothing about the baku."

"Quen," Trent complained, and the older elf arched his dark eyebrows to make Zack snicker.

Zack was probably why Quen had really left the girls to Jon, and I came into the kitchen. "What are you doing to upset Quen?" I said as I sent my arm around Trent's middle, distracting him as he drained a colander of pasta. "Mac and cheese?" I guessed.

Trent gave me a sheepish look. "I loved pasta and cheese when I was his age," he said, glancing past the open counter at Zack. "He looks hungry."

My arm tightened around his waist. "Mac and cheese is not what's bothering Quen."

Quen pointedly cleared his throat, and I eased my hold on Trent. Pointed tips of his ears reddening, Trent dumped the drained pasta into a huge bowl and added the cheese. "He's fifteen and his magic isn't working. How much danger can I be in?"

My eyebrows rose, and Trent avoided my gaze. We both knew how much danger Zack could be. Those had been upper-level charms he'd been trying to hit me with. "Your magic isn't working, either," I said as I snitched a chunk of cheese. Trent's mac and cheese was not the usual fare, and the sides of my mouth almost hurt, the cheese was so sharp.

"True." Trent stirred the cheese in, then began rummaging in an upper cupboard for a second bowl. Setting it on the counter, he leaned in, breath tickling my neck as he whispered, "You're going to tell me who that demon is later, right?"

I nodded, gaze flicking up to Jenks, Quen, and Zack. Later sounded good. I could now, seeing that Hodin had spilled the beans about himself. I hadn't done it.

"You cannot shelter a dewar elder," Quen said sourly, his arms behind his back, "especially when he's only fifteen."

"You want to take him in? Really?" I eased out of the kitchen, and Zack shrank down under my hard gaze. "In your compound with the girls," I said flatly. "You do know he's Landon's replacement." No wonder Quen was here.

"Was," Zack said, his angry, melodious voice sounding at home among Trent's casual wealth. "I was. I'm not anymore."

"Enemy of my enemy," Trent said with a little twist to his lips, but his smile worried me.

"Still . . ." I lowered myself to sit down across the table from Zack. "Seems risky. For both of you. You talked to Trent for five minutes—"

"It was twenty," Jenks said from across the room. "Then Quen showed up, and poof, no more talking. Just a lot of glaring and whispering."

No doubt. "Twenty minutes," I amended, "and you figure Landon is lying and Trent is the next coming of Gilgamesh."

Jenks landed on my shoulder, smelling like jasmine. "Jeez, Rache. I thought you said go easy on the kid," he said as he chewed a chunk of dried nectar.

"I'm not a kid." Zack's cheeks were red and his green eyes were bright as Trent slid a bowl of mac and cheese in front of him. "I'm almost sixteen. Landon is lying. The Sa'han's story makes more sense."

"Oh, so he's the Sa'han now." I put my elbows on the table and leaned in. Quen nodded his approval and dropped back a step, content to let me take up his battle. "Some guy makes you mac and cheese, and you believe every word he says. Zack, we need to talk."

Zack frowned sullenly, fork in hand. "I didn't come to that conclusion because of a bowl of pasta. Trent isn't lying. I can see it more clearly than if I had a truth amulet."

"Maybe Trent's a better liar," Jenks said from my shoulder, lips smacking as he ate the last of the pollen from his fingers.

"Landon was right about the demon babies, though," Zack said, his eyes on his as yet untasted dinner. "And how you kill people who try to stop you from repairing our genome."

"Well, I'm pleased to hear that." Quen took up a wide-footed stance at the far end of the table to look dark and threatening.

"That's in my past." Motions abrupt, Trent ran a soapy rag over the cheese-dusted counter. "I do not kill people anymore simply because it's easier than dealing with them."

"But you *did* save the demons," Zack said, still not having touched his pasta.

"And that's not going to change," Trent said as he ladled out a second small bowl of mac and cheese. "Ever. And you can tell Landon that when you see him again."

"I'm not going to see him again," Zack said, and I looked up, startled, when Trent put the second bowl in front of me.

"I doubt that." Trent put a fork beside my bowl. "You'd be smart to begin to prepare for it."

"Um, thanks, but I'm not hungry," I said softly, then flushed when Trent glanced pointedly at Zack. The young elf still hadn't taken a bite, and it suddenly hit me that he was probably worried that it might have been tampered with. "But it smells great," I added, taking a forkful. Yes, Al was still in seclusion and my hopes of jumping the lines had been crushed under the Goddess's uncaring heel, but Trent knew what to do with cheese and pasta.

Grumbling something inaudible, Quen eased back.

"This is really good," I said as my appetite woke up, and I pulled the bowl closer. Across the table, Zack took a careful forkful, and I stifled a smile when I heard a tiny moan of appreciation. Trent grinned as he returned to the kitchen, inordinately pleased.

For a moment there was only the sound of forks, but finally Zack began to slow down and sneak glances at me. "Did you really make the new ever-after?" he asked. I could understand why. I didn't look like much. "I'd never seen Landon that angry as when I asked him."

"She did." Quen leaned close, expression still sour. "She's the demons' premier tulpist."

"Bis helped," I said, slumping as I imagined his conversation with his dad. *It will be okay, Bis. We'll find a way.* "And it wouldn't have held without the combined efforts of the demons."

"Then you did make it? The new ever-after?" Zack's eyes went between me and Jenks, who nodded. "How about the St. Louis arch? Did you really drop it on assassins?"

"That was Trent," Jenks said, and Quen winced, confirming it.

"He was trying to make a deal with Ku'Sox to get Lucy back," I added. "Lesson one, Zack: never make deals with psychotic demons. I'll give you that for free." I hesitated, hoping I hadn't just broken my own rule.

Quen leaned in over the table. "Since you *are* here, tell us about the baku."

"Um . . ." Zack glanced at Quen before scraping the last cheese from his bowl and wedging it off his fork with his teeth. "I told you. He's working with it to kill Trent."

"How?" Quen said patiently, and my eyes tracked Trent as he took off his apron and came to sit beside me at the table. "How is Landon controlling it?"

"He isn't." Zack looked at the thin scrapings left in his bowl before reluctantly dropping his fork in and pushing it away. "Landon thinks he's in charge, but he's not. I can see a shadow of the baku in Landon's aura even when he's awake now. I think the baku is making all those people kill each other to waste time. Every day it's in Landon, it's eating away at his soul until"—Zack made the sound of a soft explosion, his hands mimicking it as well—"no more Landon."

"It's going to take him over?" I said. "Can't Landon kick it out?"

"Sure, if he wanted to." Zack looked longingly at the empty bowl. "But he won't until it's too late and he can't. Landon really wants you dead," he said with a low chuckle.

He was looking at Trent, and I didn't like it. Neither did Quen.

"So when the baku attacks someone . . . ," Trent prompted, and Zack shrugged.

"The baku only leaves Landon at night to look for her." Zack's eyes touched on mine, then darted away. "You know what gets me? I've told them the baku is using him, but not one of those old farts seems to care why the baku is taking so long to find you."

I slumped at the table. The baku knew *exactly* where I was, and I pushed my half-eaten bowl of pasta away. *Where are my no-doze amulets?*

"Landon says the baku is using weaker individuals to hone its skill before trying to control the dream of a demon, but I think it needs the time to acclimate to Landon before taking him completely over. His aura is looking sicker every day, and no one cares to question why."

It thinks, I mused silently. *If it thinks, it can be reasoned with.*

"But no one is interested in my opinions," Zack finished sourly.

"Landon can talk to it?" Trent questioned, and Zack bobbed his head.

"He sort of meditates." Zack glanced at my half-eaten bowl of pasta.

Trent nodded, his focus distant. "This makes sense. If it can push Rachel into killing me, it will be free to take

Landon over and have Landon's body and my stolen political power both."

"I know, right?" Zack said cheerfully, but this was bad. As soon as the baku felt it could take Landon over, it would quit messing around, attack me again, make me kill Trent, and rule the dewar as Landon.

Quen crossed his arms over his chest, a glimmer of worry marring his pox-scarred face. "Have you searched your mother's journals?"

Trent glanced at Zack and sat up straighter. "The ones I found, but there are pages missing, and I got the feeling that it didn't happen the way they wanted it to."

"Maybe she destroyed them so as not to incriminate herself," I suggested.

Trent's brow furrowed. "You should go over them yourself, Quen. It might trigger something," he said, and Quen nodded, not looking happy about it. "Zack," Trent said louder, and Zack jerked, startled as he covered a yawn. "How about a room for the night? We'll figure out what to do with you tomorrow."

"Thanks." Zack pulled himself out of his slouch. "I've not had a good sleep in a week."

Trent smiled in understanding, but it faltered and he took my hand under the table, giving it a squeeze. I didn't know about Trent, but I wasn't sleeping tonight. Sure, one of us could stay awake and watch the other, but I didn't like Hodin's claim that every attack left more damage, making succumbing to it easier.

"Rachel, perhaps I should take you home," Quen said, and I froze. He was going to take me home because I couldn't do it myself. It hadn't seemed to matter much until Bis and I had done it.

"Why?" Trent said, eyes wide. "I was hoping that we could keep each other awake tonight. We have a lot of research to do."

"I'm in," I said, but Quen's jaw was clenched. I didn't care if we'd made his night more difficult. I didn't want to go back to that empty boat.

"As you wish it, Sa'han. If you will excuse us?" Quen said stiffly. "Zack, it's this way."

"Quen, be sure to tell Zack the Wi-Fi password," Trent said as he stood and took first my bowl, then Zack's. "I doubt his phone will work out here."

"I ditched my phone last week," Zack said sourly as he stood and scuffed his feet. "Who would I call? Everyone I know is on the other side of the continent."

He was alone, and something in me shifted. I knew how that was.

Trent went into the kitchen and set the bowls in the sink. "I'm sure Landon would appreciate knowing you were okay."

Zack's expression flashed to a rebellious hardness, convincing me that he really thought he'd abandoned the dewar, but I knew better. He couldn't just leave the dewar. Not when he was being trained to lead it one day. I frowned as I remembered the spells he'd tried to use. *And Trent wants his help to figure out how to make their magic work again?*

"This way, short stack," Jenks said, his wings spilling a bright silver as he landed on Zack's shoulder to make the kid jump. I wasn't surprised that Jenks was trying to win Zack over. The kid was too much like all of us to ignore: rebellious, powerful, in search of something better . . . vulnerable. *Alone . . .*

I met Trent's eyes, totally understanding why he hadn't turned him in to social services.

"Relax. I won't kill you," Jenks said as they followed Quen to the stairs. "Unless you do something stupid like try to hurt Rachel. Or Trent. Or his kids. You can off Jon if you want."

"You're . . . ," Zack started, his words trailing off as he looked over the edge and saw Trent's great room. "Wow. You could land a helicopter down there."

"I'm what?" Jenks asked, turning to give Trent a thumbs-up. "Serious? Yeah. You think I wear this sword to look butch?"

And then they were on the stairs, their voices going faint as Quen trailed along behind.

Sighing, I ran my hand across the table to see if it was clean.

"I know what you're going to say." Trent began to rinse the bowls. "But what choice do I have? I'm not going to force him to go back to Landon, and he can't continue eating food off your stoop and sleeping on Ivy's couch. Quen will adapt."

"No, you did the right thing." I stood, going into the kitchen to lean against the counter. "I just want to make sure you know how dangerous he is."

Trent ran the sink full of water and squirted in some soap. "He's looking for something to believe in," he said, getting it totally wrong and totally right all at the same time. "That makes him more dangerous than all the spells at his disposal, which, by the looks of it, are considerable."

"Don't underestimate him," I said as I took up a dish towel.

Trent sank his hands into the water. "Besides, it's really going to cheese off Landon when he finds out where he's been staying."

"And there's the real reason," I said, and Trent grinned, but it faded fast.

"No." Trent dropped his eyes, his fingers amid the soap slowing. "It's because he's been taught and told to be this thing," he said softly. "And it's a really wonderful, amazing, powerful thing, something he's already good at and he likes, but he's not sure it's what he wants to be. He might not even know *what* he wants, but to not have the chance to find out . . . ?"

I took a slow breath, understanding. We'd both been forced into paths we were good at but didn't necessarily want. Actually, now that I thought about it, it was that realization that had let me begin to forgive Trent for what he'd done. I found his hand, drawing his attention with a soft squeeze. "Tell me if you need help convincing Quen," I said, and Trent nodded. Hard or not, risky or not, Zack would be given the time and space to work things out. We'd simply have to roll with it if Zack ended up screwing us over as he became himself.

"Thanks." Trent sighed, his shoulders slumping. "I'm going to ask Zack to help me explore why elven magic isn't working," he said. "Unless you think it's a bad idea."

"No, it's a good one." I took the bowl he was rinsing. If someone had told me last year that I'd be standing in Trent's kitchen doing KP duty, I'd have said they were crazy. "Just be careful," I added as I stacked the bowl where it belonged.

"Aren't I always?" He smiled at me, rinsing the big cook pot and setting it to drip-dry.

"No. What's this about Jenks telling me about you burning your eyebrows off?"

Trent's lips parted, and then his brow furrowed. "What's the point of having a curse to fix yourself if you don't use it?"

He was smiling, but I still didn't like the idea of Zack inside Trent's first defenses, down one floor. "Trent, I know I brought him over here, and I see why you're doing it, but Quen has a point. What happens when I leave tomorrow and you're here with the girls?"

Mood soft, Trent laced his hands behind my back and tugged me into him. "Quen will be here, and Jon. Add Jenks to that, and I'm safer than you, half a city away. He needs to believe in something, Rachel. He wants to believe. Let me give him a choice. That's all he wants. Who am I to deny him that?"

"That doesn't make him trustworthy," I said, my hands now behind his neck. "He could be working for Landon and not even know it. Have you looked for bugs?"

Trent's grip on me eased. "That's why Jenks is taking him downstairs."

"Okay, but—"

I blinked, not expecting it when Trent leaned in and kissed me. For an instant, there was just him and me, and my arms around his neck, and then he drew back, his head tilted as he worked to meet my eyes. "It will be okay," he said, but it still felt like a wish. "We're both going to be awake all night. What could happen?"

I sighed, feeling alone when he stepped back and my hands slipped from him. *What could happen?* Exactly my question.

CHAPTER
19

MY FINGERS FELT SLOW AS I SET THE YELLOWED JOURNAL on the coffee table atop the rest. After a night of dipping into Trent's mom's thoughts, I had a feeling that I'd have liked the woman if she still lived. Trent had once told me that my dad had been with her the night she died trying to get an ancient elven DNA sample. Honestly, it was amazing that Trent even *liked* me.

It was nearing seven a.m. Seven was an ungodly time to be up if you were a witch, especially one who hadn't slept at all. How Trent did this every day was beyond me, but I didn't nap for four hours at noon, either.

The entire compound was quiet with Zack at the pool and Trent in the kitchen, cheerfully making waffles. My hair was damp from the shower I'd taken to try to wake up, and I'd put on the upscale casual-professional white-and-cream outfit I'd found in the closet. Ellasbeth had probably ordered it and never come to collect. Fatigue pulled at me despite the no-doze amulet, and I slumped in the living room with my back to Trent, staring at the huge black TV.

I hadn't found anything new in Trisk's journals. They made fascinating reading, though, mostly because of the weird relationship she'd had with Trent's dad. Sort of an amorous disgust. She clearly had feelings for him even as she despised the man.

I yawned and shut my eyes, counting on the no-doze and Trent in the kitchen to keep me awake. It was hard not to see the parallels between Kal and Trisk, and Trent and myself, though I don't think Trisk ever lost her anger that Kal never evolved into the man she thought he could be.

And was that his fault or hers? I wondered, my closed eyes twitching as the memory of Trent slamming my head into a tombstone and choking me swam up from nowhere. We'd narrowly escaped the ever-after, and Trent had learned not only that I was a demon, but that his father was to blame for me surviving. Killing me would've not only ended the demons' rebirth, but probably started another war. He would've done it, too, despite the fact that I'd just saved his life and given him the DNA sample that would enable his species to again thrive.

He tried to kill me for what I was, not who I was.

A flash of old fear struck through me, and I pushed it down. But it kept returning, laying a heavier and heavier coat through my disjointed half-asleep thoughts. Trent had tried to kill me, I had sacrificed my freedom to save his, and he tried to choke the life out of me because of what I represented, what I was. He was more than an ass, he was repellent.

Suddenly, his scent in the afghan over me was vile, and I threw it off me. I stood, looking at him in the kitchen, flour on his apron as he ran a finger along the inside of the bowl to taste the batter. The elf had tried to kill me, and I *slept* with him?

Lip curling, I caught sight of my reflection in the black TV. My aura flared, and I wondered how I could see it. It wasn't even *my* aura, tainted with the dusky darkness of something other than smut—as if it was lacking something.

The sound of Trent slurping his coffee struck through me, as familiar as his voice, and with it, my aura flashed a weird purple and orange. I'd never seen its like, and as I shuddered, a wave of hatred cascaded over me. I'd say I was being possessed, but there was no one in my mind but me. He'd hunted me like an animal, put me in a cage, let Jon torment me, dumped me in a rat fight to kill for him, tried to blackmail me into being his mancipium—a virtual slave.

My breath trembled in my chest, and I stared at my reflection, the gold of my aura was swamped by purple and orange. Kalamack's life strewn around me seemed smothering: his rooms, his couch, his blanket, his life.

He needs to die, I thought as silver sparkles began to dart through the alien haze lifting off my skin, sparkles of demand, of search and action.

Resolve lifted through me, and when Trent began to run the mixer to whip up the egg whites, the urge to blast him to hell grew stronger. My hands shook, and I clenched them. He had to die before I could feel whole again. He had stolen my pride, my anonymity, and my future. I had to take it back. If I took everything he was, I'd find peace again.

I took a step toward him, then another, then another until I came into the kitchen. His head was down over the bowl, and the mixer was loud. Buddy was at his feet, and seeing me, the dog lifted his head, his lips pulling back in a silent threat.

It will be easy. The thought spilled through me, and I tapped a line, glorying in it as it flowed and backwashed at my theoretical extremities, tingles rising with the promise of satisfaction. He'd tried to choke me to death because of what I might do. I should choke him to death for what he had done. Feeling his struggles weaken and cease would be intimate and rewarding. His hair against my cheek would be soft and cool, his struggles violent against me. He couldn't stop me. I was trained for this.

But as I reached for him, still oblivious in the confidence of his security, I decided choking was too good for him. He was an elf. He should die with a curse designed for an elf— one that put him in excruciating pain and made him fully aware as he died, one that was slow enough that he would realize the depth of his folly. Smiling, I dropped into the collective to steal one. He had hurt me, and there was no forgiveness in me. None at all.

The weapons locker, I thought, but when I reached my

awareness inside, I was rebuffed, thrown out with a sharp crack of loosed ley line energy.

I jolted awake with a yelp of pain, staggering as the power of the collective dropped away.

Near panic washed through me. I clenched my hands and hid them, breath fast as I realized I was standing in the kitchen. Buddy was barking wildly at me, and I wavered, remembering having gotten up from the couch and walking in here. *Holy crap on toast, not again!* I thought as the roar of the mixer continued, my fingers tingling as I let go of the line.

I'd been angry at Trent, so angry I'd wanted to kill him over something I'd forgiven him for a long time ago. If the jolt from the weapons locker hadn't woken me up, I would have done it.

The baku, I thought, turning to look at the couch. Shit, I had fallen asleep. It had been waiting for me.

But Buddy was still barking, and finally hearing him, Trent flicked off the mixer, looking at me in surprise. "Are you okay?" he said even as he shushed the dog. "You look pale."

"Um. Tired," I lied, looking at my hands before hiding them again. *Damn it, I'm never going to sleep again.* "I'm, ah, I just wanted to tell you I'm going down to check on Zack."

"Okay," he said cheerfully, oblivious that if not for the automatic safeguards on the weapons locker, he'd be dead. *My God. I could have killed him.* "I'm almost done. You want to get him out of the pool?"

"Sure." I turned away, heart pounding. I couldn't tell him. The hatred had been real. It had been mine. But it was no longer, and I was ashamed of it: shocked and ashamed.

Eyes down, I headed for the stairs to the lower floor. Buddy slipped from Trent to follow, looking cowed and sheepish as he wagged his tail as if asking for forgiveness for barking at me. *I'm not safe anymore,* I thought as I started down the stairs.

I'd forgiven Trent a long time ago for everything he'd

done to me, having understood the why better than he'd ever know. I loved him, trusted him, but it had been as if all that understanding and forgiveness had never existed. The baku had stripped everything from me that made me who I was.

Only now, as I wove through the silent room full of empty chairs and low tables, did I understand why Dali refused to fight it. It was a true monster, making those it attacked kill the ones they loved with anger that was long dead. Worse, if I told Trent what had happened, he'd insist that I go into seclusion with Al and leave catching the baku to him. I couldn't do that. He wouldn't understand how devious it was and would be taken in turn. Neither of us was strong enough on our own. Together, though, with elven and demon magic combined, we might be.

Scared, I came to an uneasy halt at the window wall, arms over my middle as I watched Zack swimming laps in the sunrise. The new light glistened on the ripples arrowing out from his unhurried, smooth strokes. Seeing him, Buddy trotted through the wall to sit at the edge of the pool, tail swishing when Zack swam past. High above, Bis was asleep on the waterfall rock. Once, I would've known where he was by his light touch in my thoughts. Now I just knew where to look.

My gaze shifted to the table that someone, probably Quen, had set for three before the window, having used the seldom seen dishes and flatware from the bar tucked in the back. Trent had wanted to eat in the great room this morning, perhaps to show Zack that he was more sophisticated and worldly than mac and cheese in a tiny kitchen. The girls were too messy to eat over carpet yet, or perhaps he ate here every morning I wasn't with him. I didn't know. With the scattered tables and chairs, it reminded me of dining in an upscale hotel, especially with the view of the pool and the waterfall.

I shivered as I stepped through the window wall and out onto the tiled pool deck, the energy from the ward tingling through me to remind me of the mystics. It was cold, and I was 100 percent awake now. Fear was better than six cups of espresso.

"Zack?" I called, my eyes on Bis's lumpy shadow among the rocks. He knew he could come in, but the cold didn't touch him, and I think he was still mourning what we'd almost had. As much as it hurt me, it probably hurt Bis more, seeing as it was his entire reason for existing in his eyes. "Zack!" I called louder, but the kid kept swimming.

Tapping a line, I marshaled a small ball of energy in my hand and threw it into the pool. "Zack!" I shouted as I let the energy go. Water and air rushed in with a clap of sound to replace it, and he stopped, flicking the water from his eyes with a toss of his head as he tread water.

"Breakfast ready?" he asked, and I nodded, not comfortable with his obvious assumption that people were there to do things for him. And yet . . . I went to get the towel that Jon had left beside the slippers and the robe as Zack angled for the edge and levered himself up and out.

The towel I recognized, but the slippers and the robe were new. Someone had gone shopping. That gold-and-black swimsuit Zack was sporting wasn't anything I'd ever seen before, either.

His childhood has probably been as perfect as Trent's, I thought sourly, until I remembered that Trent's childhood had been as bad as mine in a way. We'd both lost parents, both fought and lost power struggles with our peers as we figured things out. Zack, too, though clearly having grown up in the luxury and the privilege of the dewar, had probably never known his parents, having been groomed and taught from infancy to replace Landon. I know I would've given up a lot to have my dad back. *Maybe not so different from me after all.*

Steam rose from Zack's lean body as he padded forward, leaving wet footprints behind on the November-cold tile. Buddy stood, tail waving. "Hey, Buddy," Zack said, voice high as he gave the dog a brisk head rub. "Maybe I can get you in the water next time." His delight with the dog still lingered in his eyes as he took the towel from me.

"Thanks," he said as he dried off. "I can't believe how warm the water is."

I looked at the whorls of steam rising from the stilling water. Quen would probably be out here after breakfast to pull the insulating cover over it, but for now, it was nice to look at. "Trent knows I won't get in it if it's not like bathwater," I said, my thoughts still on what I'd almost done. "He's thinking about putting a dome over it for the winter. I told him not to bother if it was just for me. He'd be out here in the snow."

Zack shrugged on his robe, completely missing Bis as he ran his gaze over the waterfall. "That would be amazing." He scuffed into his slippers, eyebrows rising as he looked me up and down. "You didn't sleep at all, did you," he added, focused on my amulet.

"No." Uncomfortable, I headed inside. Zack coaxed Buddy into following, the dog's nails clicking until he was inside and only his jingling collar gave him away. Trent hadn't come down yet, and I sat at the table with my back to the stairway. The journals that Quen had gone through were stacked on a nearby end table. Worried, I looked out over the steaming water and sipped my coffee. I wasn't going to sleep until this was done. We had to do this, and we had to do it fast.

Zack hesitated for a bare moment before taking the chair across from me with his back to the enormous fireplace. It would leave Trent on my right, which was fine with me, and I slid the coffee carafe across the table. "Help yourself." *I* wasn't going to serve him.

"Thanks." Looking as if he seldom had to, Zack awkwardly poured himself a cup. Syrup and butter were already waiting, and the scent of cooking batter drifted down. My stomach rumbled, and I slumped as I ate a fall raspberry. I wasn't sure how I was going to get through today. The caffeine was starting to work, though, and I took three more raspberries.

Zack slurped his coffee, and I smiled at his slight grimace.

"You want tea instead? We've got green, blue, white, black, caffeine, no caffeine. . . ."

"Coffee is good," Zack said, convincing me he didn't really like it when he added cream and three spoonfuls of sugar. Yeah, I remembered forcing down a cup, trying to impress my older brother, Robbie. Even so, it was hard to say that Zack didn't look at home there in a green robe with his hair in disarray from his swim and a dog at his feet. A fleeting thought rose and fell: was this what it would be like to live with Trent full-time? *Probably not.*

"Can I ask you something?" Zack said.

My head jerked up, and I eyed him warily. "Sure."

Zack scratched the side of his face and the soft fuzz just beginning to show. "Last night. When the mystics cloaked you . . . That was the same demon, right?" he asked, eyes pinched. "The one who told me not to talk about him?" I nodded, and he leaned toward me, an intent gleam in his eye. "He did a charm so the mystics couldn't see you anymore."

"It was a curse, but yes," I said, and a flicker of quickly hidden revulsion crossed him.

"What did you give him?" he asked. "He didn't even *try* to abduct anyone."

"Oh." I took a sip of coffee, feeling tired from more than a lack of sleep. "Demons don't do that anymore." *I hope.* "But you're right. It wasn't free. I promised Hodin I wouldn't tell anyone about him, but Al would have done it for free if he had known how."

"Your teacher," Zack said, his smooth face screwed up. "What did you give him for *that*?"

But it was obvious by his look what he thought I'd given, and it wasn't my soul. "I gave him my trust," I said, focus blurring as I remembered Al's shock when I had brazenly asked for a way to summon him without the safety of a circle, trusting that he would adhere to our bargain. He had, but only after I'd forced him into it.

"No way." Zack pushed back from the table in disbelief.

"Way." I stretched for the coffee and topped off my cup.

"I wouldn't advise it, though, if that's what you're thinking. Anyone else would be gargoyle chow. But I'm a demon, so . . ."

Zack smirked with the misplaced confidence of youth. "No, you aren't. I mean, Landon calls you one, but that's just . . ."

"Propaganda?" My smile widened, perhaps becoming somewhat mean. "Not all demons have goat-slitted eyes." I touched a finger to his mug, and it began to steam.

Zack's smirk faltered. "But the mystics *like* you," he said, sounding betrayed.

"Yeah. A little too much."

He shook his head in denial. "You can't be a demon if the mystics like you."

I stretched for the raspberries and pulled them closer. "Zack, demons could talk to the Goddess better than elves if they'd trust her again." Feeling sassy, I ate one. "Deal with it."

"They do not."

I smiled, enjoying rubbing his nose in it since it bothered him so much. "And that's why you can't hold a simple circle anymore and I was lovingly covered in mystics." I eased up, not wanting to alienate him. "Zack, there was more truth in those five minutes you watched Hodin hide my aura than Landon could tell you in ten years, but you won't see it unless you let go of the dewar propaganda. And you know why?" His eyes narrowed, and I leaned back with my coffee cradled in my hands. "Because Landon thinks knowledge is power, and he doesn't want to give it up. Especially to you."

"Then why did you let me watch?" he asked, more angry than listening.

"Because Trent knows *truth* is power, and you're going to have a hard time surviving without it."

Silent, he looked upstairs at a sudden crash and swearing. Zack's eyes shot to me as if expecting me to rush up there and help Trent. Then he frowned when I sat there, content to let Trent handle it himself. "I can't believe he doesn't have any servants," Zack said when I continued to do nothing. "How can you have demons in your living room and no servants?"

In his living room? How about his bed? "Right. You think he vacuums this on his days off?" I said, waving an expansive hand.

"But he's making breakfast. . . ."

I nodded. "While you were enjoying yourself in his pool," I said. "Who do you think ran out last night and bought you that swimsuit? That's not Trent's robe or slippers you're in, either." I closed my eyes as the sun finally crested the vegetation around the pool and found me. "Trent has staff, but he knows they make me uncomfortable, so he gives them the weekends off."

"Everyone? He doesn't even have any security," Zack said, but his tone had lost a lot of its lordly sound.

I opened one eye. "You're looking at his security, bud," I said, and Buddy swished his tail, thinking I was calling him. "You need to take off your dewar rose-colored glasses before they kill you."

Zack fiddled with his cup of coffee, quiet again. Relenting, I sat up and sifted a half teaspoon of sugar into my mug. "I think Trent first excused his staff to prove to me he could be a normal guy and that he knew how to wash his own socks, but I think he's finding an unexpected pleasure in making things for others to enjoy." I hesitated, spoon clinking as I stirred. "And if you ruin that, I'm going to be pissed."

"Me?" Zack's eyes went wide.

"Yes, you." I couldn't smell waffles anymore and I listened to the quiet upstairs. "You didn't see Trent's face when you ate your mac and cheese last night, but you made his day. He connected with you. To his own past. That means a lot to him. More than it should, but maybe that's one of the things I love about him."

Zack's brow furrowed. "It was just a bowl of pasta."

"It was until you scarfed it down and made him feel good. So think about what you want in the long term before you screw this up. You want lip service kudos from a man who sees you as a potential threat? Or the guidance of someone who wants to nurture and fledge you? You're too smart to not see that Trent's giving you the chance to choose between what everyone expects you to be and the chance to find out what you want to be, and I think you've felt the trap Landon has built around you enough to see what a gift that is." I leaned in over the table, squinting to hammer my next words home. "If you hurt him as you figure things out, I will hurt you."

Trent's soft steps scuffed at the high landing, and I smiled as Buddy's tail thumped and Trent made his slow way down with a tray. "He is all I have," I said, my thoughts going to waking up in the kitchen with a long-dead anger filling me. "And I will do anything to keep him alive. You understand?"

"I didn't come here to kill him." Zack's voice was soft but there was anger in his eyes.

"No, but maybe that's why Landon let you escape."

"He didn't let me escape," Zack said.

I shook my napkin out and draped it across my lap. "No? You've been on the run for how long? Ditching your phone only buys you a day." The sound of pixy wings was a bare warning, and I leaned back. "Hi, Jenks."

"Morning, Rache." Jenks circled the table once, smirking at my weary confidence and Zack's brooding mood. "Daybreak really isn't your time. You look like cold troll shit in December."

"Thanks," I said sourly, but I smiled as Trent wove his way through the couches and chairs. He looked rested in a fresh outfit of dress pants and a crisp shirt that showed off his eyes. There was no tie yet, and the top two buttons were still undone to peg my meter. "Wow," I said as he set down the tray of cereal and fruit. "I'll never understand how you look that awake."

"Practice." Trent flushed as Zack eyed the cereal, the scent of waffles still clinging to him. "Ah, this okay?" Trent said, and Zack bobbed his head and reached for a bowl.

"Hey, Zack. Be a pal and pour some of that syrup onto a

plate for me, will you? Rachel hates it when I get my dust in the syrup."

"Sure." Zack hesitantly poured out a dollop of syrup. "I thought we were having waffles."

Trent grimaced at the dry sound of cereal clattering into his bowl. "Me too."

I hid my smile, glad I hadn't gone up at the crashing and swearing.

"That's okay. This is good." Zack set down the syrup, fascinated when Jenks took a pair of chopsticks from his back pocket and began ladling sticky syrup into himself, head tilted back.

"Trent, you mind if I take some of this back to Izzy and Jumoke?" Jenks asked, surprising me. He never let me buy him anything.

"Not at all. Forage all you want."

"Thanks." Wings a blur, Jenks rolled his chopsticks in the sticky syrup, dusting an odd shimmer over them to cake it up and make what looked like cotton candy on a stick.

Silent, I filled my bowl and poured the milk. Watching Trent trying not to watch Zack worried me. I knew that he was seeing himself in the kid and that Trent hadn't had much of a relationship with his own dad. Combined, it made for a dangerous situation.

My mood darkened as Trent chatted lightly with Jenks and Zack, engaging them both. This was something Trent wanted that I couldn't give him. *What am I doing here?* I thought, not for the first time. I knew the demons weren't happy about my relationship with Trent. And it wasn't as if there were any elf babies available for adoption. God knew he wouldn't get any from me. I wasn't barren, but the chromosomes didn't line up right between an elf and a demon. Worse, elven society demanded children from their leader—or they weren't a leader long. It was a barbaric, but understandable, belief that had sprung from their cascading genetic failure and subsequent near extinction. That I'd helped Trent regain the DNA that allowed everyone else to have healthy kids didn't mean a thing.

"This is pleasant," Trent said, so focused on Zack that he missed my mood. "I should have breakfast down here all the time. Was the pool warm enough, Zack?"

"Plenty, thanks," Zack said as he hunched over his bowl and inhaled his cereal. "I swim laps at the dewar's pool a lot, but someday, I'm going to learn to surf." His expression shifted, part anger, part anticipation, and enough fear to worry me. "Now that I'm not going to be a dewar stooge," he added. "I lived above Black's Beach. Did you know that? And I've never been allowed to dip a toe in," he finished angrily. "Do you know what it's like seeing half of San Diego on the beach and not being allowed to even go out because some old fart thinks you might get a sunburn?"

He's been in a prison, I thought, seeing by Trent's closed expression that he'd felt those same bars of circumstance and expectation. Never allowed to risk anything in the pursuit of self, never allowed to be *normal*: skin your knee, break a bone, eat too much chocolate. I knew how that felt, but it must have been worse when there wasn't a medical reason for the invisible bars.

"I don't swim." Jenks sat on the edge of my cup, the two sticks of maple cotton candy in his grip dripping. "The water makes my wings heavy. Besides, I'd freeze my nubs off out there."

Zack's gaze flicked to me as he slowed down. "Rachel says you might enclose it."

Trent's expression cleared, and he sipped his coffee. "I might. Still deciding. The waterfall makes it tricky, but if we manage it, we could make the window wall more permeable and up the humidity in the main house. I know everyone would appreciate that."

Zack searched the bottom of the bowl to find a wad of soggy flakes. "Why not move the ward on the window? If you set the anchor out far enough, the natural arc from the top floor down should enclose it."

"Perhaps." Trent ran his gaze across the top of the window, wincing. "I was thinking something more permanent." Zack hesitated, clearly waiting for more, and Trent added, "It only takes someone with the right know-how to bring down a ward."

"Yeah." Jenks snorted. "The first time Rachel touched it, she turned the whole thing gold."

"Jenks, maybe you should get those sticks to Jumoke and Izzy before they drip all over Trent's table," I said, and the pixy rose up, saluting me with one hand.

"Back in a sec," he said, wings humming as he darted off.

Buddy's collar jingled as he watched Jenks, then the dog inched closer to Zack, begging with wide brown eyes. I settled back with my coffee, thinking the ward was a dangerous topic. Zack sitting there eating cereal like any other kid was dangerous. Everything was dangerous. Trent had defenses, but everything could collapse with the right word, and he knew it. So why was he being so free with himself? Trent was more cautious than that.

Unless he is trying to draw Zack into a mistake? Even more dangerous, and I eyed Zack in speculation as he shook more Raisin Bran into his milk to use it up.

"Rachel . . . ," Trent drawled, and I jumped, not realizing I'd been glaring. "I've been giving it some thought."

"What?" I asked, putting my attention on my own cereal.

"The curse Hodin taught you. The one that separates an aura into its constituent parts?"

"Ah, yes?" I said, wondering about his timing when Zack slowed his spoon on its way to his mouth.

"Do you think the baku might have left a residue aura on its victims?" Trent asked, cup held so the steam bathed his face. "And if so, would it show if you parceled their aura out?"

I hesitated, remembering that weird purple-and-orange aura on me when the baku had attacked. Curses before breakfast. I bet that was not how they did things in the dewar. And I wasn't so innocent as to not suspect that everything we said might land in Landon's ear along with a description of the casual openness of it all.

But then Trent made a barely perceptible head nod to

Zack. He *wanted* Zack to be included, wanted him to see that our goals were lofty even if our methods involved demons. He wanted Zack to see that you could get more done sharing knowledge than hiding it. *Sure, why not?*

My tension eased. "Maybe." I turned to Zack. "What do you think, Zack? You said you could see the baku in Landon's aura." *Please don't say it was purple and orange, please.*

"Um." Zack hesitated, clearly thrown by our conversation that up until recently would have gotten you branded a black witch and thrown into Alcatraz. "It's not what you see in Landon's aura that indicates the baku is in him. It's what you don't."

Which didn't make much sense, and I leaned in. "But you *can* see the difference."

"Oh, yeah. Big one." Zack looked at the box of cereal, and Trent pushed it closer to him.

"Then maybe I can quantify it as Trent suggests," I mused aloud as Zack filled his bowl a third time, this time adding more milk. "If we can find it on the suspects, we can prove they were possessed and not to blame."

"Perhaps." Trent sipped his coffee. "The I.S. appears to have turned a blind eye, and the FIB doesn't have the right tools. If not us, then who?"

"Yea-a-ah," I said, echoing Trent's thoughts. The Order had probably threatened the I.S. to back off, and seeing as the I.S. likely didn't care one way or the other, it was no skin off their nose. That the baku had taken out a living vamp wouldn't mean much to the old undead. But bringing that up in front of Zack wasn't a good idea. "It might be worth a try," I added. "If we can prove they were forced into attacking someone in their sleep, the I.S. would have to let the suspects go."

Trent smiled. "I'm sure they'd appreciate that. What can we do to help?"

We? I glanced at Zack, wondering if Trent wanted me to entertain/babysit/evaluate. "Ah, I'm not sure. I have to modify the curse to show the inner shells. It's going to take some time."

"Why?" Zack asked.

"Because it's a new curse, and modifying curses can get you killed if you aren't careful," I said shortly. My worry came out as anger, and Zack wiped the milk off his chin.

"No," he said, ears red. "I meant, why do you need to look at the inner shells?"

"Oh." I hid behind a sip of coffee, embarrassed. "Ah, I think the baku attacked me twice," I said, more determined than ever to keep this morning's attack a secret when Trent stiffened. "Once when I nodded off outside my church, and then yesterday morning. If there was anything out of the ordinary in my outer shells, Bis would have said so when Hodin did a spectrograph on it yesterday. Whatever we're looking for must be in the inner shells. The ones we haven't seen." *The ones that color our personalities with past experiences and make us truly individuals.*

"Rachel . . ."

Guilt pinched my forehead as I hid the truth from him. He'd only tell me to sit this out, and that might prove to be fatal. "I'm okay," I insisted, but Hodin had said the more you were attacked, the easier it would be to attack you again. "I thought they were just nightmares at the time. Nothing happened. I woke up. It went away." I smiled thinly, hiding behind a sip of coffee. "I should call Ivy," I said, ignoring Zack's wide eyes. "See if she can get me some blood samples from the suspects. There's probably a way I can store the prep in the collective to make it faster."

"Mmmm." Trent eyed me suspiciously, the worry clear in his eyes. "Do you think you could modify the curse to actively seek out the baku's presence within Landon's aura?"

"Probably not," I said. "But if we had a vial of Landon's blood, we might be able to see if there's any damage to his inner shells."

Zack poured the last of his sweet milk into his coffee,

turning it even lighter. "I could do that," he said, and immediately Trent shook his head.

"No," he said before I could, and Zack frowned. "I mean, I'm sure you could," Trent amended. "But until we can get elf magic working enough to at least make a decent circle, I'd prefer it if you stay here."

Zack leaned back, chair creaking as his arms went over his chest. "I can take care of myself," he said, but being still wet behind his ears and in a borrowed robe kind of ruined it.

"No question about it," Trent said, ignoring Zack's ire. "Anyone who can live on the streets for a week in the Hollows has enough smarts and skills to take care of themselves."

It seemed to satisfy Zack, but I had my doubts. The I.S. had probably had a pool going as to when I'd find Zack squatting in my church and how badly I'd break his nose. Honestly, the entire I.S. force was pretty loose on what laws it enforced when there was no one complaining.

"But the real reason is that I don't want you anywhere near Landon until I know you're not working with him to bring me down," Trent said, and Zack's expression fell.

"Oh." Zack eased his chair back onto four legs. "That would be easier to prove if you let me do something."

"True." Trent glanced at me, and I shook my head. I wasn't going to have him with me when I was spelling. Mistakes happened, especially when you thought you had everything under control. "I could use some help in trying to get the Goddess to look on us more favorably," Trent said, and Zack made a sour face. "Being from the dewar, you might have a few ideas I've not thought of."

"Trent," I whispered, and smiling, he gave my hand a squeeze and let go. Zack had no idea how ruthless Trent could be when pushed. If Zack betrayed him, the kid might end up dead, and that would haunt Trent forever. This wasn't any safer than spelling with me.

"I'll get a fire going in my spelling hut," Trent said as he folded his napkin and set it aside. "That way, Rachel won't be in any danger if the Goddess puts in an appearance."

Zack laughed, then went ashen when he realized Trent was serious.

"Give me ten minutes to get a fire started." Trent stood, his motion slowing when he glanced at the small stack of journals waiting on a side table.

"Go ahead," I said as I saw his dilemma. "I'll ask Ivy to meet me at the church."

Trent jerked to a quick halt. "I thought you'd be working here. Do you want the spelling hut? Zack and I can find somewhere else. I've got six kitchens on the grounds, and that's not including the stables."

I shook my head, wincing at the thought. Spelling and horses did *not* mix.

"What's wrong with my spelling hut?" Trent rocked back, arms over his front. "It's a nice area to work in."

"In the summer," I said, loving Trent but not his appreciation for the old ways. "If you don't mind not having any air-conditioning or running water. Or a bathroom," I finished, and Zack choked on his last swallow of coffee.

"You don't have running water in your spelling lab?" he said when he could talk again.

Trent's ears colored. "If it was good enough for my mother, it is good enough for me," he said. "It's highly secure. Zack, you wouldn't even be able to find it if I didn't show it to you."

Zack's eyes lit up and he stood. "Cool."

But I had already made my choice, and I set my bowl of sweet milk on the floor for Buddy. "Thanks for the offer, but no. I probably have everything I need in my old room, salvaged from the kitchen. And the garden is right there if I don't. Hodin left a slate table in the sanctuary, and there won't be any Weres since we didn't pay them last week." I hesitated, seeing Trent's misgivings. "Running water in the bathroom," I added, thinking, *Peace and quiet*.

"It's too cold for Jenks," Trent warned. "You need someone to watch your back."

"The heat is on. Jenks will be fine." I poured myself a last cup of coffee to take with me. I could leave the mug at the gatehouse, five miles down the road. "I'll call Ivy before she leaves work and see if she can get me some blood samples from the suspects, and maybe a few ringers to sanction the results. Do a blind study."

Trent glanced at Zack, the kid clearly eager to check out Trent's spelling space. "Then that leaves you with me," he said, a smile quirking his lips. "You may want to get dressed."

"Oh, yeah." Zack looked at his scrumptious robe, and jiggled on his feet. "Be right back."

Zack jogged to the stairs, and Trent tensed as he thundered up them, taking them two at a time, Buddy in hot pursuit. "No running on the stairs," Trent whispered, and I knew he was echoing something from his childhood.

Guilt hit me, and I rose, fumbling to stack the dishes. "Thanks for breakfast. Don't worry about the waffles. This was good."

"Rachel . . ."

His tone was introspective, and his eyes were pinched in worry as he looked at the third floor. I touched his hand, and his gaze returned to me. "Do you think I'm making a mistake?" he said, clearly knowing the threat Zack represented, not just to his life, but perhaps to his heart.

I shook my head, pulling him close and rocking slowly as I breathed him in, relishing the scent of cinnamon and good coffee. "No," I whispered, but I thought that maybe I was.

CHAPTER

20

THE STREET WAS QUIET AND SUNNY, HOMEY, WITH LEAVES piled at the curb, and I frowned at the truck parked outside of Keasley's old house. A new sapling had been planted in the front yard, and it somehow made me feel left out. I missed the old man who had stitched up my vamp bites and gave out wise-old-man crap when I needed to hear it, but he'd vanished shortly after I figured out who he really was, which was probably safer—for him. "Have you been to visit Jhi?" I asked Jenks, now huddled on my shoulder for the quick trip from Trent's borrowed car to the church.

"No." Jenks's wings pressed cold against me. "She wasn't sure there'd be anyone in the house by winter, much less if that person would like pixies. She's hibernating this year."

His worry was obvious, and I forced a smile. "She'll be fine. She's young and in good health." Fatigue pulled at me as I took the stairs to the front door, weaving through the offerings left by thankful freed familiars. And then I stopped, shocked to see the doors wide-open before I remembered that I'd magicked them that way when catching Zack.

"Great, they've been open all night," I whispered, grimacing at the coming heating bill. "Sorry about that, Jenks. You want to check for squatters while I get these shut?"

"Don't worry about it," he said, and then he was gone, inside to do a quick perimeter.

Let go! Let go! I thought as I grabbed one of the doors and tugged, finally unsticking it with a swift yank. Mood bad, I slammed the doors shut behind me, boots crunching on the leaves that had blown in. Frowning, I tapped the thermostat, satisfied when I heard it click on.

"No squatters downstairs, Rache," Jenks said as he came back and slammed both feet against the light switch to turn it on. "I'm going to check the belfry."

"Thanks," I said, but he was already in the foyer's stairway. My bag slipped from my shoulder, jerking the to-go cup of coffee I'd gotten at Junior's and making it spill. I sighed at the brown puddle among the wet leaves, tempted to leave it, but I could hear Ivy in the back of my thoughts clearing her throat.

I was tired, and it didn't help that I'd had to borrow one of Trent's cars to get here. No-doze amulet swinging, I strode to the stage. My purse and the bag with my new spelling robe went on the couch, and the dripping paper cup on the slate table. There was a sawdust-covered box of tissue on one of the end tables, and after I pulled a few, I went back to blot up the mess.

There wasn't enough caffeine to get through today.

Soggy mess in hand, I headed for the fifty-five-gallon trash barrel only to slide to a halt when Jenks darted right in front of me, wings clattering.

"Watch the hole," he said, and I blinked, two feet from walking right into the crawl space.

"Maybe I should cover that back up," I said, and Jenks nodded.

"Belfry is clear," he said, his dust a dissatisfied green as he rose through the hole in the ceiling to inspect the narrow space between the roof and the false ceiling. "They haven't done a slug-slimed thing! There's still only eight inches of insulation up there."

"That happens when you don't pay them." Depressed, I tossed the soggy tissue into the trash barrel and returned to the stage. It was the story of my life. I was among the most powerful people in Cincinnati, and I was basically broke, had no real job prospects, and was living on my dead, former boyfriend's boat. "Maybe I'm doing this wrong," I whispered as I brushed the sawdust off Ivy's couch and sat down.

Jenks's sparkles dimmed as he dropped to the rafters. "There's no right way to live, Rache. It's just a bad patch. You need anything from the belfry?"

"Um, magnetic chalk?" I said, remembering I didn't have any, and he darted off, content.

But I was anything but. The silence was oppressive as I unpacked what I'd brought from the boat. The feeling of being displaced was hard on me, and my fingers felt clumsy as I set my snips and hunk of beeswax from Trent's hives on the table. I should have been able to jump here, not have to borrow Trent's car. I felt stunted, lacking, and my mood darkened as I ran one of Trent's silk handkerchiefs over the table to remove stray ions. But feeling as though I wasn't good enough wasn't anything new. *Deal with it, Rachel,* I thought as Jenks returned.

"There's a shoebox full of ley line stuff up there," Jenks said as he skidded to a landing on the table with a broken stick of magnetic chalk. "You want anything from the garden?"

"Isn't it too cold?" I asked.

"Not for a quick trip," he said confidently, but my phone said it was, like, fifty out there, workable, but not if he got damp. Still, a quick foray would tell me his limits.

"I'm not sure yet." I unwrapped my ceremonial knife as I thought about what I might need. "Do you know if the ivy growing by the trash cans survived the fire? I've always had good luck with the aerial roots."

Jenks rose back up. "I'll go see." He touched the hilt of his sword and flew to one of the boarded-up windows and out a crack. Slowly the dust he left behind faded.

"Maybe a ten-pointed star," I muttered as I took up a stick of magnetic chalk and drew one for practice right on the table. Ten points ought to double the sensitivity of the original curse, but going from a pentagon to a ten-pointed star would be tricky. I could draw a ten-pointed star easily enough, but the space made from the star's lines was too large and disconnected from the center point, where the lines running point to point touched.

Unless I add a pentagon inside it, I thought, drawing one in the center of the star, the ten crossed lines marking the points and midsections. And like that, I had it. It wasn't a ten-pointed star I wanted, but two five-pointed stars, one shifted a few degrees widdershins. The curse would use the original pentagon start point, and if I could manage to turn it without losing the first star, I'd get a ten-pointed star.

"Oh, this has potential," I muttered, wondering how I could get it to turn. There were lots of ley line charms to turn things—just as many earth-magic fixes to do the same. Between the ley line stuff in the belfry and the herbs in the garden, I bet I could do it.

Hunched over the table, I began to make a grocery list of possibilities, listing on the slate everything I had that turned or evolved. *Cedar,* I thought, chalk whispering. It was a sun plant, and it was for getting rid of bad dreams, too. I could use that as a stylus. Chicory, which also belonged to the sun and was good in charms that unlocked doors and hearts. The moon turned. We had wintergreen out there, and wintergreen was linked to the moon. It was good for breaking hexes. I wasn't breaking a hex, but splintering an aura might be close, and I added it to the list. Dandelion because of its tenacity and divided nature, a straw from a broom for its nature to push together, and a drop of water from a spiderweb, as it reflects the world. All good choices.

From the ley line side of things, I probably had a crystal in the belfry to refract my desires. And there was the glyph itself, the ten-sided figure stemming from a five-sided glyph. Combine that with the blood samples Ivy was bringing over, and it might be enough. But even as I finished my list and began to think about how to put it all together, I wondered if maybe trying to use a dollop of elf magic might be in order. Not that I was lazy, but asking a deity to mesh everything together *would* make it easier. More powerful, too. I'd already modified the spell Trent had once used to temporarily contain my soul to capture Nina's so as to give it to Ivy. But I wasn't sure it was safe to swim in that pool anymore.

I looked up at Jenks's soft wing hum to see his low, dully glittering path just above the sanctuary floor. He was cold, and I held out my hand to give him a warm place to land. "Damn, it's like Tink's titties after a snow out there. Is this enough, Rache?"

A handful of long rootlets was in his grip, and I nodded. "Plenty. Thanks. Are you going to give me any flack about sitting tight as I get the rest?"

Jenks looked at my list, his brow furrowed. I cleared my throat, and he hesitated. "No," he finally grumbled, and I smiled.

"Good." I stood, and he settled on the rim of my cooling coffee. "Back in a minute."

"Slug snot. I'm guarding the church," Jenks said morosely as he sat on my cup, heels thumping and dust making an oily sheen on the bitter brew.

"At least you're not the librarian!" I said over my shoulder as I strode to the front door, snips and black gathering scarf in hand. My heels clunked on the old wood in a familiar sound as I skirted the hole in the floor and slipped outside. The street was quiet as I hustled down the steps, arms about my middle as I dodged the plates of food and vases of flowers. The slate path leading to the back gate was covered in leaves, and the squeak of the hinges went right through my head. But then I was in the garden, and a smile found me as I worked my way through the traditional witches' garden and into the *more* traditional witches' garden among the tombstones. This was where I'd harvest the dandelion and cedar, where death and transition made them stronger.

I lost myself among the fallen leaves smelling of both earth and sky as I lifted soggy, cold, stunted plants to find the still potent sheltered rosettes, gathering what I wanted and folding them into the scarf. A soft glint of gray turned out to be one of my stone spoons, and pleased, I rubbed it clean and dropped it in a pocket. I'd probably be finding stuff for years, scattered when the vampires of Cincinnati had blown up my kitchen.

The fading scent of zombie among the tombstones brought me up sharp, and I wondered how Glenn was going to deal with this wrinkle. I knew he was withholding information from both me and Ivy. Not to mention from his dad at the FIB. His last words were not inspiring: trust him and keep a low profile? The trust I could handle, but when had I ever kept a low profile?

Thoughts swirling, I spun to go inside, halting when I saw the burned back of the church. The missing kitchen and living room had been added on in the seventies, and the original stone wall was scorched and ugly. Only the fireplace remained, but it was cracked and would have to be torn down. It was easy to see where pipes and conduits ran, and as I picked my way over the low wall separating the graveyard from the more ordered flower garden, I wondered if it might be possible to make an inspection-solid tulpa of my kitchen. If it was like any other tulpa, it would be real. Really real. Permit and inspection real.

But as with all things, I'd pay for it. Making a tulpa the size and complexity of the kitchen would put me out for a week. Al was the only demon I'd trust to pick through my mind and separate the construct from my psyche, not to mention watch over me as I recovered. We hadn't made a construct since the mystics had talked to me. He seemed okay with how things were, but I wasn't sure he was comfortable with being in my mind anymore. But as I looked at the ruin of my church, I decided I'd ask him after Thanksgiving.

If we both survive, I thought, my anger with Hodin rising up again. Damn it, I had really believed I'd be able to help Al for a change.

A familiar *bumm* of sound pulled my attention to the street. It was Ivy's cycle, and I headed for the gate as the engine died and the soft click of her kickstand going down sounded in the new stillness.

The feeling of Camelot lost pricked my soul as I reached the gate, watching her from over the damp wood. Motions smooth and unhurried, she got off her cycle, scrubbing her long black hair into disarray as she set her helmet on the seat and took a small paper sack from one of the small side trunks. Somehow, even after a night under the I.S. tower dealing with red tape and hungry vampires, she managed to look svelte and sexy. The paper bag crackled as she strode to the church's door, her long legs eating up the distance and her boots hardly making a sound.

I took a breath to call her, but then she stopped, heel grinding as she turned right to me.

"Hey, hi," I said as her eyes found mine, and I stifled a shiver as I pushed through the gate and kicked it shut. "I thought that was your cycle."

"Hi, Rachel." Her voice was low and throaty, and my pace slowed. She'd had a hard night by the look of it, meaning she'd be on edge, quick to jump to conclusions, and hungry. "Sorry I'm late. It took me more time than I planned to convince everyone involved."

Hands full of chicory, dandelion, and wintergreen, I halted before her. "You didn't . . ."

She smiled, flashing her sharp canines at me, and I knew she was fine. "Oh, all the accused were amenable after I told them you were trying to prove they were innocent. It was getting everyone else to look the other way." She flexed her free hand as if it hurt, and her brow smoothed. "Nothing I couldn't handle. Nina got a kick out of it. You look tired."

"I didn't sleep last night," I said, deciding not to tell her about the latest baku attack. I'd handled it, and she'd only side with Trent about me sitting this out.

"Six samples." She handed me the bag, frowning at my dirty fingers. "And six donations to make sure you're seeing what's there and not inventing results. They're all labeled."

"Donations?" I questioned, and her expansive smile returned.

"Vampire mostly, but I got a witch and a Were, too."
Stretching her shoulder, she winced.

I peered into the bag to see twelve neatly labeled vials.
Ivy knew her job. "Thanks. I'm not getting you into trouble,
am I?"

"Not any more than usual," Ivy said wryly, and I looked
up, waiting for the rest of the story. Her gaze went to the
steeple after a faint thump from inside, then dropped to me.
"I was warned off," she said, anger marring her complexion. "Told that the situation was being handled and to keep
my fangs out of it."

"Crap on toast," I whispered. "It's the Order, isn't it."

"That's the impression I got. They've been around long
enough to know how to bring down one of the old undead
without getting caught, and no one will stick their neck out.
Homebody cowards. All of them." Ivy's eyes went to the
church at the muffled peal of sound from the belfry.

"Bis?" Ivy guessed, and I shrugged. *What the Turn is
Jenks doing up there?*

"If you're good here, I need to get home," Ivy said, her
thoughts clearly somewhere else. "An old undead is coming
in from DC tonight, and I need to clean."

And there's the cherry on top of my crap-day sundae, I
thought sourly. But with Rynn Cormel less than effective,
the old undead would want someone they knew—as in
someone they could control—in charge of Cincinnati's
vampires. Paper bag crackling, I put my arm around her
and gave her a half hug. "Thanks for this." It meant a lot
that she not only believed in me, but that she was right there
supporting me the only way she could.

"Anytime," she whispered, and then she pulled away, taking the delicious, dusky scent of vampire incense with her.
"Let me know what you find out," she added as she began to
walk backward, toe to heel. "I don't think the I.S. is going to
let these people go even if you prove it wasn't them. My boss
nearly popped a vein when I brought up the baku." She
winced, stretching her shoulder again. "Someone really
wants this quiet. No more murders last night, though."

"Really?" I frowned, worried. "That's good," I said, but it wasn't. It meant the baku was done messing around. It was coming for me—had come for me. *I'm never going to sleep again.*

Ivy hesitated beside her bike. "You okay?"

My wandering thoughts returned. "Yeah . . . ," I said slowly. "Jenks is with me. Tell Nina there might be one more for Thanksgiving. Zack Oborna. Almost sixteen. Elf. Dewar runaway."

Hair swinging, Ivy put her helmet back on. "Of course he is," she said as she fastened it. "See you at home."

I nodded as she started her bike and tooled serenely down the street, back to her life.

Cold, I turned to the church, my eyes following a sparkle of bright dust that shot from the crack in the boarded-up window and arrowed straight up. From inside, a bellow of anger rose. Someone was in my church, someone pissed by the sound of it, and suddenly the bell sounding earlier took on new meaning.

I whistled for Jenks. Immediately he got a bead on me and dropped like a stone. He was laughing, which wasn't much comfort when I saw his garden sword in one hand, a tuft of dark hair in the other. "Who's here? David?" I guessed from the hair, and Jenks grinned.

"Hodin," he said, laughing merrily. "He showed up, shouting about you stealing his curse. I don't know what his problem is. His hair grew right back. Almost as fast as his ear."

"Always making friends, eh, Jenks?" I muttered as he landed on my shoulder. I took the stairs, having to weave through the plates of food and frozen flowers. "Hodin?" I called as I shoved the door open. "I can hear you yelling all the way out to the street. I have to live with these people, you know." Damn it back to the Turn. He was still spying on me.

The warmth of the furnace going full force hit me, and my hair blew back to send Jenks up in a wash of dust. Hodin was at the stage, clearly angry as he looked from the writing on my table. His long hair was in disarray, and a black-and-gold sarilike garment draped all the way to the

floor. His right hand glowed with unfocused energy, and I
slowed.

"Where is that pixy?" he snarled. "He cut my hair."

"Aww, it was just a little chunk, moss wipe," Jenks
taunted, hovering close so Hodin wouldn't be as likely to
throw the ball of unfocused energy at him.

"You little bird smear!" Hodin exclaimed, furious. "Get
away from that witch!"

"Yeah?" Jenks hummed forward, slow from the cold but
willing as he drew his sword. "Here I am. Smite me, oh
powerful demon."

"Stop!" I barked as Hodin wound up, and much to my
amazement, the demon's hand dropped. "Knock it off, both
of you. Or I'll make both of you leave. Jenks, don't you
have some inventory to do for me in the belfry? I'm sure
Hodin and I can have a nice chat without any mashing,
pulping, or cutting off of any more parts."

Jenks sheathed his sword with a noisy flourish. "I'm
watching you," he threatened.

"Do I look as if I care?" Hodin said, and when Jenks's
wings hummed a threat, I pointed at the belfry. Jenks's
laugh sounded like wind chimes as he flew a low path back
to the vestibule and vanished up the narrow stair.

"He's four inches tall—," I started.

"That is no excuse for cutting off parts of my body,"
Hodin interrupted, expression dark as he rubbed his ear.

"No," I said patiently. "I mean, if you want any hope of
besting him, you need to shrink down." Hodin furrowed his
brow in thought, and I added, "And if you so much as bend
his wing back, I'll . . . be dead to you, too."

Hodin glared at me and shook out his black robe. "You
will not live long if you keep that much stock in a pixy," he
said, but he wasn't shouting anymore, and I edged past the
hole in the floor and onto the stage. I set Ivy's bag and my
collecting scarf on the table, wary. The faint scent of burnt
amber was coming from him, and I breathed it in, finding
it pleasantly rich with memory.

"Jenks has saved my life more times than you have

rings," I said, making a fist around the one of his that I still wore. "You did enter his space uninvited. He owns the church." Standing carefully sideways to him, I shook out the spelling robe he had given me and put it on over my jeans and sweater, doubly glad I'd brought it now. "Or didn't you know that?" I said, voice muffled.

"No." Hodin was looking at me as I shimmied the robe into place and tied the sleeves back, bells jingling. My God, it felt nice, all silk and elegance. Sure enough, Hodin's mood eased even more. The robe was a subtle show that he was needed, appreciated. I was just about desperate for his help now that he was here, but if working with Al had taught me anything, I knew if I asked for it, he'd want something. I was hoping that he'd volunteer out of curiosity.

"Why are you here?" I asked, and Hodin's anger returned full force.

"You have no right to steal my work," he said, eyes narrowing.

"I'm not stealing your work," I said, and when Hodin pointed indignantly at the slate table with my listed ingredients and ten-pointed star, I added, "Drawing a ten-pointed star is not stealing your work. And even if it was, we have a deal. You agreed to stop spying on me."

I jerked as Hodin strode forward. A wall of haze sprang up between us, and when he walked through it, he came out dressed in black jeans and a T, boots on his feet and wavy hair in disarray. "What are you trying to do?" he said, doing a bad job of hiding his fluster as he stood across the table from me and looked at my sloppy star. "Trying to get a wider spread? It can't be done. I've tried."

Sitting would have given him the advantage, so I put my hands on my hips and stared down at it. "That's exactly what I'm going to do, but how did you know I was doing it?" Hodin flushed, and I squinted. "Damn it, Hodin. Stop spying on me!"

"I am *not* spying on you," he said shortly, and when I cleared my throat, his eyes met mine. "I'm not, but that's my work you're building on. Everyone steals my ideas.

First the elves, and now you—everyone taking credit for my innovation and leaving me with not even a footnote of thanks. I'm tired of it. I taught you how to explode a pentagon. What are you doing with it?"

"I'm doing whatever the hell I feel like with it," I said. "And you *are* spying on me. I guess that means I can tell Dali about you, then, huh."

Hodin's anger shifted to frozen panic. I reached to get my scrying mirror from my bag, and he made an odd gurgling noise. "No, wait," he said, and I put my arms over my middle. "I'm not spying on you. I, uh, put a mirror on the table when I turned it to slate."

"A what?"

He sat down, a hand running over his head to muss his hair. "A mirror," he muttered. "Whatever is scribed on it shows up on the parent table."

"Which is in your living room, eh?" I said, feeling myself warm. "Take it off."

"I won't." Hodin looked up. "It's my table. I made it, and you're stealing my work."

"Bullshit," I barked, and Jenks zipped in, drawn by my loud voice. "It's my table. You turned it to slate, but it is *my* table. Take it off. Now!"

"Jeez, Rache. Can't I leave you for five minutes?" Jenks said as he helped himself to another mug from my coffee before perching on the rim to make an oily dust on the surface.

"Tell me what you're doing to my curse," Hodin insisted.

"Take the mirror off, and I will," I countered, and Hodin glared up at me.

"Fine. *Speculum speculorum*," he muttered, making a gesture over my table. I would have questioned it, but I felt a drop in the ley line, and the words loosely translated to *mirror of mirrors*.

"Rache. Look at what he did to my wing," Jenks said as the caffeine hit him and he rose in a swirl of dust. "Scorched it with his lame-ass line energy. I can hardly fly. See? Look at it."

But he was hovering so close, I couldn't. "Then perhaps you shouldn't have cut off his ear. You look okay to me. Hang tight, okay?"

Jenks turned in midair, spilling his coffee as he looked Hodin up and down. "Hear that, Home Slice? She wants me to hang tight."

"Keep your dust off the table." Hodin eyed me uneasily. "What are you trying to do?"

Gotcha. Smiling, I sat before him with a little flip of my robe to make the sash bells ring. "I'm trying to see the inner shells of the aura."

Hodin's lip twitched, and what I thought was guilt crossed him. "I'm sorry, Rachel. Even if you could, it wouldn't help Bis reach you through your adjusted aura."

"That's not what this is for." I shoved the heartache down. I could feel Jenks looking at me, but I didn't dare meet his eyes as I took Ivy's vials from her bag and stood them up in a row on the table. "It's for the baku. Zack said he could see the accumulated damage from the baku in Landon's aura. Bis couldn't see any evidence of its attack in my outer shells, but if it shows in my inner, and I can find the same damage in the people it attacked, then I have reasonable cause to blame the baku for the murders."

"I can vouch that the baku caused their actions," Hodin said, and I nodded, carefully opening up my scarf to show my snips of cedar, wintergreen, chicory, and tight dandelion buds.

"Fair enough, but I can't prove it. This might." I glanced at the ten-pointed star. "Or at least prove the accused were goaded into it, possessed maybe." The memory of wanting to kill Trent sifted through me, and I stifled a shiver.

"This is what comes from trying to live within a human system," Hodin said darkly. "You are a demon, Rachel."

"So I should take and do what I want?" I said, weary of the good old boy's privileged mind-set, and Jenks snickered. "This isn't only for them. Landon is using the baku to get me to *kill* Trent, and though I'm sure all the demons would be *thrilled*," I said with a bitter drama, "it would put me back in Alcatraz and Landon in power." I arched my eyebrows. "Or rather the baku when it takes Landon over. All the progress we've made integrating demons into reality won't mean goose slip. I like you all here. I don't know why. All of you seem dead set to ruin it."

Hodin frowned, slumped as he looked at the table. "I just told you you're right. Why do you have to prove it?"

"It's what we do here," Jenks said. "All are innocent until proven guilty. Even demons."

Hodin's feet scuffed the old wood floor. "How . . . quaint."

"And sometimes a pain in the ass, but it keeps me from being lynched." I used my ceremonial knife to whittle a tip on the cedar stick and set it on the table. "Want to help?"

"Help you steal my work? No." He pushed back into the chair, settling deeper into its sawdust-laden comfort. "But your efforts are sure to be amusing. You can't open a decahedron. There's too much distance between the All candle and the connecting threads."

"Ass," Jenks said, and I shifted my hair from my shoulder to lure him off the table.

"Then you won't mind if I try," I said as I took up my magnetic chalk.

"What's your plan, Rache?" Jenks asked as he landed on my shoulder, a muffled swearing coming from him when he slipped on the slick pixy-dust silk and fell into the air.

"Playing it by feel," I said, eyebrows rising when Jenks warily perched on the back of the couch instead. "I'm hoping that all I need is to double the candles and open a closed pentagon into a decahedron. If Hodin's curse is worth the salt to circle it, it will function the same."

"My curse," Hodin said possessively as he looked sourly at Jenks, now four inches from his ear. Then he added, softer, "A double pentagram?" He shifted, either to get closer to the table or farther from Jenks. "How do you propose to get a ten-pointed star from a five-sided pentagon?"

"Like this," I said as I drew a pentagon with the usual radiating lines from the center, then added five additional

lines running through the midpoints of the walls. I guessti-
mated how far I needed to go for the proposed star points,
and Hodin's eyes widened in interest. "What were the
words you used to open it?" I mused aloud, then brightened. *"Obscurum per obscuris,"* I said, strengthening my
hold on the ley line and letting it fill the glyph.

I hadn't set any candles, so I didn't know what I expected, but with a thrill, I felt a drop of energy in me, and
on the table, a perfect five-pointed pentagram ghosted into
existence, the lines more visible energy than anything else
since there was no candle ash to give them substance.

"Okay . . . ," Hodin said hesitantly, eyes intent. "But it's
still only five points."

I bit my lip, then went for the cedar twig still holding
half a dozen frost-dark leaves. "It just needs to be shifted a
few degrees," I said, reaching out.

"Rachel!" Hodin shouted as I breached the glyph. Jenks's
wings clattered in warning, but then his eyes widened as I
gave the lines-not-there a nudge, and they shifted, the
points setting at the freestanding lines like a roulette wheel
clicking to a stop. Left behind was a ghostly image of the
original placement. I had my ten-pointed star.

"Looks like a ten-pointed star to me," Jenks said smugly
as Hodin pushed forward.

"Seal it," Hodin said, and I drew back, the bells on my
sash jingling. "Name what you did, and register it in the
collective so you can do it again!" he exclaimed. "Latin.
Bind the motion with a naming. Do it, Rachel. I can't. I'm
not in the collective. This can't be forgotten."

"Oh!" I stared at what I'd done, only now realizing how
rare it was. "Um." Turning. I had turned it. What was the
Latin word for turn? "Ah, *Wee-keh Wehr-sah. Evulgo,* Rachel Mariana Morgan," I said, the last words imprinting it
on the collective.

"Vice versa?" Hodin's long face screwed up. "You jest.
That's hardly Latin anymore."

"Which is why I stuck with the original pronunciation,"
I said, embarrassed. *"Ut omnes unum sint,"* I said, and

with a slight pull on my awareness, the ten-pointed glyph vanished to leave only the original pentagon. "Look, if you don't like it, leave. I'm doing the best I can here."

"Mmmm." Hodin's fingers twitched as if looking for chalk. He took a slow breath and exhaled, his eyes touching on my no-doze amulet, then dropping to the wilting vegetation on my gathering scarf, and finally on my fingers still holding the dirt from the garden now mixed with a smear of magnetic chalk. "I'm impressed," he finally said, and Jenks nearly choked, inking a startled silver. "Will you show me your ideas, Rachel?"

My gaze flicked to Jenks, and seeing his shrug, I nodded. It was a request, and somehow that was more worrisome than a demand. A demanding demon I knew what to do with.

One who thought I was smart . . . That was a whole new game. And I smiled.

CHAPTER

21

HODIN WAS CLOSE. ACTUALLY, HE WAS TOO CLOSE AS HE sat on the couch beside me, and I shifted my knee before he could touch it with his own. An unopened pentagon with ten radiating lines waited on the slate table, pristine in its unmagicked state. The faint scent of burnt amber pricked my nose, and I glanced at Hodin scribbling notes on Ray's sketch pad with a half-busted pen Jenks had found in the floorboards. He'd changed into a spelling robe to minimize his aura contamination, this one gold at the top, radiating down to black with stars about the hem and Möbius strips on the ties. There were no bells, so I was the only one jingling.

It had been hours now, and he was getting frustrated.

"Shall we try it?" Hodin prompted as he set his notes down with a smack. "Modifying the All candle with a broom straw in place of traditional cotton should facilitate a smoother energy movement." His tone was scholarly, nothing like Al's bluster, and his expression was serious as he tried out another of my lame ideas. *"Obscurum per obscuris,"* he intoned, and I felt a dip in the line we were both connected to as he snapped his fingers. *"Wee-keh Wehr-sah."*

Breath held, I stared at the chalk lines, willing something to happen. But nothing did. My All candle sat and

burned with exactly the color one would expect from a
birthday candle.

"Damn my dame," Hodin muttered, slumping back into
the cushions. His knee hit mine, and I stiffened. Noticing,
he sat up and shifted down a few inches. "I thought your
addition of a straw in place of a cotton wick would have
changed something."

"Try it again," I said as I blew out the candle and removed it from the glyph.

"I did not draw it wrong," he muttered. Snapping his
fingers, he added, *"Obscurum per obscuris. Wee-keh
Wehr-sah."*

Again I felt a drop in the line, and with a soft hiss of
undrawn chalk, the pentagon opened and twisted to form a
perfect ten-pointed star. But without the candle, that was all
it did.

"There it is!" Hodin said in disgust, the sleeve to his
spelling robe shifting as he pointed at it. "It's got to be
something to do with the blood, not the candle. The double-
star twist isn't working when there's blood involved, and
that's the entire point."

The cushions shifted and, sash bells jingling, I pushed
forward to the edge of the couch when I began to slump
toward him. "We're missing something is all. I think we
can go back to the cotton cord if you want. Maybe we're
asking too much. Demon curses are always so . . . spare."

Hodin rubbed his chalk-stained fingers together. "Because most of the hard work is predone and stored in the
collective," he said. "But perhaps you're right." He leaned
to clean off the glyph to start over, and we both jumped
when his knee bumped mine. Again. "We need a bigger
space," he muttered, eyebrows furrowed as he looked at the
pool table.

"Don't think so," Jenks said from atop the nearby light.
"No touchy or Ivy get bitey."

I shook my head as well, and Hodin frowned. "Fine. We
continue at the kiddie table." Clearly miffed, he pulled his
notes to him, pen tip ticking our tried modifications. "The

problem isn't with the wick, or the herbs carrying intent within the wax, or the wax itself," he said. "We've changed all of that to no effect. It's the presence of the blood, and I don't understand why. Something basic in the glyph is blocking the transition of power once the blood is added. Perhaps the modification should be in the glyph itself."

"I don't know." Elbows on my knees, I leaned over to study it. We'd added words of power to attract the points, bits of our own hair to carry out intent. I even tapped directly into the collective for an energy boost, but nothing worked. "Maybe?" But the glyph was the only thing that felt right.

Hodin's fitfully moving fingers stilled. "It opened and turned fine before we added auratic samples. We both saw it." He took up my All candle and frowned at it. "Why would the addition of the substrate itself block it when it worked before?"

Hodin's attitude had shifted dramatically over the last two hours, going from annoyed instructor to puzzled peer. It was gratifying that he thought my knowledge of earth magic was valid, but I was tapped out. "Perhaps it's the twist," I said.

"I don't think so. That piece of innovation was inspired." Hodin leaned over the table, my candle in hand. "I thought of another placement word. Hang on."

Jenks snorted from the light fixture, a silver dust spilling down just shy of my elbow.

"*Explicatio,*" Hodin intoned as he set the candle where all the lines connected, fingers opening to show a new flame.

I started, grinning as my eyes found his. There was a new power rising in the glyph. It wasn't unpleasant, and by his eager smile, I could tell Hodin felt it, too. It was the best connection we'd had since sitting down, and his silk robe shifted in excitement. "Try it," I said, and Jenks poked his head over the light fixture.

"*Obscurum per obscuris,*" Hodin said boldly. "*Wee-keh Wehr-sah.*"

"Look out!" Jenks shrilled as Hodin clapped his hands, the pixy inking blue dust as he shot halfway across the sanctuary.

A surge flared in the line, singeing my thoughts. Yelping, I ducked, snapping a protection circle in place around me as a sodden thump of air and a clap of thunder hit me simultaneously.

"Way to go, Home Slice," Jenks said snarkily, back again and hovering over the power-smeared glyph.

"You okay?" I let my circle fall, and Hodin grimaced and let his own larger circle drop. It had encompassed me as well, which left me not knowing what to think.

"I guess that's a no." Mood bad, Hodin pulled his notes to him, flipping back a few pages before adding to the tried-and-failed word list. "I need a moment," he added, and I jumped when the sketchbook hit the table and he stood.

"Where are you going?" I asked.

"Front steps. I need to sit in the sun and remind myself how good I have it. Besides, I think someone left a sugar confection out there."

"Okay." I uncurled my legs and set my feet back on the floor. "Thanks for the circle."

"You didn't need it," Hodin muttered, skirting the hole in the floor as he strode to the front door, spelling robe drifting about his slippered ankles until the door shut loudly behind him.

"Thanks anyway," I whispered as I flipped through Ray's sketchbook. His hand-printed letters were razor sharp. The church felt empty without him. Really empty.

"You want anything from the garden?" Jenks asked as he drifted down to land clear of the magnetic chalk lines. "We're hitting the peak temp for today."

I shook my head, thoughts still on Hodin. He wasn't what I had expected, his attitude shifting fast at my suggestions even if none of them had panned out. My jumps of reason were clearly surprising him, and I had a suspicion he was enjoying having someone to work this out with. Until now.

Motions slow, I cleaned the spoiled glyph from the slate. He'd stuck with this longer than I would have expected, but his pleasure that I might be a worthy peer was slowly smothering under continued failure. "It should have worked," I said. "Jenks, how did you know it was going to misfire?"

Sitting atop the lamp, Jenks's wings moved fitfully. "I heard the Goddess laugh."

A stab of fear cut me as I glanced at the closed door. "Excuse me?" I whispered.

He grinned, green eyes merry. "It's an expression. Like walking over your own grave? The energy flowing through it sounded wrong, and it gave me the heebie-jeebies. Jeez, Rache. You really think I heard her? I'd probably explode in a flash of dust if she whispered in my ear." He shuddered, his dust sifting a cheerful gold.

"I didn't know you could hear curses twisting," I said, focus blurring.

"I usually can't." Jenks vaulted from the lamp. "It's like he pissed her off, you know?"

"Yeah . . . ," I drawled, a new thought tickling through me. Somewhere deep within the Goddess was a crazy demon. It was probably why the elves' magic wasn't working right, and maybe why this curse, which should have, wasn't. "Jenks, watch my aura, okay?"

"Whoa, wait. What are you doing?" he said, suddenly very much awake.

I scraped my magnetic chalk on the table to sharpen it to a point, adrenaline seeping through me in a slow, invigorating wash. "Just tell me if I start gathering mystics. Hodin can shift my aura again if necessary."

"You don't know if he's still out there." Jenks dropped down to the table. "Rache . . ."

Head down, I sketched out a new pentagon with its ten guiding lines. "We've tried modifying it with earth magic, ley line magic, and bolstering it with the demon collective. There's only one branch of magic left."

"Uhhh . . . ," Jenks drawled, his dust almost transparent. "Sure. You look okay so far."

The chalk was slippery in my hand, and the words were already a whisper in my mind. I sat straighter, remembering the fear in Al's eyes. Still, if Hodin put my aura back correctly, I could shout in the Goddess's face and she wouldn't recognize me. "If you see them gathering . . ."

"I tell you to quit and get Hodin," he said, glancing at the door. "Better hurry before he tries to stop you. He might tell you no, and I'm starting to like the guy."

"Seriously?" I stared at Jenks, and he shrugged, his dust shifting to an embarrassed red.

"I've been watching you. He fills a void Trent can't. That's all," he said, discomfited. "Tell me I'm wrong, but if you and Trent were experimenting with line energy and covered in garden dirt, you'd be playing with his hair and bumping uglies after the first half hour."

"Jenks!" I exclaimed as I glanced at the door to the church, and he laughed, gyrating his hips suggestively. "We would not." But I could feel myself warming, and it bothered me.

"Yeah, okay." He drifted down to land on the cold coffee cup. "I'm just saying that Hodin likes your ideas and doesn't have Trent's tendency to try to stop you before you do stupid things that might hurt you. He's okay. A little closed and broody, but okay. You *can* have friends, you know? Go on." He looked at the table and waved his hand at me. "Do your demon-elf thing."

Stupid things that might end up hurting me. Yep, that's exactly what this is, I thought, twice as nervous. Unadorned pentagon ready, I took up my original All candle. *Ta na shay,* I thought to set the melted monstrosity as I placed it in the center. *Hear me. See what I do.*

And a little demon magic to counterbalance it, I thought as I pricked my finger to smear more blood on the wick as I pinched it. *"Ta na shay,"* I said softly as I parted my fingers and let a tiny ribbon of line energy flow to ignite the candle.

A flickering golden flame mirroring my aura emerged. I sat back, eyes on Jenks, and he gave me a thumbs-up.

"It's humming like a two-year-old's wings, Rache," he said. "Sweet and pure."

I exhaled, feeling my breath shake. "Here we go." It was going to work. I could feel it. The hard part would be living with having mixed demon and elf magic. *Sorry, Al. Deal with it.*

"Ta na shay, obscurum per obscuris. Wee-keh Wehrsah, ta na shay," I said, my words fast but assertive. Strengthening my hold on the ley line, I snapped my fingers.

Gasping, I jumped at the sudden burst of line energy. On the table, the pentagon unfolded, shifted, and the ghostly points of an undrawn ten-pointed star misted into existence. At each point, a candle that never existed flickered, each with a distinctive auratic shade.

"It worked!" I shouted, then jumped, catching back a shriek at the crash of the door.

"I gave no permission to continue," Hodin all but barked as he strode in. "I felt a line drop."

"Since when do I need your permission?" I said, but he was right. He *was* spotting me.

Knowing it as well, Hodin took a breath to yell at me. And then he stared, eyes on the table. Lips parted, he closed the distance between us, narrowly missing the hole in the floor.

"Um," I murmured, my thoughts on mystics as I searched Jenks's smiling face.

"You're good. He knows his stuff," the pixy said, jerking a thumb back at Hodin.

"You got it to work." Hodin rocked to a halt, shocked. "What did you do?"

But I'd used elven magic, and he wasn't going to like it.

"Of course she got it to work." Proud as if he'd done it himself, Jenks alighted on my shoulder, hand near his sword, struggling to not slip off the dusted silk.

"You don't want to know," I muttered. Something, though, wasn't right with the last two candles. The flames looked like they weren't even there. I leaned to look closer, but my attention jerked up and away when Hodin reached for my hand, eyeing the pricked tip and bloodied thumb.

"You lighted it with your blood," he said, letting go. "We tried that already. What else did you do?" But when I was silent, Hodin's expression went ugly, probably thinking I was going to keep it from him.

"She asked for the Goddess's attention, Home Slice," Jenks said proudly. "Duh."

Horrified, Hodin stepped back, his eyes widening as he searched my outlines. "Did . . . ?"

"Jenks says the mystics aren't swarming," I blurted, unable to pull myself out of my embarrassed hunch. "He watched me the whole time. It worked. Your fix worked. She didn't recognize me." *Worked*. It was a funny way to describe mutilating my ability to jump the lines.

Hodin looked at what I'd done, eyebrows rising when he noticed the last two odd-flamed candles, and then his expression emptied. "Close it. Shut it down. We are demons, not elves," he demanded, and Jenks's wings clattered.

"She got it to work, moss wipe," he said as he darted from my shoulder, and his dust made the unreal candles sputter and flare. "What the firefly ass is your problem?"

My face was cold. "There's nothing wrong with the Goddess. She used to be Newt, for crying out loud."

"Close it!" he demanded again, posture stiff. "Or I will."

Fine. My chin lifted. I wouldn't feel guilty about this. *"Ta na shay, ut omnes unum sint,"* I said belligerently, and with a tweak on my thoughts, all the candles but the original vanished.

Hodin blew my All candle out, then used his sleeve to wipe the glyph away.

"Chicken," I said, but my lips parted when he took the chalk and snapped it in two. "Hey! Knock it off." I stood, and he grabbed my arm, looking as if his thoughts were so full he couldn't decide where to start. "What are you going to do?" I said as I pulled away. "Tell Dali on me?"

"You used elf magic," Hodin sputtered.

"So?" I backed up an angry, frustrated step. "The Goddess is in charge of demon *and* elf magic whether you like it or not. And by the looks of it, she's tired of letting the demons wallow in their pity party. She's not siding with *any* of her children anymore. I think she knows you aren't strong enough to survive a rebirth of the elves, so if you want to find your place in reality, you're going to have to use *all* your magic, not just the piddle pat you allow yourselves, and to do that, you're going to have to get off your high horse and ask for her help."

"Piddle pat?" Hodin said, and my eyes narrowed, head tilted to look up at him.

"Piddle. Pat," I said into his suddenly startled expression. "You can't rule the world from fear and live in it anymore. You gotta use all the tools in your toolbox to get along. I can help, but not if you're going to hang me from the tree I dig you out from under."

Jenks's wings tickled my neck, and I stifled a shiver. For a moment, I thought Hodin was going to storm off, but then he took a step back. Head down, he whispered, "I can't."

"That's a load of crap." But I froze when his eyes met mine. He was afraid.

Embarrassed, I glanced at the table and back to him. "Why not?" I asked. I knew about fear.

"Because I asked for her help, and she said no," he said, a flicker of betrayal in him.

My shoulders slumped.

"And because of that," he continued, voice iron hard, "I was made a slave to the elves, her favorites, for an eternity. I'd still be trapped if the two worlds hadn't collided."

It was what I figured, but the more I thought about it, the more that last misfire felt like a slap from the Goddess. "The same elves who can't do crap right now," I said, reaching to touch his shoulder.

Hodin jerked back, and my hand fell. "This lesson is over," he said, and the basket of ley line paraphernalia he'd brought vanished.

Angry, I pushed out from between the couch and the table. "This is *not* a lesson," I said loudly, pointing at the table. "It's a lab session, and it's not over! If you leave, I'll be working alone," I said, allowing a touch of fear to enter my voice. "You want to sit on the couch and sulk, fine, but you're not leaving until I'm done." I lifted my chin, not caring that he was mad. I could take whatever he dished out. "What else you got to do today?"

His eyes narrowed . . . and then he sat with a huff. "You'd be surprised how I fill my day."

He's going to stay? I thought, exchanging a glance with Jenks. "Yeah, well, today you're filling it sitting on my couch," I said, shocked he hadn't left. "I need a spotter. Spot me."

"What a whiny baby," Jenks said from my shoulder, and I huffed my agreement.

"I want to try this with one of the generic candles," I said, taking up the snapped chalk and sketching a new, closed pentagon with its ten bisecting lines. "See how much freedom we have now that we know what the Goddess wants," I added as I massaged more blood from my pricked finger and smeared it on a birthday candle. "And you can just deal with it," I shot at Hodin, but he was busy brooding, knees crossed as he scowled.

"Perhaps I shouldn't be so worried," Hodin said tightly. "Sloppy. You aren't even bothering to make an All candle."

"I don't have the time," I snarked back, angry. "And if there is one thing that Newt understood, it was a lack of time."

"Ah, Rache, should you be spelling angry?" Jenks asked, and I brushed his dust from my front before it could find my pentagon.

"*Ta na shay*, you crazy bitch," I muttered as I set the candle in the center. "*Ta na shay, obscurum per obscuris. Wee-keh Wehr-sah!*"

I shouted the last, clapping my hands and jerking when a wave of energy ballooned out, pushing my hair back as it flowed past me. Crap on toast, I knew better than to spell angry.

"It worked!" Jenks crowed, and I looked at my hands, horrified as they tingled. But it was just from overload, and the sparkles vanished to leave me shaken. "Look. It's exactly the same."

Hodin frowned, his image wavering through the shimmering protection bubble he'd snapped around himself. His eyes went to the table as he dropped it. His expression shifted to disbelief and then to something I couldn't name. "Huh," he muttered as his knees uncrossed.

Eleven candles burned, ten at the points, one in the middle, their colors more shades than a rainbow. Not only had it worked, but it had worked well. "Hodin, are there too many mystics?" I said as I thought I felt the Goddess laugh.

"No," he said, and I began to breathe again. Something had shifted. I heard it in his voice. *He's worried. About me?*

"Rache, how come those last two are black?"

I looked at the spread, brow furrowing when concern pinched Hodin's eyes. The last two flames weren't missing, but they weren't there, either.

"Maybe it's outside my vision," I said, and Jenks shook his head, slipping from me to hover beside Hodin. "You?" I asked Hodin, and he shook his head as well.

"They're burning black," he said, chilling me. "It's not smut. It's baku damage. How many times have you been attacked?"

"Two," I lied, and Jenks rasped his wings. "Okay, three," I added. Sure, this was exactly what I had been hoping the curse would do, but seeing the damage reflected in my soul's expression, a thread of dread wound about my heart and tightened. "But I'm not sleeping anymore, so it doesn't matter. I'm *not* going into seclusion. Hodin, help me here. I can't hide in a hole and wait to fall asleep and kill the person I love."

Hodin was silent, and slowly I sank down to sit across

from him, the bells on the scrumptious robe he had given me jingling. I wasn't begging for his help, exactly. But if he left, I'd be on my own. That was when I usually did something stupid in my efforts to not fail.

Hodin's lip twitched. Silk robe rustling, he stood to look at the pool table. "We need to set them all up at once. My workbench at home isn't big enough. But that is."

Relief filled me, but Jenks rose up on a column of angry red dust. "Whoa, whoa, whoa. Cool your draft, Home Slice. We already said no."

"I'll smooth it over with Ivy," I said as I stood and followed Hodin across the sanctuary, the tiny bells on my sash jingling.

"It's old slate." Hodin ran his hand across the pristine felt. "From an even older lake. Laid down before I was even born. Do you know how rare that is?"

"Which is why you're not going to twist any curses on it." Jenks touched his sword hilt as he hovered before Hodin, and the demon lifted his hand from the felt and turned to me.

"We need to compare them all at once," Hodin said. "I'll fix it once we're done."

"I need this, Jenks," I said, but what I was thinking was that a pool table was a small price to pay for demons to consider bringing the Goddess into their magic. Not to mention maybe keeping me from killing Trent.

"Oh, Tink loves a duck. Ivy's going to kill me," Jenks moaned, darting back when Hodin said a word of Latin and the table was engulfed in a shimmering bubble. When it cleared, the bumpers were gone and a gray table with six holes at the corners and on the long sides remained.

"I don't understand your reticence," Hodin said as he sketched six pentagons down one side with an incredible precision. "There're better uses for such large measures of slate than gaming on."

"Don't knock it until you've tried it," I said as I inched closer. "My dad taught me algebra at our local pool hall." My arms crept up around my middle. Sure, I'd twisted the curse twice with no mystics showing, but this was six, all at once.

Hodin finished and straightened. "You'll have to introduce me to it someday."

"Deal." I went back to the couch for the vials of blood, silent as I set them up in a row on the denuded pool table.

"You should anoint the candles to minimize contamination from my aura," I said, shifting to make room when Hodin came forward. "Here," I added, setting a handful of unused styluses down. "You can probably invoke them all at once."

"Me?" Hodin's reach faltered. "I'm not contacting the Goddess. You do it."

Jenks's wings fluttered against my neck to send a shiver through me. "You want Rachel to do it?" he protested. "And risk she attract the Goddess's little helpers? What a whiny sack of spider snot."

"I'll do it. They can't see me," I said as I strengthened my hold on the ley line. *"Ta na shay,"* I said as I took the first candle he handed me. *"Ta na shay, obscurum per obscuris."*

My heart pounded as I paused the curse midtwist while Hodin finished anointing the rest. *"Ta na shay, obscurum per obscuris,"* I said again at the next glyph, feeling my hold on the line deepen. A faint tingling in my fingers gave me pause, but Jenks would tell me if it was the mystics, and I followed Hodin down the table, setting the candles he anointed.

Done, I exhaled, thinking this was either very clever or was going to hurt really bad. *"Wee-keh Wehr-sah, ta na shay!"* I said, clapping my hands and stumbling at the line drop.

"Watch it!" Hodin exclaimed, catching my elbow, and Jenks took off from my shoulder.

"Jenks, move," I said as he hovered before me, presumably looking for swarming mystics. "I can't see."

"It worked," Hodin said as he let go of my elbow. "Look at that."

"Wow." Sash jingling, I waved Jenks out of the way. All six pentagons had opened and twisted. All had the ghostly candles, and all of them had that same gap, some with two candles, some with three. Worried, I looked past Hodin to my own spread still glowing on the table by the couch. Hodin had said the damage wasn't permanent, but it was like finding a hidden cancer, black and ugly.

"Interesting." Hodin fingered his chalk. "Let's see the aura spread from the people we know weren't infected by the baku."

Infected? Hodin quickly sketched six more pentagons on the other side of the table, this time using the anonymous donors' blood to set the candles and his own to light them. Uneasy, I followed behind him, beginning the curse anew. With each *"Ta na shay, obscurum per obscuris,"* my connection to the line grew deeper with wild, unreliable magic. I was shaking by the time I got to the last. Jenks gave me a worried thumbs-up, and I took a moment to steady myself.

"Wee-keh Wehr-sah, ta na shay," I said, locking my knees before I snapped my fingers.

My breath hissed in through my nose as the line surged and an unexpected warming wash of tingles cascaded through me. I blinked, shocked at the almost carnal sensation of pleasure rooting its way down and through me until it finally dissipated. *What the hell?* I unclenched my hands, gaze shooting to Jenks. Wings humming, he shrugged, but it was probably at my sudden flush rather than at any stray mystic. The Goddess, apparently, was pleased with me.

"Did it work?" I asked, wishing my ears weren't so warm.

"Admirably." Hodin crouched before the first. "They are perfect." Smile rising up to include his eyes, he beamed at me. "We seem to have a working curse."

"Good." My arms went around my middle. It was what I had wanted. But now there was no denying that I'd been attacked. And if I'd been attacked, then Zack was probably telling the truth about Landon's goal. The only difference between me and the poor slobs in jail was that I'd woken up.

Hodin's thoughts must have been similar, his smile fading as he looked across the sanctuary to my own auratic spread. "You should be in seclusion."

"I'm its target. I'm not sitting this one out," I said, scowling. "As long as I don't fall asleep, I'm good. You said the damage will mend. Let's get on with this, okay?"

My words were confident, but I knew Jenks could see through them, making me flustered as I rounded the table to stand before the six spreads belonging to the incarcerated Inderlanders. "Some of them aren't as bad. I bet you could put them in order of attack by the amount of healing already done."

Interested, Hodin flipped through Ivy's notes. "This is the earliest attack," I said as I read them over his shoulder before pointing to a glyph with two candles showing black.

Head bobbing, Hodin squinted at them. "You can almost see a hint of color." He rose, and Jenks, who had been hovering close, darted back. "This one here," he said, pointing. "He was the last. Am I right?"

I looked at Ivy's cheat sheet and nodded. "It's healing?"

"Of course," he said, and Jenks's dust shifted to a relieved gold. "Auras echo the soul, and the soul is self-mending."

"Or self-destroying," Jenks said as he landed right in the middle of the spell and stared at the black-flame candle. "Tink loves a duck, that's weird. Don't go to sleep, Rache. You don't want to lose any more of your inner shells."

"Well-done," Hodin said softly, almost to himself, and then his eyes came to me. "Well-done," he said again, louder this time.

I flushed at the real pleasure in his voice, and he studied the table. "It might need some tweaking, but I'd say there're enough examples here to register it," he said.

"Tweaking?" Jenks rose up from the table. "You mean like trying to get it to work without laying down some love on the Goddess? Good luck with that."

Hodin gave Jenks an acerbic look, then waved a hand

to lightly circle the entire table. "Register it, Rachel," he prompted.

"*Evulgo*, Rachel Mariana Morgan," I whispered, and then I shivered, feeling a slight tug on my chi as the curse registered. "I wish you were in the collective," I said, and Hodin's circle fell with a sharp, startled tug on my awareness. "So you could get credit for it," I added.

"I did very little," Hodin said, and Jenks flew back to his lamp, trailing a sour green dust.

"You stayed with me," I said, and Jenks swore something inaudible. "It was your curse I modified. I could never have come up with this on my own, only build from it."

Hodin was silent, and then I flushed, figuring it out. It had nothing to do with him not being in the collective. The curse needed the Goddess, and he didn't want his name attached. *Suck it.* Frustrated, I turned away. It was getting late, and I wanted to meet up with Trent before the day was over and he became a daddy again. Chin high, I strode back to the table where my own spread still glowed. "*Ut omnes unum sint,*" I said, almost shouting. "*Ta na shay!*"

With a tug on my thoughts, the not-there candles vanished. Hodin hadn't moved, and I snatched up the candle, now little more than a stub. I waved it out, felt the wick, and dropped it into my bag. "You want this?" I said, pointing at Ray's sketch pad, and Hodin started.

"If you don't," he said.

Not sure what that meant, I ripped off the pages in question and dropped them on the couch. I was cleaning. It was over. Time for him to leave. But he didn't, and my jaw clenched as he scuffed to a halt beside a chair as I ran a cloth over the ash and chalk, blurring it into nothing.

"Ah, do you mind if I continue to study this on my own?" Hodin asked as he picked up the sheets and stashed them in one of his sleeves.

I slowed down, thinking about that as I shoved everything in my bag. If he was going to practice, he'd have to invoke the Goddess. Shoulders easing, I turned to him, seeing a soft panic in his eyes. "You know the words, right? To garner her attention?"

"Better than you," he said, chin high.

"Then say it once for me," I said. "So I know you can."

His jaw tightened, then relaxed. He took a breath to say something, only to shake his head. "No." And then he vanished, taking my confidence with him.

CHAPTER

22

"HEY!" JENKS ROSE UP ON A COLUMN OF SILVER. "WHAT about Ivy's table!"

I sighed at the remnants of the curse: bits of the garden and slivers of wax. Hodin hadn't been able to say the words to invoke the Goddess in front of me, but I was betting he'd whisper them when alone. "I'd dearly love to see what Landon's spread looks like if he's been hosting the baku in his thoughts," I said as I reached for my phone. *Three thirty? No wonder I'm hungry.* "You know, maybe all we need to do is show it to him. He might kick it out once he sees what it's doing. Maybe then we can catch it."

"You want to show Landon a demon-elf hybrid curse?" Jenks said in disbelief.

My eyes flicked from my phone to Jenks now hovering over the curse-laced table. "It's not a curse. If anything, it's just . . . black," I said, feeling kind of stupid.

"Rache, maybe you should close this down," Jenks said, and I nodded.

"Um, *ut omnes unum sint,*" I said, adding a belated *"Ta na shay"* when nothing happened. With a tweak on my thoughts, the not-there candles vanished to leave the original.

"Jeez, jealous much?" I muttered as I hit the icon to call Trent. He picked up almost immediately, and I sat down as his melodious voice spilled out in a familiar "Hello?"

"Trent!" I exclaimed, my thoughts going back to what Jenks had said about me and Trent and thirty minutes of ley lines and garden dirt. "I got it to work. You'll never guess what it took, but I'll give you a hint. Hodin isn't happy."

"Uh, this isn't Trent," he said, and I froze, thoughts scrambling.

"Zack?" I said, and he cleared his throat in embarrassment. "You sound just like him. Is Trent available?"

"Ah, hang on a sec. He asked me to answer his phone if it was you." He chuckled. "Itchy witch, huh? You should see the picture that comes up."

Please not my old I.S. ID. Please? But it would have been like Trent to track it down and use it. He liked—no, needed—that I was real, that I had bad-hair days and got tired, and that I wasn't trying to be perfect. No, I was simply trying to survive. "Zack?" I said when there came a distinctive pop and Trent's elegant, seldom heard swearing rose up in the background. From across the room, Jenks grinned and hummed closer.

"No, I'm fine. I'm fine!" Trent said, voice irate. "Here. I'll take it. Could you . . . ? Thanks." There was a pause, and then, "Rachel."

He sounded annoyed, but I think he'd had a spell misfire, and I could relate. "Sorry to interrupt. You okay?"

"Yes." Trent sighed, and I could imagine him sitting back on a desk, table, armchair . . . whatever. "The lower magic is working, but the more complex the spell, the more resistance we're seeing. I'd swear it gets worse the longer we work at it. Were you able to modify Hodin's curse?"

I nodded, feeling good at the pride in his voice, and Jenks gave me a thumbs-up. "Yes, but I had to invoke the Goddess's attention to get it to work."

"Mmmm," he started, and I quickly interrupted.

"Stop. I'm fine. Jenks was with me, and Hodin, actually. Both of them agree there was no abnormal mystic activity. Mixing demon and elf magic did the trick, which makes me think you ought to prick your finger and put a little blood on whatever you're doing."

"Like witch magic?" he asked, voice hesitant.

"Like demon," I said, and Trent sighed.

"Why?" he protested. "Elves don't have the right blood enzymes to invoke charms."

"It's not to kindle the magic. It's to pay the Goddess," I said, and he made a soft sound of understanding. "Promising to sacrifice a goat won't impress Newt. But a drop of blood? Something she's used to? Something elves would see as a major sacrifice? It might work."

"Huh. It can't hurt. Hang on a sec. Zack?" I heard distantly. "Rachel thinks you should prick your finger and put a little blood on it somewhere. Use the knife there."

Knife? "Trent," I protested.

"Seriously?" Zack said, and hearing their voices side by side, I could tell the difference.

"Trent, don't make him do that," I protested, and Trent chuckled.

"Why not? He heals fast."

Somehow we'd gotten off track, and I strove to bring it back. "Hey, now that we've got a curse to show baku damage, we could prove Landon has been hosting it. I just need some blood and five minutes in a corner."

"Landon would simply claim he was a victim," Trent said, and I slumped.

True. "Okay. But if he makes a statement to that effect, the I.S. would be forced to act. Even if all they did was let the suspects go under the Unlawful Coercion Act, it would be something."

Again, Trent made an unsure "Mmmm," punctuated by Zack's whoop in success. "It worked!" the kid crowed, muffled. "Trent, it worked! Look at that. It finally worked!"

I smiled thinly. Elves buying success with their blood and demons getting it for free by saying please: what was the crazy Goddess up to? "Congratulations," I said sourly. "You're all going to have to pretend to be demons to get your magic to work," I said, and Trent sighed.

"This is going to be a hard sell." Trent's voice held a

heavy worry. "I might have to invest in a finger-stick company. Maybe if it had 'elf' on it somewhere, they might go for it."

I slumped, then began to shove more things into my bag. "I think the Goddess is trying to force the two branches of magic together again, laughing all the way. Hodin practically threw up when he realized he had to invoke her attention to get the new curse to work." But throwing up would have been better than shunning me, which was what had happened the last time I dabbled in elven magic. "Trent, do you think we can get a drop of Landon's blood?"

"Sure. I'll call him up and ask," Trent said sourly. The sarcasm was unusual, but he'd been up as long as I had, and we were both tired.

"Maybe that's all it will take," I said, words spilling out in a rush. "If the baku is damaging his soul, he needs to know about it."

"I think he already does." Trent yawned, and I could imagine him rubbing his chin. "But I'm not going to the I.S. or the FIB with the claim that Landon is working with a sentient energy with the intent to murder people without having seen the baku damage myself first." He hesitated, then softly, almost breathing the words, he added, "All we have is Zack's say-so. Landon could be using him to discredit me without him even knowing. I can't risk what's left of my reputation until I know for sure."

"Yea-a-a-ah," I said, wincing. Here I was worried about Trent letting his emotions make him vulnerable, and I was the one not thinking three moves ahead. "So how do we get a blood sample?" I prompted, and Jenks's wings pinked up, vibrating in anticipation. "Go in. Hit Landon on the head. Prick his finger? In, done, and out in five minutes."

"Perhaps inviting him to dinner?" Trent suggested dryly. "He'll show if Zack is there."

"But . . . if you're worried he might be working with Landon . . . ," I started.

"Exactly," Trent interrupted. "I need to see them interact."

My head bobbed as I got it. "How about Carew Tower?"
I was dead tired, but I couldn't sleep until this was over.
"Very public, and they know us." *Crap on toast, I need a
dress.*

"It's short notice, but I'll make a call. I might get through
to Landon if I mention Zack," Trent said sourly.

"Okay." I bit my lower lip, guilt rising. *Once upon a
time, there was a noble elf who lost everything because of
the one he chose to love. . . .* "I, ah, should probably go to
my boat tonight." True, it was technically Kisten's boat, but
none of his relatives had shown up to claim *The Solar.* I
didn't even know if he had any living relatives. The dead
ones wouldn't have been interested.

"To pick something up? You're staying here for the
night, right?" Trent said, and my eyes flicked to Jenks. That
hadn't been my thought, but Trent had sounded almost desperate. Grimacing, Jenks rose up on a column of blue dust
and flew away to give me some privacy.

"Um, sure," I said, thoughts churning. "None of Ellasbeth's dresses do squat to hide my splat gun. We can keep
each other awake again."

"Good. Good," Trent said, clearly relieved. "Is Jenks
still with you?"

I looked up to find him, but Jenks had darted over before
I could open my mouth. "You think I'd leave Wendy of the
Damned Boys alone when she's got a piece of magnetic
chalk in her pocket?" he said, and I pushed Jenks back with
a glare, a hand briefly over the receiver. Privacy was an illusion around the sharp-eared pixy.

"See you in about an hour," I said. "Let me know if you
get through to Landon."

"Will do." Trent hesitated. "Rachel . . . I want you here.
And not because of the baku."

"I know." I went silent, afraid to voice my fears. How
could something so good cause so much trouble? I needed
him, and he needed me, and the demons and elves just
needed to back off.

But neither one of us said anything until finally Trent sighed. "Good. I'll see you soon. Zack?" he said louder, his tone confident again. "I need your help."

My brow furrowed at the click, and then I looked at Jenks hovering at eye level. *I need your help* echoed in my thoughts as I put my phone in my back pocket. I'd be willing to bet Zack had never heard that before. "I wish you could see intentions as you can auras, Jenks. Landon could be using Zack to discredit Trent and the kid wouldn't even know it."

"Me too." Jenks's jaw moved as he worked a chunk of pollen he'd stashed somewhere in the church for emergencies. "It would make keeping your ass above the grass easier. I think I got one of those heat blocks upstairs. Give me a sec."

"Shout if you need some help," I said as he darted for the foyer and the stairs. "I'm going to clean up a little," I added, softer now that I was alone.

I stood, hands on my hips as I looked at the pool table and decided to leave the sketched glyphs. They'd freak the workmen out, but then maybe they'd stop putting their tools on it. The candles, though, were linked to people, and I plucked them one by one and dropped them in the paper bag with the original vials until I could do an incinerate-and-flush.

Everything that didn't go into the waste bin fit in my oversize shoulder bag. Landon would meet with us if Zack was there. And once we proved the baku was in him, we could see about a cease and desist.

But I knew it wasn't going to be that easy. I'd probably have to do something I didn't want to. Grim, I began to make a mental list of what I needed. New sleepy-time charms in my splat gun. A handful of zip-strips for Landon or his security. "A new stick of magnetic chalk," I whispered. Finger sticks, salt vials, a pain amulet or two. Perhaps a curse to remind Landon I was a demon. That slinky black dress that hid my thigh holster really well.

"If I'm lucky, the charms in my room will still be good," I mused, steps fast as I went down the hall. But I slowed as I pushed the door open. Everything was the way I'd left it: the closet open and empty, and the dresser top clear. The bed was stripped, and an old sheet covered it to keep the construction dust that slipped under the door from coating the mattress.

"Bingo," I said, kneeling before one of the boxes stacked in the corner. The harsh sound of the tape lifting off was loud, and I shuffled around the bric-a-brac, dropping a few things into my bag to take home until I found the little vial of pinkie-nail-size sleepy-time splat balls. The use-by date was coming up, but they were still good, and with a quick practiced motion, I refilled my splat gun's reservoir and snapped it closed. Satisfied, I dropped it in my bag and stood.

A sliding thump from the belfry pulled my head up, and I stared at the ceiling as if I could see through it. "Jenks?" Maybe he needed help moving something. "You okay up there?"

Silence came back, and then my pulse hammered at the rhythmic creak of steps. Someone was in the belfry. *With Jenks.*

I jolted into motion, swinging my bag around and fumbling inside it for my splat gun as I went into the hall. "Jenks?" I shouted as I dodged the hole in the sanctuary floor, then skidded to a stop, almost running into the shadow in the dark vestibule.

"Don't pull that, Morgan."

It was Weast, and I froze, my grip wrapped around the butt of my splat gun, still hidden in my bag. *What the hell is he doing here?* "I pull it, I use it," I said, tone hard. "What happens depends on what comes out of your mouth next. Where's Jenks?"

A thread of tension ruined his cool and relaxed stance as he glanced at the stairs to the belfry. "He's with Glenn. Something about a heat block. Apparently it's under a few boxes. I'm sure they'll be down in a moment. Meantime, you and I can talk."

"Talk. Sure." Motions slow, I took my hand out of my bag, satisfied when Weast relaxed. "Walking into a demon's church without knocking isn't smart," I said. "But I'm glad you're here. I could use your help with the baku."

"Twisting curses?" he said, and I took an instinctive step back when he came out of the shadows and into the light. His eyes were on the stripped pool table with its ten-pointed stars and melted wax as if knowing what everything was for. "On a Monday, no less."

My eyes narrowed at his flippant attitude. "It's new. I can prove the baku is attacking people with it. The I.S. is going to have to let everyone go." I hesitated. "I'm its target. They got in the way. Landon is using the baku to try to make me kill Trent."

Weast nodded, his eyes now on the underside of the roof. "That's our theory as well."

My lips parted. *Thanks a hell of a lot for telling me that, Glenn.* "And it's none of my business?" I said, bringing Weast's attention back to me. "The baku has been honing its skills for, what? Two weeks? Damaging people's souls in the process. You can see it in their auras. In mine, in theirs. I can prove Landon is hosting it. I just need—"

"Stop." Weast's voice was soft, holding decades of being obeyed without question. That was okay. Trent could do the same thing, and it never slowed me down. I had decades of experience ignoring demands from doctors with god complexes.

"Because I'm not human? You're a dick. You know that, right?"

Weast's eye twitched. "Stay out of this. Glenn thinks you're of value, but the collateral damage you leave behind is too expensive for me," he said, and my head rose at the heavy steps on the stairs behind him. "I have this under control, and your efforts are making my job harder." He turned to Glenn as he walked in, Jenks on his shoulder.

"Hey, Rachel," the tall man said cheerfully. "Jenks let me in. He needed some help." His smile faded as he took in my anger and Weast's demanding nonchalance. "Ah . . . ," he stammered, the heat block looking small in his hand.

"Weast seems to think he has the baku under control," I interrupted. "I disagree."

Jenks flew to me, wings rasping and his hand on his sword. "Sorry," he muttered, right next to my ear. "I thought Glenn was alone."

"Don't worry about it," I said, eyes never leaving Weast. "I can help," I said louder, to Weast this time. "*We* can help," I amended. "Trent and I can prove Landon is hosting the baku."

But Weast was walking away, pointing at Glenn to move out before him. "Back off," Weast said over his shoulder. "Leave Landon alone."

"He deserves a warning," I said, jolting into motion and following them. "You know he's in danger and you don't care," I said, then got it. "My God. You're using him as bait."

Weast halted, and I jerked to a stop before I ran into him. Eyes narrowed, he looked at me, hand hovering near his eagle amulet. "Glenn, give me a moment with Morgan."

"Sir . . ."

Weast turned to him, and grimacing, Glenn set the heat block on the windowsill and walked out. Unhappy, Jenks rattled his wings. Shoulders hunched, Weast pressed close until I fought the urge to back up. "If you continue to stick your nose where it doesn't belong, you will be swept up with him," Weast said, his dark eyes narrowed. "I won't warn you again."

"Try it," I said, and Weast chuckled, rolling his shoulders aggressively as he walked out.

"Let him go, Rache," Jenks said, but I wasn't about to follow him. Pissed, I tugged the door shut, appreciating the hard thud. Angry, I shifted the bar to lock the door. I'd only have to unlock it again to leave, but that wasn't the point. "You okay?" Jenks asked, and I nodded, arms over my middle. I didn't like Weast. Didn't like his threats. Didn't like how he had Glenn at his beck and call and didn't value his opinion.

"We're still going after Landon, aren't we?" Jenks said, and I nodded. I didn't like the distasteful head of the dewar, but I liked a know-it-all, clandestine group of humans who thought they could use him as bait even less.

CHAPTER

23

IT WENT WITHOUT SAYING THAT I FELT SPECIAL BEHIND THE wheel of Trent's favorite two-door. It accelerated like a startled horse and turned like a bird. The gray finish moved like smoke in the sun, and I tried to play it cool when people ogled it at stoplights. But it was hard with the wind in my hair and my sunglasses on, especially when Takata's latest, "Gritty Rainbows," came on all eight of the car's high-end speakers.

"Do you think he's still singing about you?" Jenks said from the rearview mirror. The afternoon sun was shining through his wings and dust to make him look magical.

Wincing, I lowered the volume. "I hope not." The new single was Takata's usual unrepentant, shrewd, loud anger at the system, but this time there was a hint that things might work out even if it was all going to hell. The message seemed to be on-target, as it had shot to the single digits on more than one chart and hung there since its release. That its inspiration might have been in my ongoing trials seemed likely. Why would Takata mess with what had worked in the past?

"You should have told me you were attacked this morning."

Jenks's voice was sullen, and my attention flicked from the road to him. "I handled it," I said as I made my way through the Hollows to the waterfront.

"Yeah? That's kind of the point of having me there, isn't

it?" His wings hummed, and a new sheet of dust spilled down. "Thanks for crapping all over my daisies. I feel useless enough as it is. Holed up with my kids for the winter, getting in their way. We're a team, Rache. Even if Ivy isn't part of it anymore. Maybe we're more of a team."

"I'm sorry," I said, both hands on the wheel instead of cupping around him as I wanted to. Not that he'd let me. "You're right. I should've told you. Don't blab to Trent, okay? If he knows, he'll try to convince me to go into seclusion, and then we're down half of what makes us work."

Jenks sighed, wings drooping. "You think not telling him is the easy way, but it's not."

My lips twitched in guilt. "What difference does it make as long as I don't go to sleep?" The Hollows waterfront was busy with the early-evening rush hour, and I slowed to a crawl behind a big-ass SUV plastered with witch-themed stickers. But my eyes flicked to my bag when my phone dinged. "Could you get that for me? It might be Trent."

"Sure." I slowed to a halt, turn signal ticking, as Jenks dropped down to shove things around in my bag.

"Ah, Trent says no-go for tonight, but we're on for an early breakfast at Carew Tower. He also called in a dinner order at Celeste's, and could you pick it up on your way back? Already paid for." Jenks made a rude sound. "And then he has some hearts and crap."

I smiled, even though the delay was probably Landon's ploy to give the baku one more night to get the job done. There'd be fewer people around for breakfast, which was good. Hiding a splat gun in my usual casual security top and skirt would be easier, too. "Could you send him a livelong-and-prosper emoji for me?" I asked, and Jenks groaned and dropped back down.

"Flaming fairy farts, Rache," he grumbled as he scrolled to find it and hit send. "I can't believe I'm doing this. You want me to have him check a box if he likes you or not?"

"Thanks," I said as he returned to the mirror, his cheerful gold dust telling me that despite his continued dramatic gagging sounds he secretly approved.

Finally the light changed, and after making the turn, I pulled into Piscary's empty, weeds-in-the-cracks parking lot. Ivy's cycle was in back by the truck-delivery door. Beside it was Nina's little red sports car and an unfamiliar black SUV.

Oh yeah, I thought, remembering Ivy telling me that she had guests from DC coming in. The undead didn't travel much because of the necessity of a guaranteed light-tight space to wait out the day, so it wasn't surprising that they—whoever they were—were still here. They'd probably head out tonight after catching a quick bite. Ha-ha.

Lip curling, I slowed as I drove past the overdone black-and-chrome rental to park at the quay. "You want anything?" I said as I put Trent's car in park.

"A nap." Jenks stretched, and a contented gold dust slipped down. "How long you going to be?"

I reached for the handle, fumbling when I didn't find it where I thought it should be. "I've got to go through my spell cupboard. Then my closet. Take a shower. Detangle my hair. Demark my heels. Oil my gun. Not in that order. Two hours?"

"Why do women always overcomplicate things?" he said as I got out. "I mean . . . ," he added, having darted outside to wait impatiently for me to lock the car. "Take a shower. Do your hair. Shine your shoes. I can be ready in five minutes. Clean my sword. Bam! Let's go."

I smiled as I adjusted my sunglasses. "Breakfast date or not, it's Carew Tower. If I don't look as if I belong, I'll end up in the I.S. lockup when this is done instead of chatting with the manager about how to pay for the damage."

But as I neared Kisten's boat, I decided it was likely going to be less of a breakfast meeting and more of a high-powered, magic-laced discussion that broke something. I wanted Landon's blood, and he wasn't going to give it up knowing that I would use it to incriminate him.

Jenks lit on my shoulder with a tired sigh. "I swear, it's easier being a pixy sometimes."

"Sometimes I'd agree with you." My arms swung as I

walked, and the sun felt good. I lightly touched the soggy algae-covered pylon to keep my balance as I lurched down onto the teak boards, boot heels clunking. The boat swayed imperceptibly with my weight, and head down, I rummaged for my keys as I stepped into the cool shade of the large overhang.

But I froze as I stood before the sliding-glass doors, frowning. The door was unlocked.

Ivy? I wondered, hesitating. And then the tantalizing, spicy scent of the long undead tripped down my spine, plucking every nerve ending on the way down to make me shiver.

"Hey, uh, Rache?" Jenks said in warning, but I was way ahead of him, and I took my splat pistol from my purse, backing up into the sun until my calves hit the back bench of the large canopied cockpit.

"Who the devil is on our boat?" I whispered as the shadow of a man approached the door.

I couldn't tap a ley line while over water, but damn it, someone was on my boat! Even in the semidark of the boat's interior, I could see he was in a suit coat and sported a professional haircut and a slim build. If he was a vamp, he was clearly still alive since the sun was up. If he didn't have a good reason for being on my boat, I was going to turn him into a dead one.

Expression grim, Jenks hovered beside me and loosened his garden sword.

But when the man came closer—smiling and ducking his head, actually giving me a little wave as he reached for the latch—I wondered if he *was* a vampire.

Simply put, he was not beautiful. Oh, he might have been once, being tall and having a slim build. The dead bred what they liked over the eons, and the dead liked beauty above all.

This guy wasn't it.

"Sorry for startling you," he said as he slid the door open and came out, blinking in the shade of the overhang. "I was hoping to find you, actually. Ivy said you might be

here. You're Ms. Rachel Morgan, yes?" he added, eyes
touching briefly on Jenks before returning to me.

His voice was average everything, and unsure, I nodded,
reassessing my first impression. It wasn't that he was un-
attractive, but his numerous scars got in the way. His nose
was misshapen from being broken too many times. Lines
from battle, not the bedroom, ran along his chin and one
side of his face to his eye, which was a little droopy compared to the other. His irises were brown and his complexion tan—and kind of lumpy. Short, carefully styled dark
hair showed that one of his ears had been ravaged. Early
thirties maybe.

But it was the wave of vampire incense lifting from him
that worried me. He *was* a living vampire, one holding a
great deal of status by the amount of pheromones he was
giving off. He'd been sipping on someone old for a very
long time, and probably vice versa. "Yes," I said, remembering what he'd asked me as I tried to reconcile him with
everything I knew about vampires—and came up short.

Slowly his smile faded as my eyes traveled over him,
clearly comparing him to what he "ought" to be. He pulled
himself straighter, tugging his smartly tailored suit coat down
over his linen slacks. There was no tie, but it would have
looked wrong on him. More scars peeped from his wrists,
appearing self-inflicted, not vampire bedroom play. By the
age of them, he'd been working his way up from average Joe
to someone's scion for a long time, and my pulse quickened
at both the threat and the promise that held. But it was his
unshakable confidence that drew me—confidence that said
he'd been sipping blood so old, it tasted like electric dust.

"How like a vampire, eh, Jenks?" I said, and the man's
faltering smile vanished. "No one home, so he assumed he
can go in." I put the splat gun in my bag, sure he could move
fast enough to avoid it. The keys, I kept in my fist. "Get off
my boat."

"It's not your boat," he said, unable to hide his anger as
his pupils grew and the brown rim around his pupils
shrank. "It belongs to Kisten Felps's estate, since given over

to the city of Cincinnati. I have every right to be here to evaluate the assets available to the city's master vampire. Which makes you a squatter."

"Son of a green troll fart! Who do you think you are?" Jenks said, and I cocked my hip, staying right where I was in the sun.

"I'm glad you brought that up," I said, trying to appear relaxed as the pheromones he was giving off began tripping red flag after red flag. "Before you get all excited about evicting me, check with your lawyer. The Hollows has laws on the books protecting so-called squatters when a past relationship is involved."

"Really . . ."

"Yes, really." I shifted my grip on my keys, making sure he saw the little cross charm hanging from them. "Who are you?" I added as my libido began making little bubbles of memory pop against the top of my brain, memories of Kisten, of Ivy, of the stupid things I'd done before I wrote vampire sex out of my Little Book of Rachel. This guy was clearly someone's scion. *Damn it, why do I always like the dangerous ones?*

Again he smiled, pulling something through me to make my knees feel like water. "My name is Pike," he said as he came forward a step, hand extended. "Let's start over. You must be Ms. Morgan." His eyes flicked to Jenks when the pixy hummed a warning, but he didn't take his hand back, and I slowly reached out to meet it. His fingers were tan, slimmer than Trent's, and he wore tiny cuff links in the shape of skulls and crossbones. *Cute.*

"Like the fish?" Jenks said snidely. "Cold, ugly, and lots of sharp teeth."

"You forgot mean," Pike said with what looked like a real smile as my hand fitted briefly into his. His touch was warm and callused, and I knew how his fingers would feel lightly running down my body. *Damn vamp pheromones.*

"Rachel," I said, then stifled a quiver when our fingers parted and the vampire incense swamped me with the gusto of a Sunday school song.

"Rache . . . ," Jenks said in warning, and I took a step back. The thought of throwing him overboard trickled through me, but I was smarter than I had been three years ago. I think.

"I, ah, take it you're here with the DC delegation checking out Cincy's master vampire situation." I backed up again, starting when I hit the seats.

Pike nodded. "Constance Corson would like to meet with you." He took in my sudden alarm and smiled. "Ivy and Nina are with her as well."

Oh good. One skilled, manipulative undead and her scion, one iffy-control undead, and a highly protective, possibly overreacting living vampire. What could go wrong?

"Not today. Sorry," I said, then let out a breath I hadn't known I'd been holding. That Cincy's new master vampire was a woman had me worried. I'd rather deal with a dead man than a dead woman any day or night.

"She's downstairs. Waiting." Pike tried to smile over his frown as he gestured to Piscary's back loading dock. "We leave tonight, and she'd like to use the time to meet you."

"I bet she would," Jenks muttered, now perched in the ceiling supports.

"Sorry." Pike was between me and my door, and I wished he'd move. "I can't fit another appointment in today."

"Make time," Pike almost growled, and I jerked, too slow as he stepped forward and took my arm. "As a personal favor to me," he said as Jenks's wings rasped a warning. "I'm not going back down there without you. It will only take a moment."

My fingers fisting my keys tightened, but scratching him would have only made things more awkward. Besides, if he was yanking me to the dock, then he was moving away from the door.

"Sorry about this," I said, even as a rush of good feeling spread through me when Pike flooded the air with pheromones to soothe and befuddle.

Jenks knew what was going to happen and flew clear. Pike didn't have a clue, oblivious that me tripping on my feet was really to pull his head down so my rising knee would hit his scarred, ugly chin even harder.

Pain raced through my knee as it hit him with a resounding *crack*. Pike grunted, his grip on me loosening in surprise. I ducked into him, arm twisting to lever him over to crash back first onto the teak floorboards, where he lay, legs askew.

I dropped down, pixy dust wreathing me as I put my leg across Pike's neck, my fingers twined in his surprisingly silky hair. It would have been a shame to pull it out, but I would. "Now you can tell her I hit you," I said. "She can't get mad if you tell her I hit you."

Pike blinked up at me, a not-surprising hint of appreciation and delight in him. Then it vanished in a flicker of worry.

"Don't try to bespell me," I said as I got off him and extended a hand to help him up. "You don't have enough undead blood in you to manage it, and you'll only embarrass yourself."

"Apparently," Pike muttered as I yanked him up and let go of his hand the instant I could.

"Pike, was it?" I said as he dusted off his jacket, looking both irate and chagrined. "I fully understand and appreciate Constance's schedule, but I'm not coming up with excuses because I don't want to meet her. I simply don't have time on such short notice. I've already made plans, and I need this afternoon to get ready. Shower, do my hair, practice a few new curses."

Pike frowned as he glanced at Jenks polishing his sword. "She's going to be Cincy's master vampire. This is more important than a date."

Things had shifted. My back was to the door, and he was on the outskirts in the sun. It gave me a confidence I hoped wasn't a delusion. "I really wish it was a date," I said as I hiked my bag back up my shoulder and put a hand on the door as if dismissing him. "Suffice it to say, I'm working, and I can't meet with her today. Please give her my apologies."

"You can take ten minutes—"

He was *almost* asking now, instead of demanding, which meant he was going to endure some pain for coming back without me even if I did knock him down. Vampire power structures sucked.

"It's not the ten minutes that it would take to go down and meet Constance, but the six hours after that I'd be spending with the I.S. after I smack her up to impress upon her that I will not be her underling. Maybe in a few days after I finish taking care of the baku."

Pike's expression hardened. "The baku is not your responsibility."

I glanced at Jenks, and the pixy snorted. Curious, though, that Constance knew about it. Knew and was doing nothing. "It's in my city, isn't it?" I said as I opened my door. The scent of vampire slipped out, making me wonder how long he'd been in there: waiting for me, going through my things, taking measurements for curtains. "Look, I'm sorry if this gets you into trouble."

"Trouble . . . ," Pike echoed, and Jenks dropped down to land on my shoulder.

"Tell Constance that if she wants to see me, I'd be more than happy to meet her. But not today, and certainly not in the same room where I downed her predecessor. Tell you what." Head bowed, I fumbled in my bag for one of our old cards. "Here's my cell number," I said as I extended it. "Call me in about a week. I'll probably have healed from whatever damage bringing in the baku is going to cause by then, and we can get together somewhere nice and neutral. Like the zoo," I added flippantly. "Or a coffeehouse."

Pike looked at the card, eyebrows going high at the wasp-waisted silhouette that Jenks said looked like a hooker. "You never downed Cormel."

"I was talking about Piscary. Cormel was too much politician and not enough mob boss to control the city. You know that, or Washington wouldn't be looking to replace him." I backed up into the boat, feeling safer though I wasn't. "It takes a firm hand to keep Cincy in order. We've been given free rein to police ourselves for a long time, and if you push them too hard, upset the status quo too far without an obvious, clear benefit, they will take you out. Or try to."

My thoughts went to my church, and I stifled a sigh. Misunderstanding or not, it was still gone. "I'll give Constance that for free. I'd hate to see her be responsible for losing a Cincy landmark like Pizza Piscary's because she couldn't respect another professional's time."

Pike was silent, and I resisted the urge to cover my neck as he stared at its unmarked smoothness. Ivy's scar was there, as was Al's, both invisible, both like vampire candy. *How many licks does it take . . . ?*

"Would you please get off my boat?" I said as a trill of sensation dropped to my groin from just the weight of his gaze. "I have too much to do today already."

Pike took a step back, unhappy and twitchy. "You have three months," he said, mood bad.

"Until what?" Jenks asked for both of us.

Pike lurched up onto the quay, then hesitated to look down at us. "Until you're evicted. As you say, there are laws for squatters." He looked at Piscary's, worry pinching his ugly brow. "Why the hell are you always so nice, Pike?" he said to himself, then walked away.

"Whatever." It was the best comeback I could come up with, and shaking, I shut the door to lean back against it. Damn vamp pheromones. I was going to have to air the entire place out.

"Maybe I could have handled that better," I said, nose wrinkled as I smelled Pike everywhere. But damn it, boat or not, this was where I lived.

At least for the next three months.

CHAPTER
24

"YOU THINK LANDON IS GOING TO PULL A GOPHER?" JENKS asked, and I looked up from the spectacular view of the Hollows, lights just now beginning to wink off as the sky brightened. I was logy and slow from lack of sleep despite the no-doze taped to my biceps, but he was bright-eyed and awake. Legs crossed, he sat on the rim of the sugar bowl in his usual working black tights. His usual flash of red to warn off other pixies was gone since they were all underground. By Jenks's reasoning, all of Cincinnati was his garden from November to March—and it showed.

"No, he'll be here," I said, then tucked a wayward strand of hair behind an ear, feeling special in my Carew Tower finest. My eyes flicked to the bar, where Trent and Zack stood, both in suits and ties despite the *ungodly* early hour, looking like brothers at the far ends of their parents' fertile years. "He'll show if only to try to drag Zack away," I added.

"Not on my watch," Jenks muttered. His gaze was on the honey pot that had come with my tea, but I knew he wouldn't indulge. Not when we were working.

And that was what we were doing, even if I was in a smart business dress with my hair tamed under a charm and my spelling supplies in a new leather bag. Trent looked just as nice. I hadn't seen him in a full suit and tie in weeks. Carew Tower's rotating restaurant demanded the best of a person, and I smiled and said thank you when the water attendant came over to top off my glass. It was important to stay hydrated when you were kicking ass.

The man hesitated when he saw Jenks, his eyes going to the three vacant chairs before backing away. Satisfied, I sent Jenks to the ceiling with a finger twitch, for a quick recon. Fatigue pulled at me as I dug in my purse to find Jenks's heat block under my splat gun. A quick glance to be sure no one was watching, and I artfully wrapped it in my napkin and set it squarely in the middle of the table beside the unlit ambient candle. He could sit on it when he got back, and no one would be the wiser.

Satisfied, I settled into my chair and sipped my coffee, praying for a caffeine buzz. Staying awake to stave off a baku attack was working, but I was tired, cranky, and not thinking straight. Quen was in a bad mood from researching Trisk's journals, but listening to Trent talk to his girls on the phone had been the worst, and my eyes strayed to him, now deep in conversation with the restaurant manager.

I'd already talked to both the building's and the restaurant's security, but settling things with management and promises of money were likely what would keep the I.S. from being called if things got icky. And it would get icky. I could tell already.

But despite it all, a smile grew as I watched Trent work the manager over, smoothing out the coming problems before they occurred. His hair caught the light over the bar, and he had an easy, confident stance with one foot on the rail. Beside him, Zack looked like a yearling colt: lean, elegant . . . and jumpy. His suit had narrow lapels and that extra pocket that had been popular when I'd been growing up, making it likely that it was one of Trent's old ones rather than something new. The tie, though, was this year's style, and as I watched Zack touch his sleeve and run his hand down his side, I was pretty sure he liked the way he looked in it.

"Enjoying the view?" Jenks asked, and I flushed, not having heard him drop down. He was sitting on the napkin-wrapped block, eyeing me as if knowing my thoughts. "Sun will be up soon. Do you think Landon timed this so Bis would be asleep?"

"I don't think he plans that far ahead," I said. "But Bis has a no-doze amulet. I simply have to tap a line, and he'll come."

Jenks's eyes came back from the honey. "He can find you, but can't sing you the lines?"

Eyes down, I fiddled with my teacup with the Carew Tower logo. "It's like the auras we're parsing out, Jenks," I said softly. "You can do a lot with just the surface, but for the intimate things, you need a more delicate, finicky touch."

"I suppose." He ran a hand behind his neck in unease. "I still say Landon won't show."

I followed Jenks's gaze to Trent and Zack, now headed our way and looking at home in their suits and easy confidence. At least, Trent was confident. Zack looked kind of sick. "Everything okay?" I asked as Zack gingerly took the chair with the best view of the changing cityscape. It also put his back to the elevator, and neither Trent nor I had wanted it.

Trent nodded as he sat across from me. "The manager will let us know when Landon is on his way up."

"Good." I smiled at Zack, wondering if he was worried we might give him up in return for Landon backing off on Trent. "We can relax for a second or two." I took a slice of fruit-laden breakfast bread, knife clinking on the dish as I scraped up some butter. "Have you ever been up here, Zack?"

He jumped at his name, then smiled to hide his surprise. "No. Do you think we'll be able to see your church when we turn?"

"Maybe," I said, but I knew we would. I'd checked the first time I'd gotten up here.

The water attendant swung back around, and the table was silent as he topped off the glasses and retreated. Jenks's wings made a regretful hum as he looked longingly at the honey pot.

"So, Rachel," Trent said, elbows comfortably on the table, "Quen didn't find anything in a second perusal of my mother's journals. Maybe I should let Al look. You said he knew her."

"You'd let Al look at your mom's journals?" I said, surprised, and he nodded, clearly discomfited. "Sure, but if he knew a way to capture the baku, he probably wouldn't be under house arrest." I set the bread down and surreptitiously cleaned the butter from my fingers on the underside of the tablecloth since Jenks had my napkin.

"He might be able to piece something together." Eyes pinched, Trent leaned back as if looking for some coffee. "And if not, just letting him look might make him feel better about his daughter dating an elf." Trent glanced at Zack to see what he thought, but the kid was mowing down the breakfast bread as if it was candy, and probably hadn't heard.

Daughter? I thought, then smiled slightly. It wasn't a bad comparison. The mystics made me too erratic for Al to call me a student. *Daughter* wasn't right, but I knew that Dali had made Al responsible for me. I'd been told enough times that if I screwed up, Al would take the blame.

Which then begged the question of whether Trent was getting pressure from not only the enclave but Al and Dali as well to end our relationship. Enough pressure that he felt he had to prove himself.

"Ah, Trent," I said, not sure I wanted to have this conversation in front of Zack, but Trent wasn't listening, his attention now focused on the manager.

"He's coming," Trent said, and Zack stiffened, panic flashing across him as he brushed the crumbs off himself and onto the floor.

"Okay, I'm out of here." Jenks took flight and, with a shimmering trail of dust, vanished into the restaurant's decor.

Trent, too, seemed to gather himself, his slim fingers making sure his tie was in place. "Jenks tells me Weast warned you off Landon yesterday," he said.

"Yep." I watched Zack, not liking his near fear at the prospect of Landon at our table. "Weast as much as admitted to using him as bait to catch the baku." *And how do you feel about that, Zack?* I thought, but the kid looked afraid, not angry.

"I thought as much." Cool and calm, Trent steepled his fingers. "Jon is trying to dig up some dirt on the Order. He's fried three computers so far, and the only thing he's found is that they began as one of the human-only security groups that evolved in the first few years of the Turn. Most joined the FIB when it formed. The rest went underground. Their reach, I'm afraid to admit, is far beyond mine. And unlike the FIB, they have no qualms about using magic."

Which explained that eagle amulet that Weast used to dampen my contact with a ley line. "At least they aren't a hate group." I watched the elevator, glad my back wasn't to it, as was Zack's. "They did lock up HAPA when we caught them."

"True." Trent grimaced. "But the farmer doesn't hate his cows, even as he considers them inferior and keeps them in pens." His eye twitched and his lips pressed together. "There he is."

Zack turned, his face pale when he spun back around. "I'm not leaving with him."

My jaw clenched, and I stood when Trent rose. Gawky, Zack got to his feet as well. *I swear, Zack, if you are playing us, I will put a bow on you and give you to a demon.*

Landon was in a suit, the purple ribbon of his office about his neck going well with his tie. He wore rings on his right hand, the one on his Jupiter finger looking like a more ornate version of Zack's. I'd have been willing to bet that the amulet he had on held magic. And the pin on his lapel. And maybe his cuff links. But as I unfocused my attention and brought my second sight into play, it was his aura that was the most compelling. Zack was right. Something was wrong. It looked transparent, as if something was missing. It wasn't nearly enough to go to the FIB or the I.S. with, though, and my fingers itched to do the curse and see the damage myself.

Landon's security was all in black suits and sporting

short military-style haircuts, even the woman. I couldn't help but notice they all had that same pinkie ring, and I wondered if it was part of the security package. I met the woman's eyes, reading in her quick assessment of me that she wouldn't dismiss me as arm candy as the other two had, and I lifted my chin, telling her in language older than speech that I wouldn't hurt her, if she didn't hurt me.

But she shrugged and touched her sidearm. She'd do what she had to, and I sighed and fingered my splat gun through the supple leather of my purse. It was going to be like that, then.

"I'm not leaving with you," Zack said before Landon could widen his pretend smile.

Landon ignored Zack, apart from a glance thick with annoyance, and my own eyes narrowed. "Good morning, Trent," he said, ignoring me as well as his three security detail spread out, each taking a stance at a nearby table. The few people about had noticed, their conversations becoming tense.

"Trent, don't shake his hand," I said as I looked at Landon's aura again, and Trent smoothly shifted his extended arm to a gesture inviting him to sit. Trent's aura was just as bright and clear as always, the sparkles that he and Ivy shared trailing after him like pixy dust.

"Please. Have a seat," Trent said. "Thank you for agreeing to meet with us."

I stifled a shudder and dropped my second sight as Trent came around behind Zack to help me with my seat. Zack's aura was bright green, sporting slashes of purple and those same damn red streaks that spoke of a troubled past. And sparkles. No wonder Trent liked him. I looked up as I finished scooting my chair in, surprised that Landon was still standing.

"I'm not staying," he said as Trent returned to his seat. "I'm here to collect my acolyte."

"No, you aren't," Zack said, chin high and cheeks red.

Trent paused, halfway down to his chair, and from above came Jenks's wing snap.

"Yes, I am," Landon said, and I cleared my throat as Trent pulled himself upright.

"Perhaps the gentlemen should sit down if they're going to argue over where a nearly legal adult is going to park his ass," I said with my most fetching smile. There were other people in this restaurant, and they all had phones. I'd had my fill of my bad temper landing on social media.

Landon smiled as he sat. It was fake, but Zack sighed in relief.

Motions graceful, Trent sat as well, a practiced hand beckoning the waitstaff forward.

But as we were all given the one-page menu with this morning's fare, I realized the bartender had her hands on her hips. She was staring at the waitstaff, and frowning, I began to pay attention as well. Suddenly I realized the restaurant's staff was being replaced by black-clad, trim thirtysomethings wearing running shoes. They weren't Landon's men. Or the I.S. Or the FIB.

Then I looked up at the shaved-headed server blathering on about farm to table and what was in season that went into the omelet, and I froze. This guy was from the Order.

Great. Weast's threat swam up from the back of my thoughts, and I forced my jaw to unclench. He couldn't arrest me for talking to the man, right? But the Order didn't arrest anyone. They simply shoved you in the back of a white panel van and you were never seen again.

"Coffee?" Trent suggested, his pleasant voice jerking my attention back. "If Landon isn't staying, perhaps we should start with something to drink. I'll have a coffee."

"Water," Landon said. "Still if you have it. Zack, what would you like?"

"Nothing from you," he muttered.

"Espresso?" I smirked at Landon's security. They'd all slacked off, blind to the real threat.

"Right away," the waiter who wasn't a waiter said, head high as he made eye contact with the guy manning the elevator. People were being encouraged to move to the other side of the restaurant, and the manager was almost dragged into the kitchen, protesting. Trent sighed as he met my eyes, knowing it, too. We didn't have time for pleasantries.

"Landon," I said, and the man's lip curled. "You're being used. I don't know why I care, but it bothers me that a hidden human security force thinks it's okay to use us as bait to cage something worse."

"You are amazing." Landon leaned back in his chair, arms crossed confidently over his middle. "You really think that is what's going on?"

"The Order doesn't care one troll snot that you're sending the baku to make me kill Trent," I said, deciding not to bring up that we were both surrounded. "All they want is the baku. They want it, and they're not averse to some major dewar collateral damage to get it."

Smile fading, Landon sat up, his arms unfolding. "Prove it."

"What?" Trent said dryly. "That the Order wants the baku? Or that you're sending it to push Rachel into killing me?"

Zack snorted, then tried to hide it behind a sip of water.

Landon spared an ugly glare at him before turning to me. "I'm here to collect my student. Now," he added loudly, and I put a hand on Zack's arm to keep him from bolting.

"Tell him what you want," I said to Zack. "We've got your back." *Please don't screw us, Zack,* I thought, my breath slipping from me in relief when Zack's chin lifted.

"I'm not leaving with you."

"Za-a-ack," Landon threatened, his attention jerking to me when I casually unscrewed the saltshaker and spilled half of its contents on the white tablecloth.

"It's eating your soul, Landon," I said softly as I used my nail to push the salt into a pentagon. "Give me a drop of blood, and I'll show you how deep the damage goes."

"You think I'm going to give you a focusing object?" Landon stood, clearly angry. Or maybe it was fear. He knew elf magic was wonky and mine wasn't. "Zack, get up."

"No," Zack said defiantly, and Landon went almost choleric, red-faced with anger as he reached over the table and tried to manhandle Zack up.

"Landon, let him go," Trent said tightly as he reached out as well.

"Trent, stop!" I exclaimed, feeling Zack tap a line.

There was a burst of light, and Landon yelped, hand jerking as he fell back. My eyes shot to the Order, but they didn't care, ringing us on the outside. Even the bartender was gone.

"You little whelp," Landon said, waving his own people back. "How dare you!"

Spinning his ring on his finger, Landon began mumbling. I stiffened, then strengthened my hold on the ley line running through the nearby university. Like light itself, it spilled through me, carrying the whispers of everyone else who was using it. It was community, and I soaked it in, relishing it.

"He's got this," Trent whispered, pride in his voice as he looked at Zack, the kid now standing with new confidence, pulling his shoulders down and his head up.

"Fire in the hole!" Jenks shrilled from somewhere, and I yanked ley line energy into me, spilling into my chi and overflowing to spindle in my head.

"Ta na shay, voulden!" Landon exclaimed, his expression ugly as he gestured.

Face white, Zack pushed back, a fisted hand motioning to make a field before him.

"Look out!" I shouted as Landon's spell misfired. The bulk of the energy went into the overhead light, and with a sharp crack, it burst. I ducked, invoking a bubble as the shards went everywhere. Trent, too, had gotten a circle up in time, and Zack had made one even before Landon had finished.

"You okay?" I said, then followed Zack's wide eyes to Landon. One of the shards had hit him and his face was bleeding.

"Is that what you meant to do?" Zack said boldly, and with a gesture and a soft word, his own glow of light replaced the busted lamp.

Landon stared at it. "How . . . ?" His gaze went to Trent. "Your magic works. . . ."

"Have a seat, Landon." Trent let his circle drop. "I could use your help in getting the elven community to accept the new constraints on our species' magic."

I felt the Order retreat as Landon slowly sank down. He touched his face when he realized he was bleeding, and I watched him use a napkin to dab it up, wanting it.

"You got our magic to work," Landon said, voice wispy.

Trent leaned back, his fingers steepled. "Zack and I, yes," he said, his confidence almost palpable. "He's an exceptional student. I'd like to extend an invitation for him to work with me. Say, for a semester? Whereupon at the conclusion we can revisit his tutelage."

Zack brightened. Clearly this was news to him, but Landon's awareness sharpened.

"You think to add to your family by stealing mine?" he said, and I began to push the salt into radiating lines. "How very old-school, Trent, but your pathetic attempts to add to your lineage while you cleave to a barren woman will only show your shortcomings that much clearer."

I looked up, feeling as if I'd been socked in the gut. Trent's fist went white-knuckled.

"Yes," Landon said, goading. "A barren, worthless woman who will drag you down. Rachel, has Trent told you that his Sa'han status will be restored if he marries Ellasbeth? He'd have a voice again. A thousand voices. I wouldn't stand a chance. But he won't because he's a fool."

I swallowed hard, finding it hard to breathe. It wasn't anything I didn't already know, but it was hard to hear it so openly.

"Zack, let's go," Landon said, and my chin lifted. I'd heard worse in third grade.

"Touch me, and I'll show you what else I learned," Zack growled.

"Now!" Landon barked, and from the ceiling, Jenks rattled his wings.

I'd had enough, and with a quick motion, I snatched

Landon's bloody napkin. "You don't look good, Landon," I
said, and Landon's face went ashen. "Open your soul and
say *ahhh.* . . ."

"Give that back," he said, reaching, and Trent grabbed
his arm. Landon's men pushed forward.

"Rhombus!" I exclaimed, and they slammed into the
outside of my large imagined circle. It wouldn't stand
against a determined assault, but I only had to stop them for
thirty seconds.

"Ta na shay," I said, strengthening my hold on the line,
and Landon pushed back in his chair, horrified at what I
might do—a demon using elven magic. *Hear me, you crazy
bitch of a demon. I need your help. "Ta na shay!"* I exclaimed as I smeared his blood on the table's candle and lit
it with a stray thought. *"Obscurum per obscuris. Wee-keh
Wehr-sah,"* I said triumphantly, my words spilling over
themselves as his security ran their fingers over my circle,
shouting as they looked for a way in. Head high, I found
Landon's eyes and snapped my fingers. *"Ta na shay."*

"Dude!" Zack exclaimed as the pentagon opened and
twisted with a soft hiss, the flame from the smeared candle
flickering into existence at all ten points. Landon's eyes
were fixed on the glowing glyph in horrified fascination.
Trent's sound of dismay and Jenks's muffled "Holy shit"
drew my eyes down, and I stared. All but three of Landon's
flames were black.

Lips parted, I met Trent's shocked eyes. Behind him, the
Order was taking note, but not one moved forward to stop
me. Perhaps they were interested as well.

"I'm so sorry," I whispered, meaning it, and then I
jerked as something alien and wrong seemed to slip into
me. Fumbling, I tried to push it away, physically shoving
myself back from the table. Panic took me when it slithered
past my mental barriers as if they didn't exist.

Will you fall to me today? snaked through my mind, and
I freaked. It wasn't my thought. It was the baku, and I
wasn't asleep! On the table, Landon's imagined candles

flickered, a few of the flames regaining a healthy color as the baku tried to move from him to me.

Get out! I demanded, ramrod straight in my chair as I fumbled to control my thoughts. But it wasn't like fighting the Goddess, who absorbed memories. It was trying to eat my soul!

Too fatigued to expel me, too alone to hold me, the baku thought, and I stiffened, feeling assaulted when it sank a long thought deep into my core. Panic swirled. I was awake. It couldn't take me. Unless . . . it had eaten deep enough and I couldn't stop it.

Not today, I thought savagely, and in a desperate effort to get it out, I touched my thoughts to a ley line and let it pour in, pushing the energy from my well-used channels and into the baku.

A laughing sensation rose as the baku rode the incoming tide of energy. But then its satisfaction faltered, and I felt a long finger of it pull free, and then another, and finally I took a breath as the first shimmer of nothing stood between it and my psyche. *Not today, but soon,* it agreed, and then I jumped, everyone crying out in surprise when Bis crashed heavily onto the table. With a burning pop through my thoughts, the baku was gone, and the line hung in me alone.

Immediately I dropped the ley line. My circle fell with an audible snap. Landon's security rushed forward, pulling him to his feet and dragging him away until the man shoved them off. Trent stood tall over me, his expression grim as his hand rested on my shoulder. I didn't think he knew what had happened, and shaking, I reached up and touched his fingers, grateful for him.

He was there, and the baku was gone. My soul was still strong enough to fight it off. That was four times now, each attack more effective. Sleeping under guard or charmed silver would only let it pare another layer from me. Maybe the demons were right.

"Thanks," I whispered to Bis, and the kid sidestepped the scattered curse to hop to my other shoulder. That no-doze amulet was around his neck, and even as I watched, the sun rose and a rosy haze touched the tallest buildings.

"I didn't do anything. You kicked it out on your own," Bis said, his eyes squinting at the new light, and I gave his toes a squeeze as he slumped, clearly tired.

"Kicked it out?" Trent said, and I looked up at him, wanting to tell him but afraid.

But my cold face gave me away. His grip on me tightened as he turned to Landon and the delicious scent of angry elf flowed from him like a balm. Zack was ashen, and Jenks stood on the table with his sword in hand, ready to give someone a lobotomy. Failed attempt or not, it was obvious that the baku had come from Landon. But the proof was his word against ours. Worthless.

"You've been a bad religious leader, Landon," I said. My voice was low to keep it from trembling and I didn't dare try to stand. Not yet. "The baku has eaten you to a shell."

"I have this under control," Landon said, but he looked as shaken as I felt, and I frowned. Weast had said the same thing.

"Then you don't understand what's going on," Trent said.

Landon pushed his security away. "You have to sleep sometime, Morgan," he said, and a real fear zinged through me. "You. Stop being stupid and come with me," Landon directed to Zack, and the kid twitched. "You aren't equipped to function in the real world. What are you going to do? Get a job? You don't know how to do anything."

My lips parted at the insult and Jenks rose. But Zack was twisting that ring off his finger, gasping in pain when it pulled free. Chin high, he threw it at Landon.

Landon caught it with one hand, almost as if the ring had been magnetized. Expression sour, he put it on his finger next to its twin. "Your entire life will be a waste," he said, and then he took the candle and strode away, his security hustling to keep up.

"Hey!" I said as I reached after the candle only to slump back and let my hand fall. I'd never get it back. Landon knew what it was. Or, at least, he knew that it was important.

"Don't listen to that slug snot," Jenks said as he landed on Zack's shoulder. "You got skills. You got skills leaking out of the tips of your hair. You're the one doing magic, not him. He's a hairy spider sack. Be a pal, will you, and open that honey pot?"

Clearly unhappy, Zack reached for it. It would take a long time to rub out Landon's words, and as I sat there trying to find myself, I vowed that Zack would *never* go back to the dewar. I'd stood alone too many times when ugly words were said to me—words meant to crush my confidence because I had said no. You couldn't stop people from talking trash, but Zack didn't have to stand alone. I'd make sure he didn't believe it.

The soft sound of sliding linen drew my attention, and I stifled a twitch when Trent sat down beside me and took my hand, holding it amid the spilled salt. "Are you okay?"

I nodded. "I can't go into seclusion. Trent, we have to find a way to destroy it."

"Agreed." He took a breath. "It's not true what he says," he said, and I blinked, not a clue where his thoughts were. "My Sa'han status has nothing to do with you."

Liar. And yet I nodded, my eyes dropping to our fingers twined together. It wasn't often that Trent lied. He did it very well, but I could see through it, and maybe that was why he said what he did. "I know," I lied back, pulling my hand from his.

The Order was dropping back to follow Landon. Weast's warning to leave Landon alone aside, it seemed as if the Order didn't want me. Yet.

The returning waitstaff was noisy after their unexpected break, and still shaky, I put the napkin with Landon's blood on the table for them to take. There wasn't enough remaining to do the curse again, but it was interesting that Landon's aura had cleared somewhat when the baku had left him. It wasn't too late, but by the looks of things, it was close. As close to taking him over as me, perhaps.

Bis felt my fear and tightened his grip on my shoulder. Trent settled back, his green eyes showing his worry as Jenks entertained Zack by belching his ABC's and the waitstaff brushed the salt and glass shards from the table and refreshed our drinks.

Numb, I watched the city turn beneath us as the day brightened. All I'd learned was that the baku had nearly stripped me enough to take me. That I was "too fatigued" to kick it out, and "too alone" to hold it.

Hold it? I thought, shivering when the low morning sun found me. It was afraid of being captured, which meant there was a way to do it. Maybe if we talked to it again, it might let slip how. Clearly I could talk to it as much as Landon did.

Asleep or awake.

CHAPTER

25

FATIGUE WAS A HEAVY, WET BLANKET AS I GOT OUT OF Trent's sports car. Quen had driven it and me back to Trent's house after meeting Ellasbeth and the girls at the front gate on the way in, and I jumped when his door slammed shut with an unexpected loudness.

It was nearing noon. I was finally waking up, but Trent looked awful as he got out of his big-ass SUV and began helping Ellasbeth with the cranky girls, his temper showing as the need to sleep grew. Zack stood beside them in his elegant suit, yawning and worrying his empty finger until Trent handed him the girls' diaper bag. A bunch of store bags followed, all emblazoned with the names of upscale children's clothing stores.

Their twined voices echoed in the low ceiling of Trent's underground garage. Jenks was getting in the way, distracting the girls and making a nuisance of himself as Zack tried to handle the numerous bags and ogle Trent's other cars shining under the garage's artificial lights. Bis had opted to return to the church. "To keep the squatters out," he had said, but as the high-pitched voices of the girls became louder, I thought he had other motives.

"Got that okay?" Trent asked Zack, and the kid nodded and fell into place behind Trent and Ellasbeth, each holding a nap-ready, sleepy girl as they headed to the underground entrance.

I sighed as I reached into Trent's car for my bag before shutting the door by leaning back on it. Quen cleared his throat, and I met his accusing dark gaze. He hadn't said a word on the long drive from Trent's gatehouse, but I had a guess as to where his thoughts were.

"Don't look at me like that." I pushed up from Trent's car and followed them in, low heels scuffing on the cold cement. "Zack *isn't* spying for Landon. You should have seen how he treated him. He *belittled* him, Quen. Tried to bully him into slug paste. Trent knows what he's doing."

"He's dangerous."

Quen's low, warning voice rumbled, darkness incarnate, as shadowy as the elf himself, and I stifled a shiver. "Trent knows that, too," I said, eyes on the beautiful family making their way through the kitchen entrance, their finery looking at home among the subdued wealth.

"He's not acting as if he does." Quen frowned, watching them as well.

"Keep your enemies closer?" I offered, and Quen looked askance at me. "How are the girls?" I asked, trying to change the subject. "Is Ellasbeth . . . ?" My words trailed off as he quickened his pace and left me behind. *Okay, touchy subject,* I thought as he caught up with them and held the door as Buddy ambled out to greet me.

"Hey, Buddy," I whispered, feeling alone as I came in last, which was about where I felt I ought to be. "How you doing, old boy?"

But Buddy left me, too, as I shut the door and sealed out the scent of damp cement. I'd been added to the house's security ages ago, and I hesitated to code the system to lock. Trent stiffened at the audible thump of the house-wide defense falling into play, and then his shoulders eased.

Alone, I trailed behind them past the ground-level industrial kitchens that Trent used when entertaining on a grand scale. Deeper in was the bar hidden under a long overhang, and after that was the three-story ceilinged great room, still holding a sliver of moving sun. They were already on the stairs as I paused to take in the soft hush of the waterfall, audible through the enormous ward. The sound of Trent and Ellasbeth talking as they rose with the girls was beautiful, and I was glad that Ray and Lucy could hear it and know that they were loved. Quen had engaged Zack under the excuse of taking some of the packages, and the feeling that it was time to go grew heavy.

Except that the job wasn't done yet.

If we couldn't destroy the baku, we had to find a way to catch it, even if it meant jerking it out of Landon and—*yuck*—saving him. Trap it, maybe, in a bottle like a soul. There had to be a way, or the baku wouldn't have been afraid of being caught.

My head jerked up at the sound of dragonfly wings, and I blinked, startled when Jenks was suddenly before me. "You okay for a few minutes? I want to check in with Jumoke."

Quen had turned on the stairs, his thoughts unreadable as he waited for my response to the impatient pixy. "Sure," I said, talking to them both, though Jenks didn't know that. "I have to talk to Trent about something, but I'm going to wait until they go down for their naps."

Jenks's dust shifted to a bright, cheerful gold. "Okay, back in ten," he said, and then he was gone, only his slowly drifting dust arrowing to the conservatory saying he'd ever been there.

Alone, I trudged up the stairs to the top floor, steps slow from more than fatigue, though there was plenty of that. By the time I reached the top, the girls were sitting in their high chairs, pulled up to the small table against the kitchen's half wall. Ellasbeth was behind the counter pouring Cheerios into two brightly colored bowls as Trent sat between Lucy and Ray, "debriefing" their stay with their mom. Lucy's voice was strong and clear as she told her dad about the park and the pirates they'd made of the ants they'd found. Ray stoically made a hat, or maybe a boat, of her napkin. Buddy sat panting under them, waiting for the inevitable fallout. It was beautiful, and I felt like an intruder, doubly so when Quen and Zack came out of the girls' room, their hands now empty of bags.

"Have you had breakfast yet, Trent?" Ellasbeth said pleasantly as she puttered in the kitchen, and Trent shot a look at me, sandwiched between his two girls with his tie undone and looking so domestic, it made my heart hurt.

"Yes. We ate at Carew Tower," he said, not a trace of anything in his voice.

Ellasbeth ran her eyes over his suit and loosened tie, gaze rising to Zack in his borrowed finery. Her attention landed on me last, and I flushed. "That must have been pleasant."

"It wasn't," Trent said as he helped Ray with her napkin boat. "It was a business meeting with Landon."

Ellasbeth's motion to put the box of Cheerios away hesitated, and then she smoothly closed the cupboard door. "Did it go well?" she prompted, a fake smile in place.

God, no. I came in closer so it wasn't so obvious that I didn't belong. "We learned a lot," I said as I half-sat against the back of the couch. "Trent, before I go, I want to talk to you about catching the baku."

"Go?" Trent's attention jerked up, completely missing Ellasbeth's flash of unease. Not to mention Quen's frown. "I thought you were going to . . . ah . . ."

I shrugged, smiling thinly at Ellasbeth as she brought the girls two small bowls of dry cereal. "I didn't want to assume," I said, and Quen snorted as he settled himself in the living room and brought up something security-related on his phone.

"You can't leave," Trent said, and Ellasbeth colored. "What if you fall asleep?"

"Why?" Ellasbeth said, still standing behind the girls. "What happens if she falls asleep?"

I ran a hand over my mouth, very aware of Ray watching me. "Perhaps we should . . . mmmm . . ." I turned to look behind me at the living room. It wasn't so far from the table that the girls would feel alone, but distant enough that they wouldn't be likely to listen in.

Trent nodded, a hand on each of the girls as he rose. "Zack, will you watch Ray and Lucy?"

"Sure!" Zack sprang from the couch, long legs eating up the distance to settle himself at the head of the table, where he could see them and us both. I wasn't sure what had happened on the five-mile drive from the gatehouse to the garage, but it was clear the girls liked him.

"Zack." Lucy giggled, spilling her dish as she reached for him. "Why are your ears short?"

"Uhhh." He flushed as Lucy eyed them. "Because I don't have a demon godfather," he said, and I smiled when Ray pushed one of Lucy's spilled Cheerios off the table to Buddy.

"Ray, no!" Lucy cried when Ray pushed another. "That's mine!" and I looked away, my smile fading as I found Quen frowning at me.

I spun where I was, not caring what anyone thought as I scooted down the back of the couch to land with my skirt in disarray. Trent watched in unabashed appreciation as I tugged everything where it belonged, then he settled carefully beside me to make me feel both awkward and loved. Ellasbeth glowered at Quen, willing him to move, then finally sat in Ceri's rocker, where she could stare balefully at Trent and me at the same time. Whatever.

"Why shouldn't you sleep?" Ellasbeth asked again, and Quen put his phone down.

Trent took my hand in his, and my shoulders eased as his fingers twined with mine. "Because Rachel, and anyone with a similar aura resonance, is potentially under the threat of a baku attack," he said, setting our clasped hands where Ellasbeth could see them.

Ellasbeth's gaze flitted between Trent and me as if unsure. "What is a baku?"

Lucy's sudden squeal of delight shocked through me. Apparently Zack had caught the Cheerio that she'd thrown at him with his mouth. At least, it seemed as if that was what had happened, since Buddy was busy vacuuming the floor of the misses.

"A baku is a spirit being," Quen said, his low voice pulling my attention back. "One that can invade your dreams and cause you to act out your nightmares."

"Oh." Ellasbeth frowned, clearly not seeing the problem, and I winced.

"Landon is using it to try to get me to kill Trent," I said bluntly, and Ellasbeth's eyes widened in horror. "But it could be used to get Trent to kill me," I added to be fair.

Trent made a soft sound of annoyance. "Or anyone for that matter," he said.

"It's a weapon," Quen said. "One our ancestors created to kill demons."

Trent shifted to set his ankle atop his knee. "But by the amount of carnage it's been causing in Cincinnati this last week, it has a much farther reach."

I faced Quen as Ellasbeth came to whatever conclusion she wanted. "Landon's aura shifted when the baku, ah, left him," I said, not wanting to admit that it had attacked me. Again. "It, er, said that I was too alone to hold it, which means that maybe with two people we could. We just have to figure out how," I added, not liking Quen's sudden frown. Clearly he'd put two and two together and gotten baku attack.

"It's vicious," I continued, "but not that smart, so . . . I'm thinking that maybe if we talk to it, it might let slip how it was caught before."

"Talk to it?" Quen said. "How many times have you been attacked, Rachel?"

"A couple," I admitted, and Zack's face went white.

Trent's grip on mine tightened in understanding. "No," he said. "You're not talking to it. If it takes you over, it will make you kill me. I'll talk to it. Not you."

My head snapped around. "You? Trent, no."

"I agree," Quen said. "This is a bad idea."

"Trenton?" Ellasbeth's voice quavered. "I'm taking the girls and going home."

Trent stiffened. "Lower your voice," he said softly, a harsh counterpoint to Ray's singing about a spider. "There is no need for them to leave."

"The Turn there isn't," she insisted, hands clasped tight in her lap as she sat in Ceri's chair, and suddenly I didn't feel like the outsider anymore. "Until this is finished, your house isn't safe."

Trent's eyes narrowed, and the scent of spoiled cinnamon grew. "Whether the girls are here or across the city makes no difference if Landon decides to target them. But you're welcome to stay with them in the safe room while they nap."

Quen jerked, and even Ellasbeth caught back her forming protest.

"Here?" she asked, and a thread of alarm pulled through me.

Mood bad, Trent said, "I doubt very much that Landon will target the baku to you. You can stay and watch over them as they nap. Here," he added firmly.

"Sa'han . . . ," Quen protested.

I didn't like it, either, but if they were arguing over where Ellasbeth was going to take her noon nap, they weren't thinking about how many times I'd been attacked.

Trent turned to Quen, his eyebrows high in challenge. "You should stay with her. Your aura isn't anything like mine or Rachel's," he snipped.

Quen's expression hardened to show his offense. "I'm not staying in the safe room when you're playing with a predator, Sa'han."

"Zack too," Trent continued as if Quen had said nothing. "He might benefit from a locked door that can't be opened from the outside while we talk to the baku."

Zack looked up from the table, and Lucy clapped her hands when the Cheerio on his nose fell off. His expression was a mix of bravado and fear. *Which one will win?* I wondered.

"Rachel and I can contact the baku," Trent said, drawing my attention. "If elves created it as a weapon, there *is* a way to contain it."

"There isn't," Quen said stoically. "Not anymore. Your mother and I tried."

"Pity you don't remember how," Trent said with what I thought was an unusual amount of gall, but Trent was tired, too.

Quen's lip twitched. "The failure was likely not at our end, but the Order's. Which might be why they saw fit to wipe the memory of it from us."

I inched forward and tugged my skirt to cover my knees. "What do you remember?"

"Almost nothing," he said, voice low. "The baku is like the wind or water, but even wind and water obey rules of gravity and pressure, and the baku does not."

Trent eyed Quen with a new mistrust. "Did my mother contact Al for help?"

Quen took a slow breath. "No, Sa'han."

I slumped into the cushions. At first glance, it looked easy for me to tap into the demon's wisdom—easy, and with little apparent cost. But sticking up for a demon wasn't easy, getting others to accept a demon wasn't easy, learning to live among people as a demon wasn't easy. Perhaps I paid my dues another way. Here's hoping it didn't claim my life in the end anyway.

"At least, I don't think she did," Quen said, voice introspective. "She knew I didn't like her talking to demons, so she hid it from me. Until it was too late."

Quen suddenly rose, startling me. "Excuse me," he said, an odd, surprisingly pained expression on him before he banished it. "I have a tent to set up in the safe room."

He strode from the sunken living room, leaving me frowning in thought. That had been rather abrupt—and there'd been a definite hint of long-hidden heartache. Eyes narrowed, I looked from Trent to Quen for any signs of similarity. Then I shook my head and dismissed the notion. Even with genetic intervention, they looked far too dissimilar to be related. It was obvious that Quen had loved Trent's mother, but it didn't follow that they had had, er, relations.

"A tent?" I asked, and Trent's focus sharpened.

"Indoor camping," he said, thoughts realigning. "We've

never done it for naps, but it should make sleeping in their closet seem normal."

"Lucy, Ray," Quen said as he crouched at the table to put his eyes even with theirs. "Your mother would like to nap with you. Would you like to make a camp?"

"Tent party!" Lucy exclaimed, her eyes brightening.

"What's a tent party?" Zack asked, voice loud to be heard over Lucy, now demanding to be let down out of her chair.

"Tent party! Tent party!" the little girl chanted as Quen expertly wrangled her into his arms. "Zack, open it," she demanded as she pointed at a kitchen cupboard. "Get the marshmallows!"

Ray didn't look nearly as happy, but I had a feeling it was because she was watching Trent, and Trent was frowning. "You're telegraphing," I warned him, and he shook himself out of his mood, smiling as he went to the little girl.

Ellasbeth, too, stood, but she wasn't nearly as adept at hiding her emotions. "Trent, if you're compromised, let the Order handle it," she said, telling me exactly what their conversation in the SUV had been. "You don't have to save the world."

"I'm not saving the world," he said as he lifted Ray and brushed the Cheerios from her. "I'm saving myself and my family. The Order doesn't care if Landon dies as long as they capture the baku. The entire world knows that Landon and I have a personal war going on. If he were to end up dead, who do you think will be blamed? Landon would have his success from the grave."

"But you don't have anything to do with it," Ellasbeth protested.

"When has that ever mattered?" Trent asked, then turned to Ray, setting her down and asking her to get a naptime book. Eyes on Trent, Ray reluctantly took Quen's hand and went into her room with Lucy.

"Tent party!" Lucy shouted again, and Buddy trotted to join them.

"You do this a lot?" I asked, and Trent's easy mood returned if only for a moment.

"Ah, yes," he admitted, seeming embarrassed. "But we usually set the tent up downstairs. Maybe someday, Quen will let us sleep under the stars. Excuse me. I need to talk to Quen."

I nodded, but he was already moving, and I smiled at the sound of Ray's cheerful demands.

That left me alone with Ellasbeth. My smile slowly fell as she began to clean the high chairs. She was trying to be useful. I knew the feeling. "Ah, sorry about this," I said as I brushed the remaining Cheerios into my hand and dropped them in one of the bowls.

"The baku?" Ellasbeth took the bowls and went into the kitchen. "It wasn't your fault. I appreciate you taking an interest and helping Trent with it."

Interest? I thought, wondering if she'd been listening to any of this. "No, I mean everything," I said, and she went still, turning the running water off with an abrupt motion.

"Is that remorse?" she said, her perfect eyebrows high and mocking. "Tell me, Rachel," she said, color high, "what would you have done differently? Not goaded me into acting like a jealous child by leading me to believe you were a paid whore and then an old girlfriend? Not arrested Trent at our wedding? Not encouraged him to go to the ever-after, where he was put on the auction block as a *slave*? Or perhaps opting to not help him cross the continent to steal my child?"

Oh, that. "I am an old girlfriend," I said, thinking of our time at camp. I'd been, like, eleven, and Trent thirteen, but the more I remembered from it, the more I thought we'd been sort of like friends. Or enemies with a common cause, perhaps. "I never encouraged him to go into the ever-after to retrieve the ancient elven DNA to revive your species," I added, not sure why I was defending myself. "And if I hadn't helped him reach the West Coast, you would've killed him by Albuquerque to soothe your bruised ego. *You* were the one to place that ancient demand upon him to steal his own child back instead of settling custody like civilized people. But as for arresting him at your wedding? You deserved that. It was all you, you, you. Did you ever even think to ask him what he might have wanted? Excuse me."

Chin high, I strode to the girls' room, not surprised to find the heavy door behind their closet wide open. Lucy was dragging her comforter into the space, Buddy wanting to play and dancing beside her. Inside the room, Zack was busy clearing space. Ray stood beside Quen, holding his leg as he used binder clips to fasten a second blanket to one of the cabinets. "What can I do to help?" I asked, thinking the large room looked more like a vault than a closet with its airtight cabinets of books, shelved artifacts, and paintings stacked on end.

But I stopped stock-still when I saw the small glass baby bottle sitting among the rest. I reached for it, my fingertips tingling as I took it in hand. I knew without asking that this was the bottle that had once held my soul, an impromptu container when my body was too broken to keep it intact. "You kept it?" I said, and a shiver ran through me as my finger traced the rough spiral Trent had etched into the bottom to confuse and direct my soul.

Trent looked up from fastening the other end of the tent to a shelf of ancient elven knickknacks that could probably fund the college educations of an entire high school. "Do you want it?" he said. "I couldn't throw it away, and I always thought it felt as if it had a shadow of your soul in there, like a reflection." He hesitated, wincing at Lucy now running back and forth to bring her stuffed animals in, one by one. "Ah, can you organize Lucy? Help her winnow it down, maybe? Ray needs to pick out a book yet, too."

"Sure." I set the bottle back with a small click. It was probably more secure here than on Kisten's boat. Lurching, I snagged Lucy with one hand and wiggled my fingers for Ray. Lucy laughed and giggled, swinging as she half-dragged me and Ray out of the safe room. Ray looked scared, and I picked her up, thinking she smelled like a snickerdoodle. "Lucy?" I said as I sat on one of their low beds. "Your dad says to pick three."

"All of them." Lucy pulled the animals on her bed to a blanket on the floor to drag in.

"But why?" I said, thinking my momitude needed work. "There won't be room for you."

"All of them," Lucy said again, turning to the toy box after she emptied her bed.

"Any ideas?" I said to Ray, and she clung to me, a book about a black horse in her grip.

I sighed, my eyes going to the open closet door when Trent's voice rose in unusual anger. "It's the only space contiguous to our current living situation. I'm sensitive to you wanting to leave my mother's rooms as they are, but if she doesn't have her own space here, I'm going to lose everything I've gained. I know you have a way in. If you don't tell me, I'm going to blow the fireplace apart and make my own door."

Fireplace? I thought, thinking he must have meant the monster of a hearth on the first floor. I swear, the hearth was big enough to park my MINI in. What had they done? Bricked up a wing with it?

Then I winced, flushing as I realized Ellasbeth was standing at the doorway, having heard it as well. Opening an unused wing of the estate? Ellasbeth staying over for naps, albeit on the floor? My shoulders slumped, and I felt more alone, even with Ray on my lap, patting her book as if to distract me. I knew Trent was trying to find a way to pacify everyone, and Ellasbeth moving back in, into a closed wing or not, might be enough to buy a few enclave votes.

Chin high, Ellasbeth crossed the room. "Knock, knock," she said brightly as she halted in the doorway to the safe room. "Oh, that is a fine tent. Lucy, Ray, come and see."

I didn't care if she was better at this mothering stuff than me. It sucked. "Lucy," I called, catching her hand as Ray slid from me. "Lucy, wait. Why so many?" I asked in a last-ditch effort to prove I could work with little egos, too.

Both Lucy and Ray hesitated, Lucy wide-eyed and Ray thin lipped as if she already knew and wasn't happy about it. "Gerry isn't afraid of thunder," Lucy said, touching the giraffe, and Ray's grip on me tightened. "Bruno isn't afraid of the dark," Lucy added, looking at a tiny bear. "Pettie isn't afraid of mean dogs. Spot isn't scared of snarled hair."

I suddenly realized Lucy was terrified. Her lighthearted giddiness was an act. She was scared, not of the safe room, but of why they were being asked to nap there. Ray too was afraid, though her fear was both more obvious and more obscure as she clung to my hand. They knew something was wrong, and they were trying to be brave by pretending they didn't.

Immediately I dropped down to give them both hugs, all at the same time. "Oh, Lucy. It's going to be okay," I said as her arms went around my neck, clinging as if she'd never let go.

"Don't go," she said, her small voice whispering in my ear. "Stay with me and Ray-Ray. Stay with Daddy, and Abba, and Mommy in the safe room."

It just about broke my heart. Sitting on the floor of their room, I wanted to tell them that there were no such things as monsters and that everything would be all right. But Lucy knew. She'd seen it firsthand, having been kidnapped by a psychotic demon. Ray had escaped, but she'd seen what it had done to both Trent and Quen, helpless to get her sister back. And so I sat them both in my lap, rocking them and not wanting to ever let them go.

But I had to, or nothing would ever be better again.

"I have to do this," I said, ignoring Ellasbeth's envious glare. "I have to go," I said firmly as Lucy began to whine. "You will be brave for your mother in the safe room. I won't say I'm sorry, because I have to do this with your daddy and abba. Understand?"

"Because you're a demon princess," Lucy said, playing with my curling hair, and from the closet came Trent's grunt of surprise. "And demon princesses are brave."

I hesitated, then gave them both hugs again. "Almost as much as elven princesses," I said, never having thought of it like that, but it would appeal to them, so I went with it.

The demons had spent too much effort trying to kill me to believe that I was anything other than a means to an end, and not one they particularly liked at that. "But mostly because I love you both and your daddy, too, and I can help stop the baku."

Breath shaking, I gave Lucy a kiss, and then one for Ray as well. "Take your pillows," I said as I stood them up in turn, and they silently pulled them from their low beds. "You'll be safe while your daddies and I talk to the baku."

I felt funny when their warm little hands found mine again and dragged me to the door. Zack was tugging the tent taut as Ellasbeth sat on the floor in front of it, trying to look happy as Lucy and Ray left me to give their daddies hugs and good-nap kisses.

"Thank you for watching them," Trent said to Ellasbeth when he set Ray in her lap, and the woman nodded, looking lost as she bundled Ray up in her favorite blanket.

"It's all I'm good for," she said, voice thin, and Trent put a hand on her shoulder.

"It's everything."

I backed out of the room, almost running into Jenks. The pixy had his hands on his hips as he hovered, clearly peeved we'd started without him. I didn't know what was going on anymore. I knew Trent loved me. I knew the girls looked to me for security. But I wasn't sure how I felt about sharing that with Ellasbeth. Or perhaps losing it to her. Nothing had changed in the last two months except that there was more pressure from the enclave for Trent to quit messing around and marry the woman as he'd promised, uniting the East and West Coast families.

"You said you were going to wait for me. What did I miss?" Jenks said, and I winced.

"Zack, you're with me," Quen said loudly, quickly followed by Zack's exuberant "Yes!" The kid bolted out, looking both scared and excited. Quen and Trent followed and, after a moment of coaxing, Buddy as well.

"Have a good nap, my ladies," Trent said as Quen shut the door. "Sleep well."

In the silence, I could hear Ellasbeth lock it, and then a wave of magic went up, strong enough to feel when I touched the reinforced wood. They were safe. My fingers slid reluctantly away, and I turned to look at Trent, Quen, Zack, and Jenks.

"Anyone want to tell me why you just locked your kids in a closet?" Jenks said, and I sighed, shifting my hair from my shoulder to fill him in as we went downstairs.

CHAPTER

26

"HEY, IS PIKE OKAY?" I SAID, PHONE TO MY EAR AS I SAT ON one of the couches in Trent's great room and checked in with Ivy. I'd changed from my comfortable security top and skirt back into my jeans and sweater, but it left me barefoot, and I tucked my cold feet up and under me.

"It's hard to tell," Ivy said, and I winced. Her low voice mixed with the soft background sounds of ambient nue-jazz, telling me she was home.

"Crap on toast," I said, feeling bad as I stared out the big ward window at the covered pool. "He tried to bespell me. What was I supposed to do? I told him I was busy. The undead need to learn to respect the time of the living."

"Since he's going to be in Cincy, you were going to embarrass him eventually," Ivy said.

"He's staying?" I asked as I remembered Pike's parting remark about three months to eviction. "And Constance? I thought this was an exploratory visit."

"It *was*," she said, and I slumped, pressing my fingers into my forehead at the stress she put on the last word. "It's not you . . . exactly. There's a lot of concern about Nina and me."

I exhaled long and slow. "It bothers them that you're holding her soul. It puts you and her on equal footing, and they don't like it."

"That's some of it." Ivy hesitated, and I looked across

the great room to where Quen and Trent were arguing. Trent's ears were red and Quen's jaw was clenched. "The old undead believe that *you* are the one keeping the vampires in line, not Cormel."

"Me?" I stiffened. "How would I keep the vampires in line?" Because the Cincy vampires *had* been unusually quiet as Cormel grew less and less effective. Even the news had noticed that vamp-on-vamp crimes had been decreasing over the last six months, and the vamp-on-human crimes had all but vanished.

"You have the ability to give the living vampires the power to hold the souls of their undead loved ones. It's a pretty big carrot for behaving," Ivy said, and my eyes lingered on Trent, kind of liking how he looked when he was ticked, his stance firm and his expression resolute, white hair floating as he got more and more angry. He was nothing like the man I'd once hated. He was stronger now, even as he was more vulnerable.

"The living vampires are willing to say no to their masters when it comes to you. That's what the old ones don't like," Ivy finished, and I fiddled with the hem of my jeans, uncomfortable. "I wish you'd met with Constance," Ivy added. "Nina and I are being asked to come to DC."

My lips parted, and I sat up, pulse fast. "When?"

"Before the end of the year."

Damn it all to the Turn and back. Jenks was going to kill me. I should've pretended to be weak and a pushover. But no-o-o-o. I'd had to flip Pike over and be the demon. *Son of a fairy-farting whore . . .*

"It's not your fault," Ivy said. "But downing Pike probably didn't help."

"You think?" I put my bare feet on the floor and leaned over my knees as I tried to process this. "He could have gotten back up and dragged me down there."

"I doubt that," Ivy said. "Or he would have done it. And I did warn him."

Hence Ivy and Nina going to Washington.

"It's going to be okay, Rachel. Nina and I will do the dog

and pony show and come right back. Look, can we talk about something else?"

Okay. Short trip. Breathe. I forced myself up from over my knees before Trent noticed. "Sure." I tossed my hair back and took a breath. "Have there been any new attacks?"

"Not since Sandra, no."

"We may not see any more." I fiddled with the tips of my hair as Zack and Jenks came downstairs, the pixy looking as if he belonged on the elf's shoulder as they shared a shortbread cookie. Zack appeared tired, as he had skipped his noon nap, but not as fatigued at Trent. "I think the baku is ready to make its move. We're going to try to contact it."

I hesitated. "Today."

"Isn't that dangerous?" Ivy said, and Jenks, now sitting on one of Trent's orchids, snorted. A few feet away, Zack collapsed into a chair and dragged Buddy up with him, tags jingling.

"Not as much as waiting until one of us falls asleep." I eyed Trent's stiff resolve as his stance with Quen became decidedly aggressive. He was still in his slacks and dress shirt, pegging my meter with that loosened tie about his neck. "We should be able to. I mean, if the elves created it, they had to communicate with it somehow without being eaten alive. Zack says that Landon talked to it while meditating."

Zack gave me a thumbs-up, but I didn't feel any better. "We're hoping to find a way to contain it," I said. "It as much as said it could be done the last time I pushed it out of my mind."

Ivy was silent, the quick staccato of her tapping pen obvious. "I can be there in forty minutes," she said, and Jenks waved his hands dramatically, clearly wanting her to stay out of it. I agreed. Ivy didn't do well with possession, and that was what it would be if things got out of hand.

"I'm *not* going to pretend to love a woman that I don't," Trent said loudly, drawing my attention. "I don't care how many votes it gets me in the enclave."

"Your father knew the strength of the enclave," Quen said calmly, his silhouette tall and dark as he stood before the gigantic fireplace, but his hands were clenched, and I swear I saw magic leaking from between his fingers.

Temper fraying dangerously, Trent lifted his chin. "Yes? Well, I know the strength of love."

"Ah, Quen is here to spot us," I said as I held the phone closer, hoping Ivy wasn't hearing this. They were arguing over Ellasbeth. Or me, rather. "And Jenks."

Trent turned as if to go, jerking to an annoyed halt when Quen took his arm. "Your father wouldn't have shirked his duties," Quen said, and Trent yanked from his grip.

"My *father* married a woman he despised. He was never happy, and because of it, *she* was never happy," Trent said, and I winced. Jenks flew to me, trailing an unhappy orange dust.

"Okay," Ivy said, her easy acceptance telling me she could hear everything and wanted no part of it. "It sounds as if you have enough help. Call me when you're done so I can sleep today, but if you need me, I'm there."

"Don't chip your fang. We've got this," Jenks said from my shoulder.

"Your father created an empire that those weaker than you are destroying," Quen said stiffly. "If you allow a closer tie to Ellasbeth, you will regain votes. It's that simple."

"No," Trent said, and when he tried to leave again, Quen drew him back.

"It will ensure your Sa'han status," Quen said softly, his angry voice laced with an old pain. "One word from you and the danger Landon represents will be gone. One word and the lawsuits will stop. One word and the sabotage and corporate takeovers will end. *This* is what your father made, Trent. *This* is what he gave you. He made you a prince, and your stubbornness is making you a pauper."

For a heartbeat, Trent said nothing. "I would rather have had his love." Turning, Trent strode away, and the static from his leashed magic pulled the magazines from a nearby table to the floor behind him.

My eyes widened and Buddy slunk away to hide under a chair. "Uh, I gotta go," I said.

"Call me when you're done," Ivy reminded me, and I nodded, eyes on Trent as he stood at the window and stared at nothing. His hair was floating, and he ran a hand to smooth it.

"Will do," I said, then hung up.

"Huh." Jenks took to the air. "The little cookie maker has a temper after all."

"Give him a break," I said. "His kids are locked in a safe room."

"That would put thorns in my jockstrap, too, but you're fooling yourself if you think that's what's bothering him." Wings humming, he flew to Trent, whispering something in his ear. It seemed to work, as Trent glanced at me and slowly exhaled. I'd have given a lot to know what he'd said.

"I should be the one to talk to the baku," Quen said, and I gave him a long sideways look as he stood at the outskirts and tried to pretend their argument had never happened.

"I'm the Sa'han whether they like it or not. I do it." Trent came back to sit across from me. Seeing the magazines, he picked them up and set them aside.

Quen's hands clenched and released. "It wants you dead so its proposed long-term host will have more power. The risk is too high."

Trent looked up, his face lined with worry and fatigue. "It is attracted to Rachel's aura. Mine is closer to hers than yours. I'm the clear choice. Rachel can't do it." I took a breath to protest, and he added, "Or we could do a spread on both our souls and see whose is the least damaged."

I shook my head and pressed into the couch. No way. If Trent saw, he would freak.

"Okay, then." Trent dusted his hands and pushed forward in the chair, his feet squarely on the floor. "You should zip-strip me just in case." Zack bobbed his head, his eyes wide and scared. I felt sick, and when no one moved, Trent faced Quen. "You generally have a zip-strip or two on you, don't you, Quen?"

"This is a bad idea . . . ," Quen said as he reached into his pocket.

Trent held his wrist out. "If Rachel kicked it out, I can.

I won't let it go too far. This is the best way to learn about the baku with your memory gone."

Quen's jaw clenched and I winced. Harsh but true.

Motions rough, Quen fastened the charmed silver about Trent's wrist and ratcheted it closed. Trent shuddered as his contact with the ley lines was cut off, and I winced in sympathy.

"I'll snap you out of it if you turn violent," I said, and Quen's mood darkened even more. Arms behind his back, he fell into parade rest behind Trent's chair.

"God, yes." Trent jiggled his wrist to adjust the strip. "A light trance should be enough."

"Landon meditated when he talked to it," Zack said.

"See?" Trent half-turned to give Quen a dry look. "Not a problem. I meditate all the time. If Landon can do this without being stripped to his core, I can."

But Landon's soul looked like decayed pus, and I fidgeted, nervous.

"Rachel, it will be okay," Trent said, and my eyes met his across the low table. "The baku is bound to be lurking around, waiting for you to fall asleep. I merely have to contact it and dig for answers."

I took a slow breath to steady myself. "Don't fall asleep," I said, remembering the terror of the baku digging deep, eating the best parts of myself—the parts that made living with the things I had to do to survive tolerable. "You can't kick it out if you fall asleep."

"No worry there." Trent settled his hands in his lap and closed his eyes.

Jenks took to the air and flew to Zack. "I'll keep an eye on his aura," he said as he settled on the kid's shoulder. "You smack him if he starts to talk in tongues."

This was my idea, but I didn't like it, and as Trent's breathing slowed, Quen jolted into motion. "What are you doing?" I whispered as he took what I guessed was a bag of salt from a nearby desk drawer and began spilling it into a circle around Trent.

"Fortune favors the prepared," Quen muttered as he edged between Trent and the table.

"He's strapped," I protested.

"Landon was never violent," Zack added.

"Landon wasn't trying to piece together how to capture it." Quen finished the circle and tossed what was left of the spelling salt to me.

"Trent can be circumspect." I set the bag down, and Trent sighed and cracked an eye open.

"It's hard to meditate when you're all talking."

"Sorry," I said, and he closed his eyes again.

Zack settled back in his chair with Jenks, both of them watching Trent. Quen moved so his shadow fell across the table, making it clear that he didn't approve. I sat and waited, fidgeting. Slowly the ticking of the clock on the enormous mantel became obvious. The huge, empty fireplace sat behind Trent, and I again wondered if they'd used it to brick up an entire wing. There was nothing behind it but the bluff the house had been built into. Maybe his mother's wing had been underground.

I sat straighter as a soft lassitude threatened to slip into me, and I tickled the top of my mouth with the tip of my tongue to stay awake. Trent's breathing slowed, and the memory of hearing it beside me as I slept slipped through me, soothing. I blinked fast, and I took up the bag of salt, shifting it from hand to hand to prove to myself that I wasn't falling asleep.

I'm awake. Eyes open, I dropped the bag to my right hand, then my left, all in time with the ticking clock. *I'm wide-awake.*

But it was hard to stay that way when Trent began a meditation hum. It was more of a drone really, almost singing, a gathering of power or an invitation for the Goddess to attend.

My head bobbed, the sudden snap waking me up. I frowned at Quen, who was staring at me, but honestly, it was really hard to stay awake when Trent was humming like that. It wasn't the first time I'd heard him use music while meditating, and the last hint of sleep jolted from me at a wisp of remembered anger.

Trent had been singing to the Goddess the night he dragged my sorry ass out of the freezing Ohio River. It was his fault that we'd landed there, barely surviving having the casino boat blown up around us. A dozen of Cincinnati's finest had gone to the bottom. Trent had been on his way to join them when I'd pulled his head out of the water. I could have made it to shore just fine if I hadn't been carting his elven ass with me.

Brow furrowed, I looked across the table at him. I'd almost died that night, and it had been his fault. He had been getting me into trouble ever since.

It was his fault I survived, too. The stray thought flitted through me, quickly forgotten as, with a blink, Trent's aura blossomed, visible though I wasn't using my second sight. Gold, with a hint of smut to keep it interesting, it flowed from him like the aurora borealis, flitting over his skin, red at the source, sparkles spilling off at the flares, the heat of intensity concentrating about his hands and head.

Curious. Squinting, I looked deeper to see purple and green and a shade of amber that shouldn't have existed.

And then he stopped humming and opened his eyes. I blinked. His aura was in his eyes.

"This isn't working." Trent pushed himself more upright with a sour expression.

"Sweet everlasting moss wipe of a mother pus bucket," Jenks swore softly, and I turned to him. He was staring at me from Zack's shoulder.

Damn busybody pixy, I thought as I spilled the bag of salt from hand to hand. I couldn't count how many times he had irritated the hell out of me.

"That isn't helping, Jenks," Trent said, and Jenks snapped his wings and pointed at me.

"Oh, no," Zack whispered, and Quen's lips parted when he followed Zack's attention to me.

"What?" I said, irate.

Jenks took to the air, the sound of his wings tugging at a memory. "Rachel, wake up," he said as he hovered before me.

"I'm not asleep." I dropped the bag of salt on the table before pushing back.

Zack pressed deeper into his chair, away from me. "She's not awake, either."

But I felt more awake than I'd been in a long time, and I stood, rolling my shoulders to ease their tension, and rocked from foot to foot to feel my new balance.

"It's her," Jenks was whispering as I gazed out onto the pool, liking how the sun sparkled on it. I hadn't seen the sun for what felt like forever, though I knew that was false. "It's her, but she's missing stuff," the pixy added, his eyes following me as I rose to look at Trent's books to either side of the fireplace. "It's a her that never existed," he said, and I snorted. "Like some things never happened to her that should have."

"Ah, Quen?" Trent said, and I turned from the bookcase to see Quen cut the zip-strip from him. Smirking, I spun to put my back to them all as I felt the elf take communion from the same ley line I had hung a stray thought in.

"The power of the ley line won't make you strong enough to hold me," I said, feeling confident as I plucked a book from the shelf and tucked it under my arm. It wasn't Trent's, and I wanted it back. "And stop looking at my aura," I added, knowing he was by the prickly feeling.

Trent stood, and the prickles skating over my skin worsened. "Rachel, wake up," he demanded. "This wasn't what we had intended."

"No kidding," I said with a sneer. "And it's Ms. Morgan, if you don't mind." I eyed his aura, seeing the damage I'd wrought over the last few nights he had dared sleep. He'd woken every time, pushing me from his mind, but the damage was there, his soul as thin as the demon's I was now in. He hadn't told anyone, and if I wanted him, he was mine for the taking. . . . Maybe.

Quen moved toward me with a stealthy swiftness. My head turned, and a flash of memory rose, one of his body pinning me to my kitchen floor, colored cookie sprinkles in his hair. "Stop!" I demanded, hand outstretched, and then I squirmed in pleasure, smiling at the heat of the line flowing through me. God, it felt good. Nothing like it had through Landon, and I purred a contented sound, satisfied when Quen slid to a halt, the zip-strip dangling from his hand.

"Talk to it!" the young elf said, clearly unnerved. "It's here."

The baku? I mused, dabbling my memories in the ley line like toes in a pool. But there was nothing in my mind that shouldn't have been. It was only me. I was just seeing things clearer. And Trent was a whiny little wannabe of an elf. Nothing like the spell warriors who had made me. Made me, and lost me. I would kill them all, a cancer from within.

"Quen, stand down," Trent said. "She's not violent."

"Not yet I'm not," I said, remembering how furious I'd been with Quen when he'd "tested" my skills by assaulting me in my own kitchen. I should have killed him right then and there. I didn't know why I hadn't.

But Trent had inched forward into my line of sight. He was cautious and careful, and I chuckled, thinking that he was going to "careful" himself into a grave. *I should put him out of his misery.*

"I want to talk," Trent said, a hand raised as if for patience. "Landon sent you to kill me."

"True," I said. "I didn't see the need, but perhaps he's right. You could have had everything, but are nothing."

"Stop!" Trent shouted, but he was talking to Quen, and I half-sat against a tall table and opened the book I'd taken from his shelf.

"Where's the loss?" I said as I thumbed through it. "Pathetic drug lord only concerned with his bottom line. The enclave is right to withdraw the Sa'han title from your family name." I snapped the book closed to read later. "Shirking your duties, family, and church?" I said. "Preferring my company to those who can move you forward in the world? You aren't going to have anything to show for it in the end, so why not take you out now? Make room for someone who will do something of worth. Something big." *Like take out the demon as Landon wants,* I thought, smug, because even though I was one, I knew Trent would never touch me. Love. What a waste.

"Maybe I was that person once," Trent said, a finger raised to keep Quen from moving. "But that's not true anymore. You changed me. You, Rachel."

My head jerked up at the rattle of dragonfly wings. The pixy was coming right at me, sword in hand and a pained, determined look in his eye. With a tug on the line, I threw a mystic at him.

"Hey!" the pixy shouted, spinning head over heels when it hit him, and I laughed, seeing his dust flash black for an instant under my will.

But Quen had moved in my split second of distraction, and I spun, wadding the line up in my hand, mystics dripping from my fingers until he slid to a halt, shock in his eyes. "Just so," I said, warning him off. The mystics' voices were mute, tumbled about like so much lint, mine to control. But they saw me not, and my anger thickened. Trent had stolen my voice from them. I could have been a goddess if not for him. He'd hurt me, kept hurting me. My God, I slept with the man! What kind of a glutton for punishment was I?

"Stop," Trent demanded again, frowning at Quen. "Everyone, stop. Relax. Rachel, you can kill me in a few minutes. I want to talk first. You like to talk, don't you?"

I eyed Quen, then faced Trent. Zack wouldn't dare move. He never had before. "Yes," I said, satisfied I was the strongest one here. "Hearing you lie is amusing."

That pixy, though, wouldn't stop moving. "Wake her up," Jenks said, sword held high as if ready to cut me. "It's going to eat her to a shell."

"I can't believe I sleep with you," I said, and Trent took a quick breath, the pain in the back of his eyes mirroring his aura flashing red and settling.

"Maybe I can give you something Landon can't," he

said, and I laughed, having had this conversation with him before when we first met.

"A Brimstone plantation in the South Seas? You foolish, stupid man. I want a body. Can you give me a body?" Which was really weird, because I had a body. I was in it.

Trent didn't seem to have a problem with the incongruity, though, shaking his head and inching closer, that damn pixy with him. "You can't have hers," he said.

"Why would I want to be a stinking whore of a second-class demon when I have a powerful elf for the taking?" I said, my words confusing me even as I felt a surge of confidence. "Maybe you can tell me why Landon wants me alive and you dead. Demons spared when elves are slain. Still, killing you gives Landon all the power, dewar and enclave alike. Maybe Landon is right. I'm tired of you hurting me."

Again I pulled on the line, my knees going watery as the power of the line flowed in with an unexpected force, singing through my mind as if it was angels exalting me home. *So much power,* I thought, looking at my hands and wondering why they weren't burning. Perhaps Landon was a mistake. Perhaps *this* was the body I wanted to keep. It wouldn't take much now. My eyes rose to Trent. Either way, he was going to die.

"Corrumpo!" I demanded, marshaling the whining mystics streaming through me into motion. It was a mundane curse, but the force behind it would shatter stone.

"Septiens!" Quen shouted, and Trent ducked as my force hit the circle he'd invoked around them, sealing me out. Zack yelped as my magic ricocheted, screaming past me to explode in the cavern of the fireplace. Rock chips flew like daggers, and the scent of dust and burnt amber rose.

I turned from the cracked wall as the adolescent elf skittered to put a chair between us. From across the room, a dog barked to warn me off as I pushed myself into motion.

"You will not hurt him, baku," Quen said, and I jerked. He had said these words to me before. A long time ago. He might not have remembered, but I did.

Wavering, I felt something open in my thoughts, a memory I'd never created swimming up from the sliding sound of salt spilling from one lobe of my mind to the other. "I know you," I said, letting the memory slip to the front of my mind, and I gasped as I recalled what he and that elf Trisk had done to me.

Hatred boiled up, and I took a step closer, the line screaming through me as I pulled on it until my hair floated. "You were why I was imprisoned in a worthless body," I said, hitting my chest as if I was in it still. "Decades I waited, until magic failed and I was freed." My lip curled, and my hand fisted into death. "You die first. It's personal."

"Quen!" Trent shouted, hunched in indecision.

But I was already in motion. Quen was too fast with his circles. I remembered from before, and a part of me spun in confusion as two pasts tried to make one present.

"Septiens!" Quen shouted again, and I slid to a halt, magic dripping from me, hatred rising from my pores. He'd hidden behind a second circle. *Son of a bastard,* I thought, relying on my memory, and then I jerked as a new thought, one of my newest, rose like a pearly wave of sun. I was a demon. Quen's new circle was undrawn. Without salt or chalk to give it structure, it was weak and wouldn't stand before me. Not now that I was a demon.

"Nice try," I said, and then I hauled off and slammed my glowing fist right into his barrier.

"Rachel!" someone shouted, and I ground my teeth against our two forces screaming their ego-ridden signatures. Neither would give, and I pushed on Quen's circle with my will and my energy, letting more flow through me until it slithered over the elven barrier like oil on water.

His magic would fail. I was stronger. *I was stronger!*

And with a ping that seemed to echo through me, Quen's circle fell.

I stumbled, cutting the line from my thoughts before the backlash could find me. I ducked, arm over my face as the wave pulsed through the room, rocking me back. I felt a smile on me as I lowered my arm and turned to Quen. He had bested me once, but now I was a demon, stronger than any who now lived because no one had told me there were limits.

Quen stared, his jaw slack as if he had never considered how much power I could hold.

"Oh, what pretty things I know," I said, considering what curse to use next. "After I kill you, I kill Trent." And then I yelped, going down as someone hit me from behind.

It was Trent. I could tell by the feel of his body on mine as we hit the floor, and I howled, frustrated as a band of charmed silver slid over my wrist and the line energy drained from me. "You son of a bastard elf!" I squirmed and he grunted as my elbow found him. The stink of dog filled my nose, and then there was the sound of claws on the carpet as he was dragged away.

"Wake up, Rachel," Trent gasped, fumbling for a hold. "Wake up!"

"Get off!" I shrieked, bucking as the memory of Trent caging me rose up, potent and hot. I'd been helpless. He had allowed that bastard Jon to torment me—all to prove that I was Trent's plaything. *Not again. Never again.* "You will die, and I'll be the one to do it!"

Infuriated, I pushed up, arms straining, almost getting free until Quen sat on me as well. I went down again, my air huffing out. "You murdering son of a bitch elf. I will slice your gullet and use your guts to soften my cuticles! I will skin you from your ankles to your scalp and put it back on you inside out! I will pour lava down your gullet and laugh at your screams!"

"Take a chill pill, Rache," the pixy said, hovering before my face, and I shrieked, infuriated.

"Landon never did anything like this," Zack said as he bent low to look me in the face.

"Landon is a fool," Trent said as he sat on me, and I struggled to get a hand free. Yes, Landon was a fool, but he wouldn't be when I got done killing Trent. Once Trent was dead, Landon would be mine. "Quen," Trent said calmly as he pinned me to the floor. "Do something."

Quen swooped in close. Finally I got a fist free, smashing it into his nose. Grunting, Quen fell back, a hand to his face as Trent grabbed my arm and twisted it painfully behind me.

"Let go!" I shouted, tears starting. I wasn't crying. I was furious. There was a sliver of satisfaction at Quen's anger, but the thought that Landon was right was a bitter truth. Demons were powerful, but when you cut off their access to a line, they had nothing. Once I killed Trent and took Landon's body, I'd have power that never died, that of the body politic.

"Wake her up!" Trent demanded as he sat on me. "Now!"

"How?" Quen looked at me, one hand on his nose.

"I don't know. Slap her."

"Don't you dare," I gasped. "Quen, don't you dare!" I squirmed, taking a huge breath, and tried to rise. They would die. All of them.

"My apologies, Tal Sa'han," Quen said as he bent low, and then his hand met my cheek.

Pain exploded in my face, sparkles radiating through my skull and my head rocking back. With a snap, my blurred vision steadied. Their auras were gone. The baku was gone. The anger at Quen's slap was still there, though, and I gasped, breathless from Trent's weight on me.

"What the hell is wrong with you! I swear, Quen, if you *ever* hit me again, I'll put snakes in your sock drawer," I shouted, totally pissed.

Quen pulled his hand back again, and my eyes widened.

"It's her!" Jenks shrilled, dropping down before my face. "Quen, it's her! Can't you tell?"

Eyes narrowed, Quen peered at me and let his raised hand fall. "Are you sure?"

"I'm sure, I'm sure," Jenks said, darting about as Trent got off and I rolled to sit up.

"Holy Goddess spit," Zack said, and Buddy came out to sniff me, his tail waving apologetically. "Landon only mumbled a lot when he talked to the baku."

My face flashed warm, and I sat between the couch and

the knocked-over table, horrified. The things I had said. Embarrassed and afraid, I looked at Trent. His back was to me as he righted the table, but he was slumped and looked depressed and beaten down.

"Trent?" I said hesitantly, and he didn't turn. "I didn't say those things. It was the baku." Which wasn't entirely true. Every ugly feeling that had poured through me and found voice had been in my thoughts before. It had been me, but it was a me lacking the understanding, or perhaps the ability, to forgive and love.

"I know." He came close to extend a hand to help me rise. "But they're true."

"Were," I said firmly as I fitted my hand into his and he pulled me up. "Maybe once, but they aren't now. Trent, I'm sorry," I added as he let go. I couldn't let Trent think that what I'd said was true. I loved him. What had happened before mattered, but only in that we'd overcome it.

"There's nothing to forgive," he said, but his smile was thin as he looked at the crack in the back of the fireplace. "This was . . . not helpful," he said, and I nodded, wishing he would come around the table, take me into a hug, anything.

"I said it would be a mistake." Quen stalked to the end table, stoic as he took a tissue to wipe his face.

"It wasn't a mistake. It just didn't work like we wanted it to," I said as I sat down, wondering if this was what Madam Curie had felt like when her research killed her.

"Looks like a mistake to me," Zack said as he lifted Buddy up onto the chair with him.

"I still say we can catch it. It's like antimatter, maybe," I said, remembering the feelings I'd had. They were mine, but mine untempered by love or forgiveness. Perhaps the baku was opposite to a soul, canceling mine out. "Antimatter exists," I said when Quen scoffed, then winced, a hand going to his nose.

"Perhaps, but anti-souls do not," Quen muttered as he reached for another tissue. "Zack, put that dog back on the floor."

My face throbbed where Quen had hit me. "At least we know you can *talk* to it," I said as I sat down and gingerly felt my face. *Thanks a lot, Quen.*

"Okay. But not you. Not again," Jenks said, unusually close as if to reassure himself it was still me.

"Agreed." I looked at Trent, now slumped on the edge of the couch with his elbows on his knees.

And then my head snapped up as I remembered. I had possessed the baku's knowledge when it had been in me. I knew how Trent's mom and Quen had tried to capture it. "Uh, guys? I saw how the Order trapped it. I'm not making a zombie out of anyone, but, Trent, your mom and Quen nearly had it on their own with a circle. If we can circle it, we can put it in a bottle."

"Zombie!" Jenks exclaimed as Trent looked up, hope smoothing his brow. "The Order uses zombies to catch the baku?"

I nodded. "Zombies are the living dead. Not awake, not asleep, and unlike vampires, they have souls to trap it and no will to kick it out. Because of what they are, once it's stuck in one, it can't escape even if it wants to."

Quen grunted in surprise, but Trent clearly wasn't convinced. "You can't catch an energy being in a circle," he said warily. "It just slips through the spaces between."

"But that's what they did," I insisted, then scooted to the edge of the couch. "They combined their circles into one impenetrable one. I saw them do it. Hell, I remember being angry at being trapped in it. I simply don't know how they did it. Maybe it's in her other journals."

Together we turned to Quen. He had been there. Done it.

"Sa'han . . . ," Quen said, and at his pained voice, Trent's gaze went past him to the fireplace, an unknown emotion pinching his brow.

"I'm done discussing this with you," Trent said, his voice raspy with anger. I stood, my gut twisting as he pulled on the ley line running through his compound with a savage intensity. His hand stretched out, and a violent ball of magic wreathed his fingers, gold and red, dripping with sparkles. Silent, he physically flung it at the wall. I tensed as it hit with a soft pop—but nothing happened. Gold and red slithered over the back of the fireplace until slowly it began to disappear. My shoulders slumped. Whatever it was, it hadn't worked.

But Trent was gritting his teeth, his expression tight in determination. He wasn't done yet, and his hand, still outstretched, held a faint ribbon of his power running from him to the wall.

My lips parted as I realized that his spell was in the cracks of the wall. "Get down!" I shouted, launching myself at Zack as the oblivious kid stood to investigate.

"Cum gladio et sale!" Trent shouted, his hand gathering up ribbons of strength and pushing them down the trace to the wall to force it in.

I hit Zack. Together we fell into the chair, sending it over backward as Trent's magic exploded among the mortared stones with a sharp crack and thump that shook the room's floor.

Rock chips and chunks of masonry rolled past with the scent of dust and stale Brimstone. "You okay?" I asked Zack as I got up, but the kid was faster than me and was already staring at the fist-size hole in the back of the fireplace. Jenks darted from me to Trent like a deranged hummingbird, finally vanishing into the hole when his curiosity became too much.

Trent's anger shifted to quick anticipation as he strode forward to pull more rock free. There was darkness beyond, and the sound of falling stone echoed in a small space.

"Sa'han," Quen protested, but his head was bowed and he looked beaten.

"You don't have to help, but you *will* stay out of the way," Trent said, and with a resolved reluctance, Quen sat down. Shocked, I stared at the pain the older man was trying to hide, his expression riven as Trent pried more rocks to tumble from the opening. Quen was *sitting down*?

"Quen?" Trent tried again, hope making his word soft, but Quen didn't move.

"There's nothing in there but heartache. Don't draw it into your future by disturbing it," Quen said, catching Zack's arm and pulling him back from the opening.

Pulse fast, I met Trent's eyes. The green of them held danger and drive, dropping to my core and setting something burning. Of course there would be heartache. Great knowledge always hurt. *"Leno cinis,"* I said softly, and Trent caught the blossoming globe of light as it formed.

A cool breath smelling of stale Brimstone sifted from the opening, and I carefully picked my barefoot way through the rubble to peer into the new Brimstone-scented darkness. "I'm sorry, Quen," I said, then followed Trent through the broken opening and into the dark, still air beyond.

They were Trent's mother's rooms, and I wouldn't let him go in there alone.

CHAPTER
27

THE DARKNESS WAS WARM AND ABSOLUTE AS I PICKED MY way over the broken stones, wincing at the sharp edges under my bare feet. I wasn't going to take even five minutes to find my shoes. Fortunately, the farther I went, the smaller the shards got until there was only light grit between me and a slate floor. The light from Trent's great room made a small spot of gray, doing nothing to light the silence broken only by the rasping of Jenks's wings and Trent's slow breathing.

Not a hint of movement stirred the air. I funneled more energy into the globe, pushing back the dark to see that we were in a hallway. It looked like any other hallway I'd seen in Trent's compound. Perhaps a little higher in the ceiling . . . maybe a little brighter color on the wall. The floors were slate tile—and now that we were away from the broken rock, clean.

"No dust," I said softly, hearing my voice come back flat of any echo.

A door opened up onto what was probably an office. To the right, the hall dead-ended with two waiting room chairs and a table, but it continued on to the left. The light dimmed as Trent went into the office, his shoes faintly scuffing. I turned, my gaze drawn to the bright hole in the wall.

"Oh . . . ," I breathed, lips parting in awe at the original archway showing behind the stone wall of the fireplace. It was beautiful, the carved, polished wood lifting high with its smooth lines decorated with carved birds and twining branches that held dogwood blossoms. "Everything is clean," I said as I breathed in the fading hint of Brimstone. "Is it a spell?"

Trent came back, his expression hard to read with the globe of light in his hand. "It's Quen," he said. "He's had a way in here all the time. I didn't even know it existed until I pieced it together from her journals the other night. It's right there in black and white. I don't know why I didn't notice it before. Except perhaps there's a 'don't see' charm on it, like her spelling hut."

There was hurt in his voice. And betrayal. Worried, I looked at the fading pixy dust leading into the dark. "Jenks?" I called loudly, then wished I hadn't as my voice came back in a hissing echo.

"I remember someone having an office here," Trent said as he came even with me and we continued forward. "I think it was Quen, or maybe Jonathan, but it could be used for anything."

Like a day nursery, maybe? I thought, recognizing a hint of anticipation in his voice. He needed space for Ellasbeth. Quen seemed certain that if she lived or worked in the Kalamack compound, then the elven enclave would listen to him.

One word, I thought. Trent would have been a fool to ignore the chance to regain his political standing. I saw his frustration every day at the lack of invites to public events, the slow tapering off of interviews to nothing, the slights and snubs from people who'd once vied for five minutes of his time, each knowing that with *one word* he could change everything. It was gone. Because of me.

"Guys!" Jenks shrilled from the dark. "You gotta see this! It's like she just walked away!"

Sounds promising, or really painful. Our pace quickened as we passed down the short hall, following Jenks's voice. One side was mortared brick behind the floor-to-ceiling windows, the other held three-by-five photos. Trent glanced at them and continued on, and I reluctantly kept pace with him. There was a younger forest, a smaller stable, a pond that didn't exist today. There was no research building, and the cars in the small lot were old models.

"Did the baku's thoughts give you any indication how to combine circles?" Trent asked when the hall ended and the light spilled out onto an open floor.

I squinted into the dark, seeing the outlines of the room where Jenks had been, his silver dust slowly falling from a tall two-story ceiling. The space was longer than it was wide, and probably ran beside the pool, though now admittedly covered by that waterfall. "No. I remember a lot of anger when they pulled it out of its current host, and then they caught it in a free-floating circle," I said. "It held for a while, but when Trisk and Quen shrank it down to physically put it in a bottle, it slipped through the spaces between matter and went back into its host. That's when a group of humans—the Order, I guess—used witch magic to make its host a zombie, trapping it."

"Agnent." Trent raised the globe and I obligingly funneled more energy into it until the light redoubled and we could see bricks where high windows had once let in the light.

"Probably." My head swiveled, trying to take it all in. These weren't living quarters. It was a lab of some sort. "It would explain the zombies. They probably escaped when the lines went down a few months ago. The one Ivy and I caught looked about twenty years undead." Which was an uncomfortable thought, because there was only one baku and at least six zombies. Either the Order had practiced on innocents, or their aim had been bad.

Trent and I inched through the room following the sound of unseen pixy wings. A long, continuous workbench ran along the entire back wall, ley line equipment filling the cabinets above. Another bricked-up window sat before a smaller workbench, and I wondered if it would have looked out onto the pool. It reminded me of my mom's spelling lab at Takata's oceanside mansion, and a pang went through me. "Your dad bricked up all the windows," I said.

"And built a waterfall over them," Trent added grimly.

Somber, I dropped my gaze. Quen had said Trent's mother and dad had hated each other, but that was not the feeling I'd gotten from the journals. Maybe it was a little hate and a little love both.

"This would be an amazing place to work," I said as Trent played the light over the long, empty room. But then my shoulders slumped. Ellasbeth. Change that outer office into a day nursery, and she'd never leave.

"How do you mesh two circles?" Trent said, a determined slant to his jaw as he strode into the dark, the light pulling me into his wake. "They just don't. I mean, that's the entire point behind making them. Do you think the demons might know?"

A hint of a tickle pricked through my toes, and I jerked to a halt before stepping into a huge circle inlaid on a massive, unbroken sheet of slate. Seating benches made a hundred-and-eighty-degree arc around it and I winced, imagining Al standing frustrated and peeved at its center, making deals with the intent to abduct Trisk if she made a mistake.

"I very much doubt it," I said as I crouched to take a closer look. "If they knew how to merge circles to capture the baku, they wouldn't be hiding from it." A quiver rose in my chi as my finger met the old silver, and I pulled my hand back. It would be a fast circle invocation with such a base to work from: silver poured onto a slate floor with no cracks or seams.

Trent cleared his throat impatiently and I rose. "I'm betting it was elven magic," I said, wiping my hands on my jeans as we headed for the open door at the end of the room.

Jenks darted out of the door, an odd green dust spilling from him. "I found the lights," he said as he came to an abrupt halt before us. "I can't trip them. I'm not heavy enough. There's, like, no cameras down here, and it has its own ventilation."

"Helpful when you're dealing with demons," I said, thinking about the observation benches around that large circle.

"I haven't found how Quen is getting in here," Jenks added. "Trent, wait until you see your mom's office. It's like she just stepped out for a coffee."

This is going to hurt. Stomach clenched. I dropped back to let him go first. He strode past me with a wash of spoiled cinnamon to leave me in the dark. I slowly followed, hesitating on the threshold.

Trent stood before an ornate desk, the legs carved with flowering dogwood and birds. His head was bowed, and it looked as if he was struggling. Jenks perched on the antique lamp on one corner, his excitement gone as he probably realized how much this was hurting Trent. My globe was sitting beside an outdated computer and a desk pad dated nineteen eighty-nine. An ancient-looking keyboard and an even older intercom sat in a forgotten silence. Again, no dust.

The wall facing the pool was entirely bricked up, but curtains hung at the outlines of a large sliding-glass door. A leather couch with pillows and a knitted throw stood against the wall across from the desk. Beside it were a matching chair and lamp. Two more walls were entirely bookcases filled with leather bindings.

And the fading scent of coffee? I wondered, seeing an empty cup on the small table. Beside it was an ornate teacup. It was dry, the brown rings saying it had evaporated a long time ago. *Twenty years?* I wondered as I came forward, my bare feet finding a tight-pile rug as I put a hand around Trent's waist and tugged him sideways into me. "You okay?"

Nodding, he pulled away, his eyes on the desk.

But he didn't look okay as he reached for the photo propped up beside the pencil cup, his jaw clenching in obvious heartache. The woman had long dark hair, but the gleam in her eyes and the tight grip on the reins in her hand reminded me of Ceri. She was on an alert, ear-pricked silver horse. A little boy sat before her, no more than three. It had to be Trent, sweet in his riding outfit and scowling at the sun despite the hat. He was thin and gaunt, and I recognized the look of one who had been in and out of the hospital too often. Two more boys sat on their own ponies beside her, healthy and strong, their pride obvious.

"Trent," I said in awe, and he seemed to shake himself back to life. I hadn't known his mom was a dark elf. No wonder there were no other photos of her. *No wonder Quen had been in love with her.*

Hand shaking, Trent set the photo down. "You want to check the books?" he said, voice throaty as he began pulling open drawers.

I hesitated, then went to the shelves, not sure how much sympathy he wanted. "Sure. Her missing journals have to be here somewhere." But as I began to run a finger down the spines, my hope faded. They were all textbooks—outdated and pretty much useless.

I turned when the shadows shifted. Trent's head was bowed and his fingertips pressing into his forehead. A shudder rippled through him, and when Jenks's dust paled, I came over. "Trent . . ."

"I'm okay," he said as he stepped past my reaching hand to go to the bookshelf. "Jenks, where was that light switch?"

The pixy rose up, somber and quiet. "It's over here."

"I'll get it," I said, though I was loath to turn them on and bring everything under sharper scrutiny. Jenks was hovering beside an obvious switch, and wincing, I flicked it on. But only the lamp on the desk lit, bathing everything in a soft, warm glow. Satisfied, I let my hold on the ley line go, and my globe of light on the desk vanished.

"Oh, look at the rug," I said in awe as I realized it was an elaborate yin and yang of embroidered swirls and swoops holding the shapes of birds and insects.

Silent, Trent continued down the shelves with methodical precision. His back was stiff, and the scent of spoiled cinnamon was growing stronger.

"What's in there?" I said as I noticed the door just off the bricked-up sliding-glass doors.

"Bathroom," Trent said, not turning. "I think I remember going from the pool to her office to use it once instead of the one we were supposed to. My dad was angry, but Mom—" His voice broke, and I slumped, wondering if he'd ever said the word in his entire adult life. "Mom gave me a hug and told me to use it whenever I wanted," he continued, his voice thready and his back to me as he pretended to read the spines. "I remember being scared that I'd get in trouble for getting her wet when she gave me a hug and told me it was okay." Head bowing, he fisted his hands.

"Damn my father for erasing my memory of her," Trent whispered. "I was ten when she died. Ten years of memories would have been enough."

"I'm so sorry." Eyes welling, I went to him, curving my arms around him from behind and resting my head on his back. I felt his breath shudder inside him, and I turned him in my arms, holding him as he struggled. His hands shook as they slipped about my waist, and he exhaled.

"I don't know what I would do without you," he whispered.

And then Jenks snapped his wings in warning.

Adrenaline was a quick pulse through me, and we parted at a soft scuff at the door.

It was Quen. Worry stiffened my spine as he halted on the threshold. His shoulders were hunched, his always upright mien having dissolved into heartache. His nose had stopped bleeding, and the obvious pain in his expression said this was hurting him, too. But for a different reason.

"I come here once a year," he said, his gaze going to the couch and the empty coffee cup. "On the day she died," he added, voice breaking. "I promised her I would destroy it so you wouldn't follow in her footsteps. You had a knack, you see." He hesitated, steadying himself. "But when your father bricked it up, I couldn't bring myself to do it. I thought . . . I thought if you never found it, my promise would be good. Trent—"

"You selfish bastard," Trent interrupted, his steps anger-fast as he snatched up the photo on the desk and brandished it. "How could you keep this from me? Where are her missing journals?"

Quen hesitated, his torn confusion clearing at Trent's harsh demand.

"Where are they!" Trent shouted.

Slowly Quen pulled himself upright. He stood on the threshold, his past with Trent behind him, his future uncertain before him. "I don't know," he said, voice steady. "But they aren't here. It doesn't matter. I may not remember what we did, but I do remember it didn't work. You can't maintain two merged circles to make a stronger one. If you could, we wouldn't have failed. Sa'han—"

"Get out of my sight," Trent ground out from between his teeth.

I jumped when Jenks dropped to my shoulder, his green dust reflecting his uncertainty. I knew I was. Uncertain, that is. Quen had practically raised Trent after his father died, but I'd always gotten the impression that Quen had held himself apart, seeing to the task of giving Trent the tools to survive . . . but not what he might have emotionally needed.

And Quen . . . bowed his head, turned, and walked away.

"ARE YOU OKAY?" I ASKED TRENT. IT WAS THE THIRD TIME IN about five minutes, but he was clearly not handling this well. I could feel Trisk's presence everywhere. It was everything he'd been made to forget, everything that his father hadn't wanted him to be: compassionate, understanding, tolerant.

"I'm fine," Trent whispered, but as I watched, he slowly sank to the floor, his back to her desk and his knees bent. One hand held the photo of her to his chest, the other traced a swirl on the carpet as if it were a touchstone, bringing back a childhood memory. "Her horse's name was Inertia," he whispered, looking miserable as his fingers stilled and he closed his eyes. "Because she never wanted to stop. I remember . . . but not enough," he finished brokenly.

I gave Jenks a head nod to go make sure no one else was lurking in the dark, listening, and he hummed away, his dust a somber orange. Slowly I sank down beside Trent, feeling his warmth where our shoulders touched. There was another circle here. I could feel it humming just under the carpet. It wasn't there to spell in. No, it was there for defense. *Against what?* I wondered. *Al, should he escape? Her husband that she both loved and hated?*

"I'm sorry," I whispered, and Trent found my hand. His breath slipped out, and I let my head drop onto his shoulder.

Slowly he set his mother's picture down to tuck a strand of my hair behind my ear, his hand lingering as if needing the reassurance that I was there.

"Hodin shifted your aura. Twice now," he said, surprising me with where his thoughts had gone. But he was good at hiding his grief behind work. "If our auras were the same—I mean, *exactly* the same—maybe our circles could mesh, seeing as it's our auras that define them."

"That's a good thought." I lifted our twined hands and kissed his knuckle.

"All we have to do is lure the baku out of Landon, catch it in a meshed circle, shrink it down, and drop it in a bottle," Trent added.

I turned our clasped hands over to see Hodin's ring. "You want me to call him? He's going to want something ridiculous for payment."

Trent nodded. "If it works, it will give him an in with his kin. Maybe that will be enough. You said they were scared to death of it."

And so, as both of us sat on the floor of his mother's office as he must have done sometime in the past while waiting for her to finish her work, I twisted the ring and opened my thoughts. *Hodin?* I sent out through the private channel the ring afforded.

Nothing. My thoughts were empty.

My lips pressed in annoyance. *Hodin, I'm trying to figure out how to mesh two circles into one thick enough to hold the baku. If you don't help me, I'm going to Dali.*

Trent's head lifted at the faint peal of a bell coming from the lab.

"He's here," I said, scrambling up and falling against the desk as a sudden great gust nearly knocked me down. My jaw dropped, and I reached for Trent, pulling him up and out of the way as something big beat the air, its wings brushing the sides of the large office. The lamp fell and the light flashed against the walls and ceiling. Claws scraped on the slate floor, and I strengthened my hold on the ley line, wondering if I should have invoked the circle around the desk.

"What in great green troll turds is that?" Jenks shrilled as he darted in, sword bared.

There were huge bat wings, a long, sinewy neck, and an even longer tail—and then it was gone, vanishing in a wash of pearly white mist to coalesce into the increasingly familiar narrow-shouldered, black-mop-of-hair demon dressed in black silk and leather.

"You can't mesh two circles into one," Hodin said, clearly annoyed.

"That was a dragon!" Jenks exclaimed, weaving about until Hodin threatened to flick a tiny ball of magic at him. "You were a dragon? That is so cool. How come Al can't turn into a dragon?"

"Because he was never enslaved to a decrepit, psychotic elven priest who enjoyed pitting wolves against larger prey," Hodin said bitterly, and Jenks's dust dulled, his wings tickling my neck as he landed on my shoulder. "Excuse me a moment. Your goyle and I were sporting in the wind. He's worried about you. The Goddess knows why."

"Bis?" I said, startled. "It's daylight. What were you doing with my gargoyle?"

"I told you. Sporting in the wind." Hodin seemed to hesitate, and I recognized that vacant look as him talking silently to someone. Then Bis popped into the room, startling me.

"Rachel," the kid said breathlessly as he oriented himself and flew to me, his red eyes wide and that no-doze amulet around his neck. "Hodin took me flying." He landed, bird light, on my shoulder, his tail lying across my back and wrapping around my opposite arm. "I didn't know the updrafts were so amazing during the day. Where are we? Trent's?" He grinned at Trent, wide and toothy. "We're behind the waterfall, aren't we?"

"Yea-a-ah." I frowned, not liking Hodin's scrutiny—as if I were a bad gargoyle mom for not taking him flying during the day. "I'm sorry, Bis. I didn't know that you wanted to fly in the sun."

"It's okay," Bis said, but his tail didn't ease its grip. "Neither did I until I did it."

"You really don't deserve him," Hodin said, and I wondered if he was jealous. He sniffed, tugging his elegant robes as he gazed at the books. "Where are we?"

"My mother's spelling lab," Trent said. "My father bricked up her rooms after she died."

Hodin leaned to look at the rug. "It smells of Brimstone."

"You noticed that, too?" I said as I sat against the edge of the desk.

"You're Hodin, yes?" Trent said, his usual upright pose beginning to reassert itself. "I've held to our agreement and not told anyone about you."

"Hence, you still breathe." Hodin stared at the bricks behind the sliding-glass door, curious.

"Are you two done yet?" I said as I righted the desk lamp, and Jenks snickered.

Hodin's red, goat-slitted eyes found me, narrowing as if smelling something rank. "Your goyle is right to be worried about you," he said as he looked me up and down to leave my skin crawling. "You were stupid. I can see it in your aura. You tried to talk to it," he accused.

"Uh . . ." I moved from the desk, taking a step sideways as Hodin reached for me. Bis's tail tightened, and Jenks was suddenly between me and the demon.

"Whoa, whoa, whoa, Home Slice," Jenks said, wings clattering. "No touchy."

Hodin dropped back, his hands politely clasped before him, but that prickly feeling was tripping over my skin again as he examined my aura. "You've damage in your outermost shells," he accused, and Bis's wings shifted nervously against me.

"I'm fine," I said, then exhaled in relief when Hodin turned his scrutiny to Trent.

"You're not fine, unless the meaning of *fine* has changed in the last two thousand years." Hodin squinted at Trent.

"Your aura looks as thin as your elven consort's has been eaten to."

My lips parted as I remembered what the baku had said. "You've been fielding attacks?" I accused, and Trent's expression became irate. "And didn't tell me?"

"What good would it have done?" Trent's voice was tight in his throat. "You would have told me to stay out of it. That I'm a businessman and to let the professionals do their job."

"Damn straight," Jenks said as he hovered before us, and I softened.

Trent had been told to be "the businessman" all his life, but it wasn't what he wanted and I knew how that felt. Grimacing, I waved my hands in defeat, forgiving him even as I decided we were going to have to come to some understanding about not keeping things from each other.

"Touching," Hodin mocked, but his attention was on the books. "And typical. Your elf is bad for you, Rachel. But most of them are. Bad, I mean."

Bis's grip tightened, and I put a hand on his feet. I didn't like Hodin talking trash about Trent, either. "It was my idea," I said, tracking Hodin as he went to the bookshelf. "And the intent was that Trent talk to it, not me."

"You can't talk to a baku without risking enormous damage," Hodin said, and the pitch of Jenks's wings increased until my teeth hurt.

"Which would have been nice to know before I did it," I said, tired of feeling stupid.

"Why do you think I procured the no-sleep amulets for you?" Hodin said, clearly disappointed when he saw they were only textbooks. "You invited that elven abomination to strip you down to where it will take very little to overcome you."

Bis gasped, and I gave his feet a reassuring pat. *Damn it, why is he being so blunt when Bis is right here, listening?* "You need to shut up," I said, and Hodin turned from the shelf, his goat-slitted eyes wide. I glanced sideways at Bis on my shoulder, and the demon's lips pressed.

"Fortunately for you it will heal in time," Hodin added,

but the damage had been done, and Bis's grip became painfully tight.

"Rachel, ask him if he'll help or not," Trent said, sounding tired.

Hodin hesitated while reaching for a book, his fingers curling under as if it might harm him. "Circles can't mesh together. That they're separate and distinct is their entire form and function."

"My mother and Quen did it once," Trent said. "But it didn't hold."

"Pre-e-e-cisely," Hodin drawled.

"Rachel says the baku remembers them losing control when they shrank it down to drop it into a bottle." Trent moved to stand behind his mom's desk, looking as if he wanted to sit in her chair but didn't dare. "If they did it, we can do it."

Hodin tapped a book as if expecting a shock, and when nothing happened, he pulled it from the shelf. "As I said, you can't do it. But even if you could mesh your circles, a bottle won't hold it," he said as he thumbed through it. "Even glass has space between the particles it's made from."

"But demons hold souls all the time," I said. "Al has at least three. Or he did," I said, not sure how much he'd saved when the original ever-after shrank to a singularity and vanished.

"The baku isn't a soul," Hodin said, expression holding old anger. "It's energy. Only another form of energy, such as a soul, can hold a baku."

"I still say if we can get it in there, a soul-bottle spiral will confuse it, keep it contained," Trent said patiently. "I kept Rachel's soul contained for three days while her body healed from her fight with Ku'Sox."

"Rachel's soul is not a baku," Hodin said distantly. And then he hesitated, turning with that book splayed open on his long-fingered hand. "He really put your soul in a bottle? For three days?"

Both Bis and I nodded, the gargoyle's white-tipped ears pricked in hope. "He modified the elven curse that moves the souls of dewar leaders into newborns," I said, my thoughts going back to the baby bottle I'd found in Trent's safe room. *He kept it in the safe room.* But if Trent's gut feeling was right, it held a reflection of my soul, and like all magic, it could be lifesaving in the hands of those you trust, and life ending in the hands of those you don't.

"That is a particularly nasty elf charm," Hodin said, then snapped the book shut to make Jenks, perched on the desk lamp, slip dust in surprise. Slow in thought, Hodin replaced the book and turned. "You might be able to contain the baku in a bottle that held your soul for three days. A demon tends to leave a shadow of his soul on the body that contains it. A much-needed evolutionary trait to keep a demon intact when he shape-shifts or travels the lines. But you still can't get it in there. You'd need two people with identical auras to even hope to mesh circles."

"So shift my aura to look like Trent's," I said, and Hodin shook his head.

"Even with your twisting pentagon, I can only see your outermost shells. At your core, you are as different as fish and birds. You will fail," Hodin predicted, and on my shoulder, Bis slumped.

"Unless . . ." Hodin's lips pressed in thought.

"Unless what?" I said, and Hodin's attention flicked up. "Unless what?" I said again, not liking how he was frowning at Trent. "You got something or not?"

"Um, it's old magic," Hodin said, and Jenks's humming wings stilled as he landed on Bis's shoulder. A gentle heat began to emanate from him, and I encouraged Bis to park it on the desk instead of on me.

"How old?" I asked, not seeing anything wrong so far.

"From when I was a slave," Hodin admitted, shooting Trent a baleful look. "Its intent isn't to protect but to equalize the energy balances between demons and elves so that no one gets hurt."

Energy balance? I thought, puzzled. *As in a power pull?* "A demon sex curse?" I blurted, and Hodin flushed as Bis giggled, sounding like rocks in a blender.

Unfazed, Trent raised a finger in question. "Ah, how does a curse created for pleasure lend itself to being able to merge our circles?"

"It blurs your auras into one unique expression." Hodin glared at Jenks as he whispered in Bis's white-tufted ear to make the kid snort. "Which in turn facilitates an equal balance of power between a demon's naturally higher carrying capacity and an elf's higher resistance to ley line energy."

"Oh." Arms crossed, I sat back against the desk again, Bis and Jenks on one side, Trent on the other. Such a curse would allow for toe-curling sex without the fear of accidently frying your partner with line energy. It didn't surprise me that the elves had found a way to even the playing field. That demons could hold more line energy than elves had always been a sore point. Trent and I didn't even play with line energy when, er, playing. "How come Al doesn't know it?" I asked.

"Because he wasn't in an elven harem for a thousand years," Hodin said bitingly, and I winced. "But don't worry. I can *guarantee* the curse won't instill any desire. The aura blending is a side effect," he added. "The baku won't be able to find you for at least thirty-six hours. If nothing else, you could get some sleep. Maybe shower and clean up. You both look like paupers."

Sleep. I looked at Trent, seeing his weariness on him like a mask. Even if we couldn't master blending our circles into one, sleep would be most welcome. "We'll do that," I blurted, and Bis nodded, clearly in favor of it.

"And in return, we will continue to give you our silence that you exist," Trent said.

I jerked to a wary stiffness, pushing from the desk and waving my hand. "Hold up," I said as Hodin bristled. "No. I'm not agreeing to that. I'm not blackmailing Hodin. I'm sorry, Hodin. This is not what we discussed." Hand on my hip, I turned to Trent, utterly mortified. "What are you doing?" I almost hissed.

Trent brushed nonexistent dust from his nonexistent sports coat. "Bargaining."

"No, you're pissing him off," I said, shooting Hodin an apologetic glance. "Would you mind if I handled it?" I asked, and Trent gestured in an obvious "Be my guest."

I faced Hodin, suddenly unsure. He looked ready to walk away. I didn't blame him after that. "Helping us capture the baku will give you a solid in with your kin. It's in your best interests."

Hodin eyed the rings on his hand. "No. They will ignore my efforts as they always have. I want you to stand beside me. Stand up and say no when they try to bury me in a hole again, embarrassed at the things I did to survive."

I knew all about breaking the rules to survive, and with a few misgivings, I nodded. "Okay. You've got a deal. Trent, tell him you'll stand up for him before the demon collective."

Hodin's arms dropped and he stared at me in surprise. "Okay?" he said, his goat-slitted eyes wide in the desk lamp's light. "Do you have any idea how much they hate me for swimming in a pool they're too afraid to dip a toe in?"

"Probably more than they hate me for existing," I said, and Trent frowned.

"Rachel . . . ," he cautioned, but Hodin hadn't asked for a demon mark, or my firstborn, or even a date. He'd asked me to stand up for him. It was something I was probably going to do anyway. Eventually. *God, I'm such a bleeding heart for wild cosmic powers on the skids.*

"Blackmailing him is safer," Trent insisted, but when I gave him a look of disbelief, he pinched the bridge of his nose, knowing he was beat. "Twist your curse," he said. "We will both stand beside you if the demon collective should come against you for your *past* transgressions."

Smirking, Hodin flung an expansive hand. Energy seemed to crawl over me, and both Bis and I jumped, my head swiveling to see what had changed. But the only thing that had was Hodin, and his tall, dark-haired presence was now lost behind a threadbare spelling robe that might have once been red. His eyes narrowed at my questioning look, and then he turned away. He had such nice spelling robes, why he was slumming it now was beyond me.

The inkpot he took from the ratty folds of his robe made me even more nervous. It looked old, pinched together, not thrown on a wheel. I'd used ink that wasn't ink before, and I was willing to bet that whatever was in it was nothing I'd seen before. "If you'd remove your shirt, Rachel?" Hodin said as he set the pot on the desk with an attention-getting click.

"Whoa, what?" I said as Jenks's wings clattered and Bis swished his tail tip in uncertainty.

"Just what kind of a curse is this?" Trent asked, clearly uneasy.

Hodin set a paintbrush beside the pot of ink instead of a stylus. "One that has to be applied," he said dryly. "You may drape yourself for modesty, but I need access to your back."

"Fair enough," I said, not willing to let our bargain fall apart because of showing a little skin. And before Trent could protest, I went to the couch, spun to put my back to them, and pulled my sweater and chemise up and over my head in one motion. The cold touched me, and I hunched, very aware of the both of them as I pulled the silken knitted throw from the couch and draped it around my neck to leave my back bare. It smelled like Quen, and I stifled a frown. *Once a year, huh?*

When I turned, Hodin was politely focused on his paintbrush as Trent squinted mistrustfully at him. Jenks stood with his hands on his hips with Bis, and the small gargoyle was glowing an embarrassed ruddy color. Hodin held the inkpot, the tiny thing almost lost in one hand, the other holding the brush. It didn't look as if he'd picked it up at the dollar store, and I wondered if the brush was made of his hair.

"Try not to twitch," Hodin said as he moved to stand behind me. "The pattern is not one you will forget. Ever."

"What's the ink made of?" I asked as I gathered my hair and pulled it forward and out of his way. "Is it blood?" I added when he didn't answer.

"It's plant based, as is the brush," Hodin said stiffly, clearly loath to say more. "I'll leave it with you both, and if you can do it correctly upon your elf, I'll tell you what it is."

"How can I do it correctly if you don't tell me how?" I complained, and then I jumped, breath catching when the brush touched me. It was like a ley line itself, burning with an icy heat as he painted from my right shoulder down my back, curving to my left and rising in a smooth arc just above the small of my back. I shuddered as the sensation multiplied upon itself. I could hardly stand it, that deliciously tantalizing itch you can't reach, and I put a hand to the desk for balance.

"Tap a line," Hodin muttered, and I did, gasping when the excess magical intent that had been building up in me spilled away to leave only a hint of connection.

"You're communing with the Goddess," I breathed, and Trent's expression went empty.

"Be still," Hodin muttered, his voice tight behind me, and I heard Bis's leathery wings shift. "I'm not talking to her. You are. Be still and listen."

But he *was* communing with her, even if the words he began to chant were unfamiliar. My shoulders slumped, then tightened as he continued to paint the curse onto me, each shift of motion sending jolts of tingles through me. Suddenly I realized the curse was being carried into me by ley line and paint and song, all soaking into me much as smoke from a distant fire taints the grapes on the vine and turns them rank.

"*Un soom ou un ermoon es un soom ou un om,*" Hodin intoned, the monotone words tickling a memory I'd never had. "*Un soom ou un om es un soom ou un ermoon,*" he echoed, only two words shifting place. I'd have given just about anything to know what he was saying. Old magic. It wasn't elven; it wasn't demon. It was a mix of them both, and I stifled another shiver as he coated me in power older than the universe. Hodin was asking for the Goddess's help, and I bowed my head, knowing the pain he was opening himself up to if she shunned him again and it didn't work.

His words softened, becoming thick in my head until he was breathing the chant, the brush never lifting from me as he went clockwise, then doubled back in widdershins, and then back again, making smaller and smaller arcs until tracing a final arc encompassing all the loops before rising up to my left shoulder, making a sparkling line between my neck and the knitted throw.

My eyes widened as Hodin shifted to stand before me. He looked like nothing I'd ever seen before as his plea to the Goddess spilled from his lips, begging her to help for my sake. His eyes held a thick torment. I knew he was breaking his own promise, one made in anger and humiliation. He'd been a slave because the Goddess had said no. He had suffered because she turned her back on him. And now he was asking again, opening himself to rejection from someone he loved and hated, despised and needed. I bowed my head in understanding, grateful.

His motion never slowing, never quickening, Hodin traced the ink in a shallow curve, staying above my breasts as he mirrored the glyph on my back but in a much smaller size—tingling against my skin. *"Un soom ou un ermoon es un soom ou un om. Un soom ou un om es un soom ou un ermoon,"* he whispered as he finished the last interior arc, the final swoop curving around the small glyph and rising up to touch the point on my shoulder where he'd begun.

Only now did he lift the brush from my skin. I staggered, and Trent's hand was there, gripping my elbow as, without warning, the ley line wasn't moving through me, but around me.

"Mirror it on your elf, and you should be able to merge your circles," Hodin said, but I was still trying to find myself. I was wrapped in a ley line, the warm humming protecting me from everything, tingling as he shifted the blanket to cover me fully. The ink was already dry. "As long as you are both conscious, your combined strength may hold it."

Too alone to hold me, echoed in my thoughts. "Hodin, this isn't an elf or demon curse. It's both," I said, pulse fast. "Is this why they hate you? Because you mixed elf and demon magic?"

Hodin's eyes flicked to Trent standing resolute beside

me. "Constantly," he said. "And now I'm doing it again."
He shook his head, grimacing. "You'd think I'd learn after
two thousand years of penance." His eyes came to me, and
I quailed. "But we're both half what we could be apart, and
I can't bear it. Don't make me suffer them alone as I try to
survive their anger."

Them being the demons. I didn't think the elves would
have cared, except it would have made the demons more
powerful yet. I swallowed hard, fingers damp as I twined
them in Trent's. "We won't," I promised. "Thank you," I
added, and Hodin seemed to find a shadow of peace.

"You felt the how of it?" he said as he scuffed back.
"Can you do it again?"

I nodded as I pulled the knitted throw closer about me.
I didn't have to see the glyph painted on me. I felt it, knew
its every turn and convoluted shift. "Maybe not the words,
but the pattern," I said, and he nodded sharply, as if having
expected nothing less.

"Then I'm done." Hodin tugged his threadbare robe
close as if it were fine silk.

"Hodin, wait." I stepped from Trent, and the demon
slumped. "I mean it. Thank you," I said again, nervous. "I
know . . ." I hesitated, not wanting him to think I understood what he'd done. How could I? His Goddess had
turned her back on him, allowing him to be enslaved. His
kin had shut him out, reviled him for not just practicing but
relishing an art of magic that they considered foul and
wrong. And all he had from me was a promise that I
wouldn't do the same when they found out he was alive and
came for him again. "I'll do what I can," I said, realizing
how expensive a promise I had made. "With the rest of
them."

It seemed to be the right thing to say, as Hodin nodded
and looked from me to Trent. "Bis, you will best serve Rachel outside while she twists the curse upon her elf," he
said.

"Yes, sir." Bis's leathery wings beat the air once, and he
landed atop Hodin's shoulder, looking embarrassed.

"What am I? Chopped fairy farts?" Jenks said as he rose up on a column of silver. "Zack is probably eating something. Give me a minute, and I'll join you," he added, and Bis nodded.

"I'll be on the roof," Bis said, and with a tweak on my awareness, he and Hodin vanished.

Again the bell rang from the other room, the pure note assuring me they had left. Jenks gave us a two-fingered salute and hummed out into the darkness in search of something to eat. We were alone. I looked at Trent, nothing but that silky throw between me and the world. Oh, and the curse, wrapping me in a ley line. We had a chance, and I gave his hand a quick squeeze.

"Your skin glowed. Did it hurt?" Trent asked, and I shook my head.

"No, it felt good going on, actually," I said as I picked up the brush and the inkpot sitting on the desk. There was considerably less "ink," but I knew for a fact Hodin had never lifted his brush. "Shirt off. Tap a line," I directed at Trent. "Let's see if this works."

Trent glanced once at the open door before beginning to undo buttons. I'd seen Trent in far less, but seeing him before me, waiting for me to paint a curse on him, made him brand-new, and I resisted the urge to touch his smooth skin and defined shoulders, his abs shaped by his almost daily rides with the girls. *Thirty minutes of garden dirt and ley line magic . . .*

"Okay, let me know if something doesn't feel right," I said, and then he shuddered, breath coming in fast as I set the brush to his shoulder.

Ta na shay, I thought, knowing I'd never get the words right as I began the first long swoop down Trent's back. But then Hodin's words rebounded in my memory with a new meaning. *"Un soom ou un ermoon es un soom ou un om,"* I whispered, and goose bumps blossomed on Trent. *The soul of the one is the soul of the all,* I thought, not knowing how I knew, only that I did. *"Un soom ou un om es un soom ou un ermoon." The soul of the all is the soul of the one.*

Breathless, I kept the brush moving as I traced the pattern to blur our auras into one. The words rose from my mind as if I was in the collective, evoking a feeling of protection, of belonging, like that of a wolf pack. The words and spell were elven, but it was as if both the enclave and the collective had taken us in, sheltering us even as we lent our souls to protect theirs. The ink never thinned as I finished the large glyph on his back and turned, coming to his front to create a smaller shield atop his upper chest.

"Un soom ou un ermoon es un soom ou un om. Un soom ou un om es un soom ou un ermoon," I intoned, my words sounding apart from myself as if others were repeating them, not me. *"Ta na shay,"* I whispered to make it wholly Trent's as I traced the final loop and rose to find the beginning. My skin tingled, and I wasn't sure why.

I looked into the pot to find the ink was gone. "That should do it," I said, my words sounding crass as I lifted the brush from him, and he shivered, his hand reaching up to grab mine.

My eyes darted to his, and I froze at the unexpected desire in them. Suddenly I realized that I was still wearing that afghan, which was basically wearing nothing at all. "That was the most erotic thing you've ever done to me," Trent whispered, and my pulse quickened.

"Is that so?" I said, eyes closing as his hands reached around my middle and pulled me closer. "How about the time—Oh! Mmmm," I gasped as he bent his head and nuzzled my neck, his teeth fastening on me in a brief gentle tug. There was no preamble. It was raw need in him, and it sparked my own with a surprising urgency. *Damn demonsex curse anyway.*

"Yes," he muttered when his lips let go. I couldn't think. His hands rose to my breasts. The drape hid his movements, and feeling dove to my groin, making me squirm in desire.

Sensation welled up, and a desperate need to see this to the end filled me. "Hodin said it didn't instill any desire," I said as I set the empty pot and brush aside. Hands free, I eagerly traced my hands down him, tugging his waistband until our hips touched. "You think he lied?"

"No. It's all you," Trent said, and then we gasped as one when, by chance, our fingers laced together and the glyphs drawn singly upon us resonated with the same exhilarating feeling. Breathless, I looked at Trent. He felt it, too. *The soul of the one is the soul of the all,* I thought as the sensation of connection snapped through us, ebbing and flowing through our fingers.

"Interesting," Trent said, his smile turning wicked, and something in me quivered.

"Uh, I don't think this was Hodin's intent," I said, wondering how I was going to get Trent's pants off if I couldn't let go of his hand. I knew I didn't want to. Feeling his desire echo through me was so erotic, I could hardly bear it.

"Not my problem," Trent said, and giving in, I found his mouth with mine.

Sensation redoubled, spilling through me, through us, our desire amplified by the still new and unblemished curse painted on our skins. My mouth moved against his, tingles racing through me, making my pulse beat fast and my hands skate over him, tugging him closer. The silky yarn between us was a cool wash on my skin, tingles trailing wherever it moved.

In wild need, I reached for his zipper, gasping when he pushed me back to the wall beside the couch. The shock jolted through me, and our hands parted. The snap of disconnection raked over my soul, and then it was just my desire making my breath quicken. But even that was exhilarating, and he quivered when I laid my hand atop the inked pattern on his chest and I could feel his love for me again.

"So it's like that, then?" I whispered, the throaty rasp of my voice making his smile heated as he took my hand from him and pinned my wrists to either side of my head.

"Ever and always," he said, and then I groaned, leg twining in his as he dropped his head and began nuzzling past the knitted throw for my breasts, finding one, then the other with his mouth until I nearly climaxed right there.

"You're wearing too much." I tugged my hand out from under his, and this time he let me. I fumbled with his zipper, his feet tangled in mine. He gasped in relief as I finally got his zipper down, shimmying everything to his knees with a careful foot. And then I found his mouth again, my tongue lightly twining with his, my hands behind his neck as he worked my jeans off and I shuddered, the cold hitting me to raise goose bumps.

I pushed from the wall, breath fast as he diverted my motion to the couch, pressing me back against the wall again with a thump. My eyes flashed open, seeing the hunger in his eyes, knowing it matched my own. Lean body taut, he pressed into me, holding me still as he found my mouth and filled my thoughts with wanting more.

A rising desperation was growing in me, little trills of emotion plinking one by one, sensation following every touch and caress. I was feeling everything twice, my desire and his, the need and hunger almost unbearable. Desperate to find all of him, my hands fisted in his hair and my legs twined with his. The tangle of our pants was lumpy under our feet. Breath fast, I tugged him closer, nails digging into him as he bore down hard enough on my neck to make me gasp. He was raw with need, strong with desire, all the passion he kept hidden under a suit and tie and the trappings of civilization gone. It made me want him all the more.

My hands skated over him, feeling his muscles move as I traced the lines of the curse from his back to his front, dropping down to search him out. I ached, wanting all of him. "Now," I whispered, and he shook his head, leaning to find my breast, biting, tugging, pulling until I moaned, shivering with the need to do more. My hands fell to seek him out, desperately wanting to guide him in, wanting to get lost in feeling.

"Not yet," he said as his lips left me, and he pulled me closer, not letting me open myself to him. "Not yet," he said again, his voice hard with demand.

Goose bumps rose as he pulled the knitted throw from me, then traced the path of the curse on my back. Trails of sparking sensation rose. I was beyond thinking, and he cupped my face with his hands, his light kisses jolting me. I was going to die. It was that simple. One person could not hold this much.

"Oh, God. Trent. The couch," I whispered, and his grip tightened. "The couch," I insisted until Trent held me tighter and lifted. My arms went around his neck and my legs tightened about his waist, and he shuffled to the couch, sighing as he eased me down and his weight covered me. I wedged a foot into his slacks and pushed to free his feet. With a tug, he did the same for me.

The sudden freedom raced through me like fire, and I pulled him lower, arching up to find him. I needed him. Now. I wanted to feel him move within me, to move with him. But he wouldn't let me, and as I ran my hand over him, he dropped his head to find my breast again. Sensation arched through me with his every pull, and I groaned softly, feeling him against me. Again I traced the lines I'd painted on his back, and he shuddered, his breath coming fast. In a sudden motion, he pinned my hand to the couch and found my mouth with his. I met him with my own desire.

Our breaths twined and our motions against each other became more certain. Reaching down, I guided him closer. My breath escaped me in a moan as he slipped inside me to his full length in one satisfying motion. I gasped, and his hands found mine, holding them down as we moved together with a rhythm older than the curse echoing our every move.

"Oh, God, now," I whispered, straining, and it tripped Trent over the edge. Groaning, he deepened his motion, sending fulfillment crashing through us. I shuddered, my hands springing from his light grip to pull him deeper, closer as I climaxed, wave after slow wave seeming to echo as they built one upon the other, over and over, until they finally died away, leaving us exhausted.

And then there were just the rasping of our breaths, his fingers twined in my hair, and the knowledge that Trent wasn't really the calm, collected businessman he showed the world, but that the demons were right. He was an elf, ruthless and savage, his needs as demanding as my own. If he didn't love me, he'd use and discard me with no thought. But he did love me, and my soul resonated with the knowledge. He loved me, and I knew to the bottom of my being that he'd turn that same ruthlessness toward ruining the world if it meant I would be safe.

Spent, I blinked at Trent, loving the way he looked above me, loving the way he felt atop and in me. *How could I ever leave him?* I thought, my fingers tracing a line of ink.

"Wow," Trent rasped, and I laughed. "Hey, watch it!" he protested at the sudden clenching of my inner muscles, and I pulled him closer, not wanting him to leave. There was the small issue that he *couldn't* leave yet. Maybe in a few minutes. Trent had never complained, but it was still a source of embarrassment for me. By the looks of things, it might be a while.

"Don't ever leave me," I said, playing with the tips of his pointy ears, and he shifted his weight, putting all of it on the flat of one arm so he could catch my hand and kiss my fingertips.

"Promise," he said, but as our breathing slowed and my thoughts turned introspective, I wondered if anyone would bother to check on us if we spent the night here, encircled by the strength of the ley lines and our love for each other.

CHAPTER
29

THE SOUND OF PIXY WINGS PULLED THROUGH ME, STIRRING me awake. My eyes opened to the dim, increasingly familiar lines of Trent's room and his sparse, smooth-lined furniture. A fading line of pixy dust showed where Jenks had been, but he was gone now, and I smiled, feeling hungry and loved, but mostly loved. Trent's arm was over me, heavy and secure. After having fallen asleep on his mom's couch, we'd stumbled back through the fireplace sometime after sunset to find Trent's bed. The clock on the side table and the light leaking in from around the curtains on the window wall said it was now just after sunrise.

God, save me from elven schedules, I thought as I spooned up into the curve of Trent's body behind me. A smile quirked my lips as my eyes shut. He might not have been awake, but he was up.

Feeling me move, Trent pulled me closer. He smelled really good, of cinnamon and wine, and a hint of leather from his horses. But my wish to fall back asleep for a few more hours was crushed when I heard Zack talking to someone in the outer room, his voice low and melodious. The scent of brewing coffee became obvious and Trent's breathing quickened. He was waking up.

My shoulders itched, and my fingers touched the curse

that Hodin had given me. *Old magic.* And as I idly traced the path from my back to my front, a sensation of connection spilled into me.

Trent stirred. Wondering if he felt it, too, I pulled my hand away, my fingers curling under my palm. "What time is it?" he whispered, his voice soft with sleep.

"Just after sunup." I sighed, knowing he'd leave me. Zack and Jenks were talking, and the faint drone of the TV was becoming obvious.

Sure enough, he groaned, his arm tightening around me. "I don't hear the girls. You don't think Ellasbeth ignored Quen and stayed in the safe room, do you? It's been over twelve hours."

More like fifteen. I spun in his grip to see him, liking how soft he looked with sleep dulling his usual sharp expression. "That's your first thought?" I teased, my fingernails raking his stubble to make his eyes open. But inside, I cringed. Ellasbeth was coming back into his life. Not only because of the girls, but to keep his head above the political waters. It was the right thing to do, but it still left me aching.

Trent's smile became more certain as my nails found his throat. His legs shifted, imprisoning mine. "My first thought was how nice it was to be able to sleep. My second was how right it felt to wake up beside you. Ellasbeth was about fifth on the list."

I played with his hair, wishing we didn't have to get up. "What was between them?"

Trent pulled me close, his fingers drifting low down my back to send a tremble-worthy sensation spilling through me. "You," he said. "Both third and fourth."

His head tilted, and he found my lips. Desire rose from nowhere, and my mouth moved against his, my legs twining tighter.

"Maybe fifth, too," he added as our lips parted, and I tucked my head under his chin.

"You want to try merging our circles?" I said, reluctant to move. My fingers brushed over his smooth skin, and I smiled as I pulled goose bumps into existence. It had been forever since I'd felt this complete. Maybe this was what it would be like if I never went back to my boat.

"Yes, and yes, it would," Trent whispered, and I leaned back to look at him.

"How do you do that?" I said, a feeling of contentment rising at the love in his eyes.

"I told you before." His voice rumbled through me. "Every thought crosses your face."

"Mmmm. What am I thinking now?" I said as I played with his ears, and he smiled wickedly.

"Something that doesn't involve circles."

But Zack's voice from the other room was getting louder, and the coming pressures of the day slowly pushed out the feeling that we could just lie here together and let everything pass. I reluctantly sat up against the headboard. "Should we scribe one, or make it free-floating?"

"Free-floating," Trent said with a yawn. "That's what you said they caught it in."

I loved how he looked there among the pillows, still soft with sleep as he sat up and tucked an arm behind me to tug me closer.

My internal energy balance made a little jump as he tapped a line. But that wasn't unexpected, seeing as most of our length was touching. I did the same . . . and then my eyes went to his at the unusual linked sensation. Frowning, Trent sat up even more.

"Curious," he said, clearly feeling it as well. "The ley line tastes different."

I took his hand and the feeling strengthened. "It's darker, like moss on a moonlit night."

He smiled and tucked a strand of hair behind my ear. "I was going to say it was electric and dusty, like a demon." He turned my hand over in his and traced a pattern on my palm to make me shiver. "You want to make a circle, and I'll overlay it?"

I nodded, breathless at the sensations tripping through me. "Sure." There were better ways to use this knowledge, and sitting in bed making circles wasn't one of them. But Hodin's curse would only last for thirty-six hours. If we didn't have the baku captured and in a bottle by then, we'd have to paint it on again. We were out of whatever had been in that hand-pinched pot.

So with more than a little reluctance, I forced my thoughts from the tingling sensation warming my core to a small space over the foot of the bed. *Rhombus,* I thought, using my circle word, whereas I usually only willed it to happen.

Trent jerked, his grip on my hand tightening as the circle swam into existence with an unusual hesitation. But it was thick. So thick I couldn't see through it. "Damn," Trent swore, a nervous smile on him as he glanced at me. "I didn't even set one. It just happened. That's good."

"Is it?" I frowned at the potential problem. It wasn't like the slave rings where the person who had the master ring supplemented his power with whoever wore the slaver. It was a direct link, as if the two were one. "What if all our magic is supplemented by each other?"

"Is that a problem?" he asked, and I took a slow breath.

"Not necessarily, but we should find out. *Leno cinis,*" I said with a flourish, directing my attention to the already running circle floating in the middle of the room.

Energy zipped through me, shocking and hot. It raced to the circle . . . and then it exploded into existence. A white-hot glow threw back the comforting gloom of the morning, making Trent grunt and me wince. It was like a miniature sun, and I dropped the line. Darkness flooded back, and the purple blot from where I'd burned my retinas danced like an annoying will-o'-the-wisp.

"I'd say yes, that's a problem," Trent muttered. "Unless you meant it to be that bright."

"No." I blinked, trying to get the haze to go away. "Let me try again. *Leno cinis,*" I said, letting only a trickle of energy invoke the curse. My shoulders eased and I leaned back into Trent as a more normal light brightened the room.

"That's better." Trent looked at it, clearly relieved. "What's the ratio?"

I snuggled back against him. *Soul bottle, check. Merging circles, check. Lure the baku from Landon and catch it . . . not so easy peasy.* "About half?" I guessed, then jerked when the lighted circle dropped. I hadn't done it, and after the first shock, I smiled at Trent. "That takes some getting used to," I said as I snuggled closer, reluctant to get up.

"Don't bother," he said as he traced a path down my arm. "I figure we have until three a.m. tomorrow, and it will be gone."

But then my expression blanked as a new voice twined with Zack's, one feminine and dark, like gray smoke in fog. *Ivy.* "Crap on toast. I forgot to call Ivy." Pulse fast, I sat up.

"It's okay," Trent said with a yawn, looking tousled and sexy in his PJ bottoms and nothing else. "I asked Jon to call her when we came up at sunset."

"Then why is she here?" I swung my feet off the bed and stood. *Where's my robe?*

"I've no idea," he said as he slid from the sheets and stretched. He looked absolutely yummy as he reached for his robe and slipped it on. I watched, feeling my body react and wanting him all over again. Yesterday had been amazing, and afterward, I'd never slept better.

"You don't think Ellasbeth kept the girls in the safe room all this time, do you?" he said as I put on my own robe, then gave him a hug from behind. My head hit the back of his shoulder, and I felt my gaze go distant.

"I'm sure Quen has them. It's hard to sleep when Lucy is awake," I said.

Trent turned in my grip, his head dropping as he tied my robe shut. It didn't cover the front half of the glyph, and I was struck with how old the curse was, older than the original ever-after maybe. Though the words had been demon, it was obviously Goddess based. *No wonder they want Hodin dead.*

"True," Trent said distantly, and my thoughts went back to their argument. I could see the hurt of Quen's betrayal on him, and I wished I could make it go away. "I don't know how you do it," he said as his tight expression eased and he gave me a squeeze.

"What?" I said, touching my hair since his eyes were on it.

Our bodies pressed together, and he gave me a loving kiss. "Look so fantastic in the morning," he whispered, and I smiled, wondering if the glyphs were warming or if it was just his presence. "It takes me an hour to look that good."

"You're sweet," I said, appreciating the white lie. But the reality was that despite sleeping, I felt too tired to look good. He dropped back, and our fingers still twined, we went out into the main room, blinking at the sudden glare of light.

"Good morning," Trent said, a hint of concern on him as he looked from Zack and Jenks making oatmeal in the open kitchen, to Glenn and Ivy in the sunken living room, a loaf of pull-apart bread between them on the table. "The girls aren't still in the safe room, are they?"

"No." Zack stirred the oatmeal, his bangs moving in the steam. "Quen took them and Ellasbeth into the conservatory so you could sleep. I'm making them breakfast," he added proudly.

"I'll let them know you're up," Jenks said, then hummed straight off the balcony and down to the great room, his sparkles cheerful and bright.

"Glenn?" I said, a flash of worry running through me as my fingers slipped from Trent's and he made a beeline to the kitchen and the brewing coffee. "Something bad happened, didn't it."

But Ivy was smiling as she uncoiled herself from the chair, licking the glaze from her fingers before reaching for a napkin. She was in her working black and high boots, clearly having come right from work. "Glenn quit the Order," she said, smug as I wobbled down the two steps.

Glenn shrugged sheepishly as he turned off the TV. "Quit stealing my thunder, woman," he said as he came forward, and smiling, I pushed past his offered hand to pull him into a hug, breathing in the odd scent of gun oil, tomato paste, and basil. Ivy was in there too, making me wonder. He looked good in his casual jeans and black shirt.

"You can't quit the Order," I said when I pulled back. He was built wider across the shoulders than Trent, less thin about the waist. "At least not without a lot of missing memory."

Glenn's smile widened. "As Weast pointed out, I'm a probational member. I know enough to keep my mouth shut, and little more." His brow creased. "Are you okay? Quen said the baku damaged your aura when you tried to talk to it."

Thanks, Quen, I thought sourly. "I'll heal," I said, embarrassed. Buddy was underfoot, the reason obvious when Zack slipped the dog a walnut. Seeing it, Trent frowned but said nothing as he poured coffee into two mugs. That oatmeal smelled great. I hadn't eaten in hours.

"Are you sure?" Ivy said as she looked me up and down, her worry obvious.

"I'll be fine." My arm went around her in a half hug to feel the strength in her slight build. The cloying scent of the long undead lifted from her skin, making me wonder how she was doing in the I.S.'s lower tower. "I feel a lot better since getting some sleep. Even better, Trent and I can merge our circles for the next twenty hours or so. We just have to go and get it."

Glenn cocked his head and smiled. "Rachel, your *fine* can put anyone else in the hospital. I'm sorry. I should've warned you about the baku, but I thought Weast was going to start sharing information. I feel bad about that."

"It's okay," I said as they stood before me, so different yet the same where it counted. "Welcome back."

"Yeah, welcome back," Jenks said as he rose up from the great room, and I thought I heard the girls in the distance. "You do anything that dumb again, Glenn, I'll cut off your 'nads and make a coat out of them."

Zack choked on his laugh, and content, I sat in Ceri's rocker. "Though letting the Order turn Landon into a zombie has a certain appeal," I said as Ivy and Glenn returned to the couch. It would be awful, though, living an eternity without sleeping. Which made me wonder if zombies were a lot more coherent when they started out, gradually losing their cognizance along with their body cohesion.

"It's how they got it the last time." Glenn nodded to Trent in greeting, and I gratefully took the mug Trent was extending before he went back to the kitchen to help Zack with the oatmeal. "Weast has been tracking the baku for the last three weeks," Glenn continued. "Once it settles into a body, he will turn him into a zombie and put him with the rest."

Nasty. Even if it was Landon they were going for, no one deserved that. It was as illegal as all hell, but the Order had put themselves above the law, and I didn't like it. Even the I.S. was looking the other way in the face of "the greater good."

"Not if we put it into a bottle first," Trent said as he adjusted the two high chairs at the table. "Much as I'd like to see Landon as a zombie, the dewar might get off our case if we save him."

"You really think you can do that?" Glenn's expressive face grew hopeful.

"Yep," Jenks said from my shoulder, wings stilling. "She and Trent spent all night learning how to mesh things together. Oh, baby, oh, baby, oh, baby!"

"Damn it, Jenks, you were supposed to be keeping watch outside!" I blurted, then flushed, realizing I'd confirmed everyone's suspicions. "Just shut up," I muttered, pulling my robe tight and hiding behind a sip of coffee as the pixy laughed all the harder.

"A bottle?" Glenn prompted, ignoring Jenks.

Trent touched the curse peeping from his robe. "I think we have a good chance."

Ivy was looking at me for confirmation, and I nodded. My eyes went to Zack and Trent in the kitchen, again noticing how much they looked alike. "Zack, does Landon know about the Order?" I asked him, and he jumped, startled.

"No," he blurted. "At least, I don't think so."

"Then warning him and offering a way out might convince him to help us," Trent said as he took two primary-colored bowls from a cupboard and set them on the counter. "I'm going to go help with the girls. Zack, will you ladle some oatmeal out to cool? I need to talk to Quen."

Which was of course the real reason he wanted to go downstairs, and I grimaced.

"Sure," Zack said, clearly uncomfortable. Ivy eyed me in the new silence, a knowing expression on her face at the almost hidden tension in Trent's voice. Frowning, I turned to Jenks. The pixy couldn't have kept his mouth shut if his life depended on it, and what Quen had withheld from Trent was sweet enough gossip to keep a faire of pixies alive through the winter.

Nice going, I thought, staring at him, and he dusted an embarrassed red as he sat on Zack's shoulder and pointed out where the big spoons were.

Jaw tight, Trent strode to the stairs as the girls' voices rose high in the great room. Somehow he managed to look fully in control despite being in a robe and barefoot. I wasn't sure how this was going to play out. It felt as if something had broken between Quen and him.

"Daddy!" Lucy shouted, but upstairs, an uncomfortable silence had begun to grow.

"Uh, any new attacks last night?" I asked Ivy.

"I have no idea," she grumped, and Glenn bobbed his head in sympathy, his mouth full of pull-apart bread. "The flow of information has stopped. I say baku, and everyone looks at me as if I've got fangs coming out of my nose," she said, and from the kitchen, Jenks snorted.

"It's not funny," Ivy said, and Jenks laughed like wind chimes.

"Yes, it is. See?" he said, and I quailed as he stuck his chopsticks in his nose and pretended to be a Hollywood vampire and bite Zack's neck.

Ivy's eyes narrowed, and Glenn stifled a laugh. "Don't let the girls see you do that, or you will be banned from the

Kalamack compound," I said, and Zack twisted, almost knocking Jenks off his shoulder as he tried to see.

Annoyed, Ivy crossed her knees and bobbed her foot. "I gave them your findings. The I.S. still intends to shove these people into the system and let them drown to shut them up. No one deserves to be locked up because someone practiced killing Trent with them."

Hungry, I sipped my coffee and watched Zack fill a third, larger serving bowl with oatmeal, adding nuts by the handful and drenching it with equal portions of milk and maple syrup. If I hadn't seen his fear at the top of Carew Tower, I'd have been concerned that this was going to land in Landon's ears, but today . . . I had other things to worry about.

"Glenn and I are arranging a press release tonight. The six o'clock news," Ivy said, and I jerked my eyes from Zack. Was she crazy? The I.S. wanted this buried.

"This is *great*!" Jenks said sarcastically as he dropped down and helped himself to the maple syrup clinging to the bottle top. "Glenn is quitting the Order. Ivy's going to get fired. Hey, Glenn, you could go into partnership with Ivy and Nina since Ivy's ditching Rache and me."

"I am not ditching you," Ivy protested as she shifted on the couch. "I'm quitting the firm."

Glenn stiffened. "You didn't tell me you weren't going back to the church."

She frowned, eyes furtive. "Nina and I have been asked to come to DC to present ourselves to the long undead. Now." Her eyes flicked to mine. "I'm sure we'll be back by Christmas."

"I thought you said you weren't leaving until the first of the year," I said, alarmed, and she shrugged, looking helpless. For a moment, there were just the sounds of the girls making their slow way upstairs. Clearly Lucy was happy to see her dad. "Christmas is good," I said, though once she was out of Cincy, there was no guarantee that she'd come back.

"It's only a few weeks," Ivy said softly, but I could hear the unsaid issues—issues that came with having the will to say no to the undead. It only made them more eager to find the point where you broke and said yes, and Ivy was very good at saying no. It drove them crazy with bloodlust.

"Hey, uh, would it help if Trent or I went with you to explain about the auratic shells?" I offered, trying to change the subject. "Trent could use the good press."

"It would," Glenn said, hunched over his knees as he looked toward the sound of giggling girls. "But I don't want either of you involved in the initial release."

Because of the girls, I thought, guilt sliding through me. "We're already involved. Up to our necks involved," I said. "We could do a private town meeting if you'd rather."

Glenn winced, and Jenks chortled rudely. *The last one wasn't that bad,* I thought, but Ivy, too, was shaking her head. "I'd rather do it publicly," she said. "Behind closed doors gives the undead too much of an advantage. How reliable is that curse that proves the suspects' souls have been tampered with?"

"Enough to satisfy me." I drank my coffee almost to the bottom of the cup, jerking when I felt Trent's sudden anger through our shared curse. It spilled through me like hot honey, tightening my gut and stiffening my back. He wasn't tapping a line, but something was sending ley line–like tingles through me. "But enough of Cincinnati thinks the demons are responsible, so that's questionable help," I finished, squirming as I worked to shunt the excess energy from me. Us.

Lucy's shout that she wanted the green one—whatever the green one was—came loudly, and Trent came up the stairs alone, his hair in disarray and his pace fast as he went to the kitchen. "Ellasbeth gave in to Lucy's every whim," he said, and I watched with wide eyes. "She's being understandably difficult. It's going to take three days to deprogram her." Mood bad, he took the bowls Zack had left to cool and set them on the table. "This is perfect. Thank you, Zack."

But Zack wasn't listening, his expression empty as he watched Quen and Ray come up the stairway. The little girl was holding his hand tightly, her face scrubbed and her hair tucked behind her pointed ears. A blanket with horses on it was in her grip, and she looked precious in a yellow sundress and matching tights. The air was tense between Quen and Trent, and it was clear words had been said, as they weren't looking at each other.

"That's so sweet it will give you diabetes, Rache," Jenks said as he hovered at my ear. But I didn't think that was why Zack had turned away, envy pinching his brow. Being raised by the dewar had probably robbed him of his parents.

And then Ellasbeth minced up the stairs with Lucy on her hip, ruining the moment.

"Look, Lucy," the woman said with forced cheerfulness as she wrangled Lucy into her chair. "Zack made you breakfast. Be a good girl and eat it up."

I thought it was a bad idea to equate being good with eating, but I couldn't help but feel a little smug. Ellasbeth was clearly tired, and her blond hair looked harsh next to Trent's and Zack's transparent whiteness. It was hard to tweak the elven genetic code to get that traditional elven wispiness. Trent's dad had insisted on it while his West Coast counterpart had not, and it showed.

"No!" Lucy protested, pushing at Ellasbeth as she tried to put a bib on her.

"She might be more hungry if you hadn't given her marshmallows all day," Trent muttered, and Ellasbeth flushed.

"Ray!" Lucy demanded even as she fought Ellasbeth. "Time to eat. Ray!" Expression somber, Ray let go of Quen's hand to quietly toddle across the floor, needing to sit to scoot down the stairs before walking over to me. "Ray!" Lucy shrilled again, and Buddy, waiting for fallout under the table, slunk downstairs. Quen crouched to put his eyes even with Lucy's, silent as she pressed her lips defiantly, face red as she balanced her demands with Quen's obvious disapproval.

"Up," Ray said to me, her arms reaching, and I just about melted, not caring that Ellasbeth's glare had become toxic.

"You heard her, Rache," Jenks prompted, and I set my coffee aside to take the soft, tiny person onto my lap. She smelled like snickerdoodles, and my need to see no harm come to them was so strong, it hurt. Ray wanted security, and she came to me to find it.

Her gaze was on the curse written on my skin, obvious when she was this close. "Daddy," she said in her pure, high voice as she pointed at it, and I nodded, cuddling her closer.

"Yes, he has one, too. It's to help us trap the monster," I whispered, and she carefully touched the glyph. Ivy was watching, her heartache that she'd never dare to have a child and commit him or her to the living-vampire hell she lived in almost looking like hunger. It hurt, seeing it in her eyes, but I couldn't help her, and I swallowed hard.

"Daddy . . . ," Ray said, in complaint this time when Trent came to get her, and when she clung to me, I put an arm around her, grinning as I shook my head.

Smiling, Trent sat in the chair beside mine instead, appreciating the idea that Ray would rather listen in than eat. "I'm not sure how showing a damaged auratic spread on national TV will convince people who don't want to listen," he said to continue our conversation, wincing when Lucy shouted, "Zack has syrup. I want syrup!"

"The I.S. can't hold these people if there's proof they weren't responsible," I said.

Jenks hummed his wings for attention. "Which doesn't get rid of the baku," he said as he licked the syrup from his chopsticks. "I still say me, Trent, you, and that soul bottle go pay Landon a visit. Nice and quiet like in the dewar. Then pull that snapped-wing fairy sparkle out of that lame moss wipe of a troll turd pretending to be an elf and put it in a bottle."

"I want *syrup*!" Lucy demanded, undeterred by Quen's quiet admonishment.

A quiver rose through me as I reached out and Trent

lightly twined his fingers with mine. Neither of us was tapping a line, but I could feel one nevertheless. "That's the plan, Jenks."

"I might be able to wrangle another meeting," Trent whispered, thoughts preoccupied. "We should go talk to Landon. *Warn* him what the Order is trying to do."

"What?" Jenks exclaimed, and then he inked a bright silver. "Oh! *Warn* him," he said knowingly. "Gotcha."

"Today," Trent added, frowning at Ellasbeth as she dribbled syrup on Lucy's oatmeal. "We can't afford to wait much longer. Landon already knows what the baku is trying to do and he thinks he can outsmart it. Right, Zack?"

Zack gave us all a thumbs-up from the table, his spoon never slowing.

"Agreed." I jiggled Ray, my fingers playing with hers. "But I doubt very much that Landon will meet with us again. We're going to have to break into his apartment or storm his office."

Nodding, Ivy eased back into the cushions as Glenn mowed down the pull-apart bread as fast as Zack shoveled his oatmeal in.

"It's nothing I've not done before," I said, but it felt risky with Ray on my lap. "Even if we fail and the Order turns Landon into a zombie, there will at least be a record of us trying to stop them. That goodwill gesture alone might get the dewar to ease up on me. Us," I amended when Trent cleared his throat. "Right?" I looked at Zack, worried, and he shrugged, not knowing.

Trent sipped his coffee, clearly thinking it over. "You do have an knack for turning adversaries into allies," he said, and I grimaced when he looked at Ellasbeth at the table. *As if.*

"Sure." Jenks went to snitch some icing. "Like Al, and Lee, and the coven, and you. All Rachel's newest besties."

"Or Piscary," Glenn said sourly as Ivy waved Jenks's dust off the pull-apart bread. "That turned out really well." And from the kitchen, Quen stifled a cough.

"That might work if Landon had a moral compass,"

Trent said. "Unlike Al, Lee, the witches' coven, and myself, he doesn't."

Jenks snorted as he rose up with a wad of icing. "Don't flatter yourself, Trent. You didn't have a moral compass until Rachel pulled it out of your ass and spun you north."

"Jenks!" I hissed, but Ray was focused on practicing that communication glyph with her fingers and hopefully hadn't heard.

"Well, he didn't," the pixy protested, now a bright red.

"We've got until about three tonight," I said to bring the conversation back. "Trent and I go in, do the curse, catch the baku, and get out." But as I worked Ray's fingers into the complicated glyph and earned a little-girl smile, I was less inclined to lean on luck, and my stomach knotted.

"We *all* go in," Jenks said as he landed on Trent's shoulder, and Trent nodded, his brow pinched in worry. Quen cleared his throat again, but it was to keep Ellasbeth quiet, and the woman's face reddened.

"I didn't want to speak for you, Jenks," I said softly, my gut tightening even more. "It's going to be cold until we get inside. Especially if we have to wait until dark."

"Then we go in the afternoon," Jenks said, but I was worried. This would have been easier without someone on my lap practicing calling glyphs.

"I know the access code to the dewar and his apartment there," Zack offered. "Unless he changed it," the kid muttered as he scraped the last from his bowl.

"There." Jenks rose up, wings a bright silver in motion. "We got our way in."

But I wasn't ready to risk my life on Zack's code, and by Quen's frown, neither was he.

"Okay." The word slipped from Ivy in a soft breath as she stood in one smooth motion. "I think we have enough to work with," she said as she checked her phone for the time. "Glenn, your dad should be at his desk by now. I'd rather do a press release at the FIB if he'll agree to it."

Glenn stood as well, dark hand scrubbing faint stubble.

"If anyone asks, you never saw me this morning. I don't know anything about your plans."

I got up and shifted Ray to my hip. "Trent, Jenks, and I will take the morning to plan a way in. Zack, can you give us a sketch of Cincy's dewar's offices?"

"The entire building?" the kid said, voice cracking.

Ivy crossed the room toward me, her mood placid. "They took over the Monastery on the Hill," she said, and Zack bobbed his head, eyes wide. "They haven't been in it long enough to do many changes. I'll text you the latest layout from the city planner." Her eyes on Ray, she leaned in for a quick sideways hug that included the little girl. "Be careful."

"Aren't we always?" Jenks said, his sparkles getting mixed up in it.

"Bye, Ivy," Ray said, her high voice pure and clean.

"Bye, my little snickerdoodle," Ivy said with a smile, and then she turned to me, her smile fading. "Are you sure you're up for this? You look . . ." Her words trailed off and she shrugged. "You don't look as if you slept at all," she added, her eyes lingering on the curse.

"I did," I said as I jiggled Ray on my hip. "Latest thing in demon body art. There's a back to it, too. You like?" I said, trying to make light of it.

"Trent does." Jenks hovered between us as Trent and Glenn said their good-byes. "He likes it a lot," he added, hips gyrating. "Oh, yeah! Color my daisies, big boy!"

"Jenks, grow up," Ivy said, waving him away. "Keep Rachel out of trouble, okay? Landon is desperate, and that makes him unpredictable and chancy."

Chancy. That was the word, and I looked past Trent to Quen and Ellasbeth still at the table with Zack and Lucy. Zack seemed eager enough, but I was betting that Quen wouldn't let him out of the compound until this was over. Damn it, I had no right to let Trent become more involved than he already was. Lucy and Ray were too precious to risk. Ellasbeth, staring at me with her arms over her middle, knew it, too. But what choice did we have?

"Bye, Ray," Ivy said again, beaming when she tried to make a kiss-kiss figure with her two fingers, getting her pinkie mixed up in there. "Bye, Lucy," she added when Lucy called her own good-bye.

Quen set his palms on the table and stood, becoming almost a different person as he took on his familiar security duty. "Zack, will you come with me as I escort Glenn and Ivy to the front gate? I want to hear about that pass code."

Zack froze, and then his chair scraped as he stood. "You bet." Smile thin, he fell into line behind Ivy and Glenn, starting when Quen put his arm over his shoulder and began talking softly.

"Glad I'm not Zack," Jenks said, circling me once before following them down.

Slowly their voices grew fainter, the soft sounds of Ellasbeth with Lucy at the table gaining precedence. I took a breath to gather my thoughts. Empty soul bottle from the vault, sleepy-time potions and splat gun from my bag. I was pretty sure I had enough leather here for breaking in. Maybe Trent had another jump spell. If we had to wait until dark, Bis could take Jenks's place, though it would just about kill the pixy to be left out.

Ray was still on my hip, and I turned to the table. Lucy was done, struggling to fend off Ellasbeth as she cleaned syrup from her hair. "Ray, did you have fun with your mom?"

Ray nodded, her eyes on her sister. "Lucy got red. Bad marshmallow! Bad!"

My eyes flicked to Ellasbeth as Ray pretended to cough, and the woman flushed, retreating to the kitchen to wash out the rag.

"Yes, well, that tends to happen when you try to eat them all at once," Trent said as he took Ray from me and expertly wrangled her into her high chair. Her bib was right there, and I tied it on without thought before sliding her bowl before her.

Trent leaned closer, smiling. "Anyone ever tell you that you could be a great mom?"

"My mother," I said, but then my smile froze. A child was the one thing I couldn't give Trent, the one thing that elves valued above all. But Ellasbeth could. As many as Trent might want and the enclave might demand from their Sa'han.

And the worst thing? She knew it.

"Trent." Ellasbeth had wrung out the rag and was coming back with a handful of Cheerios to occupy Lucy until Ray was done. "We need to talk."

I went still, wrapping my arms around myself as I suddenly felt out of place. It was just the three of us. Five if you counted the girls.

Jaw tight, Trent looked up. "I'm going with Jenks and Rachel. Thank you for watching the girls while I caught up on my sleep. Quen will drive you home if your car isn't here."

Ellasbeth's lips parted, a delicate flush to her cheeks as she took in his dismissal. "Perhaps I should stay until this is over," she said, pointedly sitting down at the table. "I don't mind setting up a cot in the girls' room."

Embarrassed, I slunk into the kitchen to get another cup of coffee. Actually, I was surprised she wasn't trying to stop him, but if Trent were dead, she'd have a better shot at Lucy, the legal paperwork that gave custody to Al aside.

"I appreciate your concern," Trent said doggedly, focused on the girls. "But we have breathing space, and Quen and I are perfectly capable of maintaining their safety."

Ellasbeth was looking at the sliver of glyph showing, and I pulled my robe tighter about my neck. "Putting the girls in the safe room is not maintaining a safe environment," she said pleasantly, but the girls had felt the tension and were silently watching. "I'm not leaving until this is done."

Trent's eye twitched as he stood, and his anger flickered through me via our shared curse. It was shortly followed by fear and worry. Now that she was here, she'd have to be carried out. "Your part is over," Trent said calmly, but Ray looked scared and Lucy was at a loss. "I appreciate you watching them, Ellasbeth. Girls, say bye to your mother. You will see her next weekend."

But Lucy and Ray did nothing, quietly panicking.

Ellasbeth didn't rise, her foot bobbing under the table. She clearly didn't want me hearing this, but I wasn't leaving, and I clenched my hands, willing the sparkles to fade. "Trenton, your life choices are putting Lucy and Ray in danger. Go save the world. I just want to save the girls."

"The girls are not in danger." Neck red, Trent put a fist on the table and leaned over it.

"Um," I blurted, wanting the rising energy to cease. "I have an idea. You don't have any classes until after Thanksgiving, right?" I said, not liking that my voice sounded high in my head. "Why don't you, Zack, and Quen blow off the girls' regular schedule and take them to the zoo? Trent and I can take care of what we need to do and meet you there for lunch or dinner, depending on what you call it."

For three heartbeats, Trent stared at me, his thoughts unknown. And then he shifted, shoulders easing as he took a slow breath. "What a marvelous idea," he said as he found his phone, but the lingering sparkles said he was still angry. Ellasbeth wasn't much better, but at least they weren't quietly yelling at each other. The girls, too, looked relieved, the normally vocal Lucy utterly silent. I hid behind a sip of coffee, knowing I hadn't made any points with Ellasbeth. She would follow them to the zoo, fully aware that she wouldn't be allowed back into the compound. And with Quen with her, Ellasbeth wouldn't dare try to leave until Trent joined them.

Trent signaled "Thank you" to me with a small finger twitch as he finished his text to Quen and closed his phone.

"You're welcome," I mouthed back, the expanse of the kitchen between us, and from beside Trent, Ray sighed and began to eat.

False smile in place, Trent looked up. "Okay, Ellasbeth?"

"Fine," she said shortly.

But it didn't feel fine, and I excused myself to find something more conducive to spell prep than a robe. Manipulating Ellasbeth felt risky, more risky than breaking into Landon's office so we could tie him up and perform a curse to extract a murdering energy source bent on making me kill Trent.

THE SUN WAS BRIGHT. I PUSHED DEEP INTO THE CAR'S SEAT to get out of it, and the soft sounds of Trent on his phone seemed to become louder. We were parked at a sub shop across from the dewar's new Cincinnati offices, waiting for Jenks to come back from his recon. Two cups of straight black were cooling in the cup holders. It was warm in Trent's gray sports car, but the outside temp was too close to Jenks's lower limits for my liking. *November,* I thought sourly. Jenks should be at the church manning the phones and keeping my spelling herbs drying evenly, not out on a run.

Worried, I ran my hands down my black slacks and fisted them at the knees. My matching jacket was cut long and my blouse was a stark white. The low heels, flashy jewelry, and small purse holding the soul bottle and my splat gun made me into any office worker, especially with my hair pulled back and minimal makeup. Trent was in a suit. I'd told him to put on one that hadn't been tailored yet, and the bad fit brought him down a peg from his usual CEO sharpness. He still looked good, though, albeit a tad uncomfortable at the poor tailoring—alert, graceful, and in control. *You could add* yummy *to the list and not be wrong,* I thought as I sipped my coffee.

The Monastery, where the dewar was now headquartered, looked busy with cars and foot traffic. The Cincinnati observatory had sat there in the early 1800s, but had long since moved due to light pollution. For a time, the denuded hill had hosted grapes to help make Cincinnati the American capital of wine making. Now the hill was covered in trees and parking lots, sandwiched between I-71 and 50.

The dewar had bought it to bolster their Cincinnati presence from a single Hollows-based office in a strip mall to the sprawling three-story multiuse building—the twelve-thousand-square-foot chapel included. Wedding receptions were still taking place in the huge repurposed sanctuary with its Roman frescoes and elaborate chandeliers, but no more were being booked, and by this time next year, the elven religious faction would have the place to themselves.

"If you don't hear from one of us in an hour, get them home," Trent said, talking to Quen presumably. "I don't care if you have to throw her into the moat at monkey island."

A smile quirked my lips. Apparently Ellasbeth was focused on the girls instead of her plotting, but it wasn't going well. From the conversation, it seemed Ray had perfected how to egg Lucy on, only to sit back and enjoy the show when she lost it.

A sudden clatter of wings at the window pulled me forward, and I jumped to crack the window for Jenks. "Gotta go," Trent said, ending his conversation as I cranked the car's heater. The pixy looked oddly heavy in his cold-weather gear, but his wings pinked right up when he angled them so the hot air passed over them smoothly.

"We're set," Jenks said, still clearly cold. "The side door is where Zack said it would be. Even saw someone use it with the code he gave us. I'll take the cameras out as we go."

Excitement tingled to my toes. "You want to warm up first?"

"Nah, I'm good." Jenks took a yellow biscuit from the folds of his clothes and began gnawing on it. "Two hours later, I might have an issue, but as long as the sun is high, I'm fine."

Worried, I looked across the car at Trent. "In, bottle it, out in twenty?" he offered. They were my own words, but I wasn't entirely happy. Thanks to Landon's public schedule and Zack's more personal knowledge of the man's habits, we were fairly sure Landon would be in the largest of the three on-site apartments where he now lived, napping until his late-afternoon appointments.

"When have my plans ever worked?" I whispered, then reached for the door. "Okay, I've got a spot for you on my shoulder, Jenks, and a heat pack in my purse if you want it."

"I'm fine, Rache," he muttered, but I felt better when he settled himself on my shoulder.

Together Trent and I got out, and I reached for the low hood, surprised when the nearest ley line poured into me, the warm sensation echoing through me from my front to my back.

"Rache?" Jenks questioned as my hair snarled, and I looked across the low hood to Trent. He'd tapped a line, and through him, I had, too.

"It's Hodin's curse," I said as I shut the car door with a thump and came around the front to join Trent. Ill-fitting suit or not, he looked good with the sun in his hair and his green eyes eager as he scanned the busy street we had to cross. People and cars were everywhere in the background noise of movement and sound that was noon in Cincinnati. The dewar's building stood before us on a slight rise, and anticipation quickened my feet as Trent and I headed for the crosswalk despite my misgivings. This was what I lived for, but today was different.

Trent flashed me a smile as he rocked forward to push the button, the light breeze playing in the silken strands of his hair. His eyes were eager as two more people joined us, bringing the scent of tacos and burgers with them. Trent hadn't been hurt enough to know the risk he was putting his girls in. But I had, and I vowed that he would walk away from this untouched.

His smile faltered as he saw my grim look. "What is it?" he said, his hand going to the small of my back as the light changed and we stepped from the curb. "Do we need to walk away?"

"No," I said firmly. "We're good. Jenks, any cameras?" I prompted, and Jenks rose up into the frost-emptied trees ringing the dewar's parking lot, their branches denuded by the cold.

Trent pulled me to a heel-clattering stop at the curb, and everyone pushed past us, intent on reaching their offices. We lingered in the dappled shade as we waited for Jenks, playing the part of two workers reluctant to part ways.

The monstrous building sprawled before us. The dewar had been filling it with people the last few months as they made Cincinnati their American headquarters. There'd never been a gathering of the religious order of the elves of this size in recorded history. Maybe it was because the elves had just come out of the paranormal closet, but maybe it was me, a demon wiggling into their oldest, most powerful family, that was bringing them together.

Guilt for having robbed Trent of his voice rose up, and I fidgeted. We were sneaking in when, by rights, he should have been able to demand an audience with the head of the dewar whenever he damn well felt like it. The look on his face when he'd broken a hole in the back of the fireplace said it all. He'd *opened* it for Ellasbeth. He *needed* a closer tie to the dewar and enclave. I was feeling more and more as if I didn't belong. Or that I shouldn't.

"What do you think about me not coming over on the weekends anymore?" I said, and Trent turned, the smile on his face faltering.

"Where is this coming from?" Worry pulled him straight.

The cold November wind coming up from the nearby river pushed against me, and I tucked a strand of hair behind an ear. "If you pretended to soften toward Ellasbeth—"

"No." It was a harsh utterance, and Trent put his attention back on the parking lot.

"I thought elves were all about misdirection and subterfuge," I said.

"Not this time," he said coldly as he scanned for Jenks.

"The enclave would take you back," I insisted, and Trent's brow furrowed. "My God, Trent, we're sneaking in. Last year, you could have made a phone call and had lunch with him."

"I won't pretend to like Ellasbeth to gain political sway, power that is already mine," he asserted. "She'd not only see through it—she'd use it against me. Wiggle herself closer."

"Maybe that's not such a bad thing," I said softly, thinking of the girls.

Again Trent turned, his brow furrowed. "Are you trying to break up with me?"

"No!" I exclaimed, eyes wide as I noticed his hair beginning to float and mine snarling up. I wasn't touching him, but I could feel him pulling heavier on the ley line. "Trent . . . ," I started, changing my mind when Jenks dropped out of the tree like an acorn.

"Route is clear," he said as he hit my shoulder.

Trent touched the small of my back, and a lump filled my throat at the familiar feel of our internal energy balances equalizing. I loved him, but I was bringing him down. My head bowed, and misunderstanding, Trent let his hand fall away. It only made me feel that much more miserable, and silent, we crossed the lot filled with newly purchased and rented vehicles. Zack had said that Landon's private apartment was on the other side of the building, third floor overlooking a distant Eden Park, but the easiest way to gain access was from this side.

My low heels clicked a sharp counterpoint against Trent's steps. I hadn't realized until now how often Trent touched me, and the thought of walking away, of making the smart, hard decision, sucked.

Finally we reached the side door and Trent punched in the code. His motions were sharp, and he shot me a questioning look, not knowing where my thoughts were other than I'd laid down two confusing, contrary statements. The door unlocked with a click, and Trent held it for me, scanning the lot to see if anyone was watching as I went in.

"I'm sorry, Trent," I said as I took in the stark, typical hallway with its carpet squares and blah art on the walls between lightweight fake-wood doors. "I'm just worried that this is going to backfire, and then what happens to the girls?"

Understanding cascaded over Trent. Turning, he put one hand on my shoulder, looking up and down the hallway before leaning in. "I'd rather have the girls raised by Ellasbeth and them see me in prison for having done what was right than raise them seeing me hide from what I know should be done. They will be leaders, Rachel. They must know from the start that that means equal parts strength and vulnerability."

I blinked fast, my love for him making my chest hurt.

"Now," he said as Jenks dropped down before us, "are we ready to do this? I need to concentrate, and worrying about you leaving me will make me slow."

"I'm not leaving you," I said, though it would be hard with Ellasbeth in the picture.

"Tink save me from lunkers in love," Jenks muttered, but his dust was a happy gold.

"Cameras?" I prompted, and Jenks darted away.

Trent exhaled in relief before pulling himself to a CEO's stiffness as we followed Jenks down the hall. I smiled, pulling on the line until his hair began to float. His hand flashed up to press it flat, and I gave him a grin and a shrug. Hodin's curse was a double-edged sword.

The deeper we went into the building, the more the air smelled like cinnamon and wine, sparking of magic at the edges of my mind. Chatter came from the offices we passed, and slowly the sound of keyboards and phones soothed me. My first impressions of the building began to shift as I began sensing stone walls behind the wallboard and oak floors under the carpet squares. I squinted at the ceiling, wondering if I could smell incense embedded in the thick, cracked paint. In my thoughts, the drone of prayers being offered up tickled the folds of my mind.

"Attic?" Trent said as we found an elevator alcove.

"Attic," I agreed, hitting the call button and hoping that the plans that Ivy had e-mailed me were correct and that the elevator went all the way. The stairs didn't, having been boarded up ages ago.

In a flash of sparkles, Jenks arrowed back, wings clattering a harsh warning. "Hide," he said shortly, and Trent spun to look up and down the hall. Someone was coming. The elevator still wasn't here, and Trent pointed to the stairs.

Pulse fast, I yanked the stairwell door open. "It's just one flight," someone complained as I darted in, sliding to the side as Trent surged in after me. Jenks shot up the stairwell, his dust drifting down in a slow cascade as Trent pulled the door shut but for a crack. "And the elevator takes forever," the man added, his voice louder now that they were right in the hall before us.

I hunched closer, tucking under Trent so I could see. My painted glyph seemed to warm at our closeness, and I held my breath and energy balance both. Two thirtysomethings in office wear stood before the elevators. "Easy for you to say," the woman said as she pushed the lit call button and rocked back. "You're not in heels."

But the man was angling to the stairwell, coffee in one hand, phone in the other. "I'm taking the stairs. I'll save you a seat," he promised, and the woman sighed.

"Fine," she said as she gave the closed silver doors a last look and followed him.

"They're coming in here," I muttered. Dropping back, I found my splat gun. Trent shifted to the other side of the door, and Jenks dropped down, gold dust sifting as he hovered right before the stairs. Splat gun pointed, I exhaled, adrenaline bringing me gloriously awake as I grinned at Trent and the glowing mass of magic in his hand as the stairwell's fire door swung open. The elves came in, jerking to a halt when they saw Jenks.

"Hi!" Jenks said as I took aim. "You're both up on your insurance, right?"

"Wha-a-at?" the man said, and then the woman gasped as she saw me.

"Sorry," I said, meaning it, and then she shrieked as I pulled the trigger and the puff of air shot through me.

"*Voulden,*" Trent whispered, and the mass of magic in his hand shifted, taking on his intent even as he threw it at the man.

"Too much!" I exclaimed as I felt his magic manifest as if it were my own. It was elven. I'd never seen it before, but through Hodin's curse, it was as if I had been casting it my entire life. Trent was using way too much energy. It was going to burn the man's synapses, not stun him.

Breath held, I tried to pull some of it back, but it slipped through my mental fingers like sand and I only managed a fraction of the excess. Trent's gold-and-red-smeared spell hit the man in the chest and exploded in a blinding flash as the two dropped, crashing into each other as they went down. The man practically glowed under Trent's overdone magic, and I thought I smelled burning hair as he lurched to catch them.

"Whoa, whoa, whoa, Tex!" Jenks said, his dust spilling brightly. "I think you got 'em!"

Trent straightened from easing them to the floor, his eyes wide as he looked at his hand before shaking the last of the glowing trails out. "I see what you mean about doubling the effect of your magic," he muttered, giving me a scared look. "It feels like more than that to me, though. I was only trying to knock him unconscious, not put him in a coma. Thanks for pulling some of it back."

"He's in a coma?" Worried, I pushed myself up from the wall to look at him as Trent checked his pulse. Crap on toast, Hodin hadn't been kidding. Mix this with sex, and you might never walk again, but right now it was a huge pain in the ass. The coming assault-and-battery charges were going to keep me on Kisten's boat for the next three years.

Jenks landed on the man's nose. "He's not in a coma," he said derisively. "But the headache he's going to have when he wakes up is going to make him wish he were. If you're lucky, he won't remember why." Jenks rose up, hands on his hips as he faced Trent. "You got a problem with your control, cookie man?"

"Apparently." Looking unsure, Trent stood back up. "You okay?" he said, and I nodded, unwrapping my arms from around myself. "Where should we put them?"

Head tilted, Jenks looked up the stairwell. "Not here. The elevator is slow. Most people use the stairs."

From the hall, a cheerful ding told me the elevator had finally arrived. "Then let's put them in the elevator and stop it between floors," I said.

Jenks darted out the crack in the door, immediately returning to gesture us out. I grabbed the woman under her arms and began dragging her. The man's coffee had landed on her, and she was a mess. Trent hauled the man to the door and held it open with one foot while I pulled the woman into the empty hallway, her heels making twin tracks in the carpet.

"Move it!" Jenks exclaimed, punching the call button with his feet when the silver doors threatened to close. I lugged the woman inside and propped her against the wall. "Shoe," Jenks pointed out, and I lurched out to get it, jerking back in as the doors shut.

"This isn't how I envisioned this playing out," Trent said as he propped the man up beside the woman against the wall of the lift and took their building IDs. Worried, he put the man's badge on. He didn't look too far away from Dan, but I was not going to pass for Wendy under even the lightest scrutiny.

Jenks snickered and foot-planted the third-floor button. "Welcome to my world."

"Can we just get to the attic, please?" I said as I put on Wendy's badge, then hit the button to stop the elevator between floors. An alarm began to sound, and Trent grimaced.

"*Elerodic,*" he muttered, his suddenly glowing hand turning a bright silver.

"No, wait!" Jenks shrilled, and I cowered when Trent's energy hit the panel with a burst of sparks.

"Damn," Trent whispered, shaking the sting from him as I rose from my crouch. "I tried to adjust it that time."

"Will you knock it off!" the pixy shouted, but the alarm had stopped, and the elevator was unmoving. "Enough with the magic! Use your other skills! You got enough of them!"

"Sorry," Trent said as he looked at his reddened hand, and I eased my grip on the ley line. Immediately the warm sensation in my middle vanished, and I gave Trent's hand a squeeze.

"And don't forget their phones," Jenks muttered. "Sleeping Beauty there will call someone as soon as he wakes up. Taking it might give us five more minutes."

Nodding, Trent began to search them in earnest, seeming incongruous as he crouched over them to flip jackets and explore pockets. Jenks frowned at him, then darted to me. "You okay?"

I touched my glyph through my shirt and shrugged. "Fine, but you're right. The less magic we do until this curse wears off, the better." I looked up. "Does that open?" I asked, pointing at the ceiling door, and Trent stood, handing me their phones to tuck away in my bag.

Eyes eager, Trent braced himself in the corner and cupped his hands. Jenks had already busted the lock, and at his nod, I stepped into Trent's grip. "Watch your balance," he said softly, voice strained, and with one hand on the wall, I palm-struck the roof panel. It snapped up with a pop, and I reached for it, struggling to keep it from banging open all the way.

Cool, dusty air spilled down and Jenks darted past me into the unheated elevator shaft. "Higher," I whispered, hearing the muffled complaints from the nearby closed second-floor doors. Finally I was able to scramble up. Immediately I lay down and extended my hands to Trent. It would've been easier to ride the elevator up, but it would have stopped on the second floor, and then there would have been shouting, and screaming, and pixy dust. . . .

The cold made my grip slippery, and my gut tightened as

Trent took my hands. We both knew I wouldn't be able to
lift him, and I held my breath as he used the wall of the elevator to push himself up until he could lever first one foot,
then the other through the opening and finally wedge himself up and in.

"Thanks," he whispered as he found his feet, and I gave
him a wan smile, rolling to a stand to try to beat the greasy
dust off me. If we could gain the attic, we could walk above
the offices and right to Landon's apartments. There was an
elevator bank on the other side of the building, and according to Ivy's building plans, it ran from first floor to the attic
as well.

"This should buy us some time." Trent gently closed the
trapdoor. Hands on his waist, he squinted up the dark shaft.
Now that Jenks wasn't moving, the only light was a thin
ribbon from the closed elevator doors above us. "Tell me
there's a door there, Jenks."

"If you're four inches tall," Jenks said, then snickered
when Trent stiffened. "Relax. I wouldn't have let you up
here if there wasn't a way out."

Trent gestured to the maintenance ladder, and I reached
for it, the cold in the iron seeming to soak into me. My
pulse quickened from excitement as I rose, feet scuffing as
I pushed myself into a faster pace. The bag holding the soul
bottle hit me in rhythmic thumps in time with my lurching.
It felt odd knowing I was going to use something that had
saved my life to capture the baku. Bis had held the small
glass bottle holding my soul the entire three days, according to Jenks.

I exhaled in relief when I reached the top, wrestling with
the twin panel door until Trent noticed and scrambled up
beside me on the ladder. "Go," Trent grunted when the thick,
age-darkened slabs slid aside with a squeak of dusty metal to
show a dimly lit attic the length of the building. "You first."

The doors weren't under any pressure to close, so I
slipped under his arm and made the step to the old floorboards. Trent easily swung himself in behind me, turning
to close the doors behind us.

It was even colder up here and, arms about my middle, I squinted into the dusky gray to see that there wasn't a shred of insulation, just bare boards and open rafters. Jenks's glowing dust was enough to make out the occasional sheet-draped lump as he buzzed about to satisfy his pixy curiosity. Almost immediately he came back, his glow dimmed as he landed on my shoulder. It was colder than the outside, where at least the sun shone. There was no light but for Jenks and the glow of Trent's phone as he angled it about. I could hear traffic on 71 and the sporadic sound of jays, but it only made me feel more alone.

"How you doing, Jenks?" I whispered.

"Stop being my mother," Jenks griped, but his wings were cold as they pressed against my neck for warmth, and I was worried.

"Seriously, Trent and I have this. Go back downstairs and warm up," I whispered.

"I'm fine," Jenks said sourly. "Just keep walking straight. There's another elevator about halfway down, and a third, smaller one at the end that I think will put us right beside Landon's front door. Trent, what does your GPS say?"

Trent grunted a soft agreement, the glow of his phone lighting his face. I started forward, more worried about Jenks than about someone hearing us. I jerked, sputtering when I ran into a spiderweb. No one had been up here in years.

"Almost there," Trent said, and Jenks's dust brightened. "Rachel, I like your no-plan thing. It's going to take them an hour to get the elevator open, and by then, we'll be gone."

"This isn't no plan," I said as I fumbled for my own phone to add to Trent's light. *See, I can do this without magic.* But a faint pull drew my attention and my expression blanked. There was an old hearth up here, surrounded by unfamiliar ancient glyphs. "You see that?" I whispered, and Trent shifted his phone to it as well, his light following the smoke marks to the rafters.

"Guys, you can play archaeologist later. I'm freezing my nubs off," Jenks complained.

"Take a picture," I suggested, leaving Trent to do just that as I hustled forward with Jenks, my cell phone light swinging as I followed his terse instructions to an old elevator cage on the far side of the building. It was larger than the one we'd come up in, and clearly for freight. Storage boxes were stacked beside it, and a few sheet-draped pieces of furniture. Landon had been redecorating maybe.

"Trent," I whispered, and he left the hidden hearth, his phone angling about to light the odd slice of attic. There was a call button, but using it might have triggered security. There wasn't even a lock on the elevator cage, and when I shook my head at Trent's offered hand, he tapped his phone off and lifted the hatch to the maintenance ladder. Together we looked down into the darkness. The elevator car was somewhere in the shaft. I only hoped it was below where we needed to be.

"Watch your step," Trent whispered as he started down. Jenks wasn't dusting, and I didn't like that he was still on my shoulder instead of lighting our way.

"Jenks, how're your temps?" I whispered as I gripped the ladder and found the first step.

"Not good," he admitted, and I moved faster.

The echoes of our scuffing feet hissed as Trent and I descended into the cold shaft that had never seen sun. I was never going to risk Jenks like this again. This was beyond reasonable expectation. We could've waited for nightfall and Bis.

"I think this is the right door," Trent whispered, and I scraped to a halt, arm hooked on the ladder as I leaned to look down. "Jenks, you want to do a quick recon?"

"No, he doesn't," I said, but Jenks had already lifted off, his dust utterly absent as he dropped the six feet to where Trent had wedged the silver doors open a crack. He vanished into the sudden light, and Trent let the door shut, sealing us back into the dark.

"It's warmer in the hallway," Trent said, and I nodded, only now understanding.

"How are you doing?" Trent asked, his soft voice whispering up from the dark, and my foot scraped on the ladder.

"Me? I'm fine." I stifled a shiver, more than a little jealous of how Trent never seemed to feel the cold. It was an elf thing.

"Ah, I didn't mean it when I asked if you were breaking up with me."

"I know." I was glad it was dark, and I shifted, uncomfortable. My fingers were beginning to cramp up from the cold, and I tried to flex them as I hung there.

"You just surprised me. Bringing up Ellasbeth like that."

I grimaced, not wanting to talk about it, my arm aching and worry pinching my brow. "Jenks should be back here by now," I said, and Trent sighed, silent as he wedged the silver doors open again. Relief filled me when Jenks darted in, his dust lighting the shaft when Trent let the doors shut and entombed us in the dark. "Well?" I asked as Jenks lit on Trent's shoulder.

"Empty hallway," he said, his dust already beginning to dampen. "I'm guessing Landon's apartment is around the corner since there's a big man standing in front of the door playing on his phone, but if you're quiet, he'll never hear you getting out of the shaft. Easy stuff."

Which is right about when it falls apart, I thought as Trent wedged the door open wide enough to slip through. Cold, I unhooked my arm and went down the last few rungs. Trent took my hand, and I almost fell as he pulled me into the hallway. "You good?" he asked when I found my balance, and I flashed him a smile.

"Let's do this and get in a tub of warm water before the curse wears off," I said, and he managed a smile as well.

Jenks was hovering at the ceiling to peek around the corner, and at his gesture, both Trent and I angled for a quick look-see. As Jenks had said, there was one guard outside a pair of elaborate double doors. The heavy man practically reeked of magic, and several amulets showed against his security-black slacks and shirt. There was an actual gun in a side holster, and I felt my bag for the outlines of my splat pistol. It was magic without using the lines, and my adrenaline spiked.

"Zack's code better be good," Jenks grumped. "Give me a second, and I'll lure him down the other hallway. You can slip in with him none the wiser. Panel is by the door."

"Got it," Trent said, focused on the guard. "Ready?"

"If Jenks is," I whispered, gauging Jenks's color to be good.

"I know what I'm doing," the pixy said. "Be ready to move when you hear the crash."

"Crash?" I questioned, but he was gone with an annoyed wing snap.

Trent was silent for a moment, and then he leaned close, expression worried. "If this all goes south, I want you to know that the last year with you has been the best of my life."

My thoughts jerked from the potential fight, surprised, but not. "Me too," I said, remembering how much I'd thought I hated him. "Let's make sure nothing goes wrong."

I held up my crooked pinkie, and smiling, he hooked it with his own. A vague memory threatened to spill through me as our energy balances equalized: a dusty stable, the fear of being caught, the thrill of what-if, of a shared goal and a belief that what we were doing was just, if not entirely within the rules. Jeez, how long had Trent and I been righting our personal wrongs together anyway?

Our fingers parted at the sound of a distant crash, and Trent peeked around the corner. His lips curled in a slow, faint smile. "We're clear," he said, and I followed him into the hall.

I was grimy and probably smelled like dust and grease, and I needlessly checked the propellant in my splat gun as Trent went to Landon's door and casually punched in the code. My pulse quickened when nothing happened. "Did they change it?" I whispered as I leaned close.

"I don't think so," he said, eyes on the mechanism. "Quen told me about these. It takes a pulse of line energy to open it. You want the honors? You seem to have better control than me."

"Uh, sure." Careful to allow only the barest thread of energy to spill into my hand, I winced and touched the panel.

A soft click sounded, and Trent shot me a grin. His eagerness went right to my core, and I smiled back, relieved. "See, we can do this. It just takes a light touch," he said as he turned the handle and one side of the double doors silently opened. "After you."

That light touch is going out the window as soon as the spells start flying, I thought as I stepped into the natural light now pouring into the hall. Trent followed me in, and we hesitated on the raised-tile foyer, waiting for Jenks. A bank of closets stood to one side, but from there, it opened up to a warehouselike apartment. The ceiling stretched a good twenty feet, and the thick, narrow windows cut the fabulous view of the surrounding city into little slices. The air was warm, and it was silent apart from a ticking clock. Between us and the view was a living room done in creams and browns. The floor was either tile or polished wood. I couldn't tell from here.

"Light touch, light touch," I whispered as Jenks darted in through the cracked door, and Trent closed it. The security panel on this side of the door blinked green, and we all sighed in relief. *Ten minutes,* I thought, feeling the outline of the soul bottle in my bag.

"I'll find him," Jenks said as he hummed off, the sound of his wings lost in a heartbeat.

Trent and I inched forward, senses searching, but the room was empty. The wet bar was shiny, and the TV was so huge, it was ugly. "Cat," I whispered, nudging Trent's elbow, and he crouched to lure the feline closer. True to form, the white longhair sat where she was and stared. But then her ears pricked and her head swiveled to fixate on Jenks.

"Cat!" I whispered again, louder, and Jenks made a wide swoop up to avoid it.

"Three bedrooms that way," Jenks said, pointing. "They look like Aladdin vomited up the decor, but Landon's not there. Give me a sec, and I'll check out the other side."

I nodded, and he took off under the watchful eye of the cat. *"Absidium fortum,"* I whispered, pulling lightly on the ley line. Clearly feeling it, Trent flattened his hair as he waited for my charm to fade. But the cat was only a cat, not a person disguised or trapped as one, and I frowned when it padded off after Jenks.

"He should be back by now," Trent whispered.

"Follow the cat," I said, worried, and Trent nodded, graceful as he pushed into motion. His steps were silent in his office shoes as he wove between the cream cushions and modern art, but I paused to slip my low heels off before following, holding them as we traced the cat's path through the living room, down a long, narrow hall set against the windows, and finally to a large open dining room with a spacious kitchen at the back.

"Wow," I said softly, one hand holding my shoes, the other my splat gun as I took in the view. It was the corner of the building, and there was even an outside space, potted evergreens and grasses to break up all the pale stone out there.

"Just in time for tea," Landon said from the kitchen, and both Trent and I spun.

CHAPTER

31

CRAP ON TOAST, I THOUGHT, DROPPING MY SHOES AND raising my splat gun. It would have been easier to down him while he slept, set up the curse, and wake him up when it was over.

Landon stood easy in the open kitchen behind the lengthy counter. He was in slacks and a button-down-collar shirt, his suit coat and ribbon of office draped over a barstool. His eyebrows were high in amusement, and I went cold when I saw Jenks plastered to the wall with sticky silk. The pixy was pissed, green sparkles sifting from him, and when the cat stretched to pat the wall under Jenks, fear slid cleanly through me.

"We came to talk," I ad-libbed as I hiked my bag farther up my shoulder. "Your life is at risk," I said, and Landon chuckled as he set the damp pot on the stove and lit the burner with a whoosh of flame. I couldn't hit him from here. He'd just bubble himself to avoid it. Actually, it might have been safer to throw my splat gun under a chair in case he knew how to burst the charms in my hopper and put me out with my own spells.

"Not from that gun," he mocked, and I spun it in my grip, holding it by a finger until I set it on the nearby glass table and pushed it away. It was only good against a non-magic user or in surprise anyway. My mouth could do far more damage.

Trent stood beside me, clearly uncomfortable in his ill-fitting suit. "We aren't here to hurt you. We have vital information. The baku you're hosting is slowly eating your soul," he said lightly. "Once it takes you, the Order will turn you into a zombie to imprison it."

"The Goddess help you, you're a mess, Kalamack." Lips pressed, Landon took a clay-colored pot from an open shelf. His eyes went to Jenks struggling to reach his sword, swear words spilling from him. "What did you do?" Landon glanced at the splat gun on the table. "Crawl through the air ducts?"

"The Order is using you," Trent tried again. "The baku is using you. We can pull it out. Bottle it. But we need your cooperation."

"Pull it out? It took two weeks to convince it to work with me." Landon smirked, his eyes never leaving ours as he opened a wooden box on the counter and filled the tea diffuser with something that smelled of lemons and Brimstone. "I know the Order's plans. I know the baku's, too. It's in me. Right now. My thoughts are known to it, and its thoughts are clear to me. The only discrepancy is that we disagree on who will prevail. I'll give you a hint. It's going to be me. Either way, you will be dead, Kalamack, and with you goes the threat the demons pose, the threat you have let sex blind you to."

My lips parted at the affront, and behind him, Jenks reached his sword. Struggling, the pixy got one wing free.

"Stupid bug," Landon said, lip curled as he took the sticky silk spray can from the counter.

"Hey! Knock it off!" I demanded when the thin webbing plastered Jenks to the wall again. I stumbled when Trent grabbed my arm, gasping as the line we were both holding sang in us. Shrugging Trent off, I wavered to find my balance, hating Landon. It wasn't so bad when we weren't stressed, but damn, the glyph worked better the more tense—or excited—we were.

Landon looked too satisfied to live as he set the can of sticky silk down. "I'll admit one thing you're right about,

Trent," he said as he peeled film from his fingers and let it drop. "It *is* almost worth the collateral damage to know where you stand with your underlings. There's only one person who knew the pass code to my apartments. I have sorely neglected Zack's training. I'll have to rectify that."

"Keep your claws off him," I said, and Landon's eyebrows rose in mock surprise.

"Him too?" he said, hands spaced wide on the counter. "You can't save him, Rachel. He has belonged to the dewar since before his birth."

"You can't own a person," I said, trying to keep him talking until Jenks could get free, but he was making little headway, and that cat was still under him, trying to decide if she wanted to jump or not.

"You can if you get permission before they die," Landon said, and Trent went ashen.

"My God," I whispered. "You still use that curse to move an old soul into a new body?"

Landon's lip twitched at Trent's disgust, and he set a teacup on the counter with a sharp click. "Youth and old age are easy to manipulate," Landon said, his cheeks a faint red, but it was in anger, not shame. "Both are afraid because we've convinced them they're weak."

"The Order—," I said, steadfastly not looking at Jenks. He had one hand free, struggling.

"Is outdated, outclassed, and no threat," Landon said, voice rising.

"The baku is using you," Trent tried again.

"No, I'm using it." Expression sour, Landon peered at his watch and worked a side button. "Bart, get off your phone and get in here. I've got two intruders."

"Shontol!" Trent exclaimed, and my knees buckled from the energy jerking through me as he pulled on the ley line and threw the spell.

Not knowing what it was other than elven, I ducked. The shimmer of a protection bubble flashed into play around Landon, but Trent's magic slammed into Jenks, not Landon, dissolving the sticky silk and freeing the pixy. Landon had never been the target, and with a sparkle of pixy dust, Jenks was in the air. The cat leapt at the fast movement, falling back with her tail swishing.

We can do this, I thought as Trent's anger simmered like a thread through me, adding to my own. He had properly estimated the power needed and hadn't fried Jenks. We had a chance.

Landon snarled, his hand breaking his circle as he reached for the sticky silk. Jenks laughed as he darted in and out, making Landon spin and the cat skitter out of the way as he sprayed at him, missing.

"Watch it. Jenks is in there!" I reached for my splat gun, firing three times in quick succession, missing as Landon danced about to evade Jenks's sword.

"I'm not going to hit Jenks," Trent said, and then Landon howled, hand over his neck as he fell back and sprayed wildly at the pixy.

"Jenks!" I shouted. "Get out of the way so we can down Landon!"

And then I gasped, heart tumbling into my throat as Landon swung a pan at him, hitting Jenks to send him flying across the room. "No!" I lunged to beat the cat when Jenks fell and slid to an unmoving halt under the table. I'd never reach him in time.

"Rhombus," I breathed, praying the cat wasn't already too close to be walled out. I threw myself forward, eyes on Jenks as I hit the floor and slid under the table. My fingers stretched for him, and then I jerked, hands spasming when a thunderous wave of sound slammed into me. I stiffened as the line sang, pouring through and out of me as if I were a sieve. My circle dropped as if it had never existed. *Jenks . . .* He was just before me, and my breath exploded from me in relief as I pulled him close, scared out of my mind. Trent had done something—something so big I hadn't been able to maintain my circle.

But Jenks was safe, and as I sat under the table cradling him, I could have cried. He was breathing, his wing bent and slipping dust. *Alive,* I thought, and then I looked up.

Landon wasn't in the kitchen anymore. The kettle screamed a harsh demand, forgotten. The head of the dewar was an unnerving five feet away at one end of the table, a wary, ugly look on his face as he dabbed at his bleeding ears. Trent was at the other end, magic dripping from his fingers to hiss against the tile. Ozone hung in the air, and the scent of burned cinnamon. Landon had tried to down me as I had gone for Jenks, and Trent had blocked it.

"That was a mistake," I said, hating Landon as I scooted out from under the table.

"We're trying to save your life!" Trent exclaimed, and then he spun, throwing his magic at the three men storming in instead, their mundane weapons pointed as they shouted.

"Trent, no!" I gasped as I felt Trent's pull on the line. It was too much. He was angry, and it was too much. I cowered, Jenks held close, as Trent's magic flowed through us, tainted with his anger as it struck the guards to no effect.

"Fool witch," Landon said, and then I yelped as he yanked me to him by my hair.

"Ow! Let go!" I exclaimed, but if I hit him with raw line energy, it would fry Jenks, too. And so I clutched the pixy closer and let Landon jerk me closer. His grip shifted, and I froze when his other hand wrapped around my chest to hold a knife to my neck. It was a ceremonial blade, so clean and shiny that I knew it had seen blood and bone before.

"Trent!" Landon shouted, startling at the boom of sound and the splinter of stone. Trent had thrown another spell. He was taking Landon's apartment apart. An outer wall cracked, and dust sifted from the ceiling, choking. "Everyone *stop,* or I slit the demon whore's throat!"

Trent spun, fear cascading over his face and shocking him still. His eyes went to Jenks in my cupped hands. If I dropped him to save myself, either the cat would get him or Landon would step on him. Seeing me helpless, Trent fisted his hands and put them in the air.

Immediately the three men tackled Trent. There was a muffled thump and grunt, and then they yanked him up again. His hair was disheveled and his lip was bleeding, but it was the new silver strap on his wrist that took the fight out of him. Trent stumbled, going down when they shoved him to kneel before Landon.

"That's a curious curse," Landon said, jerking my attention back from Trent. "On your neck?" he added, and I twitched when he flicked the knife tip against a painted line. "You both have them. Are they for the baku? Who taught it to you?"

I was silent. On the other side of the room, Trent tried to rise, only to be shoved back down.

"Was it Officer Glenn?" Landon said, breath hot on my ear. "It looks demon. The Order doesn't know demon magic. Yet," he added threateningly.

"Go to hell," I snarled, and his grip on me tightened.

"You're amusingly easy to manipulate," Landon said, stinking of burned cinnamon and spoiled wine. "You'd be surprised how long you might live if you'd stop caring."

"You'd be surprised how much you sound like a demon," I said as I held Jenks tighter, worried that he hadn't woken up yet. But Landon had a point. I'd been caught by my need to protect Jenks. Trent had been caught by his need to keep me safe. *Perhaps we'd get more done if we didn't try to work together,* I thought, despair rising up through me.

"We came to help," I said, panicking when Landon tugged at a hand to force them apart. "Let go!"

"Strap her!" he demanded as he shoved me at two of his security, and I almost fell, my need to keep my hands about Jenks making me awkward. At least that knife wasn't at my throat, and I did nothing, almost paralyzed as they fixed a band of charmed silver around my wrist and every last erg of power drained away. Trent's eyes were full of frustrated, helpless anger. But I wasn't helpless. I'd survived without magic before.

"The baku *will* take you," I promised, staying passive when the man searching Trent turned to me and took my phone and borrowed ID. "The Order *will* turn you into a zombie to contain it. Don't be stupid, Landon."

"Says the demon with no magic," Landon mocked as he

upended my bag over the glass table. My stuff spilled out, the bottle hitting with a crack and rolling until another of his security men set it upright among my spare sleepy-time pellets, magnetic chalk, and boat keys. "A baby bottle? Is this a joke?" Landon said, brow furrowed as he set it down with a hard click.

"It's your salvation," I said, watching his security set our phones and borrowed IDs with the rest.

"You have to sleep sometime." Landon sniffed. "It has to kill you to get what it wants, and I won't let it back into me until it does. Nice that we want the same thing. And then, when Trent is dead and the baku still in you, I will call the Order myself." IDs in hand, he paced closer, halting out of my easy reach when his security stiffened. "Your soul is ready to fall. You will be its prison," he said. "Not me."

Maybe, but I had firsthand knowledge that the baku would rather have Landon. Either way, Trent's life was in the mix. Silent, I watched Landon give the IDs to his security team and tell them to find Dan and Wendy—and fire them.

"You're making a mistake," I said, and memory sparked of me telling Lee the same thing on a windswept ruin in the ever-after. Landon wasn't going to listen, either. *Come on, Jenks. Wake up!*

"You think?" Landon sat against the glass table, ankles confidently crossed. "You're a bigger danger to the Order than me. They want you in their cell. If you're hosting the baku, even the FIB won't lift a finger to protest. Demon assassin."

And at that, uncertainty filled me. I looked at Trent, and Landon began to smirk.

"I'm curious," Landon said. "Tell me, Trent. When the baku takes her, will you let her kill you because you love her? Or will you kill her to save your life? It might be kinder than letting her live out her existence as a zombie."

My expression blanked.

"Put them somewhere quiet," Landon directed. "They look tired. They need to rest."

"Landon," I tried one last time, but Trent was silent as they yanked him up and we were shoved to the door.

"The pixy, your grace?" one of them said, and fear pulled me to a stop.

Landon's eyebrows rose as he saw me with my hands to my middle, frozen. "Put it in the garden, where it belongs," he said flatly.

"What? No!" I backed up, jerking when two men descended upon me to pull my hands apart. "No!" I protested, starting to fight. "He'll die. It's too cold. It's murder!"

But they held me still at a curt gesture so Landon could edge closer. "This *is* happening," he said as he gripped my fingers, fighting to pull them apart. "It's not against the law to kill a pixy."

"You bastard," I whispered, then gasped as he bent my fingers backward, almost breaking them. I fought to be free, kicking and thrashing until someone punched me in the gut and I bent double, gasping for air. Trent was watching, jaw tight and stiff in frustrated anger. "Landon," I rasped, eyes watering as they pried at my hands. "If you kill him, there's nothing on earth or the ever-after that will stop me from coming after you. Nothing!"

But it was their three to my one, and I screamed in frustration, thrashing wildly as they forced my hands apart. "Jenks!" I shouted in agony as he tumbled to the floor. But then he rose up, wings a harsh clatter as he darted erratically into the air to evade the reaching hands, slowly gaining height as they swung and jumped for him until he made it to the chandelier.

"Jenks, thank God," I said in relief, and he gave me a shaky thumbs-up, safely out of their reach as he held his head and sifted a sickly green dust. He looked awful, but he was alive.

"Get them out of here. And someone get me a net!" Landon shouted.

And then I was pulled into the hall, fighting the guards every step of the way.

CHAPTER

32

THE FLOOR OF THE DEWAR'S WINE CELLAR WAS COBBLES. Cold cobbles. And they were hard, too, as I sat with my back to the thick oak walls and held my knees to my chest. The air smelled like the pasta and red sauce that they had given us to eat. That had been hours ago, and we only had the stubble on Trent's face to guess at what time it was. After sundown, by the looks of it.

Worry for Jenks gnawed me like a cur chewing a marrowless bone. He was hurt and alone with an entire building of elves after him. And here I was, stuck in a hole with a band of charmed silver around my wrist. Al would have laughed his hat off, then smacked me with it for being uncommonly stupid. He'd be right.

But even Al wouldn't have been concerned about Jenks, and I frowned as I stared up at the light bulb hanging over the freestanding racks of fermented bottled sunshine. I had nothing. They'd even taken Hodin's ring in a second, more careful search before shoving us in and locking the door.

"Arrrrrah!" Trent exclaimed, arms straining as he pulled a wine rack taller than himself from the wall. The old wood frame structure groaned and leaned, finally falling until it hit one of the freestanding racks and stopped. The bottles on it, though, did not, and I looked up when several thousand dollars of trademarked Golden Wedding champagne hit the cobbled floor and burst in a wash of sound and rising scent of alcohol.

"You've never been trapped in a hole before, have you," I said, and, expression cross, Trent reached to angle the bulb to the newly exposed wall to inspect it for a way out.

"Not until I met you," he muttered, and I snorted, remembering.

"Well, I have. Lots of times," I said. "Once by you as a mink," I said idly. "Once in your woods. HAPA. That was a bad one. The demons, Alcatraz . . . The door will open. I promise."

But will it open in time? I wondered, worried. Trent had already searched the floor and ceiling to no avail. There were no windows. There were no doors other than the one we'd been shoved through. The only light was from the bulb in Trent's hand, and we probably wouldn't even have that except that the switch was in here.

Trent let the light go. Light flashed and swung until he caught it again, holding it in his long fingers until he eased his grip from it. He turned to me, his mood bad, and I looked away. The strap of charmed silver was too tight, and I worked a finger between it and me, wondering if breaking my hand was a good alternative. I wasn't sure how they thought I was going to kill Trent. I had no magic with this thing on. But maybe Landon was right that Trent would do nothing to stop me, and a broken bottle was as good as a knife. *Son of a bastard.*

"There are all kinds of cages," Trent said as he picked his way through the slosh to a still-standing rack. The cold sound of dust on glass scraped through the silence as he pulled a bottle, and then a crack when he snapped the top off by tapping it on the rack. Glass tinkled down, followed by the soft hiss of bubbles. "Mine always seem to have champagne in them."

I said nothing as he carefully lowered himself to sit beside me. But I *did* take the bottle when he offered it, spinning it to find the least jagged lip before I took a gulp.

Tart and strong, the alcohol burned my throat, and I

downed the rare Cincinnati vintage as if it were water. The bubbles burned, and I closed my eyes before they teared. At least it was champagne. No sulfites meant no headache. "Ah, Rachel?" Trent cautioned, and I came up for air and handed it back.

More restrained, Trent took a slug as well. "Mmmm," he said in appreciation, angling the bottle to look for the date before sighing and setting it aside. "Needs a few more years."

The silence grew heavy with only our breathing to mar it. I could feel Trent's warmth even though he wasn't touching me, but my anger and fear wouldn't let go. Jenks was leaking dust and not flying well. If they caught him, they'd put him in the garden to die because Landon had told them to. Never mind that he was a person. My friend.

"He's more resilient than you think," Trent said, focus distant on the slowly seeping champagne.

I exhaled, breath shaking. "I never should have agreed to this," I said. "I knew it was too cold for him if things got out of hand." I looked up when Trent put an arm around me and tugged me sideways into him. "And when have my runs never gotten out of hand?"

"He'll be okay," he said, the scent of green things rising as he pulled me even closer. "He's probably tormenting Landon as we speak. And with him free, we have a good chance of escaping."

"True," I said ruefully. When you got right down to it, Jenks was doing better than us. *He* wasn't stuck in a hole, bound by charmed silver. And then I realized that Landon was probably going to end up a zombie. I wasn't sure if I cared to lift a finger to stop it.

We both jumped at the knock on the door. Trent's arms fell away, and I sat up. *They knocked?* I thought. *That's weird.*

The door pushed open until it hit the fallen wine rack. A masculine voice murmured in surprise, and Trent stood when a muscular arm wrangled its way in and shoved the rack up until it hit the wall with a heavy thump and a tinkle of glass.

The door opened farther to show a large blond man in

security black standing on the threshold. He silently eyed the broken bottles until a small man in office attire pushed past him. Clearly nervous, he touched his fair hair to make sure the fine strands were lying flat.

My gaze went to Trent, and my eyebrows rose in understanding. Trent might have been wearing an ill-fitting suit. He might have been dirty and trapped in a hole. But under that thickening stubble, he had the cool, angry bearing of a wronged prince, and I loved him for it.

"What do you want?" I said, not bothering to get up.

The man edged farther around his security with an oddly starstruck look. "My name is Benny," he said, and I squinted at him, not hearing that West Coast accent most everyone else in the building had. "Up until two months ago, I was the dewar's single Cincinnati representative."

Trent put a hand on his waist, the other snapping his fingers to help trigger a memory. "I know you. We met at . . . ah. Halloween, wasn't it? At my charity ball. You were a Vulcan."

My suspicion deepened as Benny flushed, almost fanboying.

"That was me," he said, touching an ear. It was cropped as the ears of all the elves of his generation were, but being a Vulcan had given him the excuse to don a proper pair of ears for the day.

"What do you want?" I asked again, and Benny's eyes shot to mine, dark in the chancy light of the single bulb. His smile vanished.

"Not everyone is happy with Landon's obsession with the baku." Benny glanced at his security as if he was sympathetic to his stand. "Your associate told me that Landon taught you the spell to pull a soul from a body and put it into another."

Associate? My head jerked up. He had to mean Jenks. They'd *caught* him?

"Jenks?" I said, scrambling up. "If you so much as bend a wing—" My motion toward Benny jerked to a halt when that big man moved, blocking me. Trent shifted to stand beside me, and together we sized up the hard-faced man. He was the tallest, most broad-shouldered elf I'd ever seen—and he had to be an elf with that wispy blond hair and those green eyes.

Two against one in a small space. His chancy magic against our fists and feet. I settled back to listen.

"He's fine." Benny's smile looked ill. "Zack said he was not to be harmed."

My lips parted, and Trent grunted, clearly stunned as well. "That wily little . . ."

"Elf," I finished for him, new possibilities opening up.

"Zack's been spying on me?" Trent said, his worried expression making me wonder if he was regretting having shown him his mother's spelling hut. "You sent him to spy on me?"

"No." Benny clasped his hands in distress. "He ran away after being moved to Cincinnati. With Landon compromised, he's the head of the dewar." He winced. "Such as it is presently."

"Then you're . . . letting us go?" I said, remembered the large building we'd wound our way through to get to the wine cellar. It seemed pretty substantial to me for a faction that had, until a year ago, been meeting in coffee shops and at baseball games.

"That depends on you," Benny said, and my hope faltered in sudden suspicion.

"Landon hasn't given Zack any of the dewar secrets, has he," Trent murmured.

"Not the ones known only to the high priest," Benny admitted. "Landon is compromised, but he's holding the dewar's wisdom hostage. We don't dare oppose him."

My shoulders slumped and I eased back. Zack was not in charge. "Yet you're down here talking to us. What do you want?" I asked for the third time.

"Landon wants Trent dead and you responsible for it," he said, his gaze fixed on mine. "But as I said, he's compromised. Zack, though next in line, is underage, and while we will give on certain matters, such as if a pixy lives or dies, we can't give him sway in political matters."

"If Jenks suffers under your care, you will suffer under mine," I intoned, and Trent exhaled as if annoyed, his fingers tightening on my arm.

"You mentioned the curse to move souls," Trent prompted, and my jaw clenched.

Sure, now you're all political businessman. What happened to my vengeful warlord elf?

Benny's brow pinched to make the tiny wrinkles on his forehead deepen. "Ah, can we have a moment?" he said to his security.

"Sir," the large man said. It was the first time he'd spoken, and his voice was surprisingly deep, mesmerizing with its elven lilt and cadence. Almost like music.

"I'll be fine," Benny said. Lips pressed, Benny turned to me. "Will I be fine?"

I nodded guardedly, and Trent gave me an encouraging smile. *See? I can do political, too.*

The large man hesitated, then stepped into the hall and shut the door.

Benny's soft shoes scuffed the cold cobbles. The champagne was making inroads via the mortar lines, and the scent of alcohol was strong. "I wish you hadn't destroyed so many," he said, eyes on the broken glass. "They aren't cheap."

"Neither is Jenks," I said.

Benny's lip twitched. "Jenks said Landon taught you the curse to move souls from one body to another," he whispered, clearly nervous. "It's the dewar's most precious knowledge. Everything else is written down, but that one, because of its nature, has been passed by word and deed."

Its nature. I grimaced. It was black magic, foul and immoral. If they got caught with it, someone would be jailed in Alcatraz.

"I'll let you both out and quiet the assault charges if you agree to pull Landon's soul from his body and put it into a newborn," Benny added. "*Before* the Order turns him into a zombie."

And with that, everything changed.

Horrified, I drew back. "You still use that curse?" I said, appalled.

"Why?" Trent said shortly, and Benny's attention flicked to him.

"Landon's soul is almost gone," Benny said uncomfortably. "But it will regenerate. If the baku takes him, all his latent wisdom will go with it. His soul lineage stretches back nearly a thousand years. We already lost his predecessor's soul when he committed suicide. We can't afford to lose another. But more important, if you perform the ceremony, Zack will have the knowledge."

"Ceremony? It's black magic," I said hotly. "We're *not* going to show Zack how to do an ancient elven black curse. I won't do it."

Benny hunched into himself. "I'm told it's a spell, and what is the difference between this and what you did for your vampire roommate?"

"Ivy and Nina?" I said, insulted that he'd bring them up. "Nina was *dead*," I said hotly. "Ivy is holding her soul, not moving in and destroying it. It's not the same thing."

They would let us go, but the cost was morally too high. *Elves are just the other side to the demon coin,* I thought, not for the first time. "You do know that the *curse* destroys the original soul, right?" I said, words fast and angry. "The one that belongs to the baby?" I turned to Trent, my lips parting when I realized he was trying to balance the scales of morality. "No!" I said loudly. "I may be a demon, but the only way I can sleep at night is if I say no when no needs to be said!"

Silent, Trent scrubbed his face with a hand. Suddenly I realized that if he did this, his pull with the dewar would be restored. Damn it to the Turn and back. Why did it always have to be the hard way?

"Landon has compromised himself with his continued association with the baku," Benny continued, talking now to Trent since he hadn't said no yet. "The baku has eaten Landon's soul to where he can be taken at will. The only reason it hasn't is because it wants you dead as well, thereby increasing its political reach once it is in Landon. If the Order doesn't cage the baku in Rachel, they will cage it in him. We can avoid both if you relocate Landon's soul to a new vessel."

"Do you even hear yourself?" I said, one hand on my hip, the other gesturing wildly. "Relocate? Vessel? You are destroying a baby's soul. Even demons don't do that!"

Benny's eye twitched and he steadied himself. "If you rescue Landon's soul, the Order will turn his empty body into a zombie to capture the baku. Landon will be free to be reborn. Rachel will not be forced to become a zombie. Everyone wins."

I looked at Trent. Benny had it wrong. A body without a soul couldn't hold the baku. Hodin had said so, and he would know. "Everyone wins?" I echoed, not seeing the point in correcting him. "What about the baby you're shoving Landon's decrepit soul into?" I added, not caring if the security guard could hear. Maybe he needed to know how morally bankrupt the man signing his paycheck was. *Maybe he already knows and doesn't care.* "The baby's soul is crushed. It is a *baby!*"

Benny turned to me, a sliver of backbone in him from Trent's continued silence. "This is our tradition. And why your pixy is even alive."

My expression went slack as I figured out what that meant. "Zack?" I said, horrified. "You did this to Zack? Is that why you're listening to him? Because you think he's got some elven old-man soul in him? Is Zack here?" I said, looking at the closed door. "Ask him. I bet he'd say let Landon flap in the wind. You should listen to him. He's smarter than all of you combined. He saw the damage the baku was doing, and none of you did anything about it."

"To my point," Benny said grimly. "Zachariah was one of our most canny leaders. He will be again."

Zack. Zachariah. My God, they didn't even let them

keep their names. Just pasted the old atop the new. Maybe Al was right. Maybe elves were worse monsters when push came to shove.

Benny saw my horror and accepted it, chin high. "If you don't do this, our only option is to let Landon have his way. Once the baku is trapped in you, Landon *might* be able to be reasoned with. That's a choice your morals will have to make. Move his soul and sacrifice a newborn's, or sacrifice your lives, knowing Landon will eventually give the order himself to move his soul."

"No," I said. "I don't care if it's tradition. I don't care if my refusal only puts it off for a few more decades. I'm not going to pluck Landon's soul out and drop it into a baby like a rechargeable battery."

"Rachel . . ." Trent put an arm around my waist. Which was probably a good thing, seeing as if he had taken my arm to restrain me, I might have smacked him.

I pulled away, disgusted. Why was he even entertaining the thought? Had he learned nothing? Was he still the same man who had coldly killed his lead geneticist to keep his secrets?

But then his lips twitched and his eyes went to the rafters and the faint glow of pixy dust.

"You hold him down," Trent said, eyes shining. "And I'll punch him."

CHAPTER

33

BENNY'S MOUTH DROPPED OPEN. "NASH!" HE SHOUTED, backing up fast.

No magic. I reached for a line and found nothing, cut off by the band of charmed silver. "I got this," I said grimly as I pushed past Trent, hands in fists as I shifted my balance to start a front kick.

Jenks took off from the rack, dust sparkling. Benny's eyes went to him. Terrified by the two-inch sword, he flung himself away—slipping on the wet cobble to fall backward. Benny's head hit the wall with a dull *whap*. His eyes closed, and he slumped into a crumpled heap.

"That was easy," Trent said, and I spun to the door. It was opening.

Nash, the guard, was going to be a lot more difficult.

"Relax, Rache," Jenks said from atop Trent's shoulder. "We got a man on the inside."

Zack? I thought, but it wasn't Zack who pushed the door open.

Crap on toast, the guy looked even bigger now that I was going to have to fight him, and I retreated, making room to work. Trent moved to my side, his expression promising hurt. We'd have to be really fast, be really lucky, and, above all, stay out of his reach.

The large man looked at Benny slumped on the floor, his

chest moving slowly as he breathed. Nash's sharp gaze rose to mine. His hands flickered with a faint haze of magic, and then it vanished. "I never liked him anyway," he said, voice low.

And then Nash was shoved aside as Zack spilled into the room, smelling of cinnamon and wine, excited and animated. "Quick! We've got a small window while the old guys decide whether to side with Landon or Benny. I downed everyone between here and the door with a sleep charm."

"Your magic is working?" I said as I realigned my thinking. *Nash is on our side. Zack is here. Jenks is leaking dust from a bent wing but flying. The door is open.*

The kid grinned and looked at his hands. They were both bandaged, each carefully wrapped around the base of the thumb, where the fate line ran. "After I made a sacrifice of blood to the Goddess to recognize her demon heritage. Yep. I'm good as gold."

Trent put a hand to the small of my back to encourage me to the door. The stairway was dimly lit by the occasional light, and the steps were cut stone. "My magic is working and I didn't make a sacrifice," he said as we filed into the cramped stairway: Zack first, Trent and me second, and Nash bringing up the rear, carefully shutting but not locking the door.

Jenks snickered from my shoulder. "You're bumping uglies with her favorite godchild."

"Oh!" Eyes bright, Zack paused on the stairs, fumbling in his back pocket to hand Trent a pair of clippers. "I stole them from the armory. They should cut right through."

I glanced back at Nash, not sure why he was helping us. The stairs were cramped, and our shoulders jostled as Trent wedged the clippers over my band of charmed silver and, with a soft and certain thump, cut it. I reached for a line, sighing as it flooded in to ease my slight headache.

"You next," I said as I tucked the band in a pocket and took the clippers. Trent's brow smoothed as I cut his brace-let in turn, the silver breaking with surprising give.

I went to tuck the clippers into my back pocket with the broken band, starting when Nash stuck his big hand between us. "It belongs to the armory," he said, low voice rumbling, and I handed them over.

The stairs began to widen, and I twined my fingers in Trent's when Zack motioned us to hang back. A shiver of sensation rippled up through me as our eyes met. The patch of hall visible at the top of the stairs was lit from lights, not sunlight, but clearly the curse was still in force. For now.

Not that it matters, I thought with a flash of anger. I wasn't going to risk an untried curse on the baku if I didn't need to. And I didn't need to. I only had to stay awake until the baku gave up on killing Trent and took Landon over and the Order turned him into a zombie.

My fingers in Trent's spasmed at the flash of guilt. Misunderstanding, Trent gave them a squeeze and smiled. "I'll take care of the assault charges," he whispered as if this was going to blow over. But assault charges from Dan and Wendy were the last thing on my mind. It wouldn't be over until the Order had the baku . . . and Landon with it.

My guilt shifted to a nagging thorn of responsibility. *Son of a bastard . . . what the hell is wrong with me? I should've taken Trent up on that island in the South Seas three years ago.*

"It's clear," Zack said from the top of the stair. "Just cross the sanctuary and out the front door. Jenks, you want to go first?"

"On it." Jenks rose up. Dust spilled from his bent wing, but he looked otherwise okay as he darted out of the stairway. The sanctuary was as big as a gymnasium, the walls distressed plaster painted a soothing blue. There were no pews, no altar, though it was obvious where it had been. It was a meeting space now, for wedding receptions, and my eyes rose to the enormous chandeliers glowing with reduced power to barely light the space.

Zack ventured out, his youthful, gangly body looking awkward. I was next, but I hesitated when Trent faced Nash.

"Why?" was all he said, and I hung back, waiting for the answer.

Nash grimaced, his eyes tracking Zack's progress across the huge sanctuary. "I know what Benny asked you to do," he said, voice rumbling like distant summer thunder. "I don't agree with it. And I don't have to support it. Zack . . ." His eyes went to the far end of the sanctuary where Zack was waiting by the door, clearly wondering why we hadn't moved. "He can't help what they did to him, but he wants it to end. Landon would have it go on forever. But the reason I'm risking everything is because of what *you* did."

He was talking to Trent, and curious, I turned from watching Jenks arrow back to us.

"I've heard what Landon is saying about you and . . . Rachel," Nash continued, making me wonder if he had been going to say *your demon*. "But you were at the hospital the day my brother died. I know you don't remember it, but he had the demon curse on him really bad, like some do. You tried to help him when no one else would. And now my son is growing up strong. He doesn't have to endure what I did. He's named after my brother."

My lips parted at the heartache in Trent's eyes as he touched the big man's shoulder.

"What are you guys waiting for?" Jenks griped as he landed exhausted on my shoulder. "God to say go?"

"I can't leave yet," I said, and Trent jerked to a stop, his motion to break into a jog shifting almost comically fast. "Landon has my stuff."

Trent's lips quirked. "I'll buy you a new stick of magnetic chalk."

"He's got my *soul bottle*," I added, beckoning to Zack across the huge sanctuary.

"She's right," Trent said when Zack started back in a soft-footed run. "Landon can use it to target a noncontact spell to her."

"And Hodin's ring," I added when Zack slid to a breathless halt, a question heavy in his eyes. "If he accidently called Hodin . . . or, worse, intentionally?"

Trent turned to Zack. "You've done enough. You too, Nash. Make yourselves scarce."

"What? What's going on?" Zack asked.

"We have to get Hodin's ring and that bottle back," Jenks said from my shoulder.

"But they're going to wake up," Zack said. "We don't have time."

"Which is why you're going to hightail it out of here," I said. "Trent and I will get my stuff, and if we're lucky, Landon will still be in his rooms and I can pound him."

But Zack shook his head, arms over his chest to become virtually unmovable. "Landon wouldn't keep them there. If they were that important, he'd put them in the undercroft."

"The what?" Jenks asked for both of us.

"The vault," Zack whispered, turning to beckon us deeper into the back rooms of the sanctuary. "It's a hidden room under the church. That's where they put all the good stuff they moved with me. Let's go!"

I looked at Trent, and he looked at me. Shrugging, Trent rocked into motion.

"How do you know about the undercroft?" Nash said, clearly shocked as he followed us.

"Homework," Zack called over his shoulder.

But my unease grew as I followed Zack through the sanctuary's back rooms full of folding chairs, tables, and stacked linens. There were too many of us. *We're making too much noise,* I thought, jerking when I saw a booted foot poking out from behind a corner. Another slumped body lay behind a row of stacked folding tables. *Zack's work?* I thought, remembering the sophisticated spells he'd thrown at me, failing only because the Goddess hadn't been listening. She was now, apparently.

"Just tell us where it is," I said when Zack stopped before a misshapen door that looked as if it belonged to the fifties. It was caked with paint and had old metal hinges. A dented brass knob handle spun when Zack tried to open it. It might have led to a broom closet or a tiny ugly bathroom, but Zack persisted, spinning the door handle to no effect.

"I know this is it," Zack said, ears turning red as he tried spinning it the other way.

"Too late." Jenks rose up, bent wing rasping. "Someone found us."

"I got it," Trent said, and my breath came in fast when he pulled heavy on a ley line.

"Watch your control!" I almost hissed as he paced forward, chin high, stance confident. But then the trio of hapless office workers saw him, and an almost comical panic spread among them.

"*Entrono voulden,*" Trent said, his hand glowing with power as he gestured at them. A thread of energy pulled through me, and my breath caught at the wash of power spilling from Trent. His bright glow of power circled the terrified trio twice to bunch them into a tight bundle . . . and then swamped them.

Their faces went slack, and all three dropped into an untidy pile.

"Nice," I said, then lurched forward to help drag them out of sight. "When did you learn that?"

Trent grinned at me. His hair was tousled and his eyes sparkling. Feeling plinked down to my groin. He was everything I could ever want. Too bad Ellasbeth thought the same way. "It's my mom's," he said. "I'm hoping I find more of her work in her lab." His expression faltered. "Now that it's open."

"Guys!" Zack called, his hushed voice intent. "You got any ideas? It's magically locked."

I gave the three slumbering people a last look. It wasn't fair that they had such an even, predictable life when it was all I could do to keep mine from exploding every three months. "Have you tried *quis custodiet ipsos custodes*?" I said as Trent and I rejoined them, and then my gaze dropped to the door at the soft click.

"Who guards the guardians?" Trent said as Zack spun the knob again, and this time, the latch engaged. "Someone has a sense of humor."

"Go." Nash pressed his lips as he turned to the loud

voices approaching. "I'll lead them to the other side of the compound."

"Rache, come on!" Jenks prompted.

Zack was already halfway down another one of those cramped stairs lit by lights hanging from exposed wire, and I hesitated, taking Nash's hand for a moment. "Thank you," I said, and then Trent tugged me away. "If you ever need a job . . . ," I said as he pulled me down the stairs.

"If this gets out, I will," Nash said, and then the door shut.

"Wait," I insisted as I tugged from Trent, hesitating until I heard Nash's muffled shout and the sound of them fading. I exhaled, trusting the man I'd known for all of five minutes.

"If you ever need a job?" Jenks said pointedly as he landed on my shoulder.

Trent had gone ahead, and I felt myself warm as I began to follow. "With Ivy gone, we could use some muscle. Besides, if I don't grab him, Trent will."

The air began to smell musty—and sort of metallic. A thick rug spread where the stairs ended. The light was brighter, too, but I hustled forward when Jenks took off, stopping just inside what I assumed was a larger room.

"And demon makes three," Landon said when I came blinking out of the darker tunnel.

Trent took my arm, tugging me closer as I looked across the brightly lit, almost claustrophobically low-ceilinged room. It glittered with gold and jewels arranged in glass cases and narrow shelves. But it was Landon and the eight men and women who held my attention.

"There's *four* of us, moss wipe," Jenks said as he hovered beside Zack.

Trent twitched, and the eight security guards lifted their weapons in threat.

Guns? I thought, realizing how badly elven magic wasn't working.

Landon smirked. Somewhere between punching me in the gut and now, he'd put his ceremonial robe on over his slacks and white shirt, and the purple and green reminded me of what demons dressed their favorite familiars in. A purple sash was draped around his neck, and he even had on the flat-topped cylindrical hat. I wondered if he was trying to curry favor with the Goddess. If his security was using mundane weapons, it wasn't working.

And then my chin lifted when I realized it was Hodin's ring that he was setting on a display rack with the rest. Everything he'd taken from me was in a bowl beside him, and my lips parted when he plucked the baby bottle out from between Trent's and my phones and dropped it in his robe's expansive pocket.

"From one dead-end hole to another," Jenks muttered as a pounding began on the door at the top of the stairs. "Don't you elves ever make escape routes?"

Trent shrugged, and Jenks dropped to the floor to look for one.

"I never did like you, Zack, even before you died," Landon said, grimacing at Jenks's fading dust trail. "You made my childhood miserable. Which will make this almost a pleasure."

Expression ugly, he backed to the wall and motioned for the guards to shoot us.

My eyes widened as they readied their weapons. Surprise flashed through me, and Zack made a sound of disbelief. Heart pounding, I yanked on the ley line, pulling in energy to blow them backward and into the tapestry-covered walls. "Fire in the hole!" I shouted to Jenks, then inhaled to invoke the spell with the force of my leaving breath.

"Celero inanio!" Zack shouted at the top of his lungs, and I turned to look at him in horror. It would burst the cartridges right in their weapons!

"Rhombus!" I exclaimed instead, simultaneously imagining a circle to encompass all of us. Trent's energy poured into me, his power supplementing mine through Hodin's curse. Our thicker barrier flashed up, closing above our heads as a thunderous boom shook the air: scores of bullets exploding at once.

I ducked, looking up at the unexpectedly muffled sound. The barrier dimpled with gunfire, and I squinted past it, a hand going to my mouth as men cried out in half-heard pain and fell to the floor in the sudden firestorm.

Bullets embedded themselves in the wall. Glass shelves shattered to spill priceless elven artifacts in a mix of jewels, glass shards, and wood splinters. And then it was over and all I could hear were Trent's and Zack's harsh breaths. The cries of the downed men were muted and the air was getting stuffy. Under the influence of Hodin's curse, a circle *would* hold the baku. *If I cared to catch it.*

I slowly stood. Trent had never ducked, never flinched, ramrod straight with his eyes fixed on Landon across the dusty room. The leader of the dewar had put himself in a circle, too, but his men were dead or dying.

"Let me out," Zack said, his face ashen. "I never meant to hurt anyone." He turned to Trent, his young face pinched in agony. "I never meant to hurt anyone!"

My throat filled with a hard lump as I remembered realizing I could kill someone by just being stupid. "It happens," I said, not knowing what else to say. "Go fix it."

Trent touched the bubble, and it dropped. My gut twisted at the louder groans and pants of Landon's security. As if in a war zone, the wounded dragged themselves to the dying, their own pain ignored as they tried to save one another's lives.

Landon stayed where he was, safe in his circle.

Zack lurched to the first, his bandaged hand outstretched. Jenks was already flitting from huddle to huddle, dusting the bleeding to help stanch the flow.

"You know who I am," Trent said to the one officer who had escaped with nothing more than a shoulder wound, and the man looked up from the person he was trying to save, pain in his eyes. "This is between me and the former head of the dewar. I'm speaking now for the current head of the dewar, Zachariah Oborna. Agree to cease your actions against us, and there will be no repercussions. We'll get you medical attention as soon as we can."

But Zack was already among them, tears spilling from him as he murmured powerful word after powerful word. Landon watched in jealous disgust as his underling healed and mended with a skill and finesse that was so smooth and sure, it had to be from a lifetime of experience, a lifetime that Zack hadn't lived, but his predecessor had.

I stood straighter as Jenks came back to me, weary but satisfied. By his confident nod, I knew they would all live. Better, Zack would likely never act out of fear again. Pride filled me when Zack stood, slim and untidy in his jeans and T-shirt, his hands bloodied and a smear of red under his eye where he had wiped his youth away and become a man.

"What say you?" Trent said, his voice holding an unfamiliar formal cadence as Zack stood heartsick at what he had done.

One by one, the men looked among themselves. One by one, they set their weapons down. And one by one, they all inclined their heads to the new leader of the dewar.

Landon shook with anger as he hid in his circle. "*I* am the dewar! Me! She's a demon whore who tricked the strength of the Sa'han from him and destroyed his name. Bankrupted him! She will do the same to us. To you!"

"Why does everyone think I don't have any money?" Trent muttered, annoyed.

"Take them, or I swear your names will be struck from the rolls and you will be shunned!"

I coughed at the settling dust, then squinted up the stairway. The pounding had stopped, but I doubted the guards had given up. "We can't walk out of here and leave him," I said, and Trent sighed, clearly agreeing though it would have been easier. "Sure, these guys like Zack, but there's an entire building of angry elves up there."

"Fine," Trent almost grumped. "Try not to knock him unconscious."

"I got just the thing." I could still feel Trent's strength in me through Hodin's curse. I took my time, pacing forward as I readied a spell that Al had tormented me with for months until I figured out how to block it. It was almost a joke curse—unless you didn't know how to break it. Taking down the circle Landon was hiding in would be easy, seeing as the Goddess wasn't speaking to her so-called favorite children at the moment.

"*Corrumpo,*" I said, whispering so I wouldn't blow a hole in the wall. Power was a warming blip through me, and I smiled. I was getting the hang of this double-energy stuff.

"You can't!" Landon cried out when his faltering protection vanished. His fear was heavy on him, and I steeled myself against it. Pity had always gotten me in trouble.

He made as if to run, and my prey drive kicked in.

"*Stabils,*" I shouted, physically throwing the glowing curse at Landon—then scrambled to pull half the energy flowing through me back again. My palms itched as I funneled it into the earth, and what was left hit Landon squarely.

The man froze, my will racing over him like a spiderweb and soaking in. His momentum carried him several feet before he half fell, half slid to an undignified sprawl facedown on the glass-and-artifact-strewn rug. The watching security tensed, then relaxed when Landon began to swear, his muffled protest growing louder. Unfortunately the curse didn't affect the vocal cords. I think Al designed it that way because he enjoyed hearing people rail helplessly at him.

"You bitch!" Landon shouted. "You used a demon curse on me. *A demon curse!* Your soul is black, and you will die for this, you stinking demon!"

But I'd heard it too many times to let it bother me. Much. Still, I had to fight to keep from giving his ribs a swift kick as I went to get my things out of the bowl and his former security picked themselves up. "You owe me a purse," I said as I searched his pockets to find that baby bottle.

"This isn't over," Landon raved as Trent gathered the scattered rings one by one. "The Order wants you, not me. All I have to do is wait for you to go to sleep so it can find you."

A flash of fear lit through me and died. "All I have to do is stay awake," I said. "It almost has you, Landon . . . ," I crooned as Jenks came to sit on my shoulder. "It's only

Trent being alive that keeps it from taking you. But I'm not killing him, and when it figures that out, it will take you anyway. You will be a zombie. Forever."

Landon went ashen. In his silence I heard his knowledge that he was likely going to lose, not only his dewar position, but his life. The baku was so close now, I could pretend to see it lifting off his skin like heat. The bottle in my pocket was obvious, and guilt pinched me. I could save him. If I cared to. *Damn it all to the Turn and back, Rachel. Just let evil priests die.*

I turned away. The pounding on the door had returned, and I shifted to make room for Trent as he came closer, a pile of rings in his hands. We were still stuck down here, but at least no one was shooting at us. "Which one is Hodin's?" Trent asked as I gave him his phone back, and then I flicked through the rings in his cupped hands until I found the dented thing.

"Thanks," I said as I put it on, my eyebrows rising when Trent pocketed the rest.

"You common thief, you," Jenks said, laughing, and Trent stepped back, insulted.

"They don't belong to the dewar. They're demon. I'm going to return them. Goodwill gesture." Trent looked at the stairwell at the sound of an ax. "We should leave."

"There's only one way out," Landon spat. "Your lives are mine!"

"He's right," Zack said as he helped the last of the guards rise to his shaky feet. "There's only one door."

I took a breath and steadied myself. If Landon was right about anything, it was that I was a stinking demon. "We don't need a door," I said as I looked at Trent's stubble, wanting to run my hand across it.

Trent put his phone away, never having gotten any further than his address book. "Bis?" he guessed, and I nodded. It was dark. Bis would be awake. I was a demon, even if I didn't have a spelling lab like Al, or a job, like Dali. But I did have friends.

"He can jump us out one by one," I said. The noise of

breaking wood was getting louder, and Zack began organizing the guards, directing them to move a large wardrobe in front of the opening to the stairs. A feeling of urgency took me, and my focus blurred as I strengthened my hold on the ley line and sort of melded my mind with it.

"Goddess spit," Trent whispered, staggering as he reached for a bullet-torn chair.

My eyes flicked to his, and I gave him a weak smile. It was the curse. He'd probably never swum in a ley line like this before. *Bis?* I threw out into the ether, my smile brightening when I got an almost immediate response.

Where are you? Underground? Again? came Bis's response.

And then he was here, startling the guards and delighting Zack as he landed with a wide-eyed stare on the back of the probably once-priceless wingback chair.

"Cool." Bis gave Jenks a tiny fist bump, and the pixy went to Zack to help him direct the guards. "Where are we? The Monastery's undercroft? The Basilica has one, too, but it only has rats." He frowned at the broken shelves and scattered artifacts. "Is everything okay?"

"Sort of?" I said, then started when Hodin popped in as well, the demon appearing in the center of the room with his head nearly brushing the low ceiling. The men positioning the wardrobe against the archway cried out, and Landon, almost forgotten, began to struggle in earnest.

Jenks rose up high, a piercing whistle from his wings getting their attention. "You all just calm down, or I'm going to pix you into an itching frenzy," he said, hands on his hips as he hovered between them and Hodin. "This here is Rachel's friend, and he ain't going to abduct you." He turned to Hodin. "Right?"

Hodin shrugged.

Suspicion thickened in me, and I eyed the demon in his black jeans and T-shirt. Clearly he'd been with Bis. Again. "I didn't call you," I said. "What are you doing with my gargoyle?"

Bis's eyes widened, and he made a hopping jump to my

shoulder, his tail wrapping securely around my back. "We were just flying," he said.

I eyed Hodin, who smiled insincerely. I didn't like this. Bis was his own person, but Hodin had what it took to keep up with the kid and I clearly didn't. *Maybe I should rectify that,* I thought, stifling a surge of jealousy.

I spun at a loud thump to see the guards shove the wardrobe back into place. Zach was standing by it, looking ill.

"Busy evening?" Hodin looked around, eyebrows rising as he tracked Trent ambling about the destruction, picking things up and setting them down as if he were shopping.

Feeling my gaze, Trent turned. "We should leave before they break the back off that wardrobe."

It was solid mahogany, but they did have an ax.

"Where to?" Bis said, brightening.

"The church," I said softly. Not the boat or Piscary's, where Ivy was. Not Trent's, where the girls were. The church. My church. They could find me there if they wanted to.

Hodin brought his attention up from Landon. "I'm here because I want it," he said flatly.

"Want what?" I said, eyeing Trent's stuffed pockets. *Good God. Jenks is right. He's a common thief.*

"The baku," Hodin said, and Trent started, his green eyes sharp in warning. "I think you have an excellent chance of containing it." He looked at Landon, and the man went ashen. "And I want it," he finished softly.

"No, I'm last!" Zack said, but Bis had landed on his shoulder, and the two winked out.

"Well, maybe I want to leave him here to turn into a zombie," I said, though I didn't, and beside me, Trent sidled close, clearing his throat in a gentle rebuke to consider the future. "He tried to kill Jenks. If he got his way, he would make me kill you," I said.

"But he didn't," Trent reminded me.

Bis popped back in a flurry of leather-snapping wings, pinwheeling to snatch Jenks right out of the air. "Next!" he shouted merrily, and the two were gone to leave only Jenks's swearing to fade with his dust.

At the archway, the ax was biting through the back of the wardrobe, four men holding it firm. We had only moments.

"I want it because it tormented me for six agonizing years as they perfected it," Hodin said, his long face hard in remembered anger.

"Not to hold it over your kin as a threat?" Trent suggested, and Hodin's anger shifted into an evil-looking smile that made me stifle a shiver.

"That, too," he said.

Behind me, the guards cried a warning and moved a chair into position. My gaze dropped to Landon, silent as he waited to see how fate would fall. Maybe if I put my curses where my mouth was, the Order would take me seriously. If the baku was in a bottle, Landon might be the leader of the dewar, or he might be in prison for attempted murder. *Probably not,* I decided. He was an entitled bastard. They'd quietly demote him to where he would fester like a thorn in my foot.

But what really bothered me was the thought of having to live with myself when I knew I could have stopped it. "How long before this curse expires?" I said, taking a step back when the head of an ax bit into the chair and got stuck.

Hodin sniffed, totally uncaring. "Three hours."

Three hours. "Why do I always cut these things so damn close?" I whispered, my gaze finding Bis when he popped back in. I looked at Trent, and the kid nodded.

"Rachel first," Trent demanded, backing up. "I said, Rachel first!"

But it was too late, and they were gone.

Hodin glanced at the sudden uproar at the archway, then at me, his eyebrows high in question. Arms were snaking in, forcing hips and legs to follow.

"Change of plans, Landon," I said as I inched back to him. "You're coming with us." I looked at Hodin, pulse fast. *God, I hope I'm not making a mistake.* "I'll do this, and then I'll give the baku to you after you teach me a way to fly with Bis."

Hodin's lips parted in surprise. "You could have anything, and you choose this?"

"But I want to make one thing perfectly clear." I leaned to poke him in the chest. "If you *ever* let that thing out with the intent to do harm, I'll bring everything I have down on you. Got it?"

"Deal," Hodin said, and then I gasped as he wrapped his will around me and threw me into the ley line. *I would have taught you how to fly for nothing* came his thought into mine, somehow giving me the impression of a matte-finish blade of iron.

I would have given you the baku for the same, I thought back.

And then we were there, safe in my church.

CHAPTER

34

"I'M LAST!" JENKS SHRILLED, AN ANGRY WHITE-HOT DUST spilling as he hovered before an ear-drooping but unrepentant Bis. "I'm always last! How many times do we have to go over this?"

"It was thirty seconds," the small gargoyle said, his thick gray lips trying not to smile.

"Do you know how much trouble she can get into in thirty seconds?" Jenks said before spinning in the air and darting up into the open rafters to sulk.

Trent sidled close, his gaze coming back from the construction-equipment-strewn sanctuary lit by one of Ivy's old floor lamps. "I do," he said as he slipped an arm around me and tugged me into him. "I don't think he's traveled by line before," he said, attention going to Landon.

The elf didn't look good, huddled and trembling on the floor as he tried to process what had just happened. Traveling the lines was rough if you weren't expecting it. Up until the last few months, such journeys were usually one-way—straight to a living hell as a demon's familiar.

Suck it up, Mr. Dewar man, I thought as Trent went to check on him. The baby bottle was an uncomfortable bump in my pocket, and I took it out, setting it on the denuded pool table beside one of the glyphs. Bis rose in a pulse o sliding leather to sit next to Jenks in the rafters, clearly trying to smooth things over. Zack was staring at the six pentagons on the pool table, a hand at his slim waist and his youthful features creased in study. Hodin fidgeted, probably trying to decide if he wanted to explain it to him or leave the kid in ignorance.

I sighed as the peace of the place slipped into me, leaning back against the pool table with my ankles crossed. As messed up as it was, smelling of construction dust instead of coffee, filled with tools and lumber instead of my things, it still felt like home.

But my expression fell as I saw the head of the dewar paralyzed on my sanctuary floor. *I've got to stop doing this.*

"You said you were going to fix the table," I said, and Hodin turned from Zack.

"Now?" One by one, Hodin pushed all the rings on his right hand to the base of his fingers. "We might need a quick spelling surface."

"Lazy ass," I said, but he was right, and I began to wipe one side of it clean with a rag.

"This is abduction," Landon said, panting as he recovered. "You forced me through the lines! You will rot for this, Kalamack."

Which I thought was funny, because Trent hadn't done it. Finished, I tossed the rag into the waste barrel and scooted up atop the table to sit cross-legged. "So . . . how do we get the baku out?"

Jenks dropped down from the rafters to stand before Landon. "Let's knock it out of him," the pixy said, and Landon sneezed on his dust. "There's lots of two-by-fours."

"It won't leave voluntarily." Hodin looked sage in his black jeans and T, a wise-biker-dude-demon vibe on him. "You have to convince Landon to kick it out."

"That's not happening." I stared as the frustrated man choked and trembled, smearing his dewar robes with sawdust as he tried to break the curse holding him.

Hodin's lips pressed. "I think we're very close to where he won't be able to anymore."

"I control it." Landon's hate-filled eyes found mine. "I can kick it out anytime I want."

"Prove it," I said, channeling my inner sixth-grader, and Zack gave up on the pool table scribbles and went to stand beside Trent.

"You'd like that, wouldn't you?" Landon struggled. "You are *finished*, Kalamack. I will hound you and your children's children. I will live through the ages as a plague upon your house."

"Tink's tampons. He's monologing," Jenks muttered from Trent's shoulder.

"But for you, we'll start with abducting a high priest," Landon continued. "Transferring without consent through the lines. The damage to the undercroft alone will bankrupt you."

Bis dropped down to land on the sawhorse. "It's just a hole under the church."

"For the last time," Trent said, brow furrowed, "I'm not destitute. I have money."

I slid off the pool table and sashayed over to Landon. "How can we catch it if he won't kick it out?" I asked.

"Pull out his soul," Zack whispered, and Jenks's wings rasped in surprise as I turned to Zack. The kid's eyes looked haunted, and his face was pale. "With a soul spiral," he added, looking at Trent. "Take out his soul, and the baku will be forced to follow."

My lips parted. True, but without a soul, Landon would be dead in five minutes. You could get around that by putting his soul in a bottle and keeping his body alive on life support as Trent had done with me. It would work on paper. The only reason the demons didn't do it was because it required elven magic, and they would rather die than ask the Goddess for help. Me? I wasn't so picky.

"Whoa, whoa, whoa!" Jenks said from Trent's shoulder. "Won't Landon die without a soul? Not that I care, but the I.S. or the dewar might."

"Not right away," Hodin said, and Zack nodded, solemn and scared.

"You wouldn't," Landon whispered, his fear obvious o

his sweat-tracked, sawdust-caked face. "That curse isn't supposed to be used until I'm dead. I'm not dead!" He wiggled, random bits of glass catching the faint light, and I nudged him back into place before turning to Trent, my eyebrows high.

"How does Zack know about the soul spiral?" I accused, and both Trent and Zack flushed. "We agreed that the dewar's curse to move souls was going to die with us."

Trent grimaced. "I didn't tell him how to do the curse. I told him how I used it to save your life. A lesson on how something inherently bad can be used for a good reason and outcome."

I shook my head, agreeing with Jenks. "No. Killing Landon is bad," I said. "Even to catch the baku. And that's what we're going to get if we pull his soul out."

"Not if he's at the center of the spiral," Zack said, and Hodin nodded.

"I'm alive!" Landon said, his voice echoing in the empty space. "I'm still alive!"

Yeah? And so is that baby you want to drop your soul into. "Then kick it out," I said, and he gaped at me, his eyes round with fear.

"I can't," he whispered, and Trent gestured as if that said it all and why were we waiting?

"It would work, wouldn't it?" Zack inched closer, his eyes on Landon. "If you pull his soul out, the baku will come with it. You can catch the baku, and Landon's soul will be snared by the soul spiral and land back in his body before he can die."

Breath shaking, I turned to Trent. He was clearly ready to try it, eyes alight and eager.

"That might actually work," Hodin said from the pool table, and Zack bobbed his head.

"I'll take the responsibility if it goes wrong," Zack said, and both Trent and I stiffened. "It was my idea," Zack insisted. "With Landon compromised, I'm the dewar leader. It's my decision."

"You're going to *kill* me!" Landon said, desperate now,

and I almost felt sorry for him. Eyebrows high, I studied Trent. He'd be the one doing the magic. Though with Hodin's curse linking us, I'd probably walk away with a good knowledge of how to do it.

"I'll sketch the spiral," Trent said, the glint in his eye making him look dangerous. "If Landon is at the end of it, he'll get his soul back, sans baku. If it fails, Zack will not take the blame. Agreed?"

"Agreed." Pulse fast, I took the chalk from my pocket, snapped it in two and gave him the larger piece. Damn it, we were doing it again. "There's enough room where he is. Three turns, widdershins," I said, but Trent knew how to do this as well as I. It was just nerves, and as Zack grabbed a broom, I found my phone and texted Ivy that she might need to bail Trent, Zack, and me out of the I.S. lockup tonight if she didn't hear from me by three.

"This is *murder*!" Landon exclaimed, and Jenks hovered beside Trent, advising him on how to keep his lines even. "You are murdering me! I can't survive without my soul!"

"It's only a few minutes," I said to Landon. "Suck it up. Next time don't make deals with energy beings."

Landon moaned, terrified as the reality of the next five minutes hit him.

Nervous, I tucked my phone away. Zack moved the sawhorse out of Trent's way, and Bis, still standing on it, unfolded his wings and shivered at the rumble echoing through him.

"Can you catch it by yourself, Rachel?" Trent asked as he worked, bent double as he drew his unhurried even lines. "It's going to take all my concentration to do the curse."

I nodded, pulse quickening. Catch it, bottle it, and then try to explain to the world why Landon was dead in my church if it didn't work.

But when I saw Trent with chalk on his fingers and magic in his hair, something tightened in me. Hodin stood by the pool table, eager to get his baku but clearly not going to do anything to help. His interest was a little too keen for my liking. *Great, I'm teaching him something new. For free.*

"Jenks?" I called, and the pixy zipped over, his expression cheerful at the prospect of killing Landon, even if only for a short time. "Take Zack and get out of here," I said in a whisper, and Hodin snickered. "I mean it," I added when Jenks's dust shifted to an angry red. "Get him on a bus. Take him to the movies, or our boat, or something."

"My wing is fine," Jenks said bitingly.

His wing was not fine, but it was his pride that was going to get him killed, and I needed him. "Please," I added, glancing at Hodin. "I don't want Zack seeing this. The ability to pull a soul from a living being should end with the people in this room. And if he's somewhere else, he won't get blamed for any of it. Besides, you want him here if the I.S. or the FIB shows up?" God help us if the Order crashed the party.

Jenks spun in the air to see Zack doggedly pushing that broom, looking like the younger brother Trent had never had. "Fine," he muttered. "Troll turds, first I'm guarding the church, and now I'm the fairy-ass babysitter."

Dusting a depressed blue, he flew to Zack. "Zack. Let's go. Rachel wants you out of here."

"What?" Zack spun, the broom going still in his hands. "Why? It's the dewar's curse."

"You want this to end? End it," I said as I turned to Hodin. "I'd like you to leave, too. You aren't getting the baku until I can fly with Bis."

"A snowflake's chance in the ever-after," the demon said, laughing. He was in too good a mood for my liking. But why not? He was about to get the baku and my promise that I'd stand up for him against the demon collective both. I was getting . . . a lot of trouble. Maybe this wasn't such a good deal after all.

Trent stood from finishing the spiral, silent at Zack's betrayed look. Finally the kid threw down the broom and schlumped out the front door, slamming it hard behind him.

Jenks went with him, and I sighed, praying that he and Zack really left and didn't hang around outside to peer through the window. Then I jumped, startled when Bis flew to me with a rustle of leather wings. "Thanks for that," he said as he landed on my shoulder and wrapped his tail snugly. "He's my best friend apart from you," he added, and I touched his feet.

"You can't do this," Landon said, voice panicky. "It will kill me. Please!"

"It's ready." Trent bent to get the broom, carefully setting it to the side before looking at the three-ring spiral that began and ended at magnetic north. "Rachel, I'm thinking we need a circle around Landon and the spiral."

"To keep everything contained? Good idea," I said, and Bis went back to perch beside Hodin when I bent almost double to draw a larger circle around the spiral.

"You can't do this," Landon said as I passed him. "I'm the dewar's leader!"

Not anymore. Worry puddled up in my gut like black tar as I rose. "You getting all of this?" I sourly said to Hodin, and the demon beamed at me.

"Let me go," Landon begged, trembling to make the bits of broken glass on him twinkle. "I'll kick it out. We can come to some understanding. I won't file any charges. That was the baku, not me. You were right. It was dangerous, but I can kick it out. Rachel? Rachel! Listen to me!"

I looked away, gut souring. Trent had taken a purple ribbon from his wallet, carefully smoothing the creases before draping it over his neck. The small elven embellishment turned him from wealthy businessman into something dangerous, and my breath quickened.

"You pull souls from the living often?" Hodin said as he inched closer.

"Not because I want to," I said, then jumped when Trent took my hand. His hair was staticky and his eyes were bright. Chalk decorated his fingers, making him far away and distant from his usual boardroom calm. He was again my warlord elf, and I loved him for it.

Feeling it, he gave my fingers an encouraging squeeze, then moved to stand at magnetic north. I eyed the spiral uneasily. It had an enormous pull once invoked by memory and will . . . by drum and song.

"No hat," Trent said, flashing me a nervous smile as he touched his magic-staticky hair to smooth it. "But I think the Goddess will help anyway. She loves to make mischief."

And this is mischief with a capital M, I thought as Trent closed his eyes and began a humming drone.

The ancient sound hit me like a warm wave, shocking and unexpected. I stared at him, my palms suddenly sweaty. I flicked a glance at Hodin to see if he noticed, flushing when he did.

Landon's groan became a whimper, his eyes widening as the spiral began to glow with a faint stirring of ley line power. It pulled through me, tingles rising as I experienced the curse through both my senses and Trent's, thanks to Hodin's curse.

Tall and unmoving, Trent stood, his lips and chest moving as he breathed out the primordial sound. It spilled from him, at odds with his upright posture, soil-stained suit, and even the new scruff on his cheeks. I backed up, steeling myself against the curse-born pull of his voice. I'd always loved Trent's voice, but this time, it was the curse that drew me. I was more susceptible to it than most, having been lost to it once before.

"You can't do this to me!" Landon cried out, terror clouding his eyes and making his voice raspy. "I am the dewar!"

Trent's voice shifted to a droning chant. I could almost discern the words. They flitted like moths about my thoughts, and I tried to ignore them, feeling that if I listened too closely, I'd be lost. His words pushed the spiral into a brighter, pearly white light, and breath fast, I backed up another wobbly step. To touch the spiral now would have meant my death.

My fingers rose to touch Hodin's glyph warm on my chest. It joined me dangerously close to Trent's magic. It was as if the walls of the church were melting away, leaving me in a haze of a midnight I'd never seen but remembered through the curse he was twisting.

And then . . . the memory of drums began.

Landon groaned, his eyes rolling to the back of his head as he began to shake. The ancient sound wasn't real. It was an echo from the past, pulled into existence by Trent's voice reaching into distant history to find the original curse. It spoke of hidden mossy glens where ley lines ran, of star-filled nights with no moon, and of the elves who gathered to pool their magic into angry, aggressive, terrible deeds. It was a power so great that it had been lost to save the world. And as the drums beat into me, I was there. I was seeing it. I could smell the grass soft under my feet, feel the wind that made the leaves whisper, sense the power of the earth making me one with it.

I floundered as the power wrapped itself around me, making me less, and more, demanding I let go, and move on. Become something else. Become one with death.

My heart stuttered to match the drum's beat. Frightened, I backed up, right into Hodin.

His hand wrapped around my biceps, holding me firm. "You've walked the spiral once and survived," he said, as if not having believed me before, and I nodded, attention fixed to the glowing lines coaxing me forward to my death. I didn't care if he knew I was scared.

I'd felt this before. The lure was unmistakable. The drums were in my head and heart, the beat familiar as they tried to force my pulse to match it. I struggled to keep my breathing uneven and random, anything to be at odds with the force Trent was creating. He'd done this to me once in love to give my body time to mend on life support, and my eyes went to the baby bottle still on the pool table as Trent's song soaked into me, a muzzy warmth promising succor, an end to strife. It would grant me everything if I listened.

"Never," I whispered. I wasn't done yet. I had no rest waiting for me.

"Rachel?" Bis said, red eyes wide. And when our gazes

met, he flew to me. I sagged in relief as his feet clamped about my shoulder, his light weight and sharp nails grounding me. With a shocking ping, the haze in my mind was gone and the drums were silent.

"Thank you, Bis," I said as I risked a glance up at Hodin standing behind me.

"Get me out of here. No. No!" Landon begged, shrieking in fear when his skin began to glow—his soul was leaving him. "Please, no!" he cried. "Let me out! I'll stop trying to bring down Trent. I'll leave you alone. I'll make a retraction. Anything!"

But it was too late, and I swallowed, glad I stood between Hodin and Bis as Trent twisted his terrible magic. *Thank God Zack isn't here,* I thought as Landon began to scream in agony as his soul was pulled from him—alive.

"I'm not dead!" he shrilled, voice high. "Trent, I'm not dead!"

It's the only way to get it out, I thought, staring at him. *God, I'm sorry, Landon.*

But then his eyes bulged, and his high-pitched, piercing cries came again and again. His body was hazed with purple and black and green. It was what was left of his aura. His soul would follow.

My mouth was dry, and Hodin swore softly. The lure of the drums was gone, lost in the terrifying sounds of Landon as his soul was ripped from him. *It's a good thing we're at my church,* I thought as Bis hunched deeper against me, his ears pinned to his bony skull. It was probably the only place in Cincinnati where no one would call the I.S. if they heard such terror.

What kind of a life am I living?

"It's working," Hodin whispered, eyes fixed on Landon. "I thought you were exaggerating. He does have the skill."

Yes, Trent had the skill. And the drive, and the stomach to pull a soul from a still living body. It had been different when he'd pulled mine free. I had wanted to go, trusting Trent to keep me alive and return my soul to my body when it was healed. But this? This was not being done in love, and I thought I was going to throw up as Landon shrieked in anguish, his skin glowing with a rising blue and green.

"You interfering demon spawn," Landon rasped, the bile in his voice shocking me. "I was to be the dewar's leader!"

My breath caught. *That was the baku,* I thought, then I jumped at Landon's high-pitched agony. His eyes were fixed on me in hate, and he was no longer able to speak.

Trent stood resolute, his voice strong as he demanded obedience. I watched in breathless horror as Landon began to shake violently. His soul was being raked from him in waves of green and blue and purple in time with the drums that no longer pulled at me. A black haze clung to it, tendrils spiraling up to try to keep them together. It was the baku, and my lips parted. I could see it. There was so much unfocused energy in here, drawn from the lines like static, that the baku was glowing black.

And then Landon's cries ended. Which was almost worse in a way.

Hodin exhaled in wonder as Landon's soul wafted up from his spasming body, the man's eyes fixed to his soul even as he choked and died. The baku clung to it as if to drag it back down, and then with a snap, it let go and both the baku and Landon's soul floated free.

"Rhombus!" I exclaimed, hand outstretched as I made a free-floating circle around the black haze of the baku.

Trent stumbled, his hand reaching for support. The line poured through me, and I took all it could give, not wanting the globe now hanging over the spiral to fail because I hadn't been enough. Within it, I could see the baku as it looked for a way out.

"You got it!" Hodin said, shocked as the baku turned the inside of my circle black.

I didn't care. I was more concerned with Landon's soul, free and unfettered. Breath held, I watched as it rose alone, drifting as if unsure. If we lost it now, Landon would die; I couldn't hold the baku and Landon's soul at the same time.

"Shrink the bubble," Hodin said, mesmerized. "Damn my dame, you're going to do it."

Trent's jaw was clenched and his back hunched as his haggard gaze flicked to me.

"Shrink it!" Hodin insisted, but Landon's soul was still free, and I strengthened my hold on the line as Trent resumed his chant to lure his soul to touch one of the spirals before it simply . . . moved on. My throat tightened and my stomach hurt, but finally Landon's soul touched the outmost ring of the spiral, and with a burst of light, raced through the chalk lines to vanish into Landon with a soft and silent boom.

I waited, breathless. On the floor, Landon's chest moved. Relief fell on me, crushing, and I gripped Bis's foot, tears starting. We hadn't killed him. Landon still lived.

"You fools, shrink it down!" Hodin exclaimed, and Trent looked up, bleary from his spell casting. "Bottle it! If you wait, it will find a way out."

White-faced, Trent came to join me. His hand was damp as it slipped into mine. "Let's be done with this," he rasped, and I realized what this had cost him. Landon's screams would haunt both of us.

I took the baby bottle in hand, and together we began to shrink the circle. The ley line coursing through us began to warm, and the sphere floating over the fading spiral shone with an odd purple-and-gold shimmer. In a breath, it was as big as a beach ball. Another heartbeat, and it was the size of a grapefruit. But the smaller it got, the harder it was to hold it and the stronger the ley line burned my mind.

Struggling, I felt my body warm. My synapses began to singe as we spun the sphere before us down tighter and tighter, smaller and smaller. My breath came in with a rasp, and I held it. My hand in Trent's grew cold. "Trent?"

"I'm fine," he ground out between clenched teeth, but he wasn't, and in my moment of distraction, the bubble pushed back to its original size . . . and vanished.

"Trent!" I exclaimed as he collapsed into my arms. I

struggled to hold him as both of us fell to the old oak floor. My chest burned with Hodin's glyph as I gathered Trent to me, and Bis flew up, hissing at the door. Someone had come in, but Trent . . . Trent was unconscious. I could no longer feel the ley line through him. Hodin's curse wouldn't work if one of us was unconscious.

"It was too much for him," Hodin said, his gaze tracking Bis to the door. "He passed out and you lost control of your circle. Two female demons might accomplish it, but not an elf."

"Trent?" I sat on the floor of my church and patted his scruffy cheek. "Trent!" I looked up, not seeing the baku. Damn it, we were right back to square one.

"That's all I needed to see," Weast said from the vestibule, and my head snapped up.

Weast. My eyes narrowed as five Order agents filed in after him, all in black and all holding shimmering rods. Two more came in the back. Glenn wasn't among them, and I felt a spot of satisfaction. Bis puffed up to the size of a Rottweiler, hissing like a demented cat as he tried to keep them out . . . failing. The softhearted kid wouldn't hurt anything other than the occasional pigeon for dinner, and they knew it.

"When the I.S. told me the baku had gone to ground at the church, this was *not* what I expected to find," Weast said as he looked at Trent slumped in my arms, but I was more interested in the men and women surrounding us. Weast's amulet began to smother my connection to the lines, pissing me off.

"Get out of my church," I said, pulling in the line as if it were sunshine. But the more I gathered, the less there was, and I finally let go, hating that amulet of his as I stared at him.

Weast motioned for them to take us, and I lurched to my feet, grabbing Trent under his arms and backing up to find a wall. Hodin was gone, vanished like the chicken-ass demon he was. The bottle was on the floor, and I took it. Not that it would do me any good now. "Damn it, Trent, wake up!" I shouted, my pulse leaping when his eyes opened.

"I was to be the leader of the dewar," he said, and I dropped him in horror.

Trent's head hit the floor with a thunk. I scrambled back as he stood, hoping that I'd been mistaken. But it wasn't Trent. Not really. And my heart dropped to my gut when his green eyes narrowed, the power of the boardroom tempered by a soul older than the pyramids. "I have what I want," he said to Weast as he stood, and I quailed at the weird accent in how he was saying his vowels. "Leave me alone, and I will leave you alone."

Oh, God. The baku has Trent, I thought as Bis landed on my shoulder, his ears drooping, ashamed that he'd failed to keep the Order out. Trent had fallen unconscious, and the baku had taken him. Hodin had said that Trent's aura was as tattered as mine, that he'd been fielding attacks. But I hadn't thought . . . I never dreamed . . .

"Truce?" Weast mocked, one hand holding a glowing rod, the other hovering at the butt of his unsnapped sidearm as we were slowly surrounded. "It's not that simple." Weast looked questioningly at the agent checking Landon for a pulse, motioning him to drag him to the door when the man shrugged. "Morgan, take your gargoyle and get out of the way, or you'll end up a zombie, too."

Trent a zombie? I thought as the ring of agents passed me and began to tighten their circle around a wary Trent. *Not likely.*

Trent made a sudden dart for the last remaining window, pinwheeling back to avoid being touched by one of those glowing wands. Snarling, he threw a ball of unfocused magic, then lunged for an opening, only to fall back when more agents stopped him. Stymied, he swore in words that seemed to thicken the air. Power dripped from his fingers until Weast focused on him, his hand holding that glowing amulet. Angry, Trent retreated, his connection to the ley lines muted. Step by step, they tightened the circle, glowing batons forcing him back.

It was like hunters around a lion, and I touched Bis's feet on my shoulder, sickened.

"What should we do?" Bis said, and I glanced askance at the agent still standing beside me.

"Find Jenks. Tell him what happened. I'll finish up here," I said, launching him.

The agent moved, but not fast enough, and I swung my foot up and slammed it into his head, knocking him into the wall and dreamland. When I turned, Bis was gone.

I took a slow breath and looked over my church. The Order had Trent circled, their shouted words making him flinch and jerk. Turning him into a mobile prison for the baku wasn't going to happen, and when Weast strode forward, fingering what had to be the curse to turn him into a zombie, I panicked. But when I pulled on the ley line, it slipped through me like water. How could I break his magic when the more I drew on the ley lines, the less I had?

The Goddess, I thought, fear and excitement a thick slurry of hope. If I couldn't tap a line, I'd get my power right from the source.

"Ta na shay," I whispered, afraid she'd hear me, afraid she wouldn't, and with a trill of wild magic, a trickle of power seeped in, scintillating and untainted. The mystics were never far from me, the Goddess's eyes always looking even if they didn't recognize me anymore.

Weast spun, one hand on his zombie curse, the other on his amulet, as he tried to dampen my hold on the line. But I wasn't getting my power from the line. I was getting it from the Goddess, and I tucked my static-filled hair behind my ear. Her mystics didn't recognize me. I was safe. I sent a silent thank-you to Hodin, then cursed him for leaving me here alone.

My eyes narrowed on Weast. He was gripping that amulet as if it were a life preserver. It had to go. *"Ta na shay,"* I said louder this time, and the Goddess's laughter chimed in my soul, scaring me as more power flowed, unchecked and building. *How dare a singular think he can stop my mystics?* flooded my thoughts, scaring the crap out of me.

Ta na shay! I cried into my mind. *See me, hear me. Lend me your skill.* I took a breath. *"Sisto activitatem!"* I shouted, and with a finger snap, I flung Weast's spell back at him.

Weast cried out as the silver medallion broke in a flash of light, then ripped the line-dampening amulet from him and threw it. It slid to the waste drum, and with a whoosh, silver flames rose to lick the ceiling.

Ticked, I rose to my full height, my hair a static halo from the Goddess's mystics. Weast's hold on the lines was broken, and Trent cried out in satisfaction as power flooded into him. Hair wild and eyes alight, he pushed the agents back, power dripping from his fingers as he howled in exuberance. My smile faded. I had to wake him up to give him even a chance to kick the baku out.

"Ta na shay, non sic dormit, sed vigilat!" I shouted, hand extended as I funneled a massive amount of raw energy through me, scintillating as it took on my aura's hue along with my intent. It was the elven wake-up spell Trisk had written in the margins of her journal, and it exploded from my hand in a visible wave. It would either wake him up or kill him.

It hit them all, tumbling the Order and Trent alike along the floor, slamming them into the walls, where they groaned and lay still. The lights went out, and the flames in the waste drum hesitated before coming back all the brighter to light the sanctuary in a harsh glow tainted by new smoke. My ears were numb, but my heart leapt as Trent groaned, holding his head as he sat up. He was awake, and I gasped as I felt the lines redouble in me. Hodin's curse was working.

The baku was a smutty haze rising up from Trent, and I threw out my hand. *"Rhombus!"*

My circle snapped around it, heavy and thick. The baku recoiled, its black shadow railing against its new prison. I could feel it through the energy I'd bound it with, tainting me with its emptiness as I ran to Trent, scared as I pulled him up to sit against the wall.

"Trent? Trent!" I demanded as Weast and his men began stir, then gave him a little jolt of raw ley line energy.

He jumped, his hand going to his head as his eyes opened. "Did we get it?" he said, and relief flooded me at the hopeful expression in his eyes. It was him.

"Not yet," I said, but my hope that Trent might be able to help me bottle the baku faltered. I couldn't do this alone. *Or can I?* I thought, imagining a sly laugh lifting through my memory. I looked at my hands, quailing at the faint pure glow playing about them like water where they touched Trent.

I have an idea. My eyes went to the trapped baku as I let go of Trent and backed up. "Stay here," I said softly. "I might have knocked you too hard, and I want to try something."

Trent's head snapped up. "Ah, Rachel?" he warned, but I had already moved to stand between him and the three agents that Weast hadn't sent to put out the fire. I could handle three.

I want it in the bottle, I thought as I stared at the baku trapped in my circle, hanging in the sanctuary like a tiny eclipsed sun. *Help me. Lend me your skill.* But I wasn't sure the Goddess was listening as I took the bottle from where the blast had knocked it rolling, carefully stepping over the somnolent spiral to set it at the center. Trent and I might not have been able to shrink the circle down small enough to put the baku in a bottle, but it couldn't escape the spiral if it was in my bubble. Right?

"God bless it, Morgan!" Weast shouted, a hand to his bloody nose as he turned from the fire in the waste drum. "What are you doing?"

"Improvising," I said, telling Trent with a look to stay back as I carefully worked my way free of the spiral. Hodin wanted me to stand up for him. The entire collective needed to be shown that they could trust the Goddess. I had to trust her now.

"That's not going to work," Weast said as if I was being stupid, and giving him a smirk, I extended a magic-dripping hand, the memory of midnight drums echoing in my soul.

The words to invoke the spiral were in my mind, burne

into my very soul. Hodin's curse was warm through me, and I saw Trent touch his chest, realizing that he felt it, too. *"Tislan, tislan, ta na shay, cooreen na da,"* I crooned, and with a trill of wild magic, the spiral blossomed back to life as raw energy from the Goddess filled it. *"Tislan, tislan, ta na shay, cooreen na da!"* I demanded, trusting her. *See me. Lend me your skill.*

"What the hell?" Weast took a step forward, and Trent stood, wobbly but resolute as he warned him not to interfere. I was the demon. I was the song the lines danced to. I was the sword that the breaker of the worlds wielded to make reality from nothing. The drums beat for me, and I gloried in them, pounding wild into the night. With the Goddess's attention, I could do anything.

"You fool!" Weast exclaimed, his eyes on the glowing orb. "All you did was free it!"

The two people trying to put out the fire in the waste barrel hesitated, and the fire whooshed up, lighting the sanctuary in an odd smoky glow. *"Ta na shay. Tislan, tislan. Ta na shay cooreen na da,"* I crooned, and the spiral glowed brighter, rivaling the new flames creeping up the church's wall. And then I blew the orb with the baku into the glowing spiral.

"Get that fire out," Weast demanded, then turned to watch, his hands on his waist as the bubble shivered, rainbows of aura traversing the globe as the baku looked for escape. I held my breath as the power of the spiral pushed against me, the drums wild in the dark, the power icing through my veins. But it held no sway over me. I was the drums. I was the music. I was the words.

Become, I thought as the baku traveled the spiral and with a soft pop vanished.

Elation raced through me. "It's done!" I exclaimed, turning to Trent. "It moved on! Trent, we did it!"

He was leaning against the wall with his eyes alight, filled with his pride and love. He took a step toward me, hands outstretched.

And then I was pushed from behind as a silent wave

burst from the spiral, sending the bottle spinning across the floor and knocking me down. I hit the old oak with a thud, panicking.

"No!" I gasped as I spun to look, feeling betrayed as the baku coalesced out of the bottle like a dark shadow, free again. "I asked for your help. I asked!" I shouted as I bubbled the baku again and it beat at the enclosing circle. *Damn her. I thought she'd help. I thought this would work!*

"I told you," Weast said as his people began circling us again. "You can't bottle it. You don't think we tried that? You can spend all day catching it and dropping it in there, but it won't stay. You can't control a baku unless it's attached to a soul."

"Then I will hold it," Bis said as he suddenly dropped from the rafters.

"What? No!" I shouted. But Bis scooped up the bottle, wings beating as he set it gently at the center of the spiral. "Bis!" I called, terrified, and with sorrowful eyes, he pulled the glowing ball to his chest, and . . . touched the glowing spiral.

"No!" I cried out as he collapsed to the floor. Then I ducked, gasping as I hid my eyes from the blinding burst of light and sound that raced the spiral and vanished.

Now it is done, I thought I heard smugly in my mind.

"No," I whispered as I rose from my crouch and shook off Trent's grip. The bottle spinning at the center slowed and went still. My globe was gone. The spiral held no power. Bis lay beside it, wings outstretched, one hand touching the defunct glyph. As I watched, Bis shivered and was still.

God. No.

"Bis!" I ran to him, darting around the grasping agents. Shocked, I fell to my knees and picked up his bird-light body. He was gone. His soul was gone. He was breathing, but when I opened my second sight, there was no aura. He was gone!

My eyes went to the bottle glowing faintly at the center *Not Bis. Not Bis!*

I turned to Weast, my chest hot with anger as he stepped forward to take the bottle.

"Where's the baku?" someone said, and I stood with Bis in my arms, driving Weast back with my look alone. *What has Bis done? Why?*

"Isn't it in Kalamack?" someone else asked.

Bis was taking his last breath, and I held him tight. "I'm here," I said, though there was nothing left to hear me. "I'm with you, here at the end. You're not alone," I said, having done the same thing with my dad. And yet he took another breath, his skin lightening to a pearly white.

"I'm not the baku," I heard Trent say coldly. "Seriously. Did you not see what happened?"

Weast pushed Trent's head up to look him in the eye. "I can't tell," he said.

Trent shoved him off. "I'm not the baku!" he shouted. "It was in the bubble, and Bis . . ." His words faltered, and my eyes welled up. "Rachel. I'm so sorry."

"It's in the bottle," I whispered, voice low so it wouldn't break. "It's in there with Bis."

Weast started for the spiral. I lurched into motion, scooping up the bottle and holding it close, pressing it between me and Bis. "This is mine," I warned him, pulling on the ley line until my hair began to float. "You want a war with me, Weast? This is the way to do it. This is *mine!*"

"Ah," Weast said, eyes on the bottle, and fury cascaded through me.

"This is mine!" I shouted, and the agents putting out the last of the fire looked at us. "I've had it with all of you! If you're not going to listen to me, fine. But stay the hell out of my city!" I faced Trent, my vision suddenly swimming. "I . . . I have to go." Shaking, I started for the door. Trent's arm slipped around my waist, and I blinked fast, the tears coming whether I wanted them or not.

"Sir?" someone asked, and I stiffened when someone in anticharm gear stepped to block me.

"Let her go," Weast said. "Don't forget Landon. Someone call the dewar."

I didn't care, but the man before me moved with a relieved sigh. Above me, high on the steeple, I could hear gargoyles crying in the rising smoke, their laments echoing like thunder between the hills cradling Cincinnati. It was Bis's family: his father, his mother, his siblings, and a stoic girl gargoyle who had once hoped to share her life with him before he had bonded to me. Somehow they knew that the breaker of the worlds had saved his sword and left us. Left us all.

"Rachel?" Trent whispered, and I shook my head, leaning on him as we walked through the open door and down the steps. Though he still breathed, Bis was dead. He had done it to save me. I couldn't live with that.

But I had to.

CHAPTER

35

"ER, CAN I GET YOU SOMETHING ELSE?" MARK SAID FROM behind the counter. "We're technically closed for Thanksgiving, but I won't tell if you don't."

Closed. That was how I felt in a word. I took a shuddering breath, not trusting myself to say anything as I sat at the back table in Junior's, numb. One of my hands was on the table, wrapped around a long-cold untouched coffee. My other was cradled about Bis on my lap. He was still breathing, but he had no aura, no warmth. And when his tail curled around my finger in an unconscious reaction, I choked, throat tight.

Trent stood, his empty cup in hand. "I could use a refill. Rachel, you want a warm-up?"

I said nothing, and after giving my shoulder a squeeze, he went to the counter. His soft voice against Mark's was a bland background to the nothing my life had become.

I didn't remember Trent calling the car after walking out of the church, much less getting into it. I barely remembered Trent helping me out of it at Junior's. I did remember that it had taken two fifties to get Mark to unlock the door, but now I think he was regretting the decision.

I knew about regret. Little regret, like not remembering to send your mom a birthday card. And the whopping big regret, 'ike trusting your boyfriend with your summoning name and ending up in Alcatraz. *But this,* I thought as I looked at Bis curled up on my lap. This was going to break me.

I blinked fast, trying not to cry. Somehow, Bis was still alive without his soul—comatose and chalk white but alive. Most people would have gone to a bar to lose their memories in a numbing wave of alcohol. Not me. No, I didn't want to forget. Maybe if I remembered, I wouldn't be stupid and try to fix everything. But I doubted it.

"You sure you don't want something?" Trent said, and I looked up, not having realized he'd come back. He set two steaming cups on the table, and I finally let go of my cold one. "You haven't eaten in . . . a while."

Eat? I thought, chin quivering. My vision began to swim, and I held my breath.

"Oh, Rachel." He sat beside me, scooting closer as I dropped my head. "We will find a way to separate them," he soothed as he tugged me closer. His gaze was on the baby bottle sitting atop the table like a weird centerpiece. It contained nothing I could see—and yet it held everything.

I won't start crying again. I won't. My head began to hurt, and I exhaled in a slow, measured movement. "Why did he do it?" I said, voice low so it wouldn't break. "He knew it would kill him."

Trent gathered me to him, almost rocking me. "Because he loved you," Trent whispered, and my throat closed. "And he's not dead. We'll find a way to get him free."

Okay, he wasn't dead, but this was almost worse. I tried to take a new breath, but it escaped me in a sob. I tried to pull away, but Trent wouldn't let me, and I let go, crying in great, gasping, ugly sounds against his shoulder as he ran his fingers through my hair and made shushing noises.

"This is my fault," I said around my sobs. "I called on the Goddess to break Weast's amulet. And then I used elven magic to try to bottle the baku." I looked up, seeing the shared pain in his eyes. "Why did he do it?"

"I know it hurts," he whispered, pulling me closer, and I hid my face against him again.

Even as I melted into him, I wanted to lash out at Trent

How could he know? The only things he'd ever loved that needed him to survive were his girls, and they were fine.

But then I remembered his agony in Ku'Sox's lab, the knowledge in his eyes that he had failed. He'd taken the entire elven species into his circle long before he'd known me. The orphanages, the camps, the illegal medicines that funded the research to bring his people back from extinction: they needed him to survive. They might fight him every inch, but they needed him. And there were failures every day, large and small.

Finally my sobs slowed and I took a slow, clean breath, then exhaled, trying to let go of my heartache. But under it was even more crushing regret. Feeling it, Trent pulled me tight, grounding me without saying a word.

"He was my responsibility," I said, my voice broken as I used one of Mark's scratchy napkins to dab up the tears that wouldn't stop. "How do you do it?" I asked, and he sighed, his grip on me easing without letting go. He smelled like green under the layer of smoke and sawdust, and I blinked up at him. "You've made yourself responsible for all of them," I said. "To keep them alive. You know you can't. How do you live with it?"

Still he said nothing, and I answered my own question. *You do what you can, and what you can't do, you learn to live with.*

But this was Bis, and I couldn't. My breath shook as I pulled away and wiped my eyes. "I'm glad you're here," I whispered, and his grip on my hand tightened.

"Where else would I be?" he said, expression pinched.

I held my breath, struggling to start right back up again. But then Mark groaned softly as the door chimes jingled, and I sniffed, blinking fast when Ivy strode in, phone to her ear.

"I've found her. She's at Junior's," Ivy said in her dust gray voice, and I wadded up the napkin, numb and spent.

Trent gave my hand a squeeze and stood as Ivy wove between the tables. The new day was bright behind her and worry was in her eyes as she tucked her phone into a back pocket. She was still in her working leathers, slim and sexy, looking as if she would rip someone's throat out for me if I asked. It was good to have friends. Bad when being such shortened their life-spans.

"I'm going to get you something to eat," Trent said to me, nodding at Ivy's dark glare. "Ivy, you want anything?"

"Black coffee. Thanks," she said as she sat down across from me, and Trent slipped away. His hand was already reaching for his phone as he settled in before the counter, where he could see me and the parking lot both.

My head drooped, and I said nothing. She knew. She had to know. The heartache in her eyes was too deep to not.

"You should have called me," she said softly.

I looked up, feeling as if I'd been dragged behind horses. "What would you have done?"

Ivy licked her lips, a flash of fang showing as she watched Trent, his back to us as he quietly persuaded someone on his phone. "Taken you home instead of a coffeehouse?" she said. "I'm sorry. Rachel, I'm *so* sorry." Her hand reached out to cover mine, and I choked. "The Order is trying to keep what happened quiet, but I was with Pike and Constance when the news came in. Landon is not saying anything, either. I think he's hoping that if he claims ignorance, the dewar won't uninstall him."

My eyes dropped to Bis, his tail curled around my pinkie like a ring. "At least he's alive," I said, hardly breathing the words.

And Bis wasn't, not really.

"I wish I had something to say to make it better," Ivy said as her hand slipped away.

My hand fisted around one of Mark's scratchy napkins, then relaxed. "There's nothing to say. I asked for the Goddess's help, and she gave it. It's my fault." How many times had I been warned that when you ask a deity for help, it might be answered in a way that pleased her, not you?

"Your fault?" Ivy made a scoffing sound. "Rachel, I'm the first to say you make a lot of mistakes, but Bis made his own decision. The Goddess had nothing to do with it."

I said nothing. I knew better.

"How is he still alive without his soul?" she said when she looked around the edge of the table, and the pain rushed right back, taking my breath away in its shocking suddenness.

Mark was coming over with a cup of takeout for Ivy, sparing me from answering. Ivy reached for her coffee, frowning at me until I took a sip of that new skinny demon grande that Trent had given me. "Thanks, Mark," I said, putting off the tears with the sweet cinnamon taste, and after hesitating a moment, Mark retreated.

"I don't know," I said when I thought I could talk again. "Maybe gargoyles are different. They were created by the demons. Maybe they can survive without a soul." My gaze rose to the scratched baby bottle. "There has to be a way to get his soul out without letting the baku out, too."

"What part of *we're closed* don't you get?" Mark muttered from behind the counter, and I followed his attention to the dawn-bright parking lot. A black car had pulled up, two severe-looking men scrambling out of it as they chased after Zack and the sparkle of pixy dust. The kid was decked out in a new suit, but he was still in his sneakers. His big feet were probably hard to fit on such short notice. His eyes were wide in worry and his hair in charming disarray. It reminded me of Trent, and I glanced at him on the phone beside the front door as the chimes jingled and they came in. Crap on toast. What was I going to tell Jenks? I'd sent him away because I was afraid I'd lose him, and I ended up losing his best friend instead.

"Rachel!" Jenks darted from Zack's shoulder, coming to a dust-laden, wide-eyed, almost panicked stop at the table. "I've been looking for you all night."

"I wanted to be alone," I said as Trent closed his phone and came over with a bag of something from the cold shelves.

"That's swell. That's fine. We can be alone together," Jenks said, words tumbling over themselves as he landed on the table beside the bottle. It was as tall as him, and I averted my eyes when he touched it, wings drooping. I was going to start crying again. I knew it.

"Rache, I'm sorry," Jenks said softly, surprising me. "He made his own decision."

I looked up, my throat tight as Trent slipped back onto the bench, his arm going behind my back to give me a quick tug into him. "I don't want people to sacrifice themselves to save me," I said, trying to be angry, but it wouldn't come.

"Too damn bad, witch," Jenks said. "You'd do it for us. Have done it. It sucks like steaming green troll turds on the Fourth of July, but deal with it."

"Sing it, pixy," Ivy said, assessing Zack as he came to a fidgety halt at the end of the table. He was clearly trying to figure out what to say, but at least his security had given us some space.

"He's alive?" Zack finally said, and I nodded, hand curved possessively around Bis. "Maybe you can put his soul back," he added.

I followed his gaze to the soul bottle. "It's mixed up with the baku's. I don't know how."

"But you're a demon." Zack sat down as far from Ivy as he could get. "Maybe Hodin can."

It was nice hearing him suggest that without fear, but a flash of annoyance lifted though me. I wasn't happy with Hodin. He'd left. He'd just left. Sure, he didn't owe me anything, but who leaves like that?

The click of Mark locking the front door was loud, and he double-checked that the closed sign was lit. I appreciated him not kicking us out, and managed to give him a thin smile as he came up to the table, hands smoothing his apron. "Can I get you something, Sa'han?" he asked, and everyone's eyes went to Zack. Zack, though, was oblivious.

"He's talking to you," Trent finally said, and Zack flashed red.

"Oh! Uh, do you have hot chocolate?"

Mark seemed to stifle a wince. "We've got cocoa," he said. "That's pretty close."

Zack fiddled with cuff links in the shape of the dewar seal. "With marshmallows?"

Mark's smile began to look pained. "How about whipped cream?"

"Stellar," Zack said enthusiastically, and Mark's shoulders slumped.

"Coffee okay for the two of you?" Mark asked loudly, and Zack's security up front made happy noises and settled at a table in the sun.

Ivy's eyes flicked from the soul bottle to me. "Have you been here all night?"

I nodded. It had been hours ago, and a flash of guilt went through me. "Shouldn't you be getting ready for Thanksgiving dinner or something?"

"Nina didn't go shopping," Jenks said, now sitting on the soul bottle as if in protection. "There's nothing but a can of baked beans and some dried-up carrots in the upstairs kitchen. You don't want to know what's in the downstairs kitchen."

"What's in the downstairs kitchen?" Zack predictably asked.

"I *said* you don't want to *know*," Jenks said pointedly.

"Sorry," I muttered. I was ruining everyone's holiday. Even Mark's. And a pang of heartache pulled my eyes down. My eyes closed, and my hand cradling Bis under the table trembled. The hard way was going to break me someday. But not today.

Trent's grip on me tightened as he leaned in, his hopeful smile doing nothing to hide his worry. "I've talked to my lawyers. Dan is fine, and both he and Wendy agreed to not file assault charges, seeing as we were trying to save Landon. Landon is pretending ignorance, but there's been no talk of giving him the dewar back, and I think Zack is it."

My gaze turned from an embarrassed Zack to Trent as I realized he'd been putting out fires while I cried into my coffee. "Thank you." I was a shitty person. I had completely forgotten about the two people we'd assaulted in the dewar's stairwell. *But Trent didn't.*

"One hot cocoa," Mark said as he set a whipped-cream-covered grande before Zack.

"Thanks." Zack reached for it eagerly. "They haven't let me have any sugar since putting me in this zookeeper suit."

"Ah, sure." Eyebrows high, Mark retreated to deliver the twin cups of coffee to the guys by the door comparing phone screens.

Ivy, too, had her head down over her phone, and I wondered why everyone was here horning in on my misery. "Mark," Ivy called out, and the kid jerked as if she'd slapped him, almost spilling the two coffees. "When you get a moment, I need a venti salted caramel. No rush."

"You got it," he said with a sigh.

"Salted caramel?" Jenks's wings hummed, dust spilling from his bent wing.

My misery deepened. "You called Glenn? Thanks."

Ivy snapped her phone closed and tucked it in a back pocket. "There are fire trucks at the church. You don't think the FIB has been looking for you? I told him you were fine, and he said he wants to see what fine looks like today." A smile hinting at her relief threatened to show.

I stiffened with a sudden thought. Crap on toast. Al. I'd been sitting here for hours, and I'd forgotten to tell the demons that the baku was in a bottle. I reached for my pocket, hesitating when I remembered Al was under house arrest. I didn't have Dali's number. But Mark might. "Ah, Mark?" I said loudly, and he smiled at me from behind the counter.

"You want me to tell Dali that you're okay?" he said as he made Glenn's latte, and I nodded, quite sure I didn't like how cavalier he was about phoning demons. But the kid *was* Dali's boss.

"If it's not too much trouble," I said, and Jenks snorted, his bent wing leaking dust all over the table as he sat on top of Bis's bottle. "Could you tell Dali that the baku is in a bottle and to let Al sleep?"

"You got it." Mark pulled off his gloves and reached for his phone, clearly resigned to having lost his day off.

I hated to admit it, but between the coffee and the weird normalcy of Jenks begging Zack for a wad of whipped cream, I was starting to feel better. Zack looked utterly fantastic in a teen-crush sort of way in his suit and his new, hesitant confidence, miles away and just next door in comparison to the scared kid I'd found eating leftovers and hiding in my church. Seeing him with Jenks, I found a sliver of hope. If he was in charge of the dewar and they actually let him make some decisions, things might change.

The memory of Bis swam up, and I quashed it in a flood of hurt.

"So they made you the dewar's Sa'han," I said to distract myself, and Zack's head snapped up, a faint flush on his cheeks. "Did you learn what you wanted to about Trent in your little walkabout?" I asked between sips of coffee.

"Ah." Zack wiped the whipped cream from his lips when Jenks pantomimed the same. "He's everything that Landon said he was," he said, green eyes flicking to Trent sitting beside me, head down as he surfed the net.

"Sexy." Jenks rose up with a wad of whipped cream on his chopsticks. "Smart. Good with magic and kids."

Trent looked up from his phone, his fingers stilling and a smirk on his lips.

"Ruthless in his drive," Zack added uncomfortably. "Willing to sacrifice what shouldn't be for an end that might not be worthy. Landon was right."

"He wants the elves to succeed," I said as I gave Trent's hand an encouraging squeeze when his smile vanished. "There's nothing wrong with that."

"Then maybe we should stop trying to put him in jail for it," Zack muttered from behind his hot cocoa as if afraid to say it louder.

"See, Zack?" Jenks said cheerfully. "I told you there wasn't some old dried-up elf soul in you. No way, no how would one of those old moss wipes say anything like that."

Zack colored, but I privately thought there probably was.

He'd been too good with those healing charms. No one had died, and even I wasn't that good.

"Zack?" Mark called from behind the counter. "Can you give me a hand? I need your opinion on something."

Whatever that something was, it smelled like Thanksgiving, and Zack immediately stood, taking his nearly empty cup with him. "Sure."

Trent, too, stood, lingering until I looked up. "Do you mind if I make a few more calls before Quen gets here with the car?" he said, hand on my shoulder. "Things are going to start happening fast now that the dewar has scheduled a press release for tomorrow. I want to head off the rumors and arrange for a closed-door meeting tonight to explain what happened. I'd like you to be there if you feel up to it. And if you can get Hodin to come, all the better."

My eyes narrowed, and my hand cupping Bis under the table twitched. "I'll be there, but don't count on Hodin," I muttered, and Trent nodded, excusing himself to sit at a nearby table.

"What's up with Hodin?" Jenks said, and my anger flooded back.

"He left Trent and me in the lurch when the Order showed up," I muttered, and the pixy's wings hummed into fitful motion. I'd have liked to blame him for what happened, but honestly, I probably would have tried to work with the Goddess anyway, and I took a gulp of my cooling coffee. "Did I tell you I had a dream a few days ago about Ray getting married?" I said, my eyes dropping to Bis curled up on my lap, and Ivy brought her attention back from the sunny empty streets. "Bis was there, grown to the size of a pony," I whispered. He would have been about seventy. Just about old enough to be on his own.

"Rache, we're going to get him back," Jenks said, and then he stiffened. "Al's here."

Even with his warning, I jumped when Al popped in at the in-out circle at the back of the store. "Why are there *fire trucks* at your church?" the demon bellowed, and I winced, not turning. I could tell by his overdone accent that he was probably in full green-crushed-velvet regalia.

Mark grimaced, a tray in his hand as he stood before the oven. "I am closed," he grumbled, then asked Zack to get two more sandwiches out of the freezer.

Sighing, I turned to Al. Sure enough, he was in his top hat and full coat and tails, his blue-tinted glasses doing nothing to hide his sleep-deprived fatigue. "Because it was on fire?" I said, and Al grimaced. Resigned, I pushed a chair out for him.

"Dali said you bottled the baku." Al tugged his lace down at his cuffs and stepped forward. "Is that it?" he said, looking at it on the table before turning to Junior and Zack behind the counter, one in an apron, one in a suit. "Demon grande in porcelain, if you please," he said, then frowned at Trent, still on the phone. "Damn elf lives with that thing stuck to his ear. Tell me, Rachel, does it remove it for sex?"

"Demon grande!" Mark said, and a bell above the register rang of its own accord.

"Excuse me." Ivy rose, eyes on the Jeep that had quietly pulled into the lot. "I want to talk to Glenn before he lands in this."

I nodded, and she touched my shoulder before slipping from the table and sauntering to the door. Zack's security noticed, watching her all the way. The click of her undoing the lock was loud, and from behind the counter, Mark sighed—at the new customers, not Ivy.

"This should be interesting," Jenks said, and I blinked fast when he came to sit on my shoulder smelling of green things and whipped cream.

Shoes tapping, Al halted at the head of the table. "My God. It's really in there?" he said, making no move to touch the soul bottle. "How did you do it?" he asked, and Jenks's wings buzzed against my neck. "Dali is green with curiosity. Even Newt didn't know how to manage it."

She does now, I thought as I took the bottle in hand, and Al visibly stiffened—as if I held a poisonous viper. I was trying not to care that the church now had smoke damage in addition to everything else. *I should just walk away before I burn it to the ground,* I thought, but the church was the first time I'd felt a part of something big, something wonderful. Even if I did keep destroying it.

"I broke the rules—that's how," I said, unable to look up from the swirling pearl and blue behind the glass.

Al sat, his head tilting as he touched my chin and forced me to look at him. "Rules. You captured the baku. No one has ever done that. And totally unharmed." His fingers curled under themselves, and I looked away. "Where is my coffee!" he bellowed, and I jumped.

Jenks darted from my shoulder, wings rasping. "Bis is comatose without his soul," Jenks said, hovering belligerently in front of Al. "But yeah, she's unharmed. You demon weenie."

"Bis?" Al said, and steeling myself against the heartache, I looked down at him curled in my lap. He looked as if he was sleeping, and it hurt.

Damn it, I'm not going to cry in front of Al, I thought as I pulled myself together. "His soul is right here," I said, focusing on the blue bottle instead. "It's mixed up with the baku's. Bis dragged it in there with him. Is there any way to separate them?"

Al peered at me over his glasses, a familiar, angry glint in his eyes. "You caught it by sacrificing your gargoyle?"

My chin lifted. "Seriously? You *seriously* think I asked Bis to do this? He did it on his own before I could tell him to stop." I hesitated. "Is there any way to separate them?"

Hope stirred, but it was short-lived as Al looked at the bottle, his goat-slitted eyes unreadable as he touched Bis's head with a finger and shook his head. My throat grew a lump. "His body slumbers. Curious."

I stifled a flash of anger, but it was Jenks who rose up, almost snarling. "Curious, hell. Can you separate his soul from the baku or not?"

Al shot a peeved look at Jenks, then softened. "I don't know. The baku makes things difficult. You won't find anyone in the collective eager to try. We've all lost kin to it. Ah, here's my coffee. Thank you . . . Zack, is it?" He grinned, but it looked forced. "I *do* enjoy being served by elves. It makes one feel so alive."

Frowning, Zack backed up, returning to the counter as Mark called for him.

"Don't listen to him, Rache," Jenks said, again on my shoulder. "We'll get Bis back."

I blinked fast as I shifted my hand, and Bis's tail tightened about it.

Al cocked his head, clearly surprised at the band of white around my finger. "Keep him safe. I've never seen such a reaction from a body without a soul."

"I will." My hand curved more protectively about him.

"We both will," Jenks added, and Al sat back, apparently satisfied as the door chimes jingled and Ivy and Glenn came in.

"Rachel, I'm sorry about Bis. I should have spelled Weast with his own magic and made him listen," Glenn said as he and Ivy crossed the coffee shop. "Is there anything I can do?"

"Thanks, no," I whispered, and my shoulder went warm from Jenks's dust.

"Condolences are not required," Al said as Ivy sat at the far end of the table and pulled her coffee close. "The world breaker lives. We will find a way to bring his soul home."

I grimaced, but damn my dame if I didn't feel better with Al's thin promise. "I don't know what I'm going to say to his father," I said.

"Etude?" Al's eyes tracked Mark bringing Glenn his coffee. "Tell him you're working on it. Bis is stronger than he ought to be because of you. But I think Etude will thank you."

A surprised burst of dust slipped down my shoulder, and I almost choked on my drink. "For letting his son sacrifice his soul to save me?" I blurted, and Ivy slipped me a napkin.

Al's shoulders lifted and fell as his gaze went distant out

into the sunny parking lot. "It's long been a question if gargoyles—having been created by demons—possessed a soul. Bis has proved that they do. If he didn't, the baku would have not been snared and bottled." Al's eyes came back to me, and I read the truth in them. "Bis has given his entire species a great comfort. And as I say, we will work to free him."

I took a slow breath, feeling it shake as I exhaled. Al thought it was possible. Hell, he thought it more than possible. And until then, I would keep him safe. Both Jenks and I would.

"No one in the collective will help." Al stared at Bis's tail for a moment, then returned his attention to his coffee. "Still, there are texts lying about no one has looked at for thousands of years." He hesitated, his eyes narrowing in suspicion. "Hodin might."

"Really?" I blurted, and then Al pushed back from the table, standing to slam his fists on the top to make Jenks ink dust and the bottle threaten to fall.

"You *have* seen him!" Al bellowed as I scrambled to grab the bottle and keep it from falling. Pulse fast, I stood, holding it and Bis tight to me as I slid out of the back of the booth. Trent ended his conversation and stood, and Zack's security made a beeline to him. "This is *his* fault!" Al shouted, his eyes narrowed as he scanned the room as if looking for him. "That backstabbing, elven-rutting gigolo convinced you to treat with the Goddess, and now your gargoyle is lost and your church has *fire trucks* parked at the curb! Where is he? Odie?" Al yelled at the ceiling.

"That's not what happened." I backed up to find Trent standing behind me, grim-faced. Jenks was on my shoulder, and I held Bis and that bottle tight. "Al, I swear—"

"Show yourself, you little worm, or I'm going to sell you to the nearest elf!" Al bellowed.

And then I yelped when a soft pop of air pushed me back a step.

"Again?" Hodin said wrathfully as he stood in the center of the room, his slim build looking dangerous in his black jeans and T. A hint of purple magic flickered through his fingers, and my hair crackled with static. "Fool me once, shame on you. Fool me twice . . . Well, you won't get the chance because I'm going to send you to hell, Gally."

Glenn and Ivy slid out of the way, but I stood firm with Trent beside me. "Guys," I started, then yelped as Al yanked heavily on the nearest ley line, almost buckling my knees with the power he drew to life. He didn't even bother harnessing it with a spell, just marshaled the raw energy into his hand and threw it at Hodin.

White-faced, Mark pulled Zack to him and invoked the protection circle at the register. Zack's security dove behind the counter. Their pistols were out, but honestly, they were the least of my worries as the ball of energy sped harmlessly under Hodin when the demon vanished into a black hummingbird.

"You little pus bucket!" Al shouted, now swinging wildly at Hodin as he dove at him, plucking bits of hair and stabbing at his ear. "Putrid elven bootlicker!"

"Enough!" I shouted, and then, with Bis pressed to me, I flung a hand out. *Corrumpo!* I shouted, the expanding force of air flinging the hummingbird that was Hodin to smack into the window and knocking Al to a hand-reaching stagger. Mark yanked Zack back below the counter, but the kid immediately popped up, shoving Mark into his own circle to break it. Eyes wide, Zack started for me, only to be tackled by his own security and go down with an indignant yelp.

"I said, enough!" I shouted when Hodin, still a bird, shook himself and started for Al. "Al, leave Hodin alone."

"He is a liar and a cheat!" Al snarled, his hat gone and his glasses askew to show his bloodshot goat-slitted eyes. "And he's going to die. Right now!"

"Then you will have to go through me," I said, and Al spun comically fast. As he stared at me in horror, I felt a shiver run through me.

"Ra-a-ache-e-e-el? What did you do?" Al intoned, and Hodin flew to hover beside me, where he turned back into his usual broody dark self.

I glanced at Hodin, then took a step from both him and Trent. "I, ah, promised to stand up for him if the collective got ugly," I said. "And that includes you."

"You what!" Al bellowed, thick hands fisted. "What did he give you? Something you already had, I bet. Something you could have found on your own, or something I could have *given* you."

"You never *gave* anyone anything." Hodin sniffed and pushed his rings to the base of his fingers. "And truly, what did you expect? Your student's life was in danger, and you abandoned her for nearly a week?" He shook his head, his hair falling to hide his eyes in a mocking, threatening peek-aboo. "From the same thing you were hiding from. You don't deserve a student this talented. She did what no one else has ever done."

"At what cost!" Al shouted, and I winced. He was beginning to hurt my ears. "You are a worthless hack of a demon, fit only for bedroom games and little more. Rachel is mine."

Hodin's jaw clenched, his eyes narrowing.

"Ah . . ." I held up a finger. "I don't belong to anyone, guys."

Al turned to me, hunched and frustrated. "Fine," he said as he swooped up his hat and brushed cookie crumbs from it. "But this . . . *demon*—and I use the term loosely—is a loathsome, betraying liar unable to best even the weakest elf. Which is why he slept his way through the revolution that gave us our freedom, playing sex games and eating fruit and meat while we starved and suffered from exposure. I will *not* let you ruin yourself by associating with this . . . milksop sexpot!"

Jenks made a snorting scoff from my shoulder, and the dust spilling down shifted to an amused gold.

"No need," Hodin said, his expression twisted as if he were smelling something rank. "As long as the collective leaves me alone, I'll take the baku for safekeeping and leave you to your pathetic cosmic powers. None of you suffered as I did under it. It's mine."

I pressed back into Trent, glad for his light hand at the small of my back. Jenks was a threatening hum on my shoulder, and Ivy had made her way back to us after having convinced Glenn to sit it out with Zack and his crew behind the counter.

"You are not touching that bottle," Al threatened, and Hodin grew smug.

"It's mine," Hodin said lightly. "We have a deal. Don't we, Rachel?"

Al's expression faltered. "You didn't," he said, but I'd had enough, and pushing forward, I stood between them, pissed to the Turn and back. Bis was in my arms, and my heartache fed my anger. Boys. They were acting like spoiled boys.

"This is mine," I said, holding the bottle in one hand, Bis in the other. "Mine! Neither of you is getting it until Bis's soul is back in his body."

"We had a deal," Hodin said as he turned, his anger at Al shifting to me.

"Yep." I cocked my hip, angry at both of them. "The deal was that you get the baku after you teach me to fly with Bis." I hesitated, satisfied when Hodin's gaze dropped to Bis and he lost his bluster. "Fix this," I said, softer this time. "I can't fly with him unless he has a soul."

Hodin's stance became unsure. "I don't know. . . ."

Al laughed, the ugly sound making me shudder. "I don't know," he mocked. "Truer words have never been spoken. Very good, itchy witch," he added, and I went cold at the hate in his eyes. "I'm proud of you. It's hard to get the better of one of Odie's deals. We will talk about this unfortunate problem of standing up for him before the collective, but you did reasonably well." His lip curled as he looked at Hodin. "Hodin has more than the usual share of guile and trickery. Give me the baku. It goes in the vault."

"It goes on my shelf," I said, and Al's hand dropped, his ugly smile faltering. "Until I fly with Bis," I added. "And then it goes to Hodin."

Hodin sniggered, standing more confidently.

"I forbid it." Al looked Hodin up and down in disgust. "I'd rather give it to that troll under the bridge at Eden Park."

"Hey!" I shouted as I glared at him, and Jenks laughed, choking it back when Al's gloved hands fisted. "*Don't* criticize me and what I had to do to save your ass. *You* were hiding in a hole."

"Save my ass," Al said, and I took a step closer, giving the bottle to Trent so I had a free hand to poke him in the chest.

"Save. Your. Ass," I said as Trent pulled me back before I could actually do it. "If not for me, you'd still be there."

Hodin chuckled, and I rounded on him.

"And you!" I said, face warm as his expression suddenly went empty. "You *left* me when things got sticky. You know what?" Pulse fast, I looked back at Al. "I want both of you out of my life. You both left when I needed you. The only person who stuck it out was Trent, so if I hear one more shitty comment about elves and their lack of trust, or worth, or the dangers of calling on the Goddess, I'm going to shoot you both to the moon!"

"The moon, Rache?" Jenks questioned, but I was mad.

"You will both get out of this store and my life!" I shouted, and Ivy winced. "You leave me the hell alone until you idiots make up, shake hands, and . . . make me a cake together!" I shouted, echoing what my mom had said when Robbie and I had fought. "I've had it with both of you!"

"If it means he gets the baku, then I won't help you separate them," Al said.

Furious, I stomped my foot and yanked harder on the line. "Get out!" I shrilled, hurt that he'd put his hate for Hodin before me.

Al left in a puff of foul smoke, taking his coffee with him. Hodin was gone when I turned back, but I'd expected nothing less. Pulse fast, I wavered, suddenly breathless.

"I did it," I said, and Trent took my elbow to help me back to the table. "I told them both to leave, and they did."

"I guess you showed them," Trent said, but his smile seemed real, and I basked in it. "Rachel, if there's a way, we will find it," he promised, and I nodded, blinking fast as I looked at Bis, safe in my arms.

"To Bis," Ivy said, raising her paper cup of coffee. "Never has a truer soul existed."

I sat down before I fell over, overwhelmed as the love I felt for them washed over me. Shaky, I lifted my own luke-warm coffee. "To Bis," I whispered, one hand curved about him on my lap. "We will bring you home."

Silently we drank to the little gargoyle, and I swear I felt his tail tighten on my finger.

Trent's eyes were on mine as he lowered his cup, and he leaned closer, whispering, "I was going to wait until tomor-row, but I can't. Now that my mother's spelling lab is open, I want to give it to you."

"Give it . . . to me?" I stammered, and Jenks chuckled as if having already known. Rising up, he flew to Zack, Glenn, and Mark, who were headed our way with trays of steam-ing sandwiches in their hands.

"So you have a place to work," Trent said, the rims of his ears becoming red. "Just until the church is fixed," he added as if to convince me, and Ivy smiled. "And who knows?" He ducked his head, his eyes swimming with love when they rose again to find mine. "If you find you like my mother's spelling lab, you can stay."

I couldn't look away from him, breathless. *He didn't open it for Ellasbeth. He opened it for me,* I thought, not knowing what to say, much less think.

"You don't have to answer now," Trent said as I stared at him blankly. "You might want to stay at Piscary's for the winter since Ivy and Nina are headed for DC, but I wanted to give you the option. It's there if you want it."

Want it? Of course I wanted it. But it was a big change, one that I could never go back from. "Trent . . . ," I stam-mered, not knowing what to say, much less think.

But Mark and Zack were setting down paper-wrapped sandwiches smelling of Thanksgiving, and I smiled, the lightness of hope trickling through me.

"On the house," Mark said as he began to hand them out, the scent of turkey and stuffing wafting up to remind me how long it had been since I'd eaten. "Corporate sent them over to test in a mixed-species setting, but they weren't a big seller. Tomorrow, they will be even less." He winced. "Uh, I'd appreciate it if you'd fill out a like-dislike card before you leave."

Glenn swung a chair from an adjacent table around and sat so close to Ivy that their elbows jostled. "I'll take one," he said, and Ivy curved a hand familiarly over his leg to make his ears redden.

"One looks about right," she almost purred, and Jenks laughed from my shoulder.

"Hey, Rache," Jenks said as he dropped down and helped himself to the half sandwich that Mark had set in the center of the table for him. "How about that? Thanksgiving dinner. Right here at Junior's." He stabbed a cranberry on the tip of his garden sword and pulled it forth. "Couldn't have planned it better. No dishes to clean up, and everyone is here."

Smiling my thanks, I took the sandwich smelling of turkey and stuffing as Zack and Mark settled themselves. My eyes went down the table, finding peace as the conversations began to rise. Ivy and Glenn seemed to have a new understanding, and I wondered if he was going to stay in Cincinnati now that he had left the Order or follow her and Nina to DC. Trent was to my right, where he'd been for a very long time, only now there was a contented satisfaction in him I'd never seen before. He had given me something I needed—something that would protect me by allowing me to protect myself. Jenks sat in the middle of the table beside that bottle as if guarding it, razzing Glenn and Ivy even as he kept an eye on the parking lot for trouble.

They'd all come looking for me, bringing me hope that tomorrow was going to be better than today even if it was going to be new and different. Everyone I cared about was here.

Except Bis, I thought, jamming the hurt down deep. But I knew that with my friends, I'd be okay. Hodin would figure out how to separate him from the baku. Al would get over it. With Ivy gone, I could move into Piscary's for the winter and Jenks could come home. Unless I took Trent up on his offer and moved into his compound, complete with a space for just me. *My God. I can go anywhere from here.*

Blinking fast, I looked down the table, listening to my friends smooth the ugly parts of my life into a background nothing that could be forgotten. That big something wonderful that I thought the church held . . . was right here at this table.

ACKNOWLEDGMENTS

I'd like to thank Jennifer Jackson and Anne Sowards, one for giving me a chance to prove my work, and the other for giving me a chance to prove my work . . . again.

To save the city, Rachel Morgan will need to show some teeth in the next Hollows novel

MILLION DOLLAR DEMON

BY KIM HARRISON

Now available from Ace

Ready to find
your next great read?

Let us help.

Visit prh.com/nextread

Penguin
Random
House